Lulu Allison grew up in a small village in the Chilterns. She did an illustration degree at St Martin's School of Art and a fine art MA at the University of Brighton, where she still lives with her husband Pierre. She teaches art online and in person, and in the past has exhibited in group and solo shows, and worked as a gallery educator and arts facilitator. Her art practice consisted predominantly of site-specific installation and lens-based work. She has also worked as a cleaner, a waitress, a scuba-diving instructor and a maker of spectacle hinges in a small factory in Munich.

She came to writing accidentally while undertaking what she thought was an art project, unexpectedly discovering what she should have been doing all along. That art project became her first novel, *Twice the Speed of Dark*, published by Unbound in 2017. *Salt Lick* is her second novel, and she is working on a third, titled *Beast*, inspired by the Thomas Mann novel, *Doctor Faustus*.

Salt Lick

Lulu Allison

unbound

This edition first published in 2021

Unbound

TC Group, Level 1, Devonshire House, One Mayfair Place
London W1J 8AJ

www.unbound.com

ISBN (eBook): 978-1-78965-132-4

ISBN (Paperback): 978-1-78965-131-7

Cover design by Mecob

Printed and bound in Great Britain by Clays Ltd, Elcograf S.p.A.

Super Patrons

Jo Alderson
Amy Allison
Eli Allison
Matilda Amos
William Amos
Fizz Annand
Lily Ayre
Sara Benbow
Philipp Benke
David Biddle
Samantha Brown
Jane Carr
Geoff Cox
Mike Crump
Nansi Diamond
Sophie Dissanayake
Joanne Fleming
Paul Fulcher
Annie Gallop
Vanessa Gellard
Rita E. Gould
Ian Hagues
Liz Hale
Jacques Halé
Lucy Henzell-Thomas
Sam Hobbs
Clifford Jaine
Michael Janes
Simon Jerrome
Rebecca Jones

Patrick Kincaid
Sumitra Lahiri
Ruth Leonard
Alison Lowe
Barbara L McGonagle
Erinna Mettler
Emma Mitchell
John Mitchinson
Virginia Moffatt
Stephanie Monk
Diego Montoyer
Sarah Morris
Dan Peters
Suzie Poyntz
Jill Riches
Liam Riley
Mandy Rippon
Mike Shreeve
Keith Sleight
James Spackman
Linda Stevens
Sally Strachan
Lucy Sullivan
Caroline Sutherland
David Sutherland
Liz Thompson
Chloe Thwaites
Sarah Tinsley
Mark Vent
Debbie Walsh

Cassie Waters   Suzie Wilde
Miranda Whiting   Jonny Wilkes
Carol Whitton   Anne Williams

For Lilian and Phoebe –

The future is beautiful

Salt Lick

Water trickles through gullies in the brick, loosening bonds that have held the house together for nearly three hundred years. Rain and sea meet in the crooks, the filigree channels. Salt and fresh water seep into the brick and mortar. One wall has collapsed, fraction by fraction becoming sand, lulled back and forth by the waves. Other buildings, that once marked the back of the village before it gave way to fields, stand like rotten teeth in a mouth slack with the futility of further resistance.

A church rises from the sea, a small, solid island of grey rock. On the spire, a spike of metal, a weather vane with the only remaining arm pointing west, as if reminding the sea that it still has work to do. This way. The whole of England waits to be quenched.

A scrap of board that once boxed in some water pipes is inched from the shore by the waves, pulled to float away until caught in one of the unstable islands of waste circling slowly in the weary ocean's eddies. A piece of timber, the upright of a door frame, swollen with salt water is finally dragged away by the backwash, to find a place further along the shore. It had framed a door that opened to a small kitchen, nearest the beach at the back of the house. Later it was a utility room off a bigger kitchen. More recently, an arts and crafts shop, the back door cleared and opened to customers on a narrow lane now lost under sand. The proprietor made most of her income selling naive paintings of seagulls on distressed-to-order board, designed to look as though they had been washed in by the waves, collected by the beachcomber artist to use as a canvas. Slowly, slowly, the sea did the work for real, on the brick and board and mortar of the house crumbling on the threshold of the sea.

The wood that had fallen from the door frame was planed by hand and hung two centuries before, by a man named Matthew whose home was part of a hamlet further up the coast. A place where no land exists now. The door frame had been painted by twenty-two different hands. Some of the paint still clings in islands on the bare wood, from the first hard oily gloss of black, rubbed back for new colours, revealed by chips in the thickening paint. Then a bright sheen of white, and white again. Lastly, a pale matt blue matching the sky behind the painted seagulls. The rusted stub of a metal hook halfway along has bled out a black stain into the sea-darkened timber. It had been put there by Elsa, her red nails and freckled skin, already slipping with age between the tendons of her hands, had grappled with a blunt bradawl to get the hook to bite. She hung a notice bought from an online supplier, a stern message in a friendly script reminding the beach-holiday drifters that breakages must be paid for. Elsa had died before the sea had reached her door. But only just. In her eighties, the shop no longer open, deaf to the calls of concerned neighbours and friends, she watched the sea fretfully. She had watched her neighbours leave. All of them. She died, her nails still red, her chiffon scarf still puffing elegantly over her left collar bone, two weeks before the first storm surge licked her doorstep.

It crept up, storm by storm, washed through until the high

tide reached the other side of the house, started making for the fields; the acid-gold of rapeseed shot through with wilder brethren, no longer doused out of existence by spray-arms hitched wide as a field or chemicals dropped from buzzing drones. The sea intruded, in stormy times. The sea intruded. Another reason for the folk to make for the cities.

Jesse

1

A boy crawls on hands and knees, slowly, through a verge of cow parsley, a rippling wake in the veil of white flowers above his head. He moves along a hedge, full with summer growth. He peers through, searching for small gaps, those not close-darned with goosegrass and buttercup. The cows stand at the field edge. He creeps alongside, his hips and shoulder blades work the quiet, careful roll of his progress. He peers into the hedge, the tangle of hawthorn, knotted with dog rose, bramble, the small blue eyes of speedwell. His shirtless back is pale, small bones working under the skin. He catches a sting on his arm from an unnoticed nettle. His exclamation is answered by the breath and tread of a cow on the other side of the hedge. He stills, searches the shady green for a dock leaf to rub on the bumps of the nettle sting. The fat leaf stains his arm a little; he blows to cool the pain, then continues his stealthy way.

This boy spends hours and days out here. He fits himself into hollows and sings quiet songs. He stretches limber along branches, still young and smooth as he. Feet back on the ground, he hugs the ancient trunks, scratching his belly and arms on rough bark. His voice sometimes sounds with memories of games played with departed friends by the brook where they built a dam. He keeps up the work, overseeing the structure they made and bringing into the present, quietly, under his breath, the raucous chatter of old summers. He and Sep had done most of the work. They had done much together, the two boys. Only a few months apart in age and so alike in temperament. He recalls the flow of voices, an echo of those companionable days. *We need some moss. I'll get some more stones. That won't work. You idiot.*

He picks up a stick, makes an exaggerated pantomime of what itself was already just that, when Tammy pulled out a vape and smoked, properly. He mimics the challenge in her gaze as she loudly performed her confidence in this act of secret rebellion. It had been a shocking and bravura performance. She had moved with her family to the city by the autumn. He held the stick at his side, tilted his head back, blew from the side of his mouth. *Yeah.*

He mimes flicking a switch on the stick, tucks it into the back pocket of his jeans, then squats at the bank of the stream, picks stones out of the ground, throws them, aiming for a fern on the other side of the bank.

This boy, Jesse, goes in to the house where he lives with his mother Lena and his father Marshal. He can hear Lena upstairs, doing something. Doing one of the things she does, probably work. He sits on the sofa, big soft cushions that fold around him. He looks at the painting of the seagull on the wall. 'I don't even like it that much,' Mum says. He thinks that's funny. But she told him about the day when she was young, same age as him or thereabouts, and on a trip to the beach with her own mum. How they had visited a little gallery. 'It reminds me of a happy day, and it reminds me of all the times we remembered a happy day together,' Mum said, smiling.

The gull flies on and away, never reaching the artfully unfinished edge of the board. When they all needed to stay at home for so long, he sometimes used to sit on the sofa for hours, imagining all the things it could see below. The fireplace became a great harbour, the rug a pattern of crops in the fields.

Chorus
soon it will be time
to learn the land, boy

find its patterns for yourself

He gazes at the bird, lost in the animal comfort of warmth and rest after activity. He taps his feet, heels planted, taps one finger on another wrist, adrift. He comes awake to think of his bike, the skid he nearly managed, the daring he will achieve. He hopes he will learn how to slide the back wheel of his bike round, spraying stones in the sweep. He imagines himself doing that.

School has got smaller again. The Thatchers and the Wilsons have moved to the city. Jesse is sad that Sherrelle won't be at school any more. They had often played together after school. Once, when they all had to stay apart, they had both built camps in their own bedrooms and talked all night, he thought, on screens, pretending they were out in the woods. They told each other scary stories. Jesse had secretly opened his door to listen to his mum and dad downstairs.

That was before people left, when they were trying to keep safe. There are only seven children left now. He is about the middle in age. The parents talk about whether the school will stay open, what will happen if there is no funding for winter. But there are only six parents. Seven counting Romain's dad's girlfriend, though she doesn't have much to do with school. They have come to understand that they are powerless, come to accept that they will just have to make the best of it.

Lena is the teacher; she promises the parents that she is not going anywhere. 'As long as I am here these children will have a teacher,' she says often, defiantly. And why shouldn't the county just keep the school open? Pavel's mum and dad have just put up their own new solar tiles, they can do the same, team effort, for the school. 'We've all lost enough already, let's for goodness sake try and keep that level of normality going, give the children a school to go to.'

Jesse finds himself repeating the mantra to himself sometimes – *we've all lost enough already*. Without analysis, he understands it is a stepping-stone, a push toward small acts of defiance. He notices the grown-ups say it when they want to do something brave. It helps them to be courageous. Or they say it when they want something to stop. *We've all lost enough already*.

Chorus

we have

we have in days and ages,
in place and purpose

we've lost worlds

and never does it seem to be enough
for you

all our slow and watchful lifetimes

and still,
we never understood
your insatiable need
your wide arms, piston driven, lightening charged, grasping
gathering,
dragging in

as though your lives depend on it

So Lena kept teaching the children. The children kept drifting away. The community, become now so small, takes every opportunity to share thoughts and fears. Each knows just how close the others are to leaving, how determined they are to stay. Sometimes there are surprises. The Wilsons had been adamant that they would stay, now that Lewis was buried here. They weren't going to leave, no matter what. But Nora's insulin became an issue. Jesse doesn't know what Nora's insulin is. But he knows it is the reason that Sherrelle and her parents, and her little sister – the other side of the gap left by Lewis – have moved to the city.

He thinks about Sherrelle, about her brother Lewis who died and her dad, who took it all so bad, even though he got better. He thinks about a camp he made with her in the garden, before Lewis and all the others got sick. It's still light outside, and he is allowed to play outside if it is light. He goes out of the back door into the long garden. The lawn is edged with some digging that might become a wavering vegetable patch. 'One day, Jesse,' his dad had said with good cheer. 'Can we grow cherries and cucumbers?' Jesse had asked. 'God knows,' replied Marshal, smiling, crinkles at his eyes.

A blackbird sings, the notes rise from the old apple tree at the bottom of the garden. A gnarled, arthritic hand, thinned with age reaching from the long grass, the bright and agile birdsong reaching higher still. The sun is behind the house next door, where Paul and Arty used to live. Arty had died too, in the October Flu pandemic, and Paul was a bit like Sherrelle's dad. He went to pieces. And then he also died. Jesse looks to the fence that was between the two houses. Sometimes they would pop their heads over. They had seemed too happy to have died. Both had suntans. Paul always wore fancy hats; he made silly jokes and called Jesse 'Me Old Mate'. Once they went on holiday and brought back a cap with buffalo horns on it for Jesse. He wishes they were still there.

He turns and listens to the blackbird. He starts to move, softly creeping, into the singing. He walks very slowly, keeps moving within stillness. He thinks he is part of the garden.

2

Jesse is sitting at the kitchen table, half listening to the radio, fiddling with a salt cellar. The voices on the radio are talking about things that make them angry. Lena is angry about them too.

'For goodness sake, why not just ban cars in the cities? That's where the pollution is. We've got enough to deal with here. How are people going to get to the jobs that there are? It's insane.'

Jesse looks at her, aware that in her anger she is, kind of, talking to him.

'Are they going to take the car?'

'They keep saying they will but I am sure they will back down; they did last time. Bloody idiots.'

Chorus

the power of storms
you made the power of thunder and speed
inside beasts snorting up all air for their dirty burning lungs
all that might, given over to
the harms

the takings
the stealings
the killings
all that and all you did with it

There is a knock on the door, Euan is on the step, his bike lying across the path behind him. Jesse sighs inside. Today he wants to go to the woods on his own. The friendship of the older boy is hard for Jesse to live up to. It's all speed and might with Euan, it feels like a competition and Jesse is nervous about it. Euan comes round so early though, now Guy Wilson has left.

'Is Jesse coming out to play?'

Jesse checks Lena, she smiles and nods OK, he slides off the kitchen chair and picks up trainers by the back door.

'Don't be out too long Jesse – you have to do some school-work before tomorrow.'

Jesse gets his bike from the side of the house, Euan waits on the road. They cycle over to the cul-de-sac – the newest houses in the village, but all now empty. The wide front gardens are perfect for bikes, as there are only occasional small flowerbeds that divide the lawns, no one built walls or hedges between. Except for Mr Arnott. But he was the first to abandon the cul-de-sac. The first villager to die in the pandemic. His house is at the end of the close and doesn't break the sweeps of grass and tarmac interrupted only by the odd unruly ornamental shrub.

The grass is growing high in the gardens now. The two boys alone don't create enough wear, find it harder to keep the bike paths open between the course of jumps and bumps they had set up.

'Let's go and look for a knife to cut back the paths,' Euan suggests. Jesse knows he means in one of the empty houses. His heart starts a little patter; he had, they all had been told not to go into any of the empty houses – they still belonged to some-one, the children would be in danger or big trouble or both. But Euan is older and Jesse wants to be tougher, like Euan, and knows he will follow him into Mr Arnott's home. All the children know that the back door is unlocked at Mr Arnott's. Tammy and Sherelle had made a camp up in the guest bed-room last summer, created a shrine of an old dresser, with flow-ers and stolen candles, melted onto Mr Arnott's saucers.

The boys walk between the houses into the back gardens, through new gaps in fence and hedge. There is a narrow strip of field at the back of the gardens, a wild tongue that pokes into the village, no longer kept tidy with crops. Jesse notices that brambles growing at the field edge are coming into the gardens, creeping through the long grass. The village is com-ing undone at the edges. Jesse remembers a word – fray. He remembers Lena stitching a turn-up into his trousers. Jesse had been impatient to get on, but Lena had made him wait until she had hemmed the edge. She wasn't used to sewing and the stitches had come undone.

'I'll do it again or they'll fray,' she had said. 'Leave them on the back of the chair.' But Jesse hadn't left them on the chair, and Lena hadn't chased him up. The back of the trousers now hang in a line of thready rag. It was the same with the village. All the edges are coming undone.

Chorus

sweet child
this is not an undoing
but a remaking
measured on a pattern
older than time

A neighbour had cleaned Mr Arnott's kitchen after he died, took out the food and cleaned the fridge, but it is dowdy and feels grubby. Old fashioned. The kitchen is dimly lit, light seeps through a floral blind pulled down over the front window. Jesse pulls out a kitchen chair, starting at the screech, looking fearfully to the window for a moment. Euan rummages in drawers that stick, slow to reveal their contents. There is one small knife that won't be useful for scything grass. A large pair of silver scissors he hands to Jesse.

'What about the garden shed?' Jesse says. He is pleased with the smile Euan gives him, an older boy's recognition of a good idea. They run out to the back garden, once an ordered mosaic of annual colour, vivid petunias, pelargoniums, lobelia; now home to the meeker, hardier scatter of wild-flower ancestors. Stars where there were once suns. A shed stands at the side of the patio. The padlock won't give but there is a window, Jesse can see shears hanging on the wall. They look at each other, a silent agreement that yes, they will break the glass.

'Wait,' says Euan. He goes into the house and returns with a cushion, orange with white trim, and a metal coffee pot. He takes over management, his style lifted from cop shows and though they have a whole free day, there is an urgency in him.

'Shield your eyes, OK. Let's…' He holds the cushion over the window then hits it with the coffee pot. Jesse is peering through his fingers. He giggles when the coffee pot bounces off but nothing happens to the glass. He stifles the laugh, but it bubbles back up when Euan starts hammering the cushion with the bottom of the coffee pot. The safety glass doesn't break. Jesse is fully laughing now.

'Fuck off,' says Euan. 'Have you got a better idea?'

Jesse quells his mirth and says no, he doesn't. Maybe if Euan used something thinner than the cushion?

'Well, go and find something then.'

Jesse goes into the house. There are coats hanging by the front door. Maybe an anorak? He feels a nervous slide across his shoulders at the thought of dead Mr Arnott's clothes. But then, he notices a key rack. A board with a fancy bevelled edge, the word Keys helpfully burnt in above two rows of hooks. He picks them all off and takes them out to Euan.

'Genius!' says Euan, finding the small padlock key almost immediately.

The boys put the keys back in the house but leave the padlock key under a stone next to the shed door. They head out to the front, armed with sheers and edge trimmers. Keeping lazy watch for anyone they start to hack at the long stems of grass, reforming the paths for their bikes. It's hard work with the blunt blades. They clear the main drag then decide to hide the tools, stashing them under a shrub growing under the kitchen window of Evie and Arno's old place. They can do the rest another day.

Euan stands with his legs apart, hands on hips, surveying their work with satisfaction. Without noticing the shift in his limbs, Jesse mimics his pose.

'I'll go first,' says Euan, inevitably.

Jesse wheels his bike home, ready for some food. He has grass stains on one knee, and a pain that he has been pretending not to feel. He did a brilliant skid, but the skid became a wipe-out. No shame in that, unless you cry; the laughter of the two boys had made the pain bearable. Jesse had tried an experimental 'Fuckenell' as he lay sprawled still on the ground.

'Epic!' Euan had said.

His knee throbs though, now. A car passes him. A beep and a wave, it's Euan's mum on her way out of the village. Jesse wonders whether they've decided to take the cars yet. Maybe it

will be OK. He doesn't know what pollution is, but he knows
it kills people. He leans his bike against the side of the house
and goes to the kitchen to find some food.

Chorus

make yourself ready for the world, boy
oh, we wish we could keep you safely here
we wish we could make you stay

People are sick of pollution. Lena too. It's one of the reasons
that even now she refuses to move to the city. And she knows
it's for the best, for everyone, if the lung-shrinking invisible
smog seeping out from the new city micro-industries are
finally halted. People have grown tired of etiolated children,
wheezing slenderly, some tagging a tank onto their backpacks.
People have grown tired of uncles, mothers, cousins dying of
new and vicious lung cancers. The pandemic – that couldn't
be helped. But for god's sake, they could do something about
particle pollution without making the lives of people left in the
countryside even harder. No one, it seems, had expected a ban
on private vehicles to be part of the solution. The radio was
full of talk of rail links, of shrinking rural populations, of public
transport infrastructure investment. But those outside the cities
will really struggle. A radical solution, so disarmingly close to
what people want yet so dramatic a change. Such step changes
are becoming more common since the disarray of the pandemic. Crisis still jangles in the air.

You would've thought that so many people dying would at
least have had a positive impact on air quality. *There has to be
some upside*, she thinks bitterly.

She feels a helplessness that infuriates her. Jesse comes into the kitchen, his pale brown hair falling over his eyes. *How would he manage in London*, she thinks? If they had to move, what would it be like for her fawn, her little leveret, her brindle child?

'Come and give me a hug, Jessymallessy.' Jesse walks over to Lena, sitting at the kitchen table, and hugs her, speaks into her shoulder.

'I'm hungry, do we have any biscuits?'

'Oh, you're always hungry! Yes, should be some in the cupboard, but only have a couple – we'll eat soon.'

Jesse goes to the cupboard. He pulls out a packet that he doesn't recognise, he spells out Maltetto-Bics.

'They didn't have the usual ones.' Lena sighs – everything's always different. 'But these are pretty nice.'

Jesse takes a couple, waves the packet at Lena, who shakes her head. She smiles, watching her son walk into the living room and settle on the sofa.

'Mum?'

'Yes, bubba?'

'I did a really, really good skid on my bike today.'

3

With so few children, school takes place over a few hours in the middle of the day and the mornings are free. The next day, Jesse heads out to play by himself, earlier than usual to miss the call-up of Euan. He walks along the lane that cuts through the farm, past the field of Fresian cows on one side and the empty farm buildings on the other. The cows are scattered across the field today. He leans, hands on the top bar, looking through the gate. He tries a moo. A couple of the cows look at him but they don't come to investigate. He feels the gate's tubular steel bar press into his chest, straightens his arms and lowers his body down to hook his chin over it. A rash of rust prickles the skin under his jaw. He experiments with a moo again, enjoying the strangeness of the sound, squeezed through his taut throat. He sinks further, hanging from the top bar, feet pressed onto the bottom. He pretends he is wind surfing.

'Shhhwhooo.' He twists his shoulders to take a wave, makes a sound that means slicing through wind, the sound of silent speed.

He turns off the lane into a small patch of slender trees and grass, behind the farm buildings. Tucked against the stone wall of the barn, in a scrub of greenery, he sees something – a little brown face. A puppy. He stops, stands still. He knows that there are wild dogs about, abandoned during the pandemic, or when people left for the cities, lost in the chaotic aftermaths of sometimes several deaths in one household. He is scared of a big angry mother but is drawn to the small creature in a way that can't be resisted. They look at each other, mirroring the same anxieties, the same desire to connect. The puppy is shy, the more wary of the two.

Jesse's heart bumps with excitement but he stays still, talking to the puppy quietly. It looks at him, the dark marking of hopeful, sad eyebrows on its brown face. It makes little moves toward him, little tail wags, but backs away again to the wall, doesn't come to Jesse. He crouches down, slowly, sits on the ground, pushing aside grasses, jack-in-the-hedge and ragwort, so that the puppy can still see him. He waits. The puppy waits too. It sits down, yawns a yawn that turns into a little bark. It rests its chin on its paws, now and then making the sad, curious eyebrows up to Jesse, sitting in the grass a few meters away.

Jesse starts to talk quietly, an unthought stream with intention. He speaks slowly and evenly, instinctively, slightly lifting the pitch of his voice, lowering the volume.

'You look like Mr Malik's dog, Polo. Was she your mum? Are you on your own? Did you get left when Mr Malik died? Where's your family, Mr Malik's baby dog? Mr Malik's baby dog. Hey, Mr Malik's puppy dog, shall we be friends? Shall we be friends, Mister Maliks? Yes, let's be friends.'

The puppy, pretending to stretch, inches closer to the boy, sing-songing them into friendship.

'Come on then, Mister Maliks, come and say hello.' Jesse holds out his hand. 'Licks and sticks, Mister Maliks. Come and say hello.'

He coaxes the puppy to him and soon the two sit together.

He is thin and has a slightly weepy eye. Jesse tries to pick him up to carry him home, but the puppy takes fright.

'It's OK, Mister Maliks, we're friends. We're friends.' He sits still, stroking the puppy behind his ear, feeling the tiny bump of a skull under the skin. He gently traces the slopes and dips of bone with his fingertips, filled with a terrible awareness of the little creature's delicacy. He hums a soothing rhyme. 'Licks and sticks, MicksMaliks, licks and sticks, MicksMaliks.'

The puppy edges closer to the boy, drops to the ground, the slim curve of his spine resting against Jesse's leg, folded on the ground. The puppy closes his eyes, as though at last come to sanctuary and blessed rest. Jesse lifts his other hand and feels under his own hair, tracing up his neck, finding the edge of his skull. For the first time he imagines the bones inside his body. He is torn between fear and fascination, intuitively feeling the inside of the body is secret, the key to life and death. Tummy, blood, tubes. He pulls away from those dark coils, turns back to the woodlands, the buzz of warmth, the back of the puppy's head. He is moved momentously by the frailty of bone, the thinness of the skin under his softly stroking hand. He could almost cry with love, already, for the little animal.

Chorus

soft bones
and tendons
roping us to life

It is time to leave, if he's not going to be late for school. But he has work to do first. He stretches carefully. He wants to take the puppy home; somehow he will persuade Mum and Dad.

He has to, it has to be that way. But that is a risky play and the puppy is still nervous about being picked up. Jesse is scared of frightening him away for good. Or of dropping him on the road if he wriggles too much, of losing him in a place where the puppy will be confused and never come to him again. He speaks as he soothes.

'Mister Maliks, I'm going to come back, right away, with some food for you, and then I have to go away again for a while. I have to go to school, but I swear I will come back. Look, you can have this, to remember that I'll be back.' Jesse peels off his t-shirt, drapes it over the puppy, who looks up at him, curious, and as always looking sad. Jesse is worried about leaving such a small thing lying in the middle of an almost open space. He wants to tuck him up next to the wall some-where. He gets up slowly and coaxes the dog to follow him. There is a fallen sheet of corrugated iron that he fetches, keeping up his soothing refrain, keeping the continuity of their connection.

'See, I'm getting this to make a place for you. Then one day, you can come and live with me. But just for now, here, let's... it's a bit heavy, but wait just a minute.' He drags the sheet, snagging at the weeds, the edges sharp on his fingers. Soon it's propped up against the barn wall, tucked in behind a bush. The puppy watches, moves around in a tight space, ready for flight, just as ready to join in with the boy.

'So, here you are. I'll put my t-shirt in here and you can stay here and I'll bring you back some food, and a blanket or something.' By sitting still again, at the mouth, Jesse coaxes the puppy over, into the shelter. He lies down on the t-shirt, resting his head between his paws. Jesse gets up slowly, scared about leaving, scared of the curious sad look the puppy gives him, scared he may never see him again. He walks away, slowly, chattering quietly still, then as soon as he is back on the lane, he runs, full hard, arms and legs and chest and breath all pounding together. He swings through the back door into the kitchen, grabs the biscuits, a bowl, he grabs a cottage-pie ready meal, cold on the fridge shelf. He grabs some unopened milk. He can hear Lena upstairs. Her door opens, she is speaking to him about work to finish before school. He throws everything into a bag and runs back out before she can intercept.

He runs all the way back along the lane, holding the bag awkwardly in front of him, trying not to mash up the contents. When he gets to the edge of the wooded opening behind the barn he slows, begins to talk through his breathlessness, high and soft, soothing, he hopes. He moves slowly. There is no response and he is terrified that the puppy has gone, but he keeps fear from his voice. The puppy is sleeping on the red and orange t-shirt. Jesse almost cries with relief. He runs a fingertip softly over the animal's ribs, rising and falling in sleep, down a delicate leg. The puppy bends his foot in a little shimmer of response but otherwise doesn't stir. Jesse is going to be late for school if he doesn't hurry. He is afraid that the reason for his lateness will be plain to see, easily discovered, right there in the classroom and then how would he keep the beautiful joy of Mister Maliks to himself? Someone would take over, claim him. Someone would be louder, brasher, bolder. He needs time to secure their bond.

He lays out the food around the edge of the t-shirt. A barrier of fulfilment. He regrets the lack of meat, ideally a nice juicy bone, but there is some in the cottage pie and all dogs surely love biscuits. He unwraps the pie and scoops off some of the potato with his hand, wipes it on the grass and then on his jeans. He pours the milk carefully into the bowl, tucks bottle and bowl into the shade of the shelter, out of the sun.

'Here you go, that'll help, won't it, Mister Maliks? I'll come back soon, I promise, as soon as I can.' His heart gives a lurch as he looks at the sleeping dog, surrounded by food that he is suddenly afraid might attract more dangerous creatures. He decides to block the ends of the triangular shelter. Not to keep Mister Maliks in but to keep badgers and foxes out. He hurries, finding bits of board, flint fallen from the barn wall, and covers each end of the low lean-to shelter. He feels a sadness that he doesn't understand – though he acts out of care, he feels the sadness of cruelty.

Chorus

care,
from young to young
you have it in your hearts

you do,
it's born there

Lena looks at her shifty son, shirtless and late in to get ready for school.

'Jesse, where on earth is your t-shirt? And those jeans are filthy!' She is exasperated when he tells her that he has forgotten it, he left it in the woods by accident. She takes that misdemeanour as the reason for his sketchy evasiveness. 'Well, you can go back after school and get it then, we have to take care of stuff.'

As soon as school is done, Jesse runs back home, ahead of Lena, calling out behind him that he's going out to play. He doesn't think he can take any more food without it being noticed but throwing his school bag down he runs up to the cupboard to find an old towel that he can sneak out to replace his t-shirt.

The puppy whimpers once, quietly, when Jesse approaches the shelter, then barks as he picks up the sound of Jesse's voice. Jesse pulls the boards away from the opening and is thrilled that the puppy jumps at him, tail wagging. There is cottage pie and milk all over Jesse's t-shirt. He takes the towel from around his neck and puts that in the shelter instead, picking up the sodden t-shirt.

'What a messy eater! Let's go to the stream. Come on, Mister Maliks, come with me.' Jesse picks up the t-shirt and the empty bowl. The puppy seems happy now to follow him. They take a conversational route, checking and reacting to the movement of the other, meandering through the woods until they reach the stream. Jesse hunkers down and soaks his top in the water. Mister Maliks snuffles around the clearing on the bank. He rinses the top and hangs it over a branch. He sinks the bowl at the water edge, Mister Maliks drinks some water and eats some crumbled biscuit from his hand. Jesse feels it as a tremendous achievement. They play. Sunlight falls in bright daubs on the bank, skids off the rolling water, and across the flanks of the two small, happy creatures.

At bedtime Jesse hugs Lena then Marshal, who comes upstairs with his son to turn the light off. Jesse thinks he is too old for his dad to tuck him up in bed, so if Marshal does straighten the cover, stroke his son's head, drop a kiss on his hair, Jesse still will only ask him to come up and turn the light off. Marshal knows the mind of his boy, is quick to cuddle him when the two of them are alone. But he understands the awkward reaching for age, the stretch upwards to be like the older boys, even as he knows that Jesse is happiest in his childishness, in his innocence and youth. Boys grow, and all must find their way through. All must find their way under the gaze of other boys.

Marshal was a boy who was used to being a leader. The brave and bold one. But he recognises now how much he needed the admiration of those other boys. He is moved with lurching love by his son's sunny contentment, his quiet introversion, his completeness.

Jesse has a nightly habit of getting out of bed once the door is shut and the light off, placing his dressing gown across the strip of light at the bottom of the door. It comes from younger days when he still had a night light, soon after they had moved here. It comes from days so young that he thought it would give him a bit more time to escape from his room if there was another flood. It comes from days when he hadn't worked out that their new house, this home they had lived in for four years, was high enough on the land not to be reached by the sea. Their old house had been flooded when the sea breached a bar of protecting land and now sat waist-deep in the lolling tides that tugged the living room curtains in and out. It took a young boy some time to learn that they were safe from that peril, here up on the low roll of hills that nestled the village. But cutting out the strip of landing light had by force of habit come to give him a sense of security no longer related to water. In keeping out the light, the transformed spell worked to keep out all dangers.

Chorus

this land is changed
in so many ways
fences, fields and boundaries built,
containment

and now, the edges gone

your power, less

than you thought you deserved

didn't you learn?
you have the words, the stories made for learning
and yet you didn't learn

hubris

This night, he lays the dressing gown down and crosses to the open window, sending his thoughts to Mister Maliks. The air is still and warm, gentle summer dusk, but he can't bear to think of the dog being on his own in the woods. He curses himself for not making the shelter stronger. He imagines a succession of woodland creatures and feral pets, dragging down the corrugated iron sheet, shunting aside boards in search of cold cottage pies, finding instead the moonlit sport of harassing the defenceless dog. He imagines an anthropomorphic ring of badgers, hares, wild tabby cats, taunting and scratching Mister Maliks until he lies, defeated and ragged, his last breath spent just as Jesse arrives to rescue him. He is so tormented it takes him a restless age to get to sleep.

4

Early in the morning, Marshal is getting ready to leave for the long drive to work. Jesse comes downstairs, still tired but dressed. Marshal pulls him into his side for a half-hug as he makes coffee. He has managed to keep earning, but it is getting harder. Work for a builder of glass extensions to seventeenth-century farmhouses, a converter of barns into sympathetic but modern homes, a constructor of elegant villas for wealthy city workers needing a break from financial manipulation and wealth creation, depended on the presence of wealthy people to build for. The pandemic has simply and efficiently changed the set-up, put a scythe of death, relocation or destitution through the numbers of potential customers for all trades. And newly minted government strategies had whipped the wealth away from other of Marshal's former clients.

The economic decline of the countryside, slid in first to the fields and farmlands, then to the villages, the market towns. After new employment and immigration laws bite, the work-forces and wage offers no longer matched and so the workers disappeared. Harvests were hindered by the vagaries of a local work force not used to that much work for that little pay. The supermarkets stepped up importation. And as they imported more, less was provided from within the national borders. The shift over time changed the balance of power by finally depreciating the long-steady value of land. Wages for farm workers were pinched further and supermarkets scoured other lands for their produce.

For a while, for the well-heeled, little changed. Marshal kept up his flatteringly matey friendships with the wealthy of the parish. The men, encountering their own physicality only in the pampered confines of a gym, were drawn to his way of treating them as casually manly equals. All customers spoke of his impeccable reputation for quality. Though increasingly, at the golf clubs and spas, people muttered about the economic climate. The gin and tonics were knocked back between head shakes and bluster, bitter soliloquies about betrayal. Hand-in-fist together, planning national strategies that best served them, the rural wealthy, the landed gentry, were outraged to discover that they no longer had the ear of government.

Chunks of ice clinked against comfortingly hefty glass in the tremor of a suddenly bankrupt hand. During the chaos of the pandemic, the pattern of wealth in the country shifted. Over time, the losses increased, the economic climate became harder still. Some of the rich remained rich. Some did not. There were heart attacks and suicides. The gentlemen farmers, astonishingly quickly, found that all they had to bargain with was the long habit of association with those who ruled the country. Friendship can go a long way, in individual cases; some of those bonds survived the fall from grace, but it was the developers in the towns who were courted. What was the wealth of a landowner when no one wanted land?

Marshal, quicker to spot the signs than his complacent customers has shored up some of his options by becoming an installer of new systems for bespoke, single-unit flood defences. The wealthy who remain have shifted spending from luxury and pleasure to the necessary, to insurance. He is still busy enough to feed the family, busy enough to feel too distant from them, but the days of easy wealth are behind them.

Chorus

over time
all will fade
die
and grow again

this is the meaning of natural order

perhaps your time comes to a close

yes, in many ways you spent it well
– that was a time, was it not?

but think what you could have done with such gifts

'Dad?' Jesse leans his head onto his father's side, lolling against the movement of his breakfast preparations. Marshal loops an arm around his son's shoulders.

'Yes? What can I do for you?' Jesse pauses, thoughts tumbling uselessly, realising too late that he hasn't worked out the perfect formula. But he has started now.

'Can I get a dog?'

'We've talked about this before, remember? We don't know what's going to happen, if we have to... we might not be able to look after a dog.'

'But we're not going to move now. This house won't flood.'

'No, it won't flood. But if work carries on as it is, if... I don't know, Jesse; there are still quite a lot of ifs and it would be harder if we had a dog too.'

Jesse detaches himself, sits at the table. He is thinking furiously, looking for the chink in his father's argument. Looking for a way to reframe the question. It's beyond him. He will try to talk to his mum he thinks, later, when she's in a good mood. As soon as Marshal leaves, Jesse puts on his shoes and goes to the woods. It is earlier to be out than he is used to. He notices a softness in the air, the faint hush of a day not fully awake. He pauses at the gate to look over the field, just for a moment, to check where the cows are. They are sitting down. Big as sofas. He wonders if they are still sleeping. He scurries the last yards.

The shelter is still intact. He can hear Mister Maliks inside, can see the snuffle of a black nose between gaps in the construction. He pulls away the stones – flints fallen from a breach in the top of the barn wall. The puppy is overjoyed, leaps up at the crouching boy. Jesse picks up the small body, so intent on licking his face that he forgets to be afraid of the encircling arms.

Chorus

we see you, boy
we see your gentle heart
keep it carefully
it has work to do

5

The village is bristling, agitation disturbs the smooth nap of village life. A group of white nationalists have moved into Little Denton, a village less than three miles by road and only a long mile on woodland paths. Little Denton is a quiet place, or it used to be. There had once been a fierce cricket rivalry, but neither village can muster a team now.

John, who farms cereal crops as part of a resilient if threadbare collective comes by, telling how he had seen them moving into some empty houses on Elm Close. He despairs he says. Might as well be in the bloody city.

He goes round to Gopal Malik's house. The two men had shared a passion for maintaining hedgerows for wildlife. But Gopal died. John misses him, the time spent working hard on something rewardingly beneficial followed by a well-earned pint in whichever village pub was nearest. Over the years, he came to know Gopal's two daughters, though they have never lived in the village. Chetna is spending some time in her father's house while she sets straight his affairs. John wants to warn her about the newcomers. Chetna sighs. She had thought that leaving the city might mean a break from anxiety, from the escalating tension as fears become sour and turned outwards. A weight slides over her shoulders – the donning of a wry courage she had hoped she needn't carry here.

Chorus

you need protection
you ever did
we all ever did
from the flaw of cruelty
waiting
to be called into use

put into eager, angry hands

is it in the marrow? Or in the mind?
waiting somewhere

it seems part of the design

The children are told to keep away from Little Denton, though it is beyond the range of their regular play. Jesse spends all the time he can in the clearing behind the farm and the nearby woods with Mister Maliks. He discovers new ways to sneak food out of the house. He dreams all day of a woodland patch of sun and the chance to play with his new friend.

Jesse and Mister Maliks walk long, unnoticed ranges through the woods. They explore random paths. They loop toward and away from each other, walk side by side, accelerate and fall back. They stop to investigate, Jesse with his eyes and hands,

Mister Maliks with his nose. Jesse keeps up his quiet chatter, a thread that joins and stretches between them.

'Mister Maliks, Mister Maliks, hey what have you found there? Come here, here, Mister Maliks, what's this stick? You won't find a better one, I bet. Fetch! Go on! Let's play? I'll have to teach you that game, won't I?' They roam for hours, pulling leaves and slender twigs through hands, nudging the damp blunt cup of a mushroom into a fallen branch, pressing the robust and prickly cases of old beech nuts, trying to squash them shut between finger and thumb, following the trail of a squirrel, a rabbit, a deer, alarmingly another dog. They roam until the sound of a radio, tuned to pop music, quite close, stops them. Jesse is suddenly aware of the crunch of leaves under his feet. He is aware of himself in the space, his defined edges, when moments before he was a part of all that was around him. The possibility of another human re-forms his boundaries.

Mister Maliks isn't interested in the new sound. He is chasing his loops and circles, designed for his pleasure by other creatures, eyes down, snuffling at the base of a tree then on into a clump of holly. Jesse moves back onto a path that is clearer of leaves, damp earth softening foot fall. He moves closer to look. It is the back of some houses on the edge of Little Denton. Jesse peers, confused by what he sees. There are tree stumps, recently felled, blonde and raw. There are pieces of living-room furniture, two sofas and armchairs, outside in the trees. The back fence has gone, big glass doors open out straight into the woods. There are flags hanging from upstairs windows, and one big one strung up between two trees. He takes a moment to decipher the funny spiky script, pulling the black letters out of a design of red crosses. It says Sons of Boudicca.

'Get that shit music off!' shouts a voice from inside the house. A head rises into view, from the sofas with its back to Jesse. He checks over his shoulder – Mister Maliks is still happily sniffling around some logs. The man who gets up is dressed like a schoolteacher on the telly, Jesse thinks. He has a shirt with a jumper over it, neat hair. He has a black gun in his hand, hanging loosely at his side. He leaves it there, pointing down his leg as he leans over a small table and fiddles with the speaker, changing to some classical music. Jesse is frozen in a moment of terror. He imagines, inevitably, that the man will turn slowly and point the gun at him. The crystal vision evaporates, he backs away, his heart hammering. His mind is scrambled and he feels the cold drag of shock across his skin. He walks back the way he has come, holding out a hand, urgently, quietly clicking fingers to Mister, too scared to speak to him. The map of Jesse's world shrinks.

Chorus

some of your kind
would make your ways as dull and safe as ours
some would rip out your very hearts

Jesse pushes the encounter aside. He half fears being told off for straying into a place he was supposed to avoid. He guesses that he won't be believed and any way it would be his fault. And so he turns away, or tries too. But it nags at him and is kept alive by the intuition of change, disquiet in the village. He feels insecure.

The villagers take to having meetings about what they will need to do to keep the small community going. Jesse overhears Lena and Marshal talking after one of them. Another farm has disintegrated. The family have gone, no one knows where. Malc is desperate. Malc is a tall, friendly man with a drooping moustache. He has a lovely smile that puts people at ease. He once came to school and helped the children build a dome with coppiced hazel. He is, or was, the stockman at the farm. Jesse is sad to think of him being desperate.

'Maybe we can all chip in, keep the farm going, or the milk anyway.'

'Love, we can't even start a veg patch.'

Jesse decides that now is the time to tell Mum and Dad about the man in the woods, the gun. The fear of it has held him in complicit silence till now but in this moment of shared alarm, urgently, he needs to tell them.

'I saw a man with a gun in the woods, near Little Denton.'

Both Jesse's parents turn and look at their son.

'What sort of gun, Jesse?' asks Marshal. 'Who was it? Was it one of the farmers?'

Jesse describes what he has seen. His fear rises up again and in the relieved jumble of its emergence, he mentions Mister Maliks.

'Who is Mr Maliks?' asks Lena, confused by the name of a recently deceased neighbour.

'He's a dog; he's a puppy, I found him in the woods and made friends with him, and I am going to look after him always, even if you say he can't come and live with us.'

Lena and Marshal stumble over trying to keep up with their son. Lena asks again about the man with the gun, Marshal asks about the dog, where he is now, where did Jesse find him. Lena goes to hug Jesse, who is afraid of the gun and afraid that now his parents know about Mister Maliks that something will go wrong, that he hasn't had time to carefully work him into the house. The twin anxieties overwhelm him and he cries. Lena holds her son, soothing him first.

Later, Lena phones John, taking the call into the other room. Marshal sits on the sofa next to Jesse.

'I think you should show me your new friend.'

'Dad, can we keep him? Please. Please, Dad?'

'Look bud, no promises, but let's go, and you can introduce us for starters.'

Marshal is moved by the clumsy but effective shelter, tucked behind the empty stone barn. He is touched with profound love for the secret industry of the boy, anxious and hopeful, bending down to lift away the pieces of timber. The puppy leaps out of the shelter, up joyfully at Jesse and up at Marshal with the same loving abandon. *Oh no*, thinks Marshal. How can he and Lena say no to the family acquiring a dog? They already have one, it seems.

'Look, you stay here with Mister Malik and I'll go and see if your mum has finished on the phone.'

'It's Mister Maliks... and tell Mum I'll look after him. I'll do everything; I'll buy his food and everything.'

'Easy, Jesse, we still need to talk about it. Things aren't easy, and what would happen if we had to move to London?'

'People have dogs in London, and I'd walk him and look after him.'

'I know they do, but we will need to find somewhere that will let us have a dog and that might be difficult.'

'Well, let's just stay here like we all want to?'

Lena wants to stay where they are, more than Marshal. They are pulling apart in their assessment of what will keep the three of them safest, best provided for. Marshal can't help thinking in terms of his income, his work opportunities, his ability to provide more than they need. It infuriates Lena, who knows his desire to be a man of status, like he was a few years ago. She knows he wants to provide, that this wish is core to his being and that for him it is an expression of love. But she knows too that deliberately choosing to be poorer, to suit, simply, the wishes of his wife and the nature of his child, is a hard step for Marshal to take. The fundamental characters of both are being set against the other. And the good of Jesse can play out in so many ways. Is the countryside any better than the city when white nationalists with guns are at home in the woods?

The unwelcome fact is that the nationalists have moved in, that nothing will be done about it. John had explained to Lena his attempts to access help. The new arrivals are, or at least were, a proscribed organisation, their founder imprisoned for hate crime. But now it seems, proscription is either rescinded or toothless. The local town has a police station where one administrator logs reports between the hours of ten and four. Policing in the area has more or less stopped. Police in the cities don't care that a bunch of white nationalists have moved into houses left empty by death or displacement. They are glad of the absence. 'Perhaps they think they'll do less harm in whiter parts of the country,' John says. He feels a sense of hopelessness, a rush of anger for his friend's daughter, forced into awareness of the dangers to her, dangers that patchwork the whole country. He is humiliated by his inability to counter that imposition, by his whiteness, by an unwelcome feeling of culpability that it gives him.

Chorus

yes, they would call you traitor
they would call her enemy

all in hatred called
according to their bitter fear

and what will they do,

when hatred wins
and they learn their fear prevails?

each will scythe a circle round himself
until he is the only one

Unexpectedly, Lena welcomes the addition of a dog to the family. Quietly she sees it as a further bulwark against leaving. These are strange times, and a dog may provide protection, or at least an alarm. Mister Maliks moves first into the garden, then by wheedling degrees into the house. He's not allowed food from Jesse's plate but Jesse develops a flick-or-drop technique to leave bits that the puppy will find later. Marshal and Lena are not as immune to him as they thought they would be and soon they are as charmed by the puppy as they are by Jesse's love for him. But they tell Jesse off for feeding him with his own dinner, make him pick up the food he leaves with a dustpan and brush, if they catch him. Lena talks about finding a lead, but the two of them spend so much time together, work so hard to please each other, that it isn't necessary. Without ever setting out to train him, Jesse can make Mister Maliks understand him, work with him. Their relationship is too close, too equal, to say that Mister Maliks obeys him, but that is what it amounts to. The two are bound by love, the one to please the other. Neither needs a lead. Soon he will follow and respond to Lena and Marshal too. As he grows, Lena hopes he may become a big dog. She feels the comfort of his presence and is glad of his company as she goes about the village. The other kids make a big fuss of him, are impressed by Jesse's story, comes to be told as a dramatic rescue rather than a chance meeting. They are jealous of how he walks with Jesse, untethered by a lead. How he will wait, patiently, lying down or snuffling about in the grass nearby, if Jesse's attention is pulled away to play with the other kids, to bike riding and camp building.

6

There are three days of storm. One of the big summer storms, extreme enough to keep the kids indoors. The sky is stirred into dark violence, clouds become limbed beasts lashing the ground. The grass flattens, branches bend and break. A tree falls, crashing through the red tiled roof of The Oak, a building that used to be a pub, the brass pumps delivering beer made by a local brewer alongside tanker pints of fizzy larger. Quiet tables and indifferent food. And company. It had stopped being a pub several years ago. It was for a while the converted home of Tina and Kyle. Marshal had introduced them to the builder who did the conversion work. The Oak has lain empty since the couple died in the pandemic.

Tina and Kyle had left the tarmac down, across a small car park at the back of the pub, used it as a place to store their bicycling equipment in a couple of tin sheds. A place to prop the bikes on stands and tend to them with grease and cloths and specially configured tools. A constant series of upgrades. People were used to seeing them heading off into the countryside, dressed in their lurid, light-weight cycle wear for day-long bike rides, amazed to hear them talking of where they had got to, how far they had gone, a little bored by the relentless headcam videos posted by Tina on the village web site. But people missed them now, their earnest pleasure in their hobby, their kindly, neighbourly, manner. Lena had been friendly with Tina, had been the one to find them both. When she hadn't heard from Tina, she had donned her protective wear, cautiously entering the home. She called a too-late ambulance through the muffle of her medical mask, to collect Kyle from their bed, in his pyjamas, and Tina from the living-room floor. She lay next to a spilled tray, two intact boiled eggs, one egg cup still on the tray, one rolled under the edge of the sofa, scattered there by a convulsion. Lena had taken in many details. One of the spoon handles stuck out, at a tilt through Tina's hair, pressed between her temple and the rug. The ruck of Tina's t-shirt, the pale blue stripes of her pyjama shorts. A plaster, stuck to the outside of her knee, one end loose and hanging down, exposing a small scab and a yellow stain on the padded inside. The cold mottle of Tina's thighs, a death pallor over the muscle and tan from her days riding in the sun stretched over her like a claim. Another death, framed by protective eyewear, meticulously imprinted on Lena's mind. Everyone carries these snap shots, these mosaic memories of the dead and dying.

Chorus
we too live
with the reek of death

we always have,
　since your bells, your fences, your briar walls, your hunger, your taste for our flesh, your taking of our horns,
　your docile planning for our every move, your dole out of our fattening, yielding, enriching food, your fatty, pushy, plumpy, dozy medicines

you think we do not know it, smell it, hear it, taste it?
you think because you take us away to kill us
that it is hidden?

our children?
our dear-hearted old mothers, forced to leak and mourn?

As the storm slows Marshal goes out to check that the tree will cause no damage to anyone else, particularly elderly Mrs Pym who lives in a cottage joined to the pub. There is no need to save The Oak. It was already destined for dereliction. He comes back into the house with a howl of wind and rain slicing across his shoulders, yammering disruptively into the kitchen. The wind takes the door as he closes it, with a slam.

'It's OK, I think. Gone straight across and won't trouble anyone else. But no one should be going into The Oak,' he says. As though it still kept the opening hours of years ago.

Jesse and Mister Maliks become restless – bounding games around Jesse's bedroom and jumping games on living room furniture use up so little of the energy they have. They alternate between frantic activity that drives Lena mad, and turgid laziness that irritates her. Bloody weather. Almost as bad as the bloody pandemic had been.

They use screens to connect with the other kids and teach, a bit, talk about a history project, try a couple of sums. School inspections haven't happened for nearly eight years now, but once things get back to normal, they don't want the state to have an excuse to shut them down. Lena knows though, that it won't be her failings or successes that keep the school officially open, it will be whether there are enough children to warrant the designation of school. It is already, more or less a system of collaborative home schooling. The state is busy dealing with the new chaos of cities, slowly overfilling with people moving in from the countryside, people sliding in across borders from places even more ravaged by rising tides and howling gales. Everything is changing.

Such a benign name, October Flu. It rushed invisibly up the country leaving swathes of dead. The structures of society, under pressure from a changing world were further undone. Lena lost her parents and a sister. Jesse his best friend, Sep.

People left or they died. People muddled on. Years of chaos as the world tried to be its better self in pursuit of survival. And somehow, things did just keep going along. But many things changed. The British Isles were divided finally, once more, into separate nations. Incompetence and anger could do no more to patch up the rents in society than the stockpiles of useless antibiotics. Failures of leadership and the sheer raggedness of coping left all possible. There was a stripping away of certainty which meant opportunities for some. But mostly people looked inward, into their own fearful hearts.

Chorus
disaster when it hits, hits all
– with this wretched lesson
you might learn you are made equal

a hand to soothe in sickness, strong shoulders to rebuild
children to give children playmates

kin and kind, a herd to shelter, defy the ravages not yet
brought to heel

The storm dies down and is followed by gusty warmth. The sun shines. Jesse and Mister Maliks go out after breakfast to play, before school is reconvened for later in the day.

They walk down the road, the long way around to the far

side of the field and into the woods at the bottom. The verge along the road is bright, the ground still saturated with storm rain. Jesse likes the islands of grass that are growing down the middle of the road. Slowly joining up. A streamy excess of rainwater has sluiced a promontory from the verge, a dyke of mud and stones that runs diagonally across the road. Jesse wonders if it will stay long enough for weeds to grow, make a new bit of mainland reaching toward the string of green islands that dot the tarmac. Lena tells Jesse not to play on the road, though there are so few cars that the instruction is barely necessary. But by habit, and by birthright, sharing his mother's natural caution, he heeds her warning.

Under the trees, the loam, soaked and warmed, scents the air. Damp heat from the ground is trapped under the leaf crowns. Jesse sees a deer. Momentarily still, they regard each other. The deer locks on to the presence of the boy for seconds that stretch into a timeless stillness, the two creatures connected. The deer is startled, finally, by the bounding rustle of Mister Maliks and turns, like a shadow, like a play of light, like something and nothing slipping between the trees. The sunlight flits through leaves, shaping almost-creatures everywhere.

'Let's go to the field, Mister, see what those cows are up to today. Come on, Micksmaliks, I'll race you.' They hurtle through the woods, leaping fallen branches, swerving holly and bramble. Jesse slows as he nears the field. He sees a figure on the other side of the gate. His heart beats, remembering the man with the gun at Little Denton. He gestures Mister Maliks to come over. Jesse crouches down, with a hand against Mister Malik's ribs. He peers through the trees, through the gate. Soon he recognises first the hat, then the shape and finally, when he looks up, the profile of Malc. Relief surges through him. He takes a moment to rid himself of the sickening fear.

'It's Malc, Mister, let's go and say hello.'

Malc is seated on an upturned plastic crate. His long back bends, curved over himself, black hair falling over the big rough hands that brace his jaw. Jesse knows that something is amis, but doesn't understand what.

'Hi Malc,' he says cheerfully. Malc lifts his head, slowly, looks at Jesse. His face is wrong, it sits in a way that Jesse doesn't recognise. The man isn't crying, but he looks raw, pained. He takes a moment to register the boy, awkwardly poised, waiting for a cue.

'Jesse. Hi, you OK?'

'I'm OK. Are you?' There is a pause. Then Malc takes a big breath, sighs it out. 'I'm a bit down, son, two of the cows have died and, yeah, I'm a bit sad about it.' Jesse looks around the field, noticing the two bulky shapes, no longer part of the herd. Two dead cows.

'Oh.' Jesse feels sad too. He walks quietly, uncertainly, over to Malc and puts a hand on his shoulder. Mister Maliks snuffles in the buttercups and the man and boy wait quietly for some kind of comfort that comes, each from the other.

Chorus

the stretch of grass
though succulent
it can drive us to despair
– where are the bitter greens
the petals and the leaves
where are the dark and pungent plants we need?

the sap and the bark of young tree shoots
the tender mottled shade

you make us fat with greed

and weak as any crop

we say goodbye, sweet sisters

again we say goodbye

7

Summer holidays and the children no longer have school. Days are long and drifting, gossamer seed pods caught on sunbeams glimmer as they cross the part of the sky that is at eye level. Workdays are long for adults who must often travel great distances and when not overseen or in organised activity, the children are trusted to play in nearby woods and fields as well as the streets and lanes that bear the village name. They are reminded not to go to Little Denton, particularly not the short way, through the woods.

Chetna comes to visit Lena. She has a fondness for Mister Maliks, is touched by the name, however accidentally, taken from her father, and always makes a big fuss of him. She has come to like being in her father's house. She could almost stay, she tells Lena. She is after all, alone – a daughter and grandson buried in the pandemic. Jesse listens as he plays with objects on the table, filling time. Chetna's eyes are ringed dark, her front teeth stick out over her bottom lip. They fill him with sad tenderness that makes him want to be kind to her.

She is anxious but trying to work it out. She might be a grandmother, or no longer a grandmother perhaps, but she is still young enough, she thinks, to start again; somewhere she has the space to remember her beloveds, without expecting to see them around every damn corner. But though she is used to the hatred of nationalists she is also used to those groups being proscribed and, however listlessly, prosecuted for their acts. It is frightening to know that they are free, with their flags and banners, in a village less than three miles away, with no apparent fear of censure. Lena wishes she could be sure that Chetna will be safe, wishes things would get back to normal. She wonders for the first time if normal ever was a true protection.

To keep the children occupied, Lena sets up activities for the kids. They do some art and some camp building in the woods. They measure the circumference of trees, trying to find the broadest in the area. They tie knots in string, around a label that records the species of the tree and where it is. They head along the brook toward a big oak that they all think will be the winner. But Lena suddenly remembers the new residents of Little Denton, a few hundred metres beyond the site of the oak, and stops. There are only five of them in the group; they keep walking, paying her no heed in the familiar domain. She calls them back, parses her anxiety by turning it into wily excitement, claiming the superior girth of a yew tree in the churchyard. It is so old that it is hard to tell which is still trunk but she tells them it all counts, and it is loads bigger than the oak. They turn for the churchyard, across the brook and walking slantways through the woods and on to Wright's Lane, which loops into the top of the village, where the church sits at the crossroads.

Chorus

we remember
together across ages,
over ruckled hills, wild heaths and soft green fields

– you tell stories for your memories

She tells them what she can of the legends of yew. The children are delighted to learn of anything associated with death, with rebirth, with ancient custom. She tells them about a giant yew tree where the gods would meet in the centre of the universe, in her mind putting together a research and art project they can do back in the classroom. During the short walk around the edge of the village, they discover reverence for the tree. The yew doesn't disappoint. The children enjoy the necessity of scooting under the low-hanging branches into the most shady of shade, not touched by sunlight for centuries. They enjoy the collaborative passing from hand to hand of the measuring string. It has spread so far, so tattered wide that it beats all the others, the furthest knot by far. Jesse puts his hand on the shreddy bark, strips lifting off like curls of paper. The tree is dark and foreboding but the bark is a light brown. He wonders how many years people have been standing at that spot, a hand on the bark of the yew.

Visiting their dead, waiting for their angels. The church yard yew the scion of a tree that always grew in a hallowed place, gathering villagers in with their spirits long even before the church was built, before the searing reign of Christianity. A crossroad, a small hill rise at the top of a settlement next to a brook. A place where woodsmen and women, shepherds, wheel wrights, housemaids and farm hands made their promises, made deals with fate and sought out their better selves. A place where they lie buried in the earth, under the ancient shade of yew and stone.

Just over there lies Stephen, his stone sunk, his bones sunk further. And just there, where Jesse is now, he once stood, at the gravestone of his wife, died in childbirth one year ago to the day. He had carried the warm body of his little girl in his arms, round the side of the church, past the old yew, holding her hands away from grasping the needles, reaching for the coral berries so soft and tasty looking on their poisoned stem. He had carried her, telling her of the woman who he wished her to know in her heart, through his words – the only way to know the dead. He talked to his dead wife too. 'Look, my sweet, she is bonny; she looks like you.'

He had stopped, bent his cheek to her small, snuggled shoulder, fending off the writhing fears of a dependant man. On behalf of this girl, just turned one year old, he had talked to his god. He pushed away the fears, the charge of impertinence, so as to talk man to man. 'Lord, stop the creeping closure, the theft of our lands. Are we not also your children? Must we leave for who knows what? Or worse, beg for work on land that had fed us fairly, many lives long. Lord, help me find a way, help me make a life that will keep and cherish this girl, her brothers, my darling children.'

Later, Marshal comes home, filled with worries that push out at the seams of him. He is short with Jesse and shouts at Mister Maliks who gets under his feet. Jesse is angry with his dad and goes off to play with Mister in the garden. Marshal has been presented with a proposition that is bound to cause ruction between him and his family. He has been offered work in the city and has thus been reminded once again that work as it is will not last. He is burdened with the foreknowledge of how Lena will react and it is making him feel bad. It is making him silent.

Lena reads her partner, knows something is wrong. She waits until, as he usually does, he starts talking.

'Look, I know you won't like this, but we have to think again about moving.'

'Haven't we already done that?' She reacts, her own mood tightening as she sees the direction they are heading.

'I know, Ley, but it's not going to last, what we have. And we will have to do something some time, and it may then be too late. We can't just wait until there's no option and see what turns up.'

'For god's sake, Marshal. I don't know how many times I have to say it. I don't want to move to London.'

They discuss until they argue. They fall into accusations, him to her of naivety, her to him of ambitious arrogance. These are familiar charges. These are the words they use to hurt each other. They bicker over the well-chewed, meatless scraps that lie under the table of even the most successful marriages. As the evening wears on, they slide into frustration, hate each other for the evening, but wake, mollified, wanting to repair the rift. They lie in bed turned toward each other, a hand that gently strokes a shoulder or cheek, slides back a tendril of hair, makes tender gestures that emolliate a rational discussion. They shift ground toward each other, talk through all versions and possible compromises. Nothing is agreed but a move to London does not, in the end, get ruled out.

Jesse and Mister Maliks accompany Lena to the shop. The shelves are more shambolic as the usual food is harder to buy from the wholesalers, and the gaps left by neatly packaged goods are filled with home-made jams, a few second-hand household items and baskets of garden-grown muddy potatoes. As rules tighten at the centre of the food chain, they fray at the edges. Supermarkets deal increasingly with big overseas providers and increasingly only with their own bigger stores and delivery networks. Small shops find that their wholesalers are being edged out of the supply chains. But as the edges come undone opportunities do arise. People start to sell each other their home-grown produce. Bartering, a system as ancient as farming, comes back into usefulness. Mikel and Giana, exiles from war at the other edge of the continent, have begun to run the shop as a kind of co-operative. Three years ago, they counted up their profits and took one last holiday to recover from the shredding of the pandemic and then came back prepared to do whatever it took to stay in the countryside, in the peace and quiet they cherish, in the new lives they have built, far from the ruins of the old. Profit was no longer their motivation. Instead they focused on flexibility, the necessity of strengthening a community so that they might continue to live within it. Perhaps primed by the wrench already experienced from leaving one world behind, they were more able to accept that this one wasn't going to get back to normal. That only the naive would believe in such a thing. They do not, like Marshal, throw the charge of naivety at Lena and others who shared her hopes, but when these people talked of back-to-normal, Mikel and Giana smile, they listen, they offer no opinion. Instead they make themselves resilient. They live always in a new present and a changeable future.

Chorus

yes, change awaits us all
you may yet love it, if you let it carry you

Lena still clings to that hope, the memory of a world she thinks of as the world. A way of living that she thinks is the way of living. The pandemic – it was an aberration, its effects will fizzle out, will be wiped out by the determination of people like her who will make it so. The government was making mistakes that would be corrected. 'Things will go back to normal,' she intones, looking at the jam jars of Mrs Pym's homemade oat granola, individual portions sitting like chess pieces on a shelf that used to be packed wall-tight with the bright cartoon boxes of breakfast cereals.

Jesse and Mister go outside to wait for Lena who is caught up talking over the latest news with Mikel. Pavel comes to join Jesse. The two boys throw a stick between them, over the leaping head of the dog who wags his tail and chases between the boys in game-playing bliss. Lena comes out tells the boys to go and play. *She is worried*, Jesse thinks. She says she has to make some calls.

The two boys head toward the recreation ground. Pavel nips into his house and collects a football. Most of the recreation ground is meadow. There is a forlorn chained oblong that used to be a cricket pitch, just as overgrown as the rest, though the long grass is flattened at each end. The chains confer a status on the patch of ground and by mutual consent, by new habit, it is an area where the kids go to lounge in the grass. Bigger kids at one end, anyone else at the other. There is a football pitch that people take turns mowing. Jesse is proud that Marshal was the one to set up the rota, and so far, they have managed to keep the mowers in good enough shape and the goal posts standing. Though there aren't the numbers for a proper game.

A car pulls into the ground next to the pitch. Three men get out. Pavel, as is his way, darts anxious looks at them. They stand by the car, watching the two boys, then one starts to call to Mister Maliks. He sounds friendly, but Jesse is uneasy. He stops playing and goes over to Mister. Pavel, shadow slender, falls in behind him.

'What's his name?'

'Mister Maliks.'

'Mister Maliks? What kind of a name's that?' Jesse doesn't understand; the man is laughing but there is a layer of harshness in his response that seems unnecessary, unfitted to the exchange. 'Fuckin Malik,' says one of his companions. Jesse's heart catches as he looks at the man, the blue jumper, the sensible light brown hair cut neatly above the shirt collar. He didn't properly see the face of the man in the woods, but this man, this man could be the one with the gun. The heart catch drops into a skittering beat, a battering in his ribs. His breath is high and ragged though he tries not to reveal his fear.

'What's your name? Something normal, I hope?'

'Jesse.' His voice is strained. He looks at the three men, waiting out the encounter, hoping desperately it will end soon.

'And you?' The man speaks over Jesse's shoulder.

'Pavel.'

'Christ. Ethnic Pole?' The boys are confused by this question, by the sneer under the smile. Pavel is shy, always, and now he is also afraid.

'I don't know.'

'I can't hear you. Are you a Pole?'

'I don't know.'

'Oh, right. Well off you go then. Enjoy your game.'

The two boys turn and walk back toward the pitch, but without speaking, they both keep walking. Pavel picks up the ball; they cross the grass and once on the far side of the pitch, they run into the woods. They keep running, they don't speak until they are well away from the recreation ground.

8

Half a year passes; the globe tilts for winter. November and December are blighted by unusual ice storms that were also unusual three years before, and two years before that. A fault in the electricity grid remains un-repaired. The village is cold and dark. Some solar panels, some batteries are sophisticated enough to harvest the dreggy winter sun, but not for more than a bit of evening reading or morning breakfasting. Not for heating a whole house. There is not even the pretence of urgency from the power company about making repairs. Everyone gets sick of a recorded message that talks in a reasonable voice about high levels of demand, repairs being carried out, the need for patience. In the morning darkness Mrs Pym catches a foot on her wool basket, left on the floor at the end of the sofa and falls to the living-room carpet. She lies there, conscious but in pain and unable to get up. The floor is cold. She pulls a blanket off the sofa and manages to arrange it over herself. She tries to move, but it is awkward – her dressing gown and blanket snagging at each shunt of her body, tightening and slowing her so she seems to stick to the carpet. Eventually, she reaches the side table and the phone. She calls Giana, who comes and immediately calls an ambulance. They say it will take five hours to arrive. Their resources are much depleted by the pandemic and the slew of long-term health problems left for many in its wake. Resources are already skewed to the cities. She is frightened of going into hospital and persuades Giana to cancel the call; it's just a damaged knee, some bruising on her hip and elbow.

Giana insists that she must come and live with them behind the shop, at least while there's no power. Though grateful she feels sad and alone, even in that kind company, aware of the frailty of her age. She fears her hip and knee will heal slowly in the cold weather. She's not used to being dependent and is anxious to demonstrate her gratitude, frustrated by her inability to usefully return their kindness. A strong bond grows between Mrs Pym and Giana and Mikel who take her in, but Mrs Pym feels the greyness of the short days in her marrow. She feels, finally, terribly old.

Marshal makes the best use of dwindling contacts to secure first for his home and then for the village, the newest batteries and solar panels with improved low light efficiency. Malc digs out an old petrol generator that they keep for emergencies. The village sets up a communal centre, based in the shop. Mikel builds a corner with a table where people can sit and meet, drink a coffee, make plans. Mrs Pym knits covers for the cushions. Pavel's mum and dad have the best solar power connection and they open up their home to others. Their kitchen, being large and warm and part of a house where the full-time residents can easily be elsewhere for a few hours, becomes the classroom. There is no heating at all in the school; all its systems creak and fail regularly.

The small group of people feel themselves, in staying still, to have been cast adrift. It is a perplexing and difficult time but they share a desire for something and thus are primed to be allies. It takes four weeks for power to be restored.

Chorus

you did keep us warm
we'll give you that

and some of us lived well under the care
some of you gave us
– what we would chose for ourselves

some of you found love
and kept the wolves at bay

we haven't always been enemies, have we?

'Did you hear, there's been more trouble.' Lena and Pavel's mum Mish, are resting against the kitchen counter after a school session. The news is perplexing, wearying. There is relentless tumult and a sense of danger. Jesse feels the weight, Pavel too – the weight of adult misgiving and fear. They listen and they try not to listen. They seek abstract assurances that their parents, mostly, abstractly provide. But all of them, young and old, know that the process of getting back to normal is still a long way off. It is called up like a spell, or a prayer, the earnest expression of a shared desire that is experienced now mostly as a matter of faith rather than expectation.

There are riots, new laws, bans and fights between factions. There are terror attacks, racist attacks, there is a series of devastating fires in mosques and machete attacks in rural churches. A swarm of angry people form unruly beach militias that try to stop the arrival of illegal immigrants. Trying, in effect, to drown them. Across the country, people work out ways to deal with a sudden lack of resources, ways to deal with a shift from easy abundance to deficit. Calculations many have never before faced. Often, they find the way laced with goodness, with kindness and compassion. And other times, the response is marbled bloodily with dark hatred.

Chorus

we ache for you
your hopes and wishes and your cursing hates
you've not been blessed with balance, have you?

we see two young boys, quickening loops
– hope, a winged miracle
fear, a binding cage

Jesse and Pavel want to leave behind their worries, where they belong, in the hands of their capable parents who they trust, in the way of innocent children, to make it all work out. They decide to go out with Mister Maliks, let the grown-ups put things to rights. It is cold; there is nearly a foot of snow, but the wind has dropped. The last snowfall sits along the branches, paler than the sky. The world outside has become black and white. They make a snowman and throw snowballs. They go into the woods and shake branches over their heads, laughing as the snow dump creeps into the gap at the back of their necks. Mister bounds as though on a trampoline, jumping up and landing foursquare in fresh patches of snow.

After a while, Pavel goes home to warm up. Jesse and Mister walk on up to the field where the dead cows were, where Malc curled over his sadness like the letter C at the end of his name. The silence settles around them, now the voices of the two boys don't bounce back and forth in play. Mister calms, bored of the jumps. He follows in the path left by Jesse, who drags his feet, to clear the way. The smooth brown crown of Mister's head and his dark eyes, sit atop the level of the snowfall. Jesse feels anxiety, like an echo of snow-shiver at the back of his neck, like the cold caw of a crow. He imagines dead cows under what could be mounds of distant snow, he remembers the distress of Malc and the fretfulness of his parents as they talk about what to do. He wishes they could just stay as they are and is torn between foreboding and the inability to really understand how things can be any other way.

Isolde

9

She brushes her hair down, dropping a dark curtain over her face. Her last crop has grown out, the ragged tips reach below her collar bones. She pushes aside the hair, searches a drawer for scissors. She bunches and lifts the section that covers her face, raises it above her head in a fist as though in defiant, plumed salute and cuts it, bluntly, at the hair line. She turns to the mirror. It looks startling, rawly unfashionable. She likes it.

This woman, Isolde, lays the fistful of dark fibres on the white counter, separating the strands with her fingers. She thinks about her pelt-less skin, her need to conjure warmth from other creatures. She thinks about the possibilities of clothing made from human hair. It doesn't look like it would be warm. But it would be something. A despot wearing a cloak, patterned with intricately stitched and knotted tribute, demanded from and willingly given by obsequious vassals; or roughly woven fibres parted after battle from the bodies of enemies. A garment made less for warmth than as a signifier of dominion – a savage kind of beauty. *Given all the things we do badly*, she thinks, *ritualising and embellishing power is something at which we have always excelled. Decoration employed as a malign art.*

Cupping one hand at the edge of the bathroom counter, she sweeps the hair into it and drops it into the chute. She picks up her jacket and leaves the apartment.

Chorus

beauty – she might call it that
yes, savage too

such needs they have, such hierarchy, such hopeful following

it all could be so easy

The wind blusters, the sun shines. The new haircut leaves her face exposed. She walks; the tempered, composite glass of the pavement sucks the heat and light into tiny threads under her feet. Each square foot almost useless on its own, but the threads of light and heat are myriad. They connect into channels, tubes, corridors of energy that roar beneath the streets, creating almost limitless power to fuel the great city of London. She heads toward the open market.

Isolde goes for a pause, a deliberate slowing down, in a favourite place. A way to gather herself into composure, to be ready for the strange, new ordeal that lies ahead.

She orders an espresso and pastry and sits at a small cafe table at the edge of the market hall. She enjoys watching people as they scrutinise and squeeze the ranks of apples, pears and papaws patterning the tabletops of the fresh fruit and salad stalls.

Opposite the cafe is a spice stall. Isolde watches the woman performing a kind of dance as she weighs the beautifully named powders and seeds in a copper bowl, scooping the spices into little clear bags, sealed with a green and gold label. The brass weights are tiny, like jewellery slid off a chain. She runs a finger across them, selecting by touch the size of the one she needs. Perhaps when all other sellers used digital scales it was a gimmick, but it's enjoyable to watch her dark hands thread through the gleam of the metal, the bowls heaped high with powders and seeds. These spices arrive, like all food has done for years, in the prosaic, re-usable packs on the freights, but the customers who come to the stall appreciate the small investment in theatre – a bright embellishment that pleases all.

Next to the spice vendor is a stall selling vegetables. The only place Isolde knows where these exotic, raw foods are available. Loose flowers of pak choi. Gourds, orange and knobbly like a hearth full of embers. Bunched carrots, baskets of smooth-skinned potatoes. Cooking is now a ritualised hobby for a few enthusiasts who come to the market to shop at the spice stall and the greengrocer on their afternoons off. Like most people, she orders her food at the beginning of the week from a menu – Ten Economy Meals for two, Whole Week Healthy Lunchtime packs, Comfort Food, Nearly Raw, Vegan starters. They are delivered the next morning to her apartment locker. The World Cuisine Discovery Pack for one is her current staple.

She finishes the pastry and the last sip of the coffee, then reaches into her back pocket for her device. The mail notification blinks on the screen. A confirmation letter from the Justice Department. She has been receiving a variant of the same letter every few weeks since she turned eighteen. The letter informs her that if she intends to use her rights under the Restoration of Justice Act, she is able to attend Purley Maximum Security Prison Facility today between the following hours. Today, after nearly seventeen years, she has decided for the first time that she will use this right. She has a whole ninety minutes, should she want it, to sit on a bench and stare at the man who killed her mother.

Isolde's early childhood memories are patchy – shifting, dappled sunlight on the ground beneath a wind-blown tree. Most of it is forgotten, adrift, or hidden by her own evasions. In the few years of her life before her mother died and everything was changed, she knew that she had been happy. Not because she had recollections she could count as evidence for that knowledge but because she had yearned for that time every day of her childhood. The fragments – precious, uncertain scenes – that she had reached for so many times the flimsy material was moulded into fixed objects by her handling.

Sitting on her mother's lap. A tickle in Isolde's ear as she rested her head on that warm shoulder; her mother's dark hair like unravelled rope, the texture of something useful. Mama singing in small, quiet snatches, singing and thinking. A soothing blend, doing little, holding Isolde on her lap. Time passing in drowsy harmony.

Other recollections slipped in sometimes, returning at odd moments. In her early teens, she had been sitting in the garden of the children's home, eating plums. The bladed taste, sharp and sweet, the slide of the stone in her mouth, impenetrably hard, tested by her back teeth through the yielding pulp – sensations that had served up a precious memory of her and mama eating cherries and gleefully spitting pips. They were sitting on a patch of grass. They were with a group of friends or perhaps close to a collection of strangers; either way, there were others nearby. She had wished for so long that she knew where. But over time, it didn't matter where – the place was fixed now, a memory place.

Chorus

our memories
tempered
as you shaped this land

flat planes of green boredom
dark horrors
cement, the smell of death and diesel
our children taken –

– but time loops, moves forward, and so must you
this open space, this edge of forest, these shoots and sweet
grasses now are ours

time to find new places, girl

If she chooses to, she can remember the day when it happened.
Some of it. The violence of a moment. It was a tearing rip
through everything, destroying continuity, making her life
into a thing of two pieces. Before and after. The pieces were so
unequal that it is perhaps better described as a restart, the true
beginning of her life.

The day had been sunny. The wind roared down the wide
streets and the sun shone, bouncing brightly off the creamy
white suntiles that had covered all surfaces and powered the
city one way or another for the last twenty years. The older
stone buildings lining the pedestrian boulevards were pale
grey, scrubbed clean. They were out in the city, passing
through Virgin Plaza. They had been where the bomb went
off.

It had torn through her ears and mind and smashed her hip, cut a gully down the back of her calf. It had ripped through the building behind her. It ripped through her mother, leaving her ragged, dead, lying wet and heavy across the stunned body of her daughter. Isolde's face had been slick with her mother's blood, a warm mess pooling in her eye socket. The weight, the dead weight of Mama. She was there long enough in that ringing silence, under the weight of her mother's dead body to get pins and needles. That is how her memory worked it at least. The weight of Mama and the shock. The warmth of blood that spilled onto her face and the shocked cold of her own blood, withdrawing. She lay in the silent roar, in the confusion of the signals, her head pushed painfully against the roughness of a tree planter. She had turned her head, a little, blood spilling down her cheek. Her other eye looked up to the white of the sky and the beautiful sprinkling of spring leaves that danced in the wind. The shrieking roar of silence as the leaves blew. Bright green confetti that swayed above her, rippling on supple branches not touched by the bomb but driven to a perpetual dervish by the never-ending wind.

The Restorations of Justice Act twisted into law out of the remains of two outmoded concepts – justice being seen to be done and the restorative power of connection between criminal and victim. Now, judges ruled behind closed doors; victims of crime, no longer able to take part in trials were instead given the right to observe the perpetrator imprisoned. As the statute book phrased it, they had the right not to participate in the dispensation of justice, but to observe the delivery of justice, by the state, on their behalf. The restorative qualities of the act had regressed, thuggish, to ancient and one-sided precedent – the spiteful power of being able to throw rotten vegetables at a criminal in the stocks. People are not allowed to throw vegetables. But they are invited to observe the punishment, revel in it, if they wish. To take satisfaction, or a sense of justice, or pleasure from it. Prisoners no longer merit the consideration of rehabilitation – so many of them will be incarcerated too long to consider them future citizens. The vast, automated prison complexes are geared to feeding a thirst for revenge; the infantilising bond between citizen and state strengthened by sharp doses of enemy-sharing. That the death penalty had been abolished once more was only down to a lack of taste for further deaths after the annihilations of the pandemics a few decades previously. Combined with the frighteningly low birth rate even the most ruthless authoritarians had become squeamish about state execution. Criminal lives could be lived, until they died in prisons.

Isolde had been scathing about this right that had been conferred upon her, like the crown of her victim status when she became an adult at eighteen. In common with many, she found it primitive, abhorrent. She had no sympathy for the man who had killed her mother but she disliked the pandering to a baser nature, the souped-up mob mentality that in turn fuelled or excused the excesses of the state.

But things have changed. She no longer has the means to be scathing, about anything. She is adrift. So much eludes her that she wants to go back, to dig from the beginning. Not through the mire that lead to this present moment, not working back from now. She takes a mighty leap, a pole-vault. She takes a skittering wild swerve past the weary dissatisfactions of her younger life, past the pedestrian miseries of the last years – the ending of love that she thought had reshaped her. She wants to begin again, at the death of her mother. Visiting the man in prison seems like a way to make a new start.

Chorus

all this back and forth
– in time as well as place
all this searching and seeking and never seeing
nothing changes

new starts for old stories
nothing changes

she walks for miles and nothing changes

10

She walks south. After an hour, she finds a citytrain and makes her way to Purley Max. Her device guides her with curt clarity through secure access, her thumb print opening doors. First, a walkway, a smooth negative space. Then a second coded door, a platform. She is instructed to wait two minutes for a monorail.

Inside the train uniformed workers stand near the door. A woman opposite in an expensive suit sits straight, her face alert and carefully blank. Isolde wonders about her destination, if she and the woman are there for the same reason. Has she come to observe justice, to see the punishment of a man who assaulted her, beat her husband to death in a brawl, murdered her child, burnt down her house? Perhaps it's someone she knew already. Or like Isolde, a terrorist, a stranger who had randomly changed the course of her life.

Three stops along she's told to get off. A short walk leads to an area with a coffee machine and groups of generic, minimally upholstered chairs arranged around low tables. Then, another door. As she approaches, it opens onto a long corridor, dimly lit with uneven splashes of light coming from the left side. There is a dashed row of solid oblongs, benches, down the middle. Both sides of the corridor are lined with shutters but it is only on the left side that a few shutters are raised, revealing the cells and their occupant prisoners. She wonders if it is coincidence or whether the cells on the right are open on a different day. The victim's zoo, staging staggered gawping – time-share in the pillory. She moves slowly, hesitantly. Her device blinks in concert with a light about a third of the way down above a shutter that slides silently upwards. She moves forward, her nerves ringing a distant background of alarm.

There is an older couple on the bench before the first open cell, welded together, clutching at each other for comfort in the mutually supportive posture of an ordeal. The woman pulls crumpled tissues from her pocket, pressing the white carnation to her eyes. The man, his arm around her shoulders looks about in confusion, not sure if he is holding up or holding on. In the cell before them, a young man stands side-on – tense, upright, his arms folded. He looks up at the ceiling, rocking back and forth, contained aggression tipping him on his heels. His jaw muscles work tightly. Isolde is repulsed by her own intrusion and quickly passes by, moves down the corridor to confront her own horrible intimacy, Cell D191–H14.

She wonders if the man knows she is coming. She feels anxious, socially awkward even. She stops before she is in front of the cell, waiting just out of sight of the gaping opening, the horrible reveal, to collect herself.

She moves further, nearer, and looks, half looks, through a light mesh into the space that holds her mother's killer. She breathes high in her chest, a peppering of adrenalin prepares her for a confrontation, the nature of which she can't anticipate.

Sitting on the floor, awkwardly, his back turned to her is a man. A large body, a bottle-green sweatshirt. The letters DT, for domestic terrorist, large and bright yellow, printed on the back.

She sees the back of a cropped head, rough hair above a reddish neck, a bulk of rounded shoulders. There are papers scattered next to him, more on the bed to his right. A glimpse of cheek and jowl as he turns to sort them. Fat, inelegant fingers scrabble slowly to catch a corner. A pinch that buckles the paper, eventually lifts it enough to pick up one of the sheets that disappears from her view as it goes before his.

She tries to make out what is on the pages. Paper is a specialist material, used for art and craft projects, or kept in archives. He seems to have sheets of paper in abundance, a splay of creamy sheets, yellowed at the edges. There's something printed on them. She can see something, a spill of ink. Something drawn. Little masses of black and the even greying of printed text. They're pages torn from old books. Museums, institutions have archives, some people keep books for the curiosity or antique value, but the information they contain is worthless; either converted to text or irrelevant. She cranes forward, curious. The drawings are diagrams, heavy with black lines. No colour. Unidentifiable fluid shapes, tar-like mark. Some bristle with straight black lines radiating out from the central mass to words or letters floating in the empty surround of the off-white paper.

The man on the floor moves. He's cumbersome, slow. He keels onto his braced left arm, rotating inelegantly onto his hands and knees facing toward Isolde. She still can't see his face. He pauses, his head hangs down, as if the pivot has been exhausting. He heaves, pulling on the bed frame. His face is unhealthy. Stagnant, ruddy and rough. He sits sideways on, on the bed, the bottom of two bunks. He turns to look at Isolde briefly. A nervous stillness holds them.

He slumps forward, his elbows on his knees, hands cupping

his head. It blocks him a little from Isolde's view – she doesn't mind. Looking at each other is uncomfortable. She doesn't know what to say. So she busies herself trying to decipher the paper on the floor. She hears a quiet voice.

'They're pages from a book. The human body. We are allowed books. There's hundreds. No one else wants them and there's no connection the other end.'

She looks up, but he has turned away again.

'So…' She pauses, floundering, searching for anything to say that would make sense. 'So are you interested in the human body?'

'I like the drawings. Like maps.'

She finally understands the forms – the swirls and bulbs of organs, knots of muscle, sections of bones. The cellular dance halls of membrane and mysterious fluid, pinpricks of information, storehouses of all that we are.

Moments pass, Isolde refocuses on the reason she has come. It isn't for small talk. She feels a tremble of strangeness, uncertainty. She's anxious but feels nothing more pointed. Not anger, not outrage. And she feels disappointment, a kind of disgust, as though she has been short-changed. To be unmoved by any sensation, sitting five feet from the man who killed her mother.

'Am I… Are you… are you someone I hurt?'

The voice startles her. She looks at him, a sharpening of sensations, almost to the point of anger. It was something to go on.

'Yes. I am.'

'What did I do?'

She is taken aback. How can he not know? The anger gathers, buoyed on an upwelling of relief.

'How come you don't know? You killed my mother. You

took off a chunk of my calf and broke my pelvis like a dropped plate.'

She stares at him. He doesn't respond. She feels anger radiating out from her body in the silence. She feels a surge of pleasure, indignation brought in on the cusp of her contempt. It is a helpful marking of her own boundaries, formed in the clarity of anger.

The door at the top of the corridor opens and a man in a shabby overcoat makes his way toward them in the gloom. He shuffles slowly, clutching a bag held at the neck like a sack, one of the generic food delivery bags, well worn, hanging slackly enough to look empty. He looks at Isolde briefly, tips the curtest nod, then sits at the other end of the bench.

There is a moment of strange and vivid silence.

'You cunt. You worthless piece of shit.' He speaks quietly, slowly, but with a force that stiffens his whole body, a choking catch on the words as they come up through his throat. 'I hope you are miserable for every second of your remaining years. I hope you suffer, you disgusting, vile piece of... of nothing. You're nothing, you fucker. You killed my beautiful wife. An angel. You killed her. You took her away from me.'

He grinds on, knocking the energy out of her own anger. Isolde watches him from the corner of her eye, watches the man in the cell who sits with his head held in his hands. The new visitor doesn't notice her. His aged and gravelly voice pushes on, words of bitterness that tauten the tendons in his neck, the slack skin like sails blown by a storm against the rigging of his body. Isolde doesn't move, but she retreats, pulls down into her jacket, sits still enough to fade into the background. The spill of words wind round her like a spell. She's too shocked to move.

'You disgust me. Every ounce of your fucking body is an affront. Every breath a waste. A waste. You are poison. If I could reach you, you would know, you would feel it, what you deserve, you canker, you poisonous wreck. Your blood would run like poison out of your fat veins, you fucking shitbag.'

As abruptly as he began, he stops. He sags, the tension of anger no longer holding him up. The man in the cell turns and for a brief moment the two men look at each other, the tenderness of ageless sorrow links them together in a tiny moment, unwittingly shared.

The man in the shabby overcoat tightens his grip on the bag in his hand, pulls his coat around him and walks slowly toward the exit, his body shaped in the slightest curve, like a feather.

Isolde waits, intimidated by the awful intimacy. The man in the cell rubs his bristly skull, the quiet rasp breaking the silence.

'We have grown old together.' He looks over at Isolde briefly. 'That man and I, we have grown old together. We have shared this'—he gestures vaguely, encompassing the cell, the corridor— 'for decades, I think. He's my only visitor.'

'Does he... is he here often?'

'Every time, I think. I lose track.'

'Is he always the same?'

'He has got older. But yes.'

'So his wife died at the same moment as my mother.'

The man looked up at her. 'Your mother? Yes.' He looks at Isolde, curiously.

'So, you know who I am?' she asks. He turns back, elbows on his knees, fingertips searching as if for tiny flaws in his skull.

'Yes, I know who you are. Remembering is difficult here, it comes and goes. Things come back. I know I did harm people. That there are reasons I am here, things that happened before. I forget who I know, my friends, my home. But I forget, without meaning to, so much of it. It has been such a long time.'

Isolde wants to press him, to hear him admit, as though a confession, the death he caused. The lights in the corridor come up, a sign above the exit door blinks a command to leave. The shutter begins to slide down.

'So, who am I?'

His answer stuns her.

'I knew you, your mum. You lived with us.'

11

Chorus

they get so lost, drift apart
it seems a special skill, to be lost and not to wish it so,
in a crowd, sweat and breath mingling

and they forget the way back
and they forget that joining is in their bone memory

when we drift we drift together
skin to skin we hear each other

A gentle electronic ding-ding-ding chimes, in time with the
flash of the sign over the door. Exit – This Way. The shutter
slides down closing off the stage, the lights brighten, coming
up to signal the end of the show.

Isolde is rattled. How had he known her? She's the last to
go through the exit doors. She sits in one of the chairs in the
lounge area. The couple from the corridor also linger. The
woman still clutches a ball of tissues. The man busies himself

with the coffee machine trying with mild irritation to sync it with credits on his phone.

Isolde can't help wondering what brought them here. She speculates as though poking at an animal corpse, with disgusted curiosity. She can't help it. She pictures a murdered son or daughter. It's repugnant, seeing strangers so exposed, in a situation that invites speculation about the most intimate and awful moments in their lives. She recoils at the realisation that she will be considered in the same intrusive way. She briefly pictures them, all the families, with their victim genera printed on their backs, a dark mirror of the DT emblazoned on the back of the prisoner. Daughter Raped. Mother Blown Apart. Father Died of Fright During Burglary. Like an awful parlour game, played out among this low-lying utilitarian furniture, they could guess at the horror of what was spelled out on their backs, while sipping bad coffee and trying to gauge how probing the social chit chat should become. Winner gets a chocolate bourbon. *I had you down for a dead sister, but your mother, you say? Ours wasn't a terror attack, no, it was a fight. He says he didn't mean it.*

She sits with her back to the couple, sinks as much as possible into the low chair. She doesn't want to engage with anyone, especially not another custodian of a bleak history. She examines the confusion of her own path to this place, this moment. How can he possibly have known her mother? He was a criminal, part of a long-gone terror group called The Claimants. Was it possible that he was winding her up? But he was so vague, so imperfectly present that it was hard to believe him capable. It didn't make sense. She wished she had someone she could talk to, some connection to her mother. Someone who had known her.

The only person Isolde can remember from her childhood is her godmother. Isolde has fragments of memory, a crudely spliced reel. She is playing with a soft dark cloud of hair that she sculpts with combs, pins and ribbons kept in a wooden bowl, the two of them laughing at the asymmetric and hectic result. She can remember a game with her mum and her godmother, each woman holding one of her hands, swinging her into the air as they walked. She can remember being hugged, her own hair stroked back from her face, a beaming smile. Both of them had gone, when her mother died.

She could remember her godmother crying, holding her hand, being with her at the crematorium, at her mother's funeral. She remembered burying her face, clinging to her. But then she had just gone. Disappeared. It had felt like a second loss. Moved to Manchester, they told her, and life in the children's home had begun.

Isolde, like many in the children's home, had put trauma behind her at a young age. Perhaps they rarely defeat its subtle workings but these bold, surviving children learned to keep their pain away from the focus of their daily thoughts.

After the shock, there was a petering out, a slow deadening that seemed like grief. It was something she never lost but learned to bear, learned to hide away. She balanced it the same way she balanced the loss of her mother. But there were years of loneliness, a parasitic loneliness that hooked into her so tenaciously that it seemed to need her; a wily interloper, an abusive ally. She had weathered it until it became an occasional obligation, one that no longer devoured her. Though how it shaped her still.

She was surrounded for most of her childhood by the clatter of a home filled with other kids and the adults that cared for them. There were a few deep friendships but they hadn't outlasted changes of address or fortune. Mostly they simply tolerated each other. With hindsight and the understanding of adulthood she had felt a clench in her heart when she realised that the other children – brash Evie, tough-talking Kane, chirping little Odile with her bouncy curls and bouncy smile – probably all these other kids had felt the same as her. The same practised avoidance of vulnerability. The same strategic nonchalance. The same stifled anger and dreadful longing.

There had been allegiances that kept the children going, came close to love and a sense of family. Most of the workers had been caring, even when scratchy with too much work. Few had been actually unkind. There had also been traumatic times; she had attempted to kill herself once. The weight of years of loneliness. The weight of years of hope that one day she could go back, to before, even if it were just in her memory. The dread that she would never know how to get there. It was that fear that nearly killed her; the time she stole Kwame's pills and Io's razors. She was fifteen, her cheek pressed against the tiles, throwing up into her hair and the blood on the bathroom floor.

But that busy, noisy place had taught resilience too. She had it from a young age. It just slipped, that time she took a razor in her pilled hand, to her pilled wrist. It slipped on the end of a sub-dream: the rescuer she knew to be a fantasy but she had reached for any way, until they disappeared from her dreams, in a moment of clarity, back into the un-existance and she knew that all she had was herself.

That sub-dream slipped and she did too, on the bathroom floor in the dark hours when no one should find her. But that busy, noisy place was never discreet. And soon she was put back together, clear in her mind once again that rescue was her own business.

Yes, the children's home had bred resilient children. She had carried that legacy with her into adulthood, became a young woman who was brash, tough and tender. Guarded from the perils of emotion, certain of the need to resist anything that may use up any scrap of what she needed to take care of herself. She had had boyfriends, lovers, but weathered the risk with a toughness that could be cruel. Too dependent on good times and highs in her teens and twenties, she had skittered, her tough hide the main navigational tool. She knew what she could bear and pushed forward, away, outward, over edges. And then picked herself up, bleary-eyed and tired, to do the same again. It was a life that was perilous, threadbare, frenetic. And often spectacularly joyous, moments of soulful happiness materialising like crystals in the wild concoction. It was a life that caused ructions that absorbed all of her attention in an endless string of fractured moments.

Then she had fallen in love, felt for the first time the security and protection of love, when she was twenty-eight. He hadn't, like some, fetishized the drama of her story, the ghostly scars that map it on her legs. He hadn't, like some, sought out the hazy vulnerability that lay quiet at the centre of the wild spin of her life. He hadn't been seduced by the glamour of the tough, young woman with her wide, challenging stare and cutting cheekbones, her bitten fingernails and dramatic style, who would go further, over more edges than others. But he had loved her. She, in response, had set about dissolving her toughness in order that she might love him in return. It took time. It took shouting and arguments, and several near break-ups but they persisted and found a way to make it work. They fell in love. Life became happy.

And it became ordinary. Love survived in that prosaic way it has, retreating somewhat – underground, a rhizome ready to feed, to nurture, part of the store cupboard of our strength. They decided to start a family. Conception was not impossible for them, as it was for many other couples. It was not impossible but it was elusive. The state offered up its conception stipend, the concession of a society becoming desperate about the many means the population had of fading away.

They tried, they kept trying. What started as hope became over a number of years, a matter of grim determination. They still loved each other, perhaps, somewhere, but they dropped the other's hand. They lost the means to caress and cherish each other's bodies, seeing only the completion of their task written in the flesh and bones in the bed next to them. They forgot, in pursuit of their goal, how to make each other happy.

One night, a few months before, after an evening spent in sullen silence, he left the apartment telling Isolde he needed a bit of time on his own. The next day, from an unknown place, he announced that it was the end. She understood partly, they had come to run in parallel – two steel tracks not meeting or crossing, two tracks heading determinedly the same way. The effort had made them distant. But she had loved him deeply. She had planned to love him till she died. She was destroyed by his cold implacability, by the completeness of this ending.

The tentative scrap of human life that had miraculously taken hold, unknown to either of them at the time of his departure, discovered by her in the weeks after, bled out of her nine weeks later.

She felt the absence of her dreams with terrible longing. Though her love was now tainted by a furious anger. It was another abandonment. The spark of life so longed for seemed to be a miracle, an answer to all questions. But that long-awaited child had left her too.

Part of her understands well, the family of the future, like the family of the past, is gone. She has been left behind, and she must now be that other thing. A thing she knows intimately; she must be a person on her own. Disconnected. It had been a respite, to have glimpsed a future that held more than that but there is an ugly comfort in a return to old expectations. And she hasn't yet found the way back to doing it well.

Chorus

find your family girl
let them find you

The prisoner looks down to his bare feet planted on the floor next to the bunk. They have broadened over the years, as though his increased weight has borne down on them, spreading them out. The plastic of the floor is tepid, as warm as all the space he knows, inside his body and out. He longs to feel cold. There is so little to feel. His body has got bigger, but there is less and less for it to encounter. Just endless neutral temperature that bleeds through his skin, matching inside and out. The only cold is the pooling of blood against a hard surface before pins and needles begin. Or the alcohol rub from the stub above the faucet in his cell. Sometimes he puts it on his scalp, the bones of his ankles. Sometimes he squeezes his toes until they hurt blue.

He blurs his eyes to the speckles that make up the impermeable smoothness of the floor. The compressed grains, several shades of beige and grey, will jump if he stares long enough, if he overrides the automatic tug of muscles regulating the lens of his eye. This fogginess, this self-induced dizzying, it is a way out. To the shore. Small grains, little pebbles, the beach. The sand and shingle. To begin, the smooth sand of the backwash, the sand left flat and dense by a wave. If he stares longer, trance-like and blurry, the grains jump and grow, could become the stretch between sand and mud, stony, rough, dark. Where the land takes over properly from the sea, where

the soil and sand meet, where earth cliffs wear away. Or sometimes, most beautiful of all, the rime of high-tide – bones, lids,
a part of something graceless, worn to beauty by the patient
sea.

He remembers a wash of gritty cold over bare, bony feet.
Feathers, stones and discs, the tangled shrines of sea treasure,
collected from the beach and kept on a window ledge. A treasure trove.

Here he's in a place for him alone. Too adrift these more
recent years to be lonely. But he craves something – feeling,
touch. A slug of cold sea, a rush of wind. The soft weight of
fingertips on the back of his hand. His body, less feeling than
it ever was, craves the cold, a snap of muscular action, a caress
on bone through skin. Touch. Not company even, but touch.
He twists a pinch of short hair at his temple. Not so hard that
it would pull out. Though in the past he has sometimes revived
himself with that sharp, cruel tug, practised often enough to
bruise his skin; a tenderness that whispered at the slight touch
of his blunted fingers. He brushes his fingers now across his
temple, pictures the shallow scoop of smooth bone beneath the
skin, shallow enough for the merest puddle. A wren would
struggle to bathe in it. Next, to the deeper pool of his eye
socket, a sudden depth of dark water, a plunge before feet find
the bottom, inside his skull, eyes open to keep the eye hole
in sight, not to lose oneself in the murky underwater cave of
anaerobic thought.

Why would he know my mother?

The question twists, catching the light, lures her into baffling speculation. It sounded so intimate. Tormented by the
endless, answerless loop, she calls Arthur.

They had met in the home, their paths coming from opposite directions; Arthur's parents were both in prison – political activists he would say, terrorists is what the state called them. He hadn't had an easy time. The children of the guilty were treated subtly less well than others. Onward opportunities and expectations narrowed. Other innocent children, the sons and daughters of victims, were subtly, piously elevated; innocence, fetishistically dwelt upon, was the ecstatic flip side of guilt. How beloved it was.

These two had formed their own coin, minted by the fortunes of their parents – guilt or innocence, heads or tails. They fell outside the main group of kids. Neither liked the same games, the same music, the same virtual reality immersions as the others. Isolde was drawn to the raspingly soulful rather than the gleefully popular. Arthur didn't like anything on principal that came from the centre ground. They had been surly allies, bonded in their disdain for most of what happened around them. Time had mellowed them. But their friendship, though often ignored, is built on the strong bonds of shared youthful values.

They meet in a busy park. Joggers and children run. An exercise class at the outdoor gym fills the air with barked instructions splitting the babble of children's play. Parents with young children group on the grass, hand round cups and fruit and bits of bread, wipe mouths and leap up to grab various toddlers as they set off on a determined run toward a flower bed or bike lane.

Isolde and Arthur hug; it has been a while since they have met. First in pursuit of a pregnancy, then in loneliness, Isolde had shrugged herself away from the busy, drinking, social life that had kept them connected through their earlier adult lives. They walk and Isolde talks, begins with her reasons for going to the prison, something she had sworn she would never do.

Other kids, foisted into the home by the criminal deaths of parents, had bragged about what they would say when they came into their right, how they would tell that fucker, how they were going to go there and make that person squirm. They talked as if it would redress the imbalance, weight their dead parent back into being. But others, Isolde among them, scorned the practice.

Though she is still unsettled, uncomfortable with it: something has changed; she needs information. She wants to work out the beginning of her story.

She tells Arthur about this need to start at the beginning, so as to finally reach her present self. By dealing with her past she hopes to gain agency in the present. That meant starting with her mother. The closest she can get to her is to find out why she died. Why was it necessary for that man to kill anyone? Why had he ended up killing her? She labours over the rationale for her curiosity, struggling to explain that finding the absence will lead to better knowing what surrounds it. For what is around the absences is Isolde. And in that first step, the visit to the prison, something has already complicated the task.

'When he said he knew Mum, it was like recognition. Personal recognition. So I wanted to ask, can you help me find out more? I don't want you doing anything that would be risky but you're the only one I know who's used the ghost web, so—'

'Solde, it's no problem. Taking a look is easy. Leave it with me for a couple of days.'

Chorus

bump and bustle
you jostle and swerve

and yet have so little instinct
for what connects
for the endless threads that make you herd

12

Isolde pulls on her stormsuit to meet Arthur for the second time. It has been raining hard for days, powerful winds keep people inside. She ventures into the wild and empty streets with a surge of joy. The city looks like a stage set, when there are no crowds to pull it into the mundane backdrop of a million lives.

They meet in a gaming hall at the cafe concession. They speak quietly, privately, amid the hum of the activity, the noisy excitement of the young bubbles up around them.

'You know he was a Claimant, right?'

'Yes, that's in the docs they handed over when I turned eighteen. They talked about it a bit during therapy.'

'Ha! Yes, well, as you know, we had very different experiences there, Solde, you being the innocent victim.' They both smile at the familiar joke.

Arthur, she can tell, is impatient to reveal what he has learnt. She is unexpectedly nervous. He looks around briefly, then begins telling her what he has found. He tells her what is known about the Claimants.

'The incidents alongside the one that killed your mum are the only certified times that anyone was killed by a Claimant action. There is some pretty compelling testimony that it wasn't them.' Arthur is smiling, as though pleased by this information, as though expecting Isolde to share his pleasure.

'I'm not sure how that helps me, Arthur.'

'No, no of course not. But that's... you might be glad to know all that anyway, when you hear the rest.' There is an earnest note in his voice and he looks at Isolde intently. She stops fidgeting, feels a curious prick of alarm over her scalp.

'What, what's so serious? Tell me.'

'Solde, I don't think your mum and you were just passing by. I think your mum was one of The Claimants.'

There is a pause as Isolde digests his words. She gazes off, above the heads of the excited gamers, over the flicker of the multi-screen arena. She had not gone as far as to formulate this possibility to herself but she recognises that it is what had made the past days so jumpy and uncertain, so in need of resolution.

'It would be strange, if we ended up in the same box after all.' Arthur gives her an uncertain smile. He looks at her carefully, trying to assess the effect of his words.

Though she was somehow expecting to hear what he has said, as soon as the words are spoken, she is shocked. Stalling, Isolde asks, 'What was it your parents were done for? It wasn't violence, was it?'

'Disruption. Hacking and electronic thieving. Not for gain, but to cause problems. Though I do remember a few times we seemed to be pretty flush all of a sudden.' He smiles again. 'But I'm not doing some kind of secretly gleeful pitch to put you in the same bracket as me. I wouldn't wish it on you, to be honest.'

'Do you ever visit them still?'

'They died.'

'Sorry to hear that.'

'It was grim, visiting them. They were out of it most the time.'

'The guy seemed pretty out of it too, couldn't connect who I was, then suddenly had it.'

'Dietary medicalisation. Keeps the place running smoothly with the inmates an easily managed herd at the centre.'

Isolde considers this information. 'I can't remember any news recently about prison riots, not for years.'

'No, doesn't happen now. Narcotic pacifiers that make the boredom and frustration go away. Bit of arts and crafts, a bloody enormous warehouse full of all the books that no one wants. It's a manageable system they've got going.'

'At least they rescinded the death penalty.'

'For now.'

Arthur sips at his drink, looks around the arena. Isolde turns to him again.

'I don't really know what to think, Arthur. I feel kind of OK about it, and it would explain a lot about why I know so little. But why were our experiences so different? If Mum was one of the terrorists?'

'Because The Claimants were becoming folk heroes. Their collaborative politics were taking hold. The state needed victims. They had the ideal candidates: a dead young mother and a little orphaned girl.'

Chorus

so roped you are by patterns wrought in other minds

we have escaped these binds
our ways no longer barred
we are ones
no longer set to serve

you, who can choose it,
would be wise to follow us

The shutter slides silently up. She walks to the front of the cell, less hesitant this time. Inside, the man lies on the bottom bunk, foreshortened. She can see rubber slipper soles and a mound of belly.

'Did you know my mother?'

A slow stirring on the bunk, he lifts a hand and rubs his eyes. He rolls slowly onto his side, a tangle of thin blanket pushed behind, slippered feet swing laboriously to the floor, a counter-weight to pulled him upright.

'Wait.' He pauses, searching for something. Clarity perhaps. 'Yes. I did. In a way. Not good to be too clear on... on that connection.' He looks around the cell, then at her. 'They waste no time on me anymore. No threat. But all the same...'

Isolde's heart beats, urging her to action.

'Was she a—'

'Stop. Don't make trouble for yourself.' He leans on his knees, head resting forward on large hands. He presses his fingers into his eye sockets. 'We came from the same place.'

'Where? Which part of London?'

'No part.' He yawns slowly, widely. 'It was... It was out...' He gestures with one arm. 'She was a farmer. Like me. That's all.'

'A farmer? What... That can't be. I'd remember a farm, surely?'

'We wanted to be farmers. Not like farmers overseas, with big fields, machines. We were romantic. But it worked. She was one of us. You were too.'

'What, or where, was the farm?'

He goes to the desk. Searching through the lose pages, he chooses one with a space below a diagram. He picks up a pencil, draws. He holds up the page. Isolde stands up, steps forward from the bench, nearer the thick line that demarcates her allowed space.

'It's here, near here. This village, the sea, the coast. This is where they built that sea wall. This bit. It's here.

'Is it still there?'

'I've been here too long. I don't know. I dream about it. I think about the beach nearby. Tin lids, rubbish from years ago. I hardly remember who was there then. I don't know. I hope it is.'

'Was it near the sea wall?'

'Some hours, on foot. We ran along it. Like a bridge on the sea. To the middle and back. It was beautiful.'

He pauses, the pencil in mid-air. Gazing into the memory, his face softens. He closes his eyes for a moment, perhaps a blissful moment, then turns back to his drawing. Isolde sits, once again made awkward by the proximity, the strange intimacy that has been thrust upon them.

'How did you recognise me?'

'The other one didn't have children. My mind is…' He pauses, half-smiles in helplessness at Isolde. 'It's full of holes, I know. I get, it gets all loose. But I think about the people who died and… sometimes I remember, sometimes not. You look like her. You've hit a good day.' He smiles, a little, looks back to the drawing he is making on the book page. 'There was a big road. And here, what was it called? The town. There was…' His voice fades out but he remains bent over the table, making marks with the pencil.

The door at the end opens. It's the same man as last time. The same clothes. The thin frame shrouded in a pale mac.

Clutching the same bag by the fabric at the opening. He ambles along the corridor slowly, tipping over to one side, leaning forward. He sits down next to Isolde, giving her a curt nod. He puts down the bag.

'You shit. Fucking human shit. You are a waste-pipe of shit from all the worst places. Just filth and darkness and shit, you disgusting fucking worm. My beautiful angel is dead and you sit there, a sack of fucking useless shit. Taking up money, taking up air, taking up a few fucking spare inches of floor space – even that is wasted on you.'

His voice never gets loud, but there is fierce intent, such force in it that Isolde is frozen in the slipstream. She watches him, eyes wide, too shocked to notice that she's staring. The man in the cell seems indifferent, but after some moments, he turns and speaks. Isolde realises he is speaking to her.

'He comes here all the time.'

Isolde has many more questions but there are no gaps, and she can't bring herself to speak over the quiet force of the man.

'He must have loved her so much,' says the man in the cell. Isolde is embarrassed by his openness in the face of such a torrent of emotion. He continues, only just audible above the relentless tirade. 'Yes, he must have, but I loved, I loved... I loved too...'

Isolde looks back and forth between the two men, both spewing as though the words were leaking, both seeming so inappropriate.

'You don't even know what it means to be a human, you are less than a germ. You are a scab picked off the bed sore of a dying thief. Don't you fucking sully the idea of love, don't you fucking pollute it, even the idea of it, you dirty—'

'We all tried to... I must've... She was with me. With you. When it happened.'

'I would wring your fat neck. These bony hands, they would

choke the life out of you. Cut though the life of you like wire.
I would have the strength for that, believe me.'

The prisoner keeps talking to Isolde, over the other, in short
sentences as though to gather his thoughts. 'You were there,
little scrap. In the yard. In the fields.'

Isolde searches behind the confusion, looking for a distant
signal, the wakening of a far-away memory. There is nothing.

She walks most of the way back, a cacophony competing, what
to let go, what to cling to. How to make sense of it. He had
known her, had known her mother. He was the only person
she could talk to who did. And he had killed her mother. Had
she been trying to do the same to others? Accidentally suffering
the fate she meant only to dish out? On the long walk, Isolde
can find no way to tidy it all away.

Back in her apartment, Isolde looks at the few images she has
on the main wall-screen. Her mother has become a new person. No longer the shadowy representation of an unclear but
certain happiness. Nor the innocent victim taken out of life
in the rash instant of another's anger. She is more complicated
than that. She no longer fits within the skinny boundaries that
Isolde had been given.

She picks up the page that had arrived early that morning.
Torn from an old book, tags of paper are still attached where
the stitches had held the page in place. On one side, two blocks
of text, on the other, the Eye and Vision printed in bold at
the top of the page above an illustration, it looks like a planet
mapped with rivers, Fig. 157 – view of 'Fundus of Left Eye'.

Surrounding the black of the printed drawing are grey pencil markings. It is a map. Not entirely clearly a map – she
wouldn't have known it had she not been there when it was

made. The fat bit of land, the sea wall. Those meagre instructions, or random recollections. She didn't know if he had given it to her, with unexpected subterfuge, as a map, or because of the message written at the bottom of the page. Block letters in pencil, elaborated with curlicues, a pastiche of old, formal typography, as much handwriting was in an age when no one used it. The two words are simple enough. *I'm sorry.*

The paper arrived, heralded by an official digital message asking if she was willing to accept an item from prisoner D191-H14. The envelope, marked like the scene of an accident with lurid black and yellow borders, had to be signed for with her thumb. Inside was an official letter with some bland words of explanation. Nothing from the prisoners was committed to the electronic communications networks. Too many fine lines radiating outwards. A piece of paper was mute. It couldn't be overheard. But this one shows her where she might find her mother. She picks up her device and looks for a map that shows the old sea wall project.

Jesse

13

Train lines are modernised but roads fall into disrepair. Marshal's roving journey for work takes increasing chunks out of his life. He stays away for days at a time. There aren't enough hours for him to see his family every evening. Still he clings to his job, his income; their collective failure at creating a vegetable garden does enough to convince him he has no choice. For Lena it proves only that they haven't tried hard enough, that Marshal doesn't want it enough. Eventually, in his absences, mother and son finally get properly to work, they learn from their neighbours and from the internet. Recently they have eaten their own potatoes and their own salads, saved for the weekends when Marshal can join them. It is a kind of courtship – their way of life subtly manoeuvring to seduce his.

Jesse and Mister are bigger, stronger. They rove the countryside, play themselves true in lost woodland hours and field drifts, roving absences where time and purpose blend into some other medium. Jesse is still young enough to be at the mercy of his parents' plans but old enough to feel capable of other choices. He knows that their position is perilous, that they are clinging on, just; if not yet with any sense of victory. Lena's defiance is what is keeping them there.

Mikel and Giana, on the other hand, have shown what can be possible. Their whole back garden has, for some years, been keeping them in most of the food they need. Giana has planted grape vines on the back south-facing wall, to grow slow and steady among the vegetables. Mikel has turned the garage into a workshop where he repairs and rebuilds, mends chairs, makes shelves, stacks wood to season for use in future years. They still run the shop, a place where barter has become normal once again. It is remarkable what can happen when the terms change. But the village has shrunk even further. More left, others died. The edges are more ragged, the woodland creeps in between the houses, into the empty gardens, the verge slips into the road.

There is a small herd of cows kept by Malc, and they provide milk, enough for the village, though many others left abandoned like the farms have wandered away into empty fields and the edges of woodlands. Malc, for all that he may regret it, cannot care for them all and he knows them to have a wisdom that will ensure they find their own way.

Mrs Pym, finding vigour that heals in new purpose, researches making cheese and butter, and some not entirely hopeless results have been achieved. Food still comes in deliveries but the pressure on that model increases on all sides. Vehicle licences are prohibitively expensive and roads, though emptier, are in a bad state of repair. Food from the wholesalers is expensive. One of the big food corps sets up a delivery centre in the nearby town, as an experiment, to see if the commercial success they experience in the cities can work at smaller scale in the towns and villages. But they are impatient with the patchiness of take up, the inability of the remaining villagers and countryside dwellers to understand the necessary flow of the system. It is financially draining. Even Lena has come to see that back-to-normal has changed. A new normal waits for them to discover, somewhere.

This blustery morning, Jesse walks with Mister through the woods, the way to Little Denton no longer barred by the nationalists. They made their presence felt over a number of years. Their bold aggression, their willingness to go further, to end with violence, caused more upset than their numbers should allow. The burr, the scratch, the imperfection defined the whole of the community. Lena had nearly given up her resistance to leaving in the face of them. Chetna dug in her heels, her talons and horns, her hoe, her will, her anger; she refused to bow to the pressure of their bigotry. She had found a sanctuary in the quiet village and would not leave simply to please, to make it easier, for those cowards.

Chorus

for some of us
resilience is the greatest might
with resilience we defy them

Jesse and Mister walk through the woods onto Wright's Lane. Jesse thinks about Euan. He too could handle a bit of trouble. He had that in common with the group in Little Denton. Last September three of them came through, a girl and two boys, about eighteen or so. A quarter of a bottle of whisky from god knows where – it wasn't always available for sensible money – clutched in the girl's hand, her long straight hair lifting in the breeze as one of them asked Euan for the opening hours of the shop, her smile lighting up as she offered him a pull of the bottle. He took it, smiling back. She was pretty.

Chetna had come along the road, heading for her home.

Seeing the group, she had crossed the road, pulling her long cardigan across her front, her dark eyes topped by the neat square of a frown. One of the boys shouted at her. 'Goofy fuckin paki.' Chetna glared at him, carried on her way. The girl had laughed. One of the boys turned, looking after Chetna, moving as though to follow her, watching as she opened her newly painted yellow front door. The girl curled her lip at the older woman, her fresh beauty becoming suddenly malevolent, corrupted. 'Leave her alone,' said Euan, enjoying the rise in his own anger, feeling the hurt meant for Chetna as his own indignation. An argument had started between them, then a fight. The girl smashed the bottle against the wall of The Oak, lashing at Euan. He tussled with one of the young men. The other had pulled away, temporarily nursing his jaw. Euan wavered under a punch, and the other rejoined, shoving him from behind, the bottle sliced into him again. Chetna came out of her house and pointed a shot gun at the group.

'Get away. Get away from here, you... you vermin.' The girl let the ragged glass fall to her side but laughed at the older woman. Chetna's eyes had widened, her lips had pulled back. Her anger tightened the grip on the gun she had not once picked up before, since John had brought it, tucked it behind the living room door for her safety and protection two years before. She couldn't even remember if it was loaded. She shook with a mix of fury and fear at the uncertain knife edge of this new threshold. But the three read her anger, saw determination in a face that was filled with fight. They backed away, walking a trail of blood, and on noticing how much of it there was, pooling at Mrs Pym's front gate and tramped in their footprints down the road, they began to run.

It had taken the police until later the next day to respond. The three had gone. There was no trace of them in the houses at the edge of Little Denton. That had seemed to satisfy the police. They would keep an eye out to apprehend them if found. Euan's father got himself arrested, shouting and intruding into the remains of the police centre, the Crime Reporting Hub, but he was the only one. A week later, the whole lot of them had moved out, keen to evade arrest and protect the three, apparently gone to join with a larger group in a town a little further north.

At an open edge of the churchyard, out of the shade of the yew, is a square stone, unmarked by a mason. Two sets of flowers, one tattered and brown, one fresh bunch of buttercups in a jam jar, sit at the stone edge. Euan has lain in the ground there for nearly a year now. Jesse wanders into the graveyard, replaying what he didn't see but has heard, told and retold, so many awful times.

He wonders about the difference between bravery and the willingness to have a fight. Euan had both. He knew he could fight, but he also stood up for those who couldn't; he had enjoyed that in himself, Jesse could tell. He had wanted to be a hero, had wanted to be looked up to, but he had also wanted to look out for one of his neighbours. In a different combination, the same ingredients of bravery and anger had prompted Chetna to try to save him. She had mourned his death alongside his parents, the three knotted close in a pattern that would never be undone.

Jesse sits on the stone, thoughts turning to a random drift of memories, playing football with Euan, computer games, bike rides. Negotiating a new school with the older, tougher boy keeping an eye out for him, letting it be known that there would be consequences to messing with Jesse. He thought about many times with his almost friend.

There is a darker imagining that sits, just under the surface when he remembers Euan. Blood sliding along the gutter of the village road. A strange sickness as he can't help but turn to his own mortality, picturing the threaded-out volume of his own blood, its containment, the frailty of the barrier that holds it.

He walks over to Sep's grave, an older stone in the row that marks the villagers who died during the pandemic. He wonders how Sep would be now, all these years later. Perhaps he would've already left for one of the cities. Mister Maliks busies himself around the gravestones, quantifying visitors, unravelling the wisps of fleeting presence.

Chorus

fences fall, hedges gape, we wander at our own pace
or no pace, for we don't know where we're going

a peril on the roads

it's slow, finding new ways

we amble through your graveyards and playgrounds,
your funny little back gardens
we too find ourselves anew in the world

Marshal's absences have become too difficult for the family to sustain. In an attempt to save their marriage, Lena and Marshal have agreed, finally, that they will move to London. They will try it, anyway. They promise Jesse that they will keep up a connection with the village, that they will try to remain primed for a return if it doesn't work out. Jesse is sad and worried. But he is excited too. He knows that there is so much more to find in the world, and though he can look forever at the detail of what is already in this small realm, he is excited about seeing more. Other teenagers, parties, changing scenes, excitement. He's not immune.

Marshal has a lead from someone he contracted for, a wealthy client who usefully works in one of the housing companies that hold sway over the city's real estate. She has promised to help Marshal find a home in London and comes up with either an apartment in a re-apportioned Edwardian block, somewhat shabby but with the glamour of having once been the preserve of the very wealthy, or a bigger new-build, part of a fully solar tower in a bright, new development. Marshal will be working for her company and knows he can afford either. The new build has everything, is efficient, cheap to run, easy to live in, but the mansion block has a big shared garden with mature trees that both Lena and Jesse see as a link to the home they don't want to leave.

To give hope to Lena and Jesse, to keep open the option of return, Marshal brings some of the workers from a job, and a truck of materials. They spend a couple of days, littering the house with work boots and hard hats, fine drifts of sawdust, building shutters for every window and a second skin for the front door. Various villagers come by to look, saddened that yet more people are leaving, but hopeful that such measures speak of the intention to return. While they are there, Marshal gets them to make a glazed door for the noticeboard Mikel built outside the shop. Chetna paints it the same egg yolk yellow as her front door. Lena pins up an invitation to the goodbye party and a few days later, twenty-three people gather, the whole village, to wish them well, and secretly, to wish they return not too long hence.

Marshal won't be able to take his beloved car to London. Private vehicles are priced out of the range of almost everyone by anti-pollution taxes. A car reverts once more to the status symbol of the very wealthy. He has clung on to it too long, in hope. There isn't even the option, by the time they come to leave, of claiming the tokenistic scrappage fee offered in compensation. This car cull, as it is known, has been a source of great turmoil as outraged owners have staged blockades and slow-driving cavalcades up and down the country, across city centres; more turmoil cited by the state as it brings in military models of control to re-quiet the populace.

On an evening just before they are due to leave, Marshal says to Jesse, 'Do you wanna come for a drive?' They go out to the front of the house and get into the sleek and sporty car. It is a pristine burnt orange with a recently stylish brass-coloured trim. Rather too low-slung for country life, it is at least powerful.

Jesse and Marshal hoon round the country roads, windows wide, music blaring. Marshal turns off into woodlands, skidding on leaves, bumping a dent into the rear end as they turn back from an impassable path. He turns next into one of the fields, checks Jesse has his seatbelt on, and they careen in wild circles, bumping and skidding across the grass. 'Don't tell your mum,' says Marshal, as they come to a stop in the middle of the field, father and son beaming at each other. 'What are we going to do with the car, Dad?' asks Jesse. 'I think we'll just leave it here,' he replies.

Isolde

14

The citytrain stops at the edge of London, a section of the outer ring, the 25, named after the old motorway. Eight lanes of traffic become a miniature valley, edged by grassy slopes or canyon walls of sound-baffling cement. It sprawls with small businesses and apartments. All are built, ad-hoc and low, directly on top of the road tarmac. It is a permanent shanty town, as though the engineering groundwork of the motorway prevented new roots going deep. As though homes and buildings couldn't truly settle there. But businesses as opportunistic and tough as buddleia dig in and somehow survive. Homes built without recourse to the latest styles and technologies, recombining old materials with idiosyncratic, problem-solving flourish have sprung up along sections of the 25. Here is a place for the latecomers, those unwilling to penetrate further. People who left the countryside reluctantly, all their resources used up trying to stay out of the cities.

In some sections, wealthy blocks of housing push out, refined aprons of gated and green garden estates that take advantage of the space and privately financed track extensions bringing the citytrains to a stop at their bio-locked gates. Wealthy, walled communities, large houses edged with generous sweeps of private greenery and leisure areas. Personal taxis, using a loophole in the law, wait in bays. Passenger drones come and go in an unobtrusive whirr. Serenity and space secured inside an eight-foot, sensor-topped bubble of brick.

Where Isolde disembarks from the train, life is more modest. Shops selling second-hand furniture, cheap food packs, and buckets and mops that are arrayed on cracked and weedy tarmac.

Isolde hoists her bag. If the farm still exists, it might take time to find it. Other ways of travelling the empty expanses of countryside are available, but they are sporadic and inefficient, dependent on unreliable people or restrictive systems. She wants freedom, and in this instance, the achievement of that freedom requires only time. She is going to walk. She has a storm suit and a low-slung bivouac tent, food packs for eight days or so; she carries as little as possible.

In her pocket, she has an old brass-cased compass, given to her by her lover. They had learned to use it on a walking trip in a vacation park in North Devon. She takes it out, rubs it on her sleeve – the smudgy gleam of the metal never quite comes to shine. She flips open the lid. The needle hovers in endless service. It hovers with the lid closed, always showing the way. It comforts her, the lozenge of metal that warms in the tuck of her hand, and shows the way to somewhere, any time she opens the lid.

She pulls out her device, checks levels. She'd been in two minds. Ever since she decided to leave, to go into the unknown, a sense of longing for the disconnection has tempted her into leaving it behind, but caution has prevailed. Still, she doesn't know how long it will work once outside London, so five days ago she had bought paper from an art supplier, and with Arthur's help, drew a map. It is an amalgam, overlaying the scrawl from the man in prison, a map of the country with the old towns marked and what Arthur had found on old networks and in travel journals, on forums and information pages for and about the activities of the New Agrarians, gleaned from information tucked away on the ghost web.

They had pored in wonder over the maps that revealed the wild improbability of all the land being occupied, in use, productive. Other maps mark the scarred rash of abandoned towns and the anomalies where settlements still remain. By piecing it all together, they had found what surely must be the farm. If it is still there. If it truly ever was.

She crosses the tracks to a cafe in a low-slung cabin, sits at a small rickety table outside. She orders coffee and a pastry. Weeds poke up through the terrace as though the countryside is seeping into this far edge of the city.

The weather has held. It's been several weeks since the last storm. To her left, the city centre heating under a haze of cloud. To the right, the unknown; it begins unpromisingly in a strip of pale square buildings and then a ruffle of trees.

Her apartment is secure – she has arranged for an acquaintance to stay and pay rent for a few days. All work is temporary, and her resourcing experience will hold long enough for her to slide back into employment whenever she returns. Though she doesn't know what she'll find, she doesn't even know what she hopes to find, she senses the possibility of freedom that has been missing for years.

She looks about her with curiosity and, for the first time in ages, hope. This walk, this strangely elaborate plan seems to offer an antidote to the failure, the sadness and stasis of the last year. She is tired of sorrow, tired of the lead weight of loss, and tired of rage. The time has come for her to make movements, to exit the safe and horribly tight circle of her unhappiness.

Chorus

come out to us girl, into the sweet green
where all reshaping is a slow beat
a steady, inevitable pulse

Outside of the cities is not forbidden space; it's not a poisoned wasteland slipping into the dangerous unknown. It is just empty. Wilderness regrown where food used to be farmed. Small, abandoned towns and villages slowly consumed by forests and skipped over by animals and birds. Empty dining rooms with wide open patio doors giving deer shelter from storms. People have regrouped in the cities. Now and then, a few slide out to join the hardy, the idealists that live on the land. Now and then, they give it a go but return to the relative ease, the access and certainty of city life.

Isolde doesn't know whether to expect hippy idealists, radical rebels, old-school traditionalists or an empty, abandoned building. The police did sometimes raid and arrest from settlements out in the countryside; there were occasional excited news reports about caches found, pharmaceuticals repossessed, weed crops burnt. Or anti-state terrorist organisations imprisoned. Satellite eyes and drone heat sweepers mapped and surveyed all power loci outside the city fringes. But as with all policy, there is a prevailing pragmatism: if a potential enemy is weak and without an obvious way of becoming strong, it is ignored. England, like the other, separated nations of the British Isles, is a lagoon of feral fields, untamed hills and forests, populated by a chain of city islands. The rare threats that emanate from outside the cities are, at best, bare-headed and pitchfork-armed. These rare settlements and the cities survive, by mutual consent, in avoidance of each other.

She tilts the cup for a last bitter sip of coffee, the final drop in the stain at the bottom of the cup. She looks along the 25. She can see the road she'll take, heading toward the distant crepe of greenery laid along the horizon. She is nervous but it is exciting too.

She feels finely balanced – calm and resolute in the knowledge that though she is doing a strange thing, it is something that will be done and perhaps must be. It is a moment of absolute peace.

She starts walking.

The old road, her guide, leads out under the causeway that carried the motorway full speed, across the interchange. Beneath, the bridgework has been co-opted; strangely built homes nestle under the shelter of a disused highway on the city edge. Children play in an area, an empty roundabout under the wide roof cover of the 25. Their voices echo warmly in the shady space, reaching up into the concrete eaves to mingle with the brief, woody sound of pigeons tucked into the struts and under-beams. Sparrows too, chitter in shrubs between the buildings under the disused road. Wind rumbles through gaps and around cement pillars, as though the muted ghost of combustion.

She walks on a path between two buildings. Red brick and cement blocks jostle, a calendar of patchy progress as the building filled up the space over time – scavenged materials working hand over hand.

Beyond the motorway junction is a scrubby patch of grass, a few low buildings, recently built. The road ahead is visible, a snakeskin of old and new; tarmac is interrupted by flat islands of weeds growing in the drifts of soil washed onto the surface by rain. Footpaths connecting buildings are worn back to black skeins of the road. She identifies her direction and follows the road.

Chorus

through the trees we see her, starting out
along ways pounded once
by bullish stampedes, angry steel that screamed with noise
and now is quiet
ways that ran by our dull and safe fields, our electric fences,
our pinned and trimmed hedgerows where birds would hide
ways where we now find sweet meadow herbs

we murmur through the group
take heed

we watch her through the ghosts of houses,
through empty windows, glassless, crossed now by branches

hollow shells
echo with so many dreams

A thin cast of cloud mutes the world, colour and detail slipping as though into the past. The dark windows of abandoned homes peer blindly through dogwood and hawthorn, the slender trunks of young elms. These trees will grow, their roots will push at foundations, tip the earth, unsettle walls. Each autumn leaf-fall, each creep of ivy, every mouse dropping; all of it a tiny lick, a little bite, a pull back into the ground.

Some houses have been cannibalised for materials and all

that remains is an outline, a low-walled shrubbery of brambles and bindweed. Storms have taken others more fully to ruin. They look furtive, dejected, lame. Birds sing, masters of the in-between spaces, making their homes in the disarrayed buildings. A sparrow shuffles brightly in a puddle on the flat base of the road.

There is a car dump, the metal pods tip carelessly, unwieldy shapes bonded by ivy threaded through engines, rusty body work. In front of this accidental sculpture is a circle of car seats, perhaps a hangout for the kids living under the bridge.

In the past, the road would have taken her almost to the door, in a few hours' drive. But Isolde doesn't know what a drive is. Trains are ridden, and ways are walked, drones ferry goods and people where the trains don't reach. Taxis and ambulances transported the wealthy and the sick, inside the cities.

Ahead of her, a dog barks. She searches for a stick, for protection. In the front garden of the nearest house she finds a length of tubular metal, the double handle of a kid's scooter that had bowled along this pavement to the corner shop, when money existed to be held in a pocket, a pound coin, or old coppers, tasting of dirty hands, exchanged for stickers and sweeties.

The metal clacks lightly on the road surface as she walks, her fingers overfill the ridges on the rubber handle. The dog barks intermittently, somewhere in the distance. Eventually she leaves the sound, and soon after the metal stick, behind. She stops for a rest, sitting on a wall that once marked a front garden, an area paved in slabs fringed with grasses and dandelions, like eyelashes. Where the house had stood a low buzz of foliage has grown over rubbly remains. In the back garden she sees an old trampoline cage filled with tangled growth.

Though she often takes long walks, her feet, unused to the walking boots and the backpack, ache. She wishes she could traverse the veins of old roads with the same ease that the squirrels skip along the branches. To be a creature of the air, unzipped a little from gravity's steady pull.

When they were new and happy lovers, at the beginning of their relationship, flush from a five-month gig in his job as a building engineer, her partner had used a connection higher up in the company and blown almost all of his pay on a boat and visa to Portugal. They had camped wild on the Atlantic coast. It was the only time Isolde had both the money and the paperwork to travel overseas. She remembers the discomfort of sleeping on the ground on the same thin, blow-up mat she's brought on this trip. But she remembers, too, that time outdoors will leave her sleepy enough not to care. She savours the sweetness of memory, then pushes it away.

The old town of Chelmsford lies ahead. She doesn't want to sleep in the town. There might be people still living there, and she's unwilling to enter an unknown community. She turns off the road into a clearing, shoulder-high with cow parsley, oxeye daisies and nettles. She keeps near the road, but tucked away, choosing by instinct the spot that offers the greatest sense of security. At the edge of the clearing, the older trees feel both like a protection and a menace. She is a little scared – it is anxiety born of the unfamiliar in encroaching darkness. If she stays still and quiet, she expects rationally that she will still be alone in the morning; the countryside is not inhabited by anything she need be afraid of, all the people have left.

Chorus

there are wolves
out here in fields and running through the empty streets,
pissing on a lamp-post where a house dog once felt brave
hunkered down at woodland edges

hungry, patient
but even wolves do not have the appetites of your kind
best stay out

Dusk domes the sky, peach bleeding into deep sapphire. A few stars appear in the distant blue. Setting a low light on her device, she pulls out the tent and sleeping mat. The tent goes up with a flick, the mat is inflated with a few breaths. She lies down, under a thin cover, the tent a cocoon of light. She tries not to listen to the intimate noises of the woodland. She reads for a while, then lets the device read to her, reading her, softening the sound and light as she falls asleep.

15

She wakes, restless and thirsty, in a narrow tangle of clothes and bedding. She hears sounds outside the tent, peers through an opening in the fabric above her. In the centre of the clearing is a group of feral cattle.

Chorus

join us in the sunshine
then make the way you set so clear

we amble and sway
newtread our paths
– our way is subtle
our destiny
subtler still

She disentangles her clothes in the narrow space, arranges things in loose order. The animals aren't frightening, but there are occasional reports of a trampling or stories of a bull getting into one of the wild parks and goring a holiday maker. She must be vulnerable lying so low on the ground, the tent perhaps small enough for cattle to amble over rather than step around. She dresses and moves to the shade of the trees behind her. One of the cows watches her, a languid blink, a slight lumbering shift, a ripple across the velvet brown skin, then she turns back to the grass.

The animals, moving slowly, flank to flank, seem at home on the land. Not wild, still not wild after several unfenced generations. The first corral, the first low walls and crude bells, the first selected expressions of form, markers now deeply imbedded within the beasts themselves have made them something other. The consequences of life, the weave of it, has changed them.

Feral animals are everywhere. Sheep and cows nibble down the saplings, keep clearings in the trees, enough to preserve patches of meadow in the woodland growing in once managed fields – a little snip of fresh green trying to push into the space, a grind of big teeth pulling the pale shoots of oak and beech and ash into the first stomach.

Isolde sits on a log, watching them contently as her mind and body stretch into wakefulness. A blow of breath, an occasional low moo. They seem to know each other's minds. The beasts look up occasionally, watching her, she thinks. Eyes blink slowly, long-lashed, intelligent. The lines of their spines rise and fall in ranges, the shaping of a distant skyline. The ribs look big enough to curl up inside.

It is time to get moving. She packs up, takes a last look at the cows, then walks, approximately along the direction of the road, into the woods. The compass hangs on a loop of thread, big enough to slip over her head and long enough to use without removing. She flips open the round lid, holds it before her and makes a reckoning for the direction she must take. The shade of the woodlands, the scattering of sunlight that slips through the cover of branches is, even at this early hour, a welcome alternative to the steady beat of summer sun. She's not in a hurry. The old injury in her hip aches, from a night on the ground. It brings a reminder of why she is there. Slow progress will ease out that pain before she needs to resort to the pills in her backpack.

She will portion her time in food packs. For each day's worth of food she eats, she will put aside another for the return. She will stretch it out with what she can gather on the way.

Chorus

you left the city for a kind of hunger,
but not for food

Brambles overrun the spaces between the trees. She picks up a stick, stout enough to batter back the shoots that claw at her backpack and t-shirt. Taking advantage of the slow pace, she picks blackberries, gathering them in a bag tied at her waist as she pushes through the looping switches with their offering of sweet sharp fruits and their toll of scratches.

The woods end in a meadow. Isolde spots field mushrooms and fills a second bag. She sits down in the shade of the trees to eat from the harvest hanging at her waist. Her blackberried hands stain the flesh of the mushrooms a dull mauve as she snaps the caps, putting the pieces in her mouth. Both flavours have smoky, earthy undertones. She savours the two, alternating between the dark purple and the pearly grey-white. Each has a distinct texture; the berries squashing until her teeth meet the tiny pips, the mushroom almost shearing from itself as though on myriad invisible fault lines. Opening out the bags, she arranges the two bodies, the white and the purple, lays them on the dark green of the shaded grass. How much there is to see, to taste, to smell, just in these foods. She pulls out a stem of the grass and chews on the sappy pale end, finding a tiny hint of sweetness, less acidic than the blackberries, sharper than the mushroom.

Chorus

you could join us, girl, if you had the stomachs for it

Isolde keeps some food for later, retying the two bags at her waist. She drinks water, pours some on her hands. The dark stains remain. The ground slopes down to the edge of a stream. She fills her bottle, scoops cold water over the back of her neck.

Ahead, the distant growl of heavy clouds. She stretches her back, gives her hip and leg a vigorous rub, enlivening the sting of a scratch or two, chucks her bag across the stream and jumps a narrow section. Soon she reaches a small housing estate on the edge of a highway village. She stays alert for signs of people, even though there are unlikely to be any. There is a large petrol station on the corner, the canopy still intact. At one end sits a low building with a cement ramp. The sign above the empty doorway reads Happy Burger Steak House in letters a foot high, the red faded to a coral bleed, the yellow burger, smiling, ready to eat – what? Itself? Two crows flap from a broken window and disappear above the canopy.

The wind picks up, the dense cloud edges in from the east. The gangly weeds growing in the soil on the road surface begin to move with it. Teasels and dandelion heads bop. The sky darkens. A shudder of cold runs across her bare arms as the first of the thunder hails from the distance.

Chorus

we are of the summer storm,
moving together, hide by hide

we hunker down
moisture seeps where our sharp feet trod, where our big
teeth tore
rain falls, steam rises from our hides
we warm bent blades with our furnace heat
our breath sweetens each other's breathing

find shelter girl, get rest

She sees a house partly open to the road. A fallen tree, split by lightening has knocked through the front wall. It grows still, slender branches reaching upwards from the horizontal trunk. Her boots crunch on glass as she hurries out of the rain. Behind the lattice of branches is a disintegrating carpet, shot through with unfussy bindweed. The vivid beauty of the white flowers stands out as though deliberately to vain advantage against the rotten merge of old reds and browns. Rabbit droppings scatter the floor. The rain rumbles against the roof, thunder bashes out its energetic demands across the stage of the sky.

Across the room is an armchair. A small colony of fungi grows at the hem, sprouting up like stamens from the flowers of the upholstery fabric. She brushes off a scatter of mouse droppings, gives the cushion an experimental hit. Nothing runs out or puffs up in a toxic cloud, her hand doesn't encounter a slimy sink hole. It's tattered but dry. She pulls out a cloth from her bag and opens it over the chair, sits down. Rain comes down, fills the air, turns the light a muted grey blue. The bindweed stretches out across the floor, luxuriant in the squalor of the decaying carpet. Isolde pulls out another cloth from her bag, and drapes it across her shoulders and head. She leans back and closes her eyes, drifts into silken sleep.

Chorus

she sleeps
she hears nothing

we blink, a drop on long lashes, a tongue rolls across
a wet face,
the wet inside and out meet on a fat tongue

we watch him pass by

16

The rain quiets, patters softly among the sweet sounds of the
birds who sing in the rafters and in the branches. Isolde
stretches out her legs, opens her eyes. Outside, between the
growth of the fallen tree, she sees something. A brightness. She
realises with a battering of alarm that it's a person. She looks
carefully, cautiously. It is a boy, or young man. She thinks he
must have seen her and yet has waited, has done her no harm.
She thinks that makes him safe. She eases herself quietly into a
better position, before calling out gently.

'Hello?'

The figure stands up, unfolds in a series of skinny angles that
eventually align vertically, pulling his rain cover from his head
and shoulders.

'Hi, hi. Don't mind me. I'm just...'

He cranes away, looking up and down the road.

'Do you live here?' asks Isolde, suddenly aware that she
might be trespassing.

'No, I'm passing through.' He has a northern accent that she
doesn't know how to place.

He's young, maybe nineteen. Tall and thin, dressed a little
strangely.

'Do you mind if I…?' He gestures toward the back of the room where Isolde still sits in the chair.

'No, come in.' She feels a little absurd making this invitation. She's wary but his youth and demeanour reassure her. 'I'm Isolde,' she says.

'I'm Lee.' He smiles at Isolde. She makes a clipped smile back. He has short light hair, darkened by the rain, pale skin, a hesitant way of moving that makes his skinny height awkward. The sleeves of his bright pink jacket end a few inches above his wrists, he wears some kind of shorts over some kind of bright leggings. All items reasonably fashionable, but never showcased in this combo. He has a wide orange ribbon around his neck, tied in a bow at the side. He eases tentatively toward her, then stops, holding up a hand in greeting.

'Hi,' he says again. She watches him as he peers at her through the opening at the front of the house.

'Where are you from?' she asks him.

'Ugh, you don't want to know. A small place.' A flicker, a sneer or revulsion, crosses his face.

'OK. Then where are you going?'

'London? I guess. I'm not really sure.' He looks down, studying the carpet or his thoughts, chewing the inside of his lip. He looks very young. 'I haven't got papers.'

'Well, you might be alright, depending on your back story.'

He tips a wry smile with one corner of his mouth, lifts his head. A bitter acknowledgement that he does indeed have a back story. He turns to Isolde. 'How about you? Where are you heading?'

She gestures to the road. 'North. North-east-ish, toward the coast, I think.'

He looks disappointed. 'Right. Right.' He sits down on the ground, arms hooped around bent knees. They sit in silence for a while, then a distant sound, a voice, catches their attention.

Lee sits up straight, horribly alert, eyes wide and unfocused as he listens intently. There's another sound. It becomes the noise of men talking, still a little way off – a laugh, a shout, a posse. Lee scrambles to his feet and makes for the door that leads into the house. He wrestles with it then pulls it open and scrambles through, a harsh, panicked whisper as he disappears.

'They mustn't find me!'

Isolde, also now anxious, gets up and moves behind the arm-chair. She thinks she wouldn't be seen anyway but feels the need for greater protection. The voices approach, the sound of young men, cheerfully aggressive with one another, their voices and actions buffeting around them. She peers round the back of the chair, through the branches. She can see about five of them, their short hair slick and darkly wet. They look to be on their way, harmless enough excepting the constant assault on each other's egos and the odd retaliatory punch to an upper arm that is part of the language of young men. They pass by. Their voices drift, soon quieter than the rain, as they head south.

Isolde moves back into the armchair, readjusting the cloth between herself and the dry, spore-dusted surface. She looks toward the door, waiting for Lee to reappear. After a few moments, she gets up to look for him. Behind the door is a dark corridor half blocked by a fallen ceiling panel. There is an open cupboard in the understairs space with a collection of gaudy high-heeled shoes and men's boots. She ducks to go through the triangle of space under the sheet of plasterboard, walks up the stairs. On a window ledge above the bare staircase a row of china animals stands, forever holding a straight and orderly line among a disorganised scatter of dead insects.

At the top of the stairs she calls out the unfamiliar name. 'Lee?' There's no response. She opens the first door, sees bare floor boards and a stained divan. She tries again. 'Lee, they've gone.'

His reply is quiet. 'I'm in here.' She enters the second room. Lee is in the gap between another bare bed and a wall, papered in a pale floral design overlaid with the speckles of a living fungus. He looks scared and angry, squeezed into the absurd space, his bright colours blaring in the muted decay, visible the minute she came through the door.

Isolde brushes a hand over the surface and sits on the edge of the bed. 'So, are you in trouble?'

He laughs, a small puff of air out of his nose, a set grin. 'Maybe.' He looks toward the door. 'Who were they, those people?'

'Five guys, ordinary looking.'

'Were they white, all of them?'

'Yes. I think so.'

Lee sighs, drops his head. 'Yes, then that could be the trouble that was meant for me. All in black?'

'Maybe.'

'Tattoos on their necks?'

'I wasn't close enough to see that, couldn't tell.'

'I'm pretty sure they did.' Lee untangles himself and stands up, moving to look out of the window at the back of the room. He turns around, at the same time, pulling at the end of the satin ribbon so it falls in a drape across his shoulders.

'I've got one too.'

Chorus

take heed boy,
they still hunger

your leaving gives them fear

– can you see it?
fear is fed with rage
rage in turn feeds fear
it is the failing of your kind

with dread, we hear them come

Lee stands with his back to the window, his head tilted to the side, a hand pulling away the collar of his pink jacket. Isolde can see the black mark on his neck. A symbol, a square with a zigzag of lines across it from top to bottom. Two lines of type, the top in block roman capitals, LEE CHARLES PEYTON. She cranes forward, frowning, trying to read the line underneath.

'It's my date of birth,' Lee tells her.

'So you are seventeen?'

'Yep.'

'And why do you have it?'

'It isn't something I had a choice about. I come from one of the White Towns, everyone gets this – boys on their necks, girls on the inside of their forearms. Tenth birthday. We're marked as one of the tribe.'

Isolde is surprised. 'I've heard of them, of course, but I guess I thought they were more like, I don't know, villages. A few crazy, old white people keeping the real world at bay.'

'Yeah. It's exactly that... but organised to an insane level, I mean – rituals, systems. And there are quite a lot of those crazy old people who have bred some crazy young people too. Folk to march to the drum.' Isolde looks at him questioningly, but he carries on.

'And there are at least a dozen or so communities. We're a smaller one, but we're in contact with other groups. One of them has hundreds. Every so often there's a military sweep, once they even took away some weapons. But as long as the leaders don't try and meddle with the cities, we… they just get on with it. I guess it's like the others, the farmers. Just easier to ignore them. You want to be purist whites, just do it quietly.'

'How long's it been like this?'

'Long enough for a second generation to have been born there – there's a new ceremony for them. It's all about the ceremony in the White Towns. That, and skin colour. They'll always find reasons to wave a flag and make an oath.'

'When did you leave?'

'Four days ago. It's vile there. Plus, I'm gay. I'm a taint. That doesn't go down well.' His face twists briefly, into bitterness and anger. 'I didn't even know the word "gay"; the only words I knew were "taint" or "corrupt". I was both until a while ago when I met some outsiders.'

'Why would they stop you leaving?'

'Do you think all the people my age would stay, by choice? Some of them buy into it. But it's fear that keeps them there. That and battered-in loyalty. Loyalty, loyalty, loyalty. And hate. I doubt you'd pass as white enough to get in, but you wouldn't like it, I swear.'

'What will happen if they catch you?'

'Probably be beaten up and left for a day or so tied up in the square. At the least. That's what happened when I was caught peeking at some other boys with my trousers down. And the Enforcer raped me. But that was his secret punishment, just between us.'

Isolde feels pity for the boy, but she keeps her words in the same tone as his. He hasn't asked for her pity or even her care, and she knows from experience that either, offered at the wrong time, can be an undoing.

'So they just run their own entire legal system?'

'Yep. As long as we don't keep too many guns and don't go asking for anything.'

'Hell. I had no idea it was like that.'

'For a long time, I didn't know everywhere else wasn't like that. But this incomer, he had the marks from another White Town about two days away. He told all us kids about Liverpool. God, he was a dullard. He'd come from there to find his white brothers,' Lee says with derision, 'about five years before. And in telling us how lucky we were, he filled in a lot of blanks about the world. After, we had special lessons about the corrupting dangers of the cities, trying to put the genie back in the bottle. But it was too late for me – I had a new scripture. That was only a year after I'd been raped and beaten and left tied to a pole for three days for my own good. My mum snuck out in the night to give me a drink of water. But that kind of thing can put you off a place.'

Isolde, well-practised, can see the hurt behind his insouciance. She recognises it from the children she has grown up with. She is surprised to learn that being gay is a problem. In the city, it seems people have more choices. But she catches a dawning, a hint of realisation; there is monstrousness in a version of freedom that changes to suit this or that local dominion. If rights are mutable, perhaps they are no longer rights. They have become another kind of tool. Freedom, it turns out, is so partial, so vulnerably granted that it can change its definition from one piece of land to the next.

Some of her friends have already understood that this variant of permissiveness is dangerous, dark. And she has taken on what they've said, in a careless way. But she hasn't felt it enough to see it, to feel the need to challenge or resist. She begins to wonder at how lazily, how easily she has traded her complicity. Like so many others, she has let the clouding of her own problems act as the screen behind which such a system evolves. Like many in London, she has a multiple heritage that could barely be untangled, but with her relatively pale colouring, in not being an object of hate, she hasn't bothered to read the threat, she hasn't felt the danger.

She looks at Lee who is picking at some of the peeling wallpaper. He lifts a strip and tries to extend the length of what comes away. It tears too easily. He picks with his thumbnail at another corner.

'Do you have family?'

'Yes. Still do. But they made a choice and so I had to too.'

'I'm sorry, that must be awful.'

'Well, at least Mum brought me a bit of water in the middle of the night. An older guy, in his twenties, his dad took him to the courtroom with his hands tied and a black eye when he found him with another man. That other man disappeared mysteriously. I like to hope I'll see him somewhere in the city. But I think I might have more luck digging round the edges of the Further Fields.' Lee pauses, chews the side of a fingernail. 'My dad, I think he always knew; I think they both knew. But they cared enough to pretend that they didn't, then hope for a miracle. Or that I would be celibate enough to hide our shame from the rest of them. And I was doing pretty well, until they caught me watching the boys and wanking.' He looks at her with a hardness, it is a challenge. As though she is being dared to find him disgusting, as though he is testing her.

'Well, I can promise you, you will be fine when you get to London. You'll even be able to get that tattoo removed.'

He sighs, turns back to the window glass and catching as much of his reflection as he can, re-ties the ribbon in a looping bow. Turning back to Isolde, he leans onto the windowsill. He looks worried and young.

'Do you think it will be OK?' he asks her.

Chorus

the one you remember, his hands tied still, he is there
in the ground
not by the far fields but the other way, down the gulley
rough with gorse,
  ancient shadows under the sweet scent of yellow blooms

he is there
buried in a shallow hole dug by men who laughed and felt
their urgent wickedness as a thrill, men who sought to soothe
the threat of treachery – a father, sick with his own betrayal

he is there, the young man
  his love and his pain still sing, through the clods that
fill his wounds
  we murmur words of comfort when we pass through
that shady hollow
  we show him we can hear

Lee circles some loose bricks and builds a fire in the back garden of the house, gathering dry fuel from inside the buildings.
Isolde walks back into the fields, her legs brushed wet in the
long grass. She pulls a few handfuls of naturalised barley to
augment a dried soup. In another garden, she finds a clump
of parsnips snuck in among the meadow weeds. They're small,
easily pulled from the ground – skinny pale fingers that taste of
sweet earth. It is enough food, with the mushrooms, to make
a soup for two instead of one. She can feed Lee without losing a day. Lee also finds carrots in another garden where the
previous occupants had been attempting self-sufficiency before

death or the city claimed them for good. He shows Isolde the feathery leaves so she'll know what to look out for.

Lee feeds the fire attentively, just enough to keep the pot simmering. The fire crackles, birds sing from the dripping trees, a branch taps lightly against a patch of loosening roof tiles, moved by the slender tail of the storm wind.

Isolde looks over at the boy, the near-man. The tails of the orange ribbon around his neck trail perilously close to the flames. He looks slender and vulnerable. She thinks, *He must be tough, he must have learned to be so. But he looks too young to be alone.*

'Lee, I'm going the wrong way for you. But if you feel like it, you could stay with me for a few days. Maybe going the wrong way would make you harder to find?'

Lee sits back on his haunches, thinks over her suggestion. 'Yeah, I think that would be good. Yeah, good.'

'I don't have room in my tent, and you'd have to help me find food, but you'd be doing that anyway. Or you could just head straight to London – it's a few hours, maybe five or six. But on the same road as those guys. And you'd have to be pretty unlucky to bump into them, but still.'

'Thing is, I've no idea what to do when I get there. They won't look for me forever, I don't think, but I don't really know what to do till then.'

'I don't know either, off hand. I could probably find out. I think there are amnesty papers you can get when you arrive from Out, but I've no idea how that works. Maybe because of your age they might just send you straight back.'

He winces. 'Yeah, that's my worry.'

Isolde fishes in her bag, pulls out the pack of dehydrated food, adding the contents to the simmering pan nestled in the burning scraps of wood and chair legs.

At the end of the garden is an apple tree laden with small, hard apples. Drowsy wasps buzz through the grass lurching between the fermented fallen fruits. Isolde can smell the rotten sweetness. She plucks a hard apple from the tree, bites into it. It's sharp and sweet and sour all at once. Lee collects whole fruits from the trees with the aid of a stick. Isolde hands him the second food bag, emptying the last of the blackberries as a sweet finish to their meal.

'Wait,' says Lee, wandering off to look around the plot. He parts the weeds with the stick, searching among the knee-high growth. Eventually he bends down to pick some leaves.

'Here we are, just what you need with blackberries. Pure good.' He comes back, shredding the rumpled little leaves. Though she knows the flavour extracted from it, Isolde has never eaten fresh mint before. He scatters the shreds over the berries; the smell washes her insides. He was right, the combination of the bright and bitter mint with the dark sweet earthiness of the berries is delicious. Isolde savours the taste and magnificent colour, green and blackish purple, an antidote to the pale, salty starch of the soup. Lee, having lived his whole life on the land, is an asset and will, with his knowledge of how food actually grows, most likely add time to how long she can survive, rather than diminish it.

She pulls out a bottle of water and tips some over her hands then passes it over to Lee. She makes ready to go but Lee asks her to hold on, disappears into the house. He returns with a faded floral curtain, and a fistful of long strips of satin fabric. He holds them up to her, smiling quizzically. They are slightly flared, with a point at each end. She recognises them as the neck ties worn by men in old photos.

'I've got the dandiest luggage straps ever!' Lee smiles. He drops the fabric on the ground and shows his other finds. Two small plates, a holed woollen jumper, some scraps of wallpaper, a sheet of plastic with large rings across the top – a shower curtain.

'This will keep me dry at night. And this–' he holds up the paper–'is kindling'.

Lee opens the fabric and bundles the swag in the middle, ties it with the neckties. He loops two more for shoulder straps.

He shrugs his shoulders to settle the load and looks back at the pack.

'Very fancy! Shall we go?'

Chorus

two by two along the tracks they travel
we see the boy, bright as flowers in May
so bright he hides his darkness

so he tries
and so he sometimes wins

17

They walk into the town. Trees engulf houses, fill gardens, lift paving slabs. The road is covered in leaf litter, muddy washes of dark woodland soil over-spilling the edges of the tarmac. The ruins of buildings shuffle in, closer to each other, holding out against the incursion of the forest. In the shade of the trees small puddles from the storm glitter in dips and runnels. Tracked through the earth, leaf-covered and wet from the recent storm, are hoof prints. After a few hundred yards the tracks turn into a gap between shrubs and on into an old park. Goal posts stand, curiously, with a hoof-flattened bare patch before the goal mouth. The cattle have made their own ways.

They come to what Isolde first takes, in the dense growth of young trees, holly bushes and elder, to be a fork in the road. But she sees it's a roundabout. She pulls out the secondary screen to plot their best way.

'I'm not really keen on being in the towns. It seems safer to me just to keep away from other people.'

Lee looks at the wall of trees swallowing the buildings.

'I don't expect many people will be living here,' he says.

She can see what he means. The houses look dark, dead, abandoned. The young forest has surely won back this patch of land. Birds sing in the trees, washing the gloom out of the air. But the absence of people hangs uncomfortably, like the unhinged and broken doors a few feet into the trees. This place is home to new souls, the little lives of birds and rodents who don't feel alarm at the sightless squares of dark windows. They don't feel the absence of the people behind the broken glass, or the memories that drift, indestructible, fragile waste, like tattered plastic bags in the trees.

Lee cranes forward, peering into the trees ahead. Within the wall of growth is a sign, as high as Lee and wider than his arm span. Huge chevrons in black and reflective off-white pointing road users to the left.

'The guy from Liverpool was old enough to remember cars. How about you?'

'Me? No, not quite. Though I think there were still a few around when I was little. The solar ones. Then just the public trains, drones and the freights. Have you ever been in a city?'

'No. I've been to a place kind of like this one, maybe smaller. We did some scavenging there now and then. Collecting bricks with the tractor and a trailer, that kind of thing. There were quite a few people there, but they didn't like us. The first time I went was the first time I saw someone who wasn't white. They left though, probably soon after that. Place was empty after... next time. I'm not sure if my folks had anything to do with it. But every now and then, there'd be this atmosphere. Excited. But not fun. It...'

He looks down at the ground. He turns to Isolde, pleading for understanding.

'I knew it was wrong. But all I could do about that was leave.'

Isolde feels compassion for the struggles of the boy, and feels too that his discomfort should by rights be her own. What has she done that was more than that? What has she ever done?

Rumours existed but the scale of harm has never moved her. Now she feels remiss, ashamed.

'The person you saw, the first non–white person. How did that happen? Who were they?'

Chorus

he feels a sickness in his stomach, in his chest
you have words for this
we do not

the pain of causing harm

Lee feels shame so clearly that she can read it. She can see it in the furrows of his forehead, the set of his brows, in the hunch of his shoulders. His pace slows.

'I was twelve. We had gone to find the peddler, to restock with supplies he brought out from the city. We traded things that were banned in the town – marijuana, mushrooms. We made alcohol too. We took a cart to the next town. There was a woman and a child – I guess she was about six. Asian I guess, both with straight black hair, like yours, but darker skin. There were five of us, two men and three boys. The woman and child were coming toward us. The girl was skipping along, chatting. I could hear her voice, high and cheerful. They had no reason to pick us out; we weren't close enough for them to see our necks.'

Lee pauses. He looks upward, searching for pictures or avoiding them.

'One of the men, my uncle, shouted something vile. I wasn't sure what would happen, but I could feel the change. I wished they would turn off the street, but they didn't hear the threat in his words to start with. The little girl seemed to notice us first, then her mother. It was all so quick. But I saw her change, from a bright, skipping child to a frightened one. The woman pulled her in, behind her.'

Lee's words are slow, ungainly.

'My uncle shouted again. We had slowed too but were getting closer, and they were still frozen. I could feel the relish, the enjoyment from them, these men, my family. My cousin Raif picked up a stone and threw it. Then another. Then the other boy threw one that hit the woman. She stood up, taller. I could see a mixture of anger and fear, then she turned, pulling the little girl with her and they were running back the way they had come. The girl fell over, and all these men and boys around me laughed. The mother scrambled to pick her up, then ran with her, all ungainly. It was... it was that effort, making her stumble. I just felt so... My cousin was still throwing stones. They were excited. I felt so disgusted. And then I laughed too. To fit in, to not cry. To not let them down, to not bring disapproval on myself.'

He pauses.

'The people of my family, my kin, the people I grew up with. I know they've done much worse. I know they've killed and judged and battered and belittled people. It's how they are. It's how they define themselves. I've seen cruel things. And I knew that we were supposed to be bonded, for pride, for love, for what we were, against this thing. This threat, this pollution. We were supposed to be vigilant, against the threat. This time, it was low on the scale, compared to other things that I know about now. But I saw a mother and a child become frightened, because of us. I saw my uncle, all excited. It left a sickness in me.'

Isolde hears the break in Lee's voice, feels a heartsick moment of empathy for the woman. Her easy scorn for the backwardness, the narrowness of the White Towns serves only as a solipsistic marker of her own distance from their actions. It does nothing to mitigate the harm to a mother and child, stumbling in fear in the streets where they lived – streets that should, like all homes, belong to them.

They walk on into the town in a silence still echoing with the imperfect presence of humans – the troubling memories of people they have brought with them, and the echo of the people who have left. Isolde consults her map. She holds the compass in her hand. The solid roundness of the brass casing warms, a small and comfortable weight that gives her comfort.

Ahead the trees clear, only poking now and then from broken gaps of the roads and business forecourts. A street light lies on the ground. An office block, stark white with strips of black windows, five storeys high, stands in a spread of concrete. Lanky shrubs waver on the high roof. Moss grows in senseless patterns and weeds poke up through the cracked surround. Lee speaks in a low voice.

'Look, there's someone there, watching us.'

A stooped figure, tall and thin with long, straggly hair and beard stands in the apron of tarmac at the front of the building. He watches them, still and silent. Isolde switches on a mood of entirely false but pragmatically friendly greeting, but as she's about to wave and speak he retreats swiftly, behind a rubble rock garden, into the block by the main doors. Isolde looks up the cliff-like building. Another face, another quiet blankness, watches them from a high floor.

'Do you think we might get trouble from the people here?' asks Lee.

'I don't know. I can't see why, unless they want to rob us.'

'Or unless they're far-corrupts.'

Isolde frowns at his use of words. She wonders about the degrees of deviation, the rings that spread out from the cherished, knowable centre as seen by the people of the White Towns.

'Well, you probably get plenty of those in the city, no need for them to come out here. Let's just walk, look like we're passing through.'

Around them is near silence. A dog barks distantly. Birds sing among empty buildings, flit through dark front doors. There are no further signs of people. Isolde checks the compass as they come to another roundabout. Soon, in the centre, the buildings hold their ground, the trees give way to shrubs and scramblers that make their homes in the crevices and across the surfaces. Chelmsford, like most places, was abandoned in stages. Goods from shops were sold or taken away for stocking new city start-ups. The items that were not part of this orderly redistribution have mostly been scavenged. But some fully stocked shop windows remain. Children's clothing on sackcloth figures, a stanchion of greetings cards and novelty mugs.

Lee stops suddenly.

'I thought that was…' He's looking at a shop dummy, a blank, white human form. Six of them, unclothed, serene and distant, raised on a platform in the wide glass of the window like the personal guards of some ceramic emperor. Lee looks into the window, then seeing the door into the old department store, turns back.

'Statues. Is it a museum?'

Isolde laughs. 'No, they're shop dummies, for the store to display the clothes.'

Lee doesn't move.

'They're beautiful.'

'Lee, let's keep going.'

'I just want to go and look.'

She tuts to herself, but resolves to patience, puts down her pack. Lee appears behind the glass, moving in between the figures. He runs his hand slowly down the arm of one. He disappears deeper into the shop. Isolde sighs, sits on the ground. She can feel the slight damp of the moss through her trousers. The building looks empty, so she hopes he won't be long. She strokes the lid of the compass absentmindedly, lets her thoughts drift and disappear.

Lee comes out smiling with delight. He's wearing a large, blue hat with a flaring arrangement of cerise and orange on one side. He holds his bag in one hand and a white, hairless head – the previous owner of the hat, Isolde guesses – in the other. She realises he is so delighted by these finds because they're new to him. All that is new to her is the dated styling of the hat.

'There's lots of stuff in there! Please, let's just take a look?'

Isolde smiles, catching some of his mood. She follows him through the wide doors. The ground floor is large, white and mostly empty except for the few shop dummies. The six in the window stand in orderly anticipation, as though waiting for the rapture. A disparate bunch of stragglers lag behind, some of them still wearing the odd item of clothing. The light is muted. The window glass is overgrown with mossy greenery. A squirrel looks at them for a moment, scampers along a counter and out through a broken window. The abandoned space has a strange cool emptiness, like being inside a large tank. Halfway to the back unmoving escalators lead up to the second floor. They mount the awkwardly large steps. A window above the escalators has gone. Dark ivy rumbles down from the glassless square and lies in a trail among blown-in leaf litter down the stairs, pigeon feathers are caught in the silver runnels.

Up on the second floor, goods remain on display but there are gaps on rails, piles where some of the clothing has been folded or boxed. Lee abandons the head and the hat and starts to go through the items.

'I could do with a change of clothes,' he says. Passing a stand, he pulls a couple of long silken scarves, pushing them into the side of his folded bundle. Isolde picks up a candy striped jumper.

'Nice colours!' says Lee. Isolde notices his gravitation to the bright.

'Did you… did everyone dress the same at your place?'

'Not exactly, but there were rules. And uniforms. They're kind of precious, because they aren't easy to replace. Scavengers were sent out for fabric, and there's a stockpile kept in the depot, but it was hard to earn. Things got mended a lot. And stuff got added. Awards, symbols, things sewn onto them.'

Isolde tries to picture the garments, the language of symbols sprouting among the patches and repairs. Traditions reinventing themselves, determinedly being woven into the necessities of mending; spell making.

'These will be good. And that jumper you had. And a couple of tops.' Lee drapes a pair of trousers over his arm then walks to a rack hung with stretch shirts. They are all dark, sober colours. He rifles disinterestedly. Then he picks a pack of underwear, a cap and a pack of t-shirts.

'OK, done. Let's just go and look for a better bag. Further back is a section with holdalls and cases.' She wonders whether her solar charger can be upgraded but all the bags have been there for so long and have been dead for years. There are a few backpacks. Lee picks one out and places his new attire and his makeshift pack inside. He loops the handful of ties through a stretch of elastic chord so they dangle from the side of the new bag.

In the remnants of the travel section is a shelf stand with labels showing old, cheap prices for solar cookers and water cleaners. Isolde pictures the two ghostly men they had seen gathered in the evening dark around a jaunty, vintage campsite, with a small solar fire on the roof of the white building, holding their hands out, silently waiting for the trapped sunlight to boil their leaves.

'We might as well go and look at all of it,' says Isolde.

On the top floor, birds roost on the metal beams in the ceiling. The glass skylights are clouded by algae and moss. Isolde thinks of the cool depths of a pond. A big side window is empty of glass, joining the space to the sky. There is a fabric section, stands with rolls of material, trays of haberdashery. There's a showroom of furniture and household goods. Furniture in abandoned towns is available behind almost every fallen front door.

Lee puts down his bag and jumps backwards into a deep red armchair, its arm studded with buttons of various remote controls. Isolde sits on a coffee table cast in smooth and swirling polymer, clear and opaque colours twisting through the mass.

Isolde is ready to move on. Lee follows. They walk toward a wide central staircase through the wall-less rooms on show. Past a chartreuse sofa that has its back to them. They both stop, seeing at the same moment the shape on the sofa.

They edge closer. All that remains is skeletal. A dried out form, a woman judging by the thin synthetic gown that is still intact; it falls into hollows around her bones. The bones, the dried flesh and shrunken skin of a woman wearing a pattern of pink on a stained chartreuse sofa. One foot still hangs onto a sandal, its pair lies on the floor. Objects from the showroom have been placed around the remains. On either side of the head stand two vases. Cutlery glints, ray-like among strands of long, grey hair still clinging to the skull. A china animal rests on each bony hand. Glass globe paperweights are placed at intervals, at ankle, knee and hip, on the fabric of the gown as though to stop it from blowing away. Buttons join the gaps in between, a line of coloured dots, varied sizes ordered tonally, red becoming orange then yellow as they rounded the complex, narrow bones of her feet. Isolde looks closer. There is something shining in the eye sockets – golden buttons. A ribbon has been tied, long after death, around the slender forearm bones. There is something tender and beautiful in these acts, the meaning-making of placement. Presumably, the act of a stranger; it is difficult to imagine someone would leave a loved-one for eternity in an old furniture store then come back to reclaim them in this way.

Lee slides one of his silk ties from the loop on his bag and lays it across the figure, from shoulder to shoulder. With slow care he arranges it so that the ends are tucked away, with tenderness for her and caution for himself. He makes the lightest of touches, two fingers on the silk tie, where it crosses her sternum. Isolde, deeply moved by the instinctive gesture, is caught in a curious moment of love for the two strangers – a boy she has known for a few hours and a woman she can never know. They stand silently for a moment then head back to the road.

Chorus

you keep them with you
your dead

we too
though all do the carrying

make new kin, girl
find new ones you will want to grieve for

it is the only way

love is sacred and remains in the bones

18

Incarcerated days bleed on, seep into each other. Time drips through him, the steady flow just potent enough to maintain life. The marking of time, it's a sign of life, of sorts. He seeks memories of an age when his body was strong, active, when pleasure was to be anticipated and enjoyed, when signs of life were measured least of all by time. Touch, smell, strong emotions and anticipation: the rich materials of a young life. The eviscerating certainties of love. Floods of anger, of joy, the thrill of exciting and knowable danger. Could he ever feel so much now? Emotion wells, tantalisingly, as though to test his capacity. But it barely wets. A damp stain of sadness for all that is no longer felt.

They see no one else as they walk through the town. Their feet crunch on fallen leaves, tread silently on moss, pavement glimpsed in skeins below nature's first claiming veil. In a bricked pedestrian way lies a jumble of letters from shop signage. Some of the letters are laid out in a line, but spell nothing. Bright plastic and metal dulled by weather, leaves and webs tucked into the spars between capital Es, groundsel growing through the hole of a turquoise O. A wordless babble of retreat.

A street away, sunshine hits a crumbling cement lattice. The brutalist chevrons encasing the long side wall of the multi-storey carpark are patchy, as though, at one time, subjected to a sustained spray of gunfire. A few cars rust in the shade. One corner is wound with a spiral ramp connecting the five levels.

Whether for some unknowable practicality or for the sheer joy of having the town as a playscape, an extravagant, thickly knotted rope walkway connects the fourth floor of the carpark and a big, open window high in the side of an office building. The office workers are long gone, as is now also the bridge-builder.

On the first level of that carpark, unseen by Isolde and Lee, a missing chunk of cement opens up a sunny patch of con-crete floor. A wolf basks in the sun, yawns and rises, disap-pears briefly into the shadow and appears once more, between the yellow pay barriers. She walks carelessly, stopping to listen and smell, small animal cues from the hordes of birch marching slowly, slowly into the centre, youngest first. She carries on her way. At a crossing, she casts a glance at the back of the male and female walking north through the town. The big pads of her feet skirt the broken glass of a jewellery store, chains and trinkets glinting alongside the glass as though the valueless futility of such easy wealth had suddenly hit the thief during the execution of the raid.

As though in a dream seeded by genetic memory, a dog barks, distantly, whining in fear or in terrible longing.

Chorus

oh we feel them, everywhere, wolves, loping, drifting through

after our young, the savages

a shiver from coast to coast, shakes through the branches,
waves through the grass
   to find us

the ancient fear survives
the docile years when fences stretched to keep us in
keep others out

it will never leave us

some fears we have already unlearned
though they rumble, uncertain presences that have no form

ghosts

The cities, for all their brash mystery, seem certain, knowable in comparison to the great, untethered stretches and strange possibilities of the lands and empty towns between. The density of people in London keeps most to a consensus that acts as guidance. But in other places, the continuity is broken. People are making new sense of the world. Some, like the White Towns, are re-making from the old, building on fears that were already festering before. Others make new systems. What was once floors of easy-credit consumer goods, shopping malls, can become mausoleums. Letters that no one could read become wordless spells. All it takes is the absence of other influences, one imagination on a loop, reinforcing its manifestation into a pattern. Or the ideas of a persuasive and charismatic leader adored by those looking to follow a design invented by another, looking for fate rather than creation. This way, slowly all our stories get rewritten.

As they leave the town, the buildings become wider and lower, more of them pulled down by storms. Roofs and fascia of recent utility peeling easily away in the wind. Something temporary written into the structures of edge-of-town car dealerships and tyre suppliers. Uncherished buildings that spread lazily into spaces that maintained a strange emptiness even when in use. Storage space, parking space, affordable space. An uncertain connection to town and country – the worst, perhaps, of both. But the triumph of utility bestows a strange freedom, not loaded with the age-old meanings of town and country – when in use they always felt new. Not modern, not dashing, not exciting. Just new.

A sheet striped with angular corrugations lies partially on the ground, one corner caught up in greenery. The edge squeaks against a rusted car. A sound etched out in the silence for years. Soon the buildings are left behind, trees and meadows marking open country.

'You never told me where you're going,' Lee says, ending the silence that has fallen between them.

Isolde smiles, realising that a boy who'd agreed to come along with her without knowing a destination must indeed have need of company.

'Well, it's a bit strange, I don't actually know where I'm going. But I think it's some kind of farm, or community.'

Lee's face shows his disappointment.

'What's at this farm then?'

'It might be where my mother came from.'

'How don't you know?'

Isolde tells Lee about the events that have led to her journey. In speaking, she's glad to discover that it does make sense. What makes less sense for Lee are the parts that she takes for granted. Lee doesn't ask her, wide-eyed with wonder, why she would choose to walk for several days to a place that she couldn't be sure even existed; he asks her how the prisons could be so big and still function automatically. He doesn't ask why she has started to look for her mother, he asks her how it is possible for the state to know so much that she had to meet discreetly with Arthur to talk about the past.

They stop for the night in a brightly carpeted pub. Lee builds a fire outside in what had been the smoking area. He takes out squat stools but gives up on them, unable to remove the synthetic cushion, bright and tough like a mushroom extension of the carpet. A shed, slid to the ground in a neighbouring garden, provides fuel instead.

Isolde lays out her maps on the bar, checking where they are. She finds a bump in the road, a wide curve they just walked, she finds a group of buildings that match. They are not far from the destination.

They eat at a table in the pub garden. From the road, they hear the ring of a bell, and a voice.

'Holler, holler! Hello! What can I offer you today?'

Drawn by the smoke, a man comes through the gate, beaming the trust-less smile of a salesman, bright and empty in his sun-beaten face. He holds a staff with bells on the top that jingle as he strikes the ground. Isolde has met pedlars in the city who used a similar device. He has a larger pack than is carried in the cities, where stock can be stashed and replaced more easily. He also has a motorised travel bag adapted with large wheels for the rough terrain. All of its city neatness is undone by straps, added pockets and pouches, and a bulky wrapped-and-tied bundle slung on top. He smiles again, his easy intrusion make Isolde and Lee nervous.

'Hi, I don't think we want anything, thanks.'

'Are you staying here? Is there anything I can bring you next time? I can get light bulbs, solar connectors, food bullets. Anything.'

'No, we won't be staying here, thanks.' Isolde regrets saying it as soon as she has spoken. If the pedlar does pass on to anyone that he has seen a light-haired boy with a neck tattoo, it would be better if he gave them the wrong information.

'I have treaties, sweeties, sprites delights, bubbles and fizz and gewgaws.' He smiles through his sing-song performance. 'I have almonds, lipsticks, jewels and gems, meat, batteries and pencils.'

'Do you have any chocolate?' asks Lee.

'Ah!' says the pedlar, raising a finger as if to stop himself in his own flow. He moves with dance-like gestures, elaborately, as if preparing a magic trick. A flurry in his pack, and with the gesture of a bow, he sweeps his closed hand forward toward Lee. After a second to build tension into the performance, as though Lee is a decade younger, the pedlar opens his hand, revealing a small packet of chocolate sweets.

'There. And I have other flavours.' He rummages, looks at Isolde but she shakes her head. Lee fishes in his pocket and brings out a generic credits tab. *So, he has some money at least*, thinks Isolde. *Wise of him to keep it quiet.*

'How much?' Isolde gasps at the price, but Lee pays without flinching. Living Out, he is used to the inflation of goods sold by pedlars. Road prices are always high.

The pedlar tries to push his pitch a little further, pulls a few items from his pack, including, ludicrously, Isolde thinks, some lacy pants and bras, and the lipsticks he had advertised early in the pitch. She is impatient with it, with him, and doesn't like the intrusion. One person in the emptiness of the countryside causes more anxiety than the crowds of hustlers and street sellers trying to pressure a trade on the pavements of London.

Eventually, he leaves, managing only to get a second sale

of a bag of extortionate sweets. They are discomforted by his appearance, take time to settle. Eventually they make up their beds on the red and gold carpet in the lea of the old oak bar.

Chorus

beware the pedlar, that man of gold and green
he means no harm but will hurt all to help himself

Jesse

19

Jesse takes time to find his way in the city. He disguises himself
a little to fit in. He camouflages, stands with his weight shifted
onto one side, leaning on an arm held up by a trouser pocket.
His head tips back slightly, to the side slightly, eyes closed
slightly; he deals with his quietness by displaying it as though it
is intense boredom. As if to say he would be a shouter, a josher
and a joker, a kidder, if he could be bothered. Soon enough he
makes friends. Mister eases his passage into acceptance, the way
the two of them are linked by silent understanding. The other
kids are charmed by what seems almost a special power held by
Jesse the newcomer. Some of them have family pets, but Mister
is so definably Jesse's dog.

Without drawing attention to it, Jesse finds ways to be on his
own. He slips into reveries, staring window dreams; bird flights
and cloud patterns are intensely noticed, and it seems, instantly
forgotten. He misses his time in the quiet of the woods, in
places of no thought, of being absorbed and unaware and so
fully there that his edges merge with his surroundings. The
city claims too much of his present attention to allow the same
waking dream to capture him.

He dreams of empty beaches. He dreams of forests. He

remembers younger days, very young days before the sea moved them on. Families on the beach, eyes squinting into sunshine and heat on the back of a neck bent over the high-tide mark. The feel of a sharp-edged shell made gritty with sand, clutched in his hand. The brittle stiffness of old gull feathers. The sea washing his ankles, taking his breath as he hollowed out his belly, elevated his ribs, hunched shoulders and star-fished fingers for that first gasping dip into the cold water. He isn't unhappy, now, with reliable friends and a loving family, but he feels himself taken from his true place. He feels that this new world shrinks around him. Mister dreams of the rich crochet of trails lacing the forest floor. City smells are as baffling a puzzle, but they bring him less joy.

Chorus

such noise and smell and choking of our senses
no place for us
it never ends well

a ridged ramp into the tight metal box as we shake, rattle, bellow our fear
above the roar
the race that drowns our dread
no place for us
it never ends well

So life rolls on, a boy makes friends, walks with his dog, moves through life learning how to be, how to avoid, how to learn. He no longer blots out the light under his bedroom door. Before Jesse knows it, it is time to start university. His quiet demeanour is less of a marker, needs less managing. Many of the students are just as quiet as he; others are raucous enough for all. There are groups that drink themselves silly and shout their exuberance into the night after night, groups that plan revolution, groups that talk about civil disobedience, groups that claim solutions. Some print their proposals on pamphlets, hold meetings, arrange support for what remains of the unions. Some are content to school others over canteen coffee about their failure of understanding, their lack of radicalism, their cop-out or cave-in to the system. The vast majority settle down diligently to prepare for the world just as it has been designated for them.

Chorus

but what of the world is truly written
what is truly law?
yet you name us docile

Jesse, a student of engineering, listens to all the chatter. At the canteen table, he listens again as Elise, her indignation slowly turning the dial on the volume of her voice, unravels how the beneficiaries of the move away from domestic food production were investors with links to government, hand in hand with officials who conveniently owned stakes in the vast overseas corporations. It was, she tells them, in their interests to find the problems of wage costs and low income insurmountable.

Jesse shakes his head slowly, baffled by the endlessness of disruptive greed. He is one of the people who mourns the loss of connection to the land, feels the slowly tightening grip on freedom of expression and opportunity across the whole country. He feels the closing of the map. Farmers and traditionalists rail at their loss of income, the end of thousands of years of connection, of being. Their bitterness is commonplace; popular media sends it up, reduces it to a lazy comedic trope. Moaning farmers appear in television sitcoms, old-fashioned and backward looking. Efficiency, safety of supply, price, these are the watchwords, brought into service as though they signify the only available logic. Many are thankful for the convenience, the low prices. But expediency, even when cheap, becomes expensive. Profit comes at the cost of loss. Same as it ever was.

At Jesse's university, the latest project, set by a tutor with industry links, under the auspices of a department with industry backing, is for a system that will speed up efficiency in the off-loading from the freights of salad crops. It depresses him to be funnelled toward this shrink-wrapped, distant, greenwashed provision.

Chorus

such strange conceit
to think you can transcend basic laws

what you, what we too are,
all must be –

– you are animals
and is it not enough?

– you float, uncertain
unroped from land, unanchored
and it is not enough

you are like the we
forced into sheds
you choose it even,

roofed acres on cement
no grass, no sky

at least we served a purpose –

whose crop are you?

Each day he passes a community garden. He starts to notice as plants grow and flourish under the care of the estate community. And most days, he notices one girl, about his own age; she is black, petite, stylishly individual. She is always too absorbed in her tasks to see him, her black cloud of hair tied from her face with a succession of bright scarves. He hurries to reach the railings that divide the garden from the street, then slows his pace to a dawdle, seeks her out between the raised beds, her scarf-tied hair bobbing among the greenery. Sometimes she sits, paused, on a plank bench balanced on two rounds of a tree trunk, tucked under the dark spread of an evergreen tree, gazing with a lost focus that Jesse recognises, taking little puffs on a vape. He makes unnecessary trips after college, walks by with Mister, hoping the dog will provide the circumstance for a meeting. He is too shy to talk to her but he wishes they could meet. He wants to help them with their project. Not only because of the girl, her precise beauty, her air of calm competence. He wants to build raised beds over ground that had been asphalted for half a century or more, maybe design an irrigation system. Pick and eat the crops. Put his problem solving to better use than shaving pennies off the costs of food importation businesses.

Chorus

yes, somehow you see it boy
under years and ages
stone, cement and brick
the sweetness of raw earth

clad feet ringing on hardstand
children playing on the acrid black of asphalt
for years
the black-skinned earth lay quiet
but you feel her wake

20

He finally meets her, Jada, at a session for beginners to learn about growing fresh food in the city. Jesse signs up as a volunteer, throws himself into being useful in the hope he will impress her. He takes Mister with him, and Jada does speak to Jesse for the first time after making a fuss of the dog, who takes to her with the same hopeful friendliness he offers to all.

He tells her how he found Mister, and that his full name is Mister Maliks.

'What was it like, where you grew up?'

'It was good. Yeah, I miss it actually.'

'I hear some people are making a return, doing the whole self-sufficient thing.'

'Yeah, I hear that too. I think I'm going to look into it.'

'Yeah, part of me would love that, but there's so much to do here.' Jada gestures, looks around at the garden.

'You mean here, here, or London?'

'Both. It's all got so… wrong.'

'Yeah, it sure has.' Jesse squints across the beds thinking how just at the moment, things have got pretty right. He turns back to Jada, sitting next to him on the step, takes in her profile, the glint of gold at her ear, the battered vape, the purse of her mouth as she expels an antisocial cloud of smoke that scratches at his throat.

'Do you have other work, or do you live from this?'

'God no, I wish I could. "Growing Food" was never really on the agenda as a career choice. I'm a translation overseer, took the vocational training route at seventeen, seemed like a good way out of the rest of school. I just do all my earning in the evening. Vietnamese, trade. All boring stuff. I'd imagined myself working on literary projects but it's all import protocols and storage facility data. Soon I doubt I'll be necessary, but it works OK for now.'

Jesse is impressed, wishing he had more to offer, a certain way to impress her. He thinks she is lovely, then he pulls himself up – she's too lovely, too smart, too settled into her place in the world to even notice him in that way. And as their friendship grows, he stifles his yearning so well that he barely registers it himself.

Mister gets used to his place next to the gate of the garden; he lies on a tarpaulin over the unswept, ancient tarmac, greets visitors and engages in small social exchanges with all the gardeners and volunteers. He sleeps on opened cardboard boxes in the sun, waking to greet those who come and go through the garden gates. Jesse is delighted when Jada brings a dog bed for him, to tuck in the shelter of the doorway when the weather starts to turn a little colder.

Jesse sits in the doorway next to the oval bed. Mister's nose is tucked between his paws, his eyes are closed. Jesse is filled with tenderness, lays his hand on the brindled flank of the old dog. He runs it slowly across the body. Mister's bones have begun to show now with age, as they did when Jesse first found him. He has weight, but it runs off him, pools with gravity. Jesse looks at a slight hollow, a runnel between the bones of Mister's foreleg. Without taking his hand from Mister, he reaches across, with the fingers and thumb of his other hand presses into his own arm, above the wrist, feeling the same channel in his own body. He is still firm, still young compared to Mister. But he shares the same mysteries and is arcing more slowly along the same trajectory.

Mister has grey hairs, white around his eyes and snout. Jesse runs his thumb, knowing the little flicker of response it will cause, across the tough pad of Mister's foot. He pictures himself, years from now, at the same stage in his own life. Slower, rougher, greyer. He wishes that Mister could still be with him.

Marshal, still thinned out by all the hours of work, tired from the constant vigilance needed to keep it going, is quick to argue with Jesse about what he is doing with his life, pushing him to achieve in his studies, ambitious for his grades and his future plans. He thinks the work at the community garden is a distraction and the implication of its necessity simply wrong. He doesn't believe that the state is directly to blame for anyone's situation. Things are tough because they have to be. And while he feels compassion for any individual, washed out of their homeland by sea flood and storm, by crop failure and disorder, he doesn't think it is the state's job to help because that would encourage others. He and Jesse argue often. Marshal thinks his son is naive. Jesse finds his father the same. Lena polices the extreme edges of their discussions but her sympathies lie with her son.

Jesse keeps to the fringes of the various protest groups, sharing the sentiments of many but disliking the posturing, the hierarchy, the downright bitchiness that bristles within and between the political factions and personalities. He has, though, been involved in protests and some confrontations; with uniformed thugs who believe themselves to be a militia, who believe their white skin is some kind of precious commodity that others try to take away. He feels the loss of Euan, the fear of Chetna; he feels complex emotions about the world, rendered somehow to a debt within him.

21

Then it is autumn again, and the worst fears are realised; a second pandemic comes. It is a quick and vicious upgrade. It becomes known as October Night Flu because night sweats are the first in a series of rapid-fire symptoms. And many do not live until morning.

There are fewer fatalities. But there are many deaths, and Lena is one of them. Fewer fatalities but still so many funerals. She takes ill one evening, just as she and Marshal had lain down in their bed, content for the evening to subside in gentle familiarity, lying side by side, talking over the week. She starts to shiver, to sweat. Marshal rushes in desperation through all the measures of care that have been published, futile as they are. Many do survive. Many seem inoculated perhaps by an unnoticed brush with the variant of years before. But for some it is brutal and swift. Marshal protects Lena's head as she convulses, tries not to harm her or scare her with his trapping of her body. He tells her he loves her. And she dies seventeen hours after the first shiver shook her, held in the harbour of his arms.

Jesse had been isolating with friends, but when calls go unanswered he returns to find them lying on the bed. He fears them both dead, until Marshal, speaking from another plane, says, 'She's gone, Jesse. What are we going to do? What will we do?'

Father and son struggle through the hideous process of finding a resting place and somewhere to hold a service for Lena. As happened during the first pandemic, graves become fiercely coveted property. Politicians and councillors grind into gear eventually. Lena's body is taken and stored in a converted warehouse filled with commandeered freezers, overseen by protocols hastily dug up from years before. The horrible disappearance into bleak, makeshift storage, the unseemly disorganisation – it batters the grievers.

Slowly, new burial and memorial sites are identified and buildings cleared. Promises are made that, in the future, the raw ad-hoc grave sites, bare patches still churned up by digger wheels, will be made suitable grounds for the dead and the grieving.

Finally, Lena is buried in bare, wet, brown earth on a rainy November day. Walkways of plywood and plastic mesh are laid down in a semblance of ordered paths, portioning out the land for all the bodies to come. There are seven small groups of people, carefully choreographed away from each other, burying someone at the same time as them. Seven hurried little services with immediate family only, trying not to overspill, trying to maintain the scant dignity of their slot. On another muddy path Jesse sees a man in a dark suit fall forward to his knees, his sorrow given to the ground. He is helped up. A child clings to his leg. He wipes the mud from his hands down the front of his dark suit jacket and gently cups the girl's head, holding her to him. It drizzles for days.

Chorus

so much lost

we feel for you
we feel with you
as we find our own place in this new-shaped world

you have taught us what lives of loss feel like
and we feel for you

Marshal and Jesse fall into lonely confusion.

Everyone does, it seems. The wearying misery of grief affects them all. There is no longer even a pretence that things have to go back to the way they were. Once the pandemic has been controlled, the old vaccine effectively reset, some people do try; Marshal works harder than ever but Jesse's studies have taken a fatal hit. He spends more and more time at the garden, leaning into the community of growers and hopers as though to escape the pall of grief in his heart and home. A dreary, tight silence holds father and son at bay.

Jesse feels a profound sense of loss. The loss of possibility and of love. Everything shrinks to the necessity of living. And he can't understand what living, when so reduced, means. He longs to be with Jada, feels the loss of something impossible. He misses Lena. He misses the privacy to grieve alone. Everyone gets in on it; the moment sorrow escapes, it reminds everyone, anyone, that they too are grieving. Like many, like his father, he shuts his feelings away for more private examination. He seeks solitude in walks with Mister, taking a train to the edge of the city to the relief of empty fields. He finds somewhere shielded, lies on the ground with Mister tucked like the sweetest comfort against his flank, and watches the sky.

On one long day, they get a train out a few miles from the city to an area once unpromisingly framed by the pounding thrum of the M4. Scrubby grassland, scattered with outbuildings used for city storage overspill and the horses of townsfolk, has with the flow of the last decades become quieter, more definitely rural. Their path back into the city angles toward the M4 motorway. As he gets closer he can hear the whirr of vehicles, the electric, particle-shedding speed.

A solar railway is under construction. Jesse stops to watch the building work. Earth movers force a new shape from the ground. *Once, we only had spades*, he thinks, *spades and picks*. Railways and mines were created a pick-strike and a spade-heft at a time. The worksite is complex, men and women primed for one job somehow interlock with machines that channel, shift, lay, spread. Someone had a picture of it ahead of time. Someone created efficiency in the system of building to save money, to make it faster. Someone or many someones worked it all out. Jesse is in awe of the effort. He has a reverence for the ability to imagine complex systems and create refined solutions, to have faith in a picture, invented in the mind, to have within that mind the knowledge that can call such an image into being. Once, long ago, someone working with iron imagined a bridge. 'Perhaps,' he said to himself, alone at first, 'we could make an iron bridge. I believe we could.' And then in his mind's eye, he imagined and built and corrected each step that would be necessary. Casting, moving, ordering, joining. Building pontoons and buttresses. How many horses, how many men? How much rope and of what gauge? Boats, coal, iron. Wood. Food. Fires, heat, furnaces. How much coal in the furnaces? How hot? How many spades? What future is possible?

Jesse wonders how his childhood village home has fared. If Giana and Mikel still keep things going, if Malc still keeps his inherited herd. He decides as he walks back toward the city that he won't stay in London. He'll find an alternative. He can't face the city as the only vision of his future.

The emptiness of the house rings, like a sound Marshal can't hear, but he feels it, a seasick frequency that crushes him. The air resonates, a rumbling growl of oppression. The absence of Lena shimmers in the air. The presence of Jesse, so like her, lost in his own grief amplifies the suffocating weight. He is ashamed of his inability to reach his son, to know what to do to protect him. He knows that he has finally been found wanting, that he is not the father he hoped he would be. He has failed. And he has lost Lena.

Father and son are perplexed by the opening of a gulf that echoes, unwanted by both, between them. Marshal puts all his efforts into work, shifting focus to a new strand of endeavour that becomes available to all in his trade: making space for others to home their dead. This work takes on an urgency for Marshal, driven by the need to do well by strangers, to fulfil for them an act of compassion that in his suppressed sorrow, he is unable to afford himself or his son.

Jesse too searches for distraction and finds it in more volunteering. He goes to the community garden every day, gives up any pretence of continuing at uni. For welcome hours, he turns his mind to building. There is escape, as his mind turns over pictures, makes connections, fathoms how this problem can be solved by this resource. He builds a lean-to greenhouse for Jada to bring on her seedlings earlier in the season. He learns from her about the different plants, what constitutes the right conditions, how to coax lush green growth more fully and for longer, how to entice the fruit from the tree. He makes a shelter in a corner of the garden for Mister, a timber frame with a sheet of corrugated iron, a sophisticated version of his first effort years before. He builds a rain harvest and irrigation system out of readily available scraps; there is much to be picked from the glut of old materials, buildings emptied by the two pandemics and not yet repurposed or refilled by newcomers retreating from the rising saltwater seas and the spreading tide of nettle, bindweed and wild grasses.

Chorus

old binds, old ways, old walls replace the new

place is where we are
that is all

The community garden so lushly fills its existing plot and provides so much fruit and veg for the residents that soon they take their expertise to other estates. Jesse is always happy to work with Jada to expand what they've created, to build new vegetable gardens in different communities, to grow food that is truly fresh, to strengthen the valiant efforts of city gardeners who have always known the need for people to touch and see and smell the world, unmediated by packaging and an exchange of money. A determinedly quiet movement sends out shoots, grows stealthily into the city around them. But they unfurl with care. They emphasise community; the search is for cohesion within the current reality, not power against it. Anything more would be to invite too much scrutiny, too much impatient, heavy-handed ire from a state growing tetchy with challenges to its authority in what it still insists are difficult and dangerous times.

Six weeks after they buried Lena, Marshal and Jesse find themselves together in the apartment for the whole of a long evening. They are stilted, quiet, unsure of how to connect with each other.

Jesse looks up at the seagull painting, the worn blue square, the carefully naive lines marking the outline of the bird in flight, forever flying clockwise and forever static on their living-room wall. He remembers Lena saying, 'I don't even like it, but it reminds me of happy times.' That sentence, repeated often enough to become familiar, a small tile in the complex mosaic of family lore. It was, for Jesse too, a reminder of happy times. He remembers his mother remembering, her smile, her grudging acceptance of the seagull – an ugly painting that did a beautiful job.

He remembers sitting on the big blue sofa. An antique damask cushion, naples yellow with garland stripes in pale pink and green that Lena would hold on her lap when relaxing in her favourite corner. He wonders where it came from.

Chorus

old lives, our own and others
are a mystery
not always to be unravelled
not always unpicked

the past is a whole and a fragment
take what it gives you and move

on into now

He wonders if the cushion is still there, in the locked and boarded-up house. They hadn't brought the sofa with them – it was too big. They haven't been back to the house either. It has stood empty, and as far as they know, intact, for these last years.

'Dad, do you remember all the stuff we left back in the house?'

'Well, I'm not sure. I've got a list somewhere but I doubt I can remember all of it.'

'Do you remember that yellow cushion? The one Mum used to put on her lap when she sat on the sofa? She used to say it was an antique.'

'Yeah, it was.' Marshal pauses, looking up to the top of the wall, concentrating to retrieve his memories. 'She got it from an antique shop, at least.' He smiles. 'It was on one of the first trips we made together, just before we moved into our first house.' Marshal settles back in his chair. 'We got it from the same place we got that brown lamp, the angle-poise, the one that kept blowing a fuse.'

Jesse catches another tableau: a corner cupboard behind the dining table. On the top the lamp, next to small, mismatched baskets where Lena kept glue, scissors, a notepad, bits and pieces for sewing. Things that were broken and in need of repair. Jobs for the household. When she did pick up something to mend, bent over a jacket with a broken zip, a plug that flickered at whim, she would sit in a dining chair, a pool of light spilling over her shoulder from the fully extended angle-poise. He remembered the creak it made when Lena pulled it out. The click of the white on-and-off button switch in its base, the neat mechanical economy of the way it caught in, then out, then in – a crisply satisfying double click. He remembers the exasperated telling off he'd get for repeatedly pushing the button, flicking the light on and off. 'You'll blow the fuse Jesse, stop it!'

Jesse looks over at Marshal, also lost, he can tell, in memories of Lena.

'I really want to go back,' Jesse says. Actually, he really wants them both to go back but doesn't know how to ask. Looking at Marshal, in snatched glances, he recognises the tiny movements of muscles trying to control the expression of his sadness. He feels a clutch of anxiety, perceiving the frailty in his dad. And though Jesse waits in hope, Marshal doesn't offer to come with him. But he breathes, he doesn't oppose Jesse or bring up, once again, the well-worn arguments about returning to his studies. He gives Jesse a drifting smile. 'Yes, OK, that sounds like a good idea, Jess. I'll dig out the keys.'

Isolde

22

A pale stone church rises from a sea of russet reeds swaying in the wind, like a gently ecstatic congregation of millions crowding slowly toward the door. Floods and broken river banks have brought mud into the hollow; new marshland rises over the door stone, through bricks and sandbags banked up by the last stubborn and anxious parishioners of this scoop of land, sunk a few crucial inches below sea level. Flood and drain and flood have filled the shallow basin, and after the last parishioner finally left, made a new floor in the knave – soft and silty. A floor for wading birds and reeds. Frogs hop from hollowed bell tower steps. Soft mud overlays the gravestones, the worn-out faces of the anciently rich peer blindly into it. It stains the cloth that still lies over the altar, covers the needlepoint kneelers left on the floor between the pews. More kneelers than there were people to kneel, at least for the last century of worship. Hours of work in those dense stitches, made mostly by the women. The last was completed in 1963 by Nadine, when god still meant more to her than true love. None took enough wear to need replacing after that.

Nadine moved house four times, always locally, and kept the habit of going to this church, even as her faith left her. She died in the first pandemic at the age of eighty-nine. She had stitched her kneeler with a bold design of barley heads, gold on a blue background, filled each tiny square with a thread intertwined with her youthful ardour. She kept the habit of looking out for it for over six decades. Checking it didn't lie too much in obscurity, checking it may be seen. Now the colours are dun, the stuffing too. The stitches, once as tightly packed as the seed heads they depicted, softened, decayed, bloomed out into the wet mud.

They pass the church and come to the edge of an inlet, broadened by the sea to cover the old road. To prevent a lengthy inland detour, a causeway has been thrown together by weather and by man. The construction is opportunistic. A pile-up of boats, hurled by storms up the inlet from a harbour at the river mouth, have become a walkway. The boats tipped as the water receded, the hulls leaned on their sides against each other. Across the top of the boats boards are lashed, a rope handhold next to them. Further ropes go down into the water to prevent another storm taking away what had been so usefully provided.

They make their way, a step at a time, across the uneven walkway holding onto the handrail of rope, walking on the camber of a hull, over portholes and horizontal masts, over lashed planks bridging the gaps. All of it is knotted together with yards and yards of rope. Bright nylon, red and white climbing rope, the doughty brown of hemp.

Ahead, the causeway ends in a trampled fan of mud and reeds. Firmer footing and a path shows a way into the woods. Paths always go somewhere useful. She stops to consult the map, taking it over to show Lee.

'We must be here. Which means we have about, I guess, ten miles to go. Or less.'

'Will they mind us turning up?'

'No idea. I'm not even sure we'll find anyone. Either way, we stop for the night, then tomorrow, we get to know our new friends or turn back and in three days we're in London.' Her heart sinks at the prospect.

The air is thick and damp. Isolde feels a cushion of heat across her skin. The bag has become uncomfortably heavy. She fans herself with dock leaves; they are too soft but the small stir in the air is welcome and swishes midges away. After a mile, the path reaches a break in the trees. Isolde kicks back the mulch to find the tarmac. They head north-east again, back on the road.

'I think we must be near the turn-off.'

Chorus

nearly there

heavy feet
and hearts light with hope – or just curiosity
for hope can be heavy
– tiring as any journey

we hear them come

The woodland opens out to a patchwork, clearings of grass and scrub, small stands of trees. Cattle in the open spaces chew grasses and herbs. One lows, a mellow and deep sound. There is a lane into the trees.

'I think this might be it.'

'How far down here?'

'If it's the right place, less than a mile.'

The lane weaves through birch and hazel and the straight and broad trunks of pine, rising like obelisks that solemnly pin an ancient meaning into the terrain. Isolde stops, her eye caught by a strange sight on the left of the lane. The trees are gone and there is a curtain of colour thrown across the ground. A whole area united in the pale gold of wheat. She has never seen one plant taking up so much space, so uninterrupted. Lee stops beside her.

'What? What is it?' Coming from a farming community a crop in a field isn't new to him. He imagines she has startled to a threat – a wolf, crouched warily, caught dangerously by surprise. A man with an axe running out of the woods.

'I've never seen so much of one thing growing in one place.'

'Oh.' He looks at her, baffled by her inexperience. 'It's a good sign, at least we know someone is growing crops out here.'

Isolde has nerves in her belly, anticipation mixed with slight fear. There might be no one there, the wrong people there, aggressive, dangerous people. She might just walk back to London with nothing learnt. She realises with a flash, that what she dreads most is nothing changing.

Soon they hear sounds. Children playing, someone shifting or banging or building something. Around a bend, they see a group of buildings. Isolde's anxiety rises. Her momentum has been blind, had not left room for her to plan, providing only the compulsion to start moving. She hasn't rehearsed what she will say, how she will present herself. How she will ask them, at least temporarily, to take her in to their home.

'Wait,' she says, her hand on Lee's arm. 'Just give me a moment to think, what I need to ask. What I want to know.'

Lee sits on the bump of verge, twirls a buttercup between

finger and thumb. Isolde stands on the track, her hands on her hips, biting her bottom lip.

'Well. I'm not sure to be honest, but we might as well find out if they are the right people, if this is the place.' She starts off toward the building abruptly, Lee scrambles to his feet to follow. Automatically his hand goes to the ribbon over the tattoo on his neck, checking it holds in place.

23

There is a farmhouse, with a gate and a patched brick path to a red door. All the sounds come from behind the house, the buildings and a yard at the back. It matches a description from one of the old unofficial guides to settlements that Arthur had found. Isolde unlatches and opens the woven hazel gate. It looks rickety but swings cleanly between the wooden posts, catching on vetch and campion fringing the base. They walk to the door. She pauses for a fraction of a second, her fist raised to the door as if in greeting, before her knuckles knock out a summoning. Someone speaks as they move toward the other side of the door. There is the clunk of a handle; the door swings open. There stands a woman with long hair, an open, pale brown freckled face.

'Hello?' She smiles curiously at Isolde and Lee.

'Hi, I'm Isolde. I've come from London... walking, nothing official. I wanted to ask you, or maybe someone else who lives here, or did... Sorry, I'm not making much sense. I have an idea my mother used to live here and hoped someone would be able to tell me?'

The woman's eyes are wide, her mouth falls open into a round.

'Did you say you are Isolde?' She steps through the threshold of the doorway. As Isolde answers, the woman's arms widen, moving toward an embrace. The lightest touch on Isolde's upper arms and her hands drop again. She smiles, serene and amazed.

'I'm Esther!' She opens her arms again. Isolde, puzzled and taken aback by the warmth of her greeting holds out a hand to shake.

'Pleased to meet you, Esther.'

Esther appears confused by the gesture. She repeats her words, hands held out before her, asking Isolde to find the meaning in them.

'I'm Esther?'

Isolde frowns, uncertain, a gesture of incomprehension.

'Do you not know about me? I'm your sister.' The two women look at each other closely. One, taller and fairer haired, darker skinned, knowing of the other. The other, Isolde, in baffled wonderment, her whole life changed in an instant, again. Once again, all that she has known is thrown out of shape, subject to a new arrangement.

'Amazing!' Lee exclaims from behind Isolde. 'That's grand!'

'I—I didn't know you existed. I didn't know I had a sister.' Isolde's eyes drift around the garden, a swell of shock pushing her to leave, to be alone, to create distance so that she can understand. But it is too momentous a connection to break.

'You're here!' says Esther, her voice quiet, roughened by the tears that set her expression.

'No one told me. No one told me,' Isolde repeats, anger reaching toward her, plucking at her for a hold.

'Wait, look, come in, come in.' Esther gestures past herself into the cool interior of the passageway. They both follow her inside, the sudden contrast in light partially blinding them to details. At the other end of the passage is a bright room, the first big kitchen Isolde has ever been in. Esther gestures for them to sit at a large table. She sweeps objects aside, clearing the surface as they sit down. She sits too then immediately rises again, her gaze darting constantly back to Isolde's pale, moon-quiet face.

'Would you like tea? Water? Ale? Are you hungry?'

Lee sits up, keen to have whatever is on offer, but Esther only notices the quiet shake of Isolde's head. Lee relaxes back down, a look of regret slipping momentarily across his young face. Esther comes back to the table and sits opposite Isolde.

'So, you didn't know you had a sister, that I existed?'

'No. I would've thought… I thought I would have remembered. I thought someone would've told me.' She shakes her head. 'I didn't even know that I had any connection, that Mum had any connection, or family, or anything at all, outside London. I didn't know anything.'

'Do you remember her? Mum?'

'Yes, I do. I can't remember our life, or where we lived. I remember her though.' She looks over at Esther to see if the memory will come to life from the face before her. She sees something, fleeting, a drift of connection across a forehead, in the shape of a jaw.

'I can't remember at all. I was a baby. When she died.'

Isolde looks up at her again. 'I can't believe it. I can't believe no one told me, that I didn't remember.'

Esther shakes her head too, in agreement.

'But you were tiny; you were dealing with so much. It's not you who should remember, but to have kept you away from us, that was cruel.' Esther's movements are short, abrupt, as though she can't decide what to do. She sits, staring and, letting go of her anger, smiles again at Isolde.

'It's cruel. But I am so glad you're here now. Jada said they moved you soon after she left.'

Isolde's attention snaps up at the mention of her godmother,

Jada, who disappeared so suddenly just when Isolde needed her most. 'You knew Jada?'

Esther smiles. 'Still do!' She gestures with her head to the outside.

'You mean she's here?'

'Yes. She lives here. Unofficially, she's the boss. The matri-arch of here. But she's unwell, has been for some months. She's mostly in bed in her room. She will want to see you, Isolde; she will be so happy we have found you.' The form of tears once more show in Esther's expression. 'But she'll be sleeping now. Soon, I'll go and take her a tea; I'll tell her you've arrived. You have arrived, Isolde, I'm so... grateful!'

A child walks into the kitchen through a back door that opens to the garden. Esther reaches out as she passes.

'Misha, this is your Aunt Isolde. This is my daughter, Misha. She's twelve. There's also Amber, whose seven and Bert, who's five. I think they're still outside.'

Isolde smiles, her face open, sunshine of a smile. Her family is growing by the second.

'Hello Misha, how great to meet you.' Misha stays at her mother's side, next to the chair. She waves across the table at Isolde.

'Are you the one who disappeared in London years ago?'

'I guess I am. Though it doesn't feel that way to me! But yes, I live in London.'

'Why did it take you so long to come and see us?'

'I didn't know you were here.'

Esther turns to Misha. 'You remember I told you that our mama died when I was a baby? There was kind of a muddle up, or something, and nobody knew that we were here to take care of Isolde or they wanted to take care of her themselves, so she grew up in the city. We weren't able to find her, though Jada tried.'

Isolde shook her head, slowly, again. There's so much to take in.

'Do you want to stay? Please do stay. I can find a room for you, for you both, or one?'

'No, we're not together. We met on the road.' Lee sniggers with embarrassment.

'OK, so we will be glad if you stay, you will then have a bit of time to get used to everything, to get to know who is who.'

'It seems I've got to get to know who I am too! It would be good, yes, if we could stay.' She looks over at Lee, who smiles in ready agreement.

Misha turns to Lee too. 'Do you want to come and see my rabbit?'

24

Esther takes Isolde's pack and leads her up the stairs. At the end of the corridor is a small room with a bare mattress on the floor, a table next to it with a light and a trunk. The floor is plain board with a rag rug that curls at one corner. The glow of evening sun gilds a deep-silled window above the bed. There is an armchair next to the window.

'If you give me a moment I'll get some bedclothes. If you want, just relax, have a bit of time to yourself, or we can talk some more? I never thought this would happen. I can put Lee in the barn. We call it the barn, but it's actually where some of the others live. But I hope you'll stay here in the house? I'll make you a bed, then you can decide what you want to do, and in an hour, maybe, Jada will be awake.'

Isolde stands, just over the threshold of the room. Esther puts the bag down, then, briefly, takes Isolde's hands in her own. Then she leaves the room, returning a few moments later with a pile of bedding. In a few minutes the mattress on the floor looks comfortable and welcoming. Isolde longs to lie down and shut the door. Esther brings a jug of water and a glass.

'Look, I'm going to leave you now. I can't imagine this is easy, to find this out. But I'll be either in the kitchen or vegetable garden which is right next to the kitchen back door. And any time you want to, you can come and find me. Take as long as you need. There's a bathroom on the left, enough warm water for washing. Just relax, make yourself comfortable, sleep if you want. I'll go and make a place for Lee to stay.' She stops talking, but stands in the door way for a moment, beaming a broad smile across the room at Isolde, who smiles back. Then the door, blessedly, is shut.

Isolde sits on the edge of the armchair. She stares at the patterns of light, sunlight flicking the dancing leaves outside the window with gold. She pulls out her cotton cloth and picks up the clean towels and goes to the bathroom to wash off the dust of the road.

She lies down, and though her thoughts whine for attention, she drops through the cacophony of them into a well of deep sleep.

Chorus

rest, as though in summer shade
on sweet, long meadow grass
rest, as though held in safety
in the arms of peace

rest and let all tomorrows come

An hour later, she wakes. The room has darkened. Outside she can hear Lee chattering in play with Misha and other children. A young voice giggles in delight. Isolde drinks, pours water on her hands, refreshes her face. She sits for a moment, absorbing her new status. A woman with a sister, with nieces and nephews. Connected. She finds her remaining clean t-shirt and least grimy trousers, and goes down to the kitchen.

'Ah you're here!' Esther smiles. 'I've just made tea if you want some?'

Isolde sits at the table again, taking the cup that Esther places before her. There's a jar of honey on the table. A spoon in the cup. She feels awkward – she wants to get to know her new family if for no other reason than to end the strangeness of the discovery. She watches Esther furtively, but Esther is doing the same. Like two ghost forms of themselves their curiosity bumps lightly, apologises and moves away once more to give the other space.

'Jada is awake, she is longing to see you. Do you want to finish that and we'll go to her?'

Isolde feels rushed, uncertain. It is wonderful to discover this unexpected opportunity, but she had been abandoned by Jada. She had been left to grow up alone, in the children's home when here there was apparently a whole family. She wants to see Jada, feels the edges of remembered love, but she wants time to grasp what is happening.

'Yes, OK. But I don't know if you can, maybe, fill me in a bit first on what you know?'

Esther sits down at the table and begins to talk. The story is a wonder and a fresh horror. The man in prison didn't kill her mother; he didn't kill anyone. He was a useful casualty. He is a man called Jesse, linked by Jada and their mother to an organisation designated as terrorists for political expediency. She was herself an equally useful casualty. A little victim. A photogenic tragedy. Jada hadn't abandoned her – she had been kept away, lied to. Blame recoils, sits in a tight, ugly knot in her chest. That vague, shambolic man had done nothing, wasn't responsible for her loss.

'They made it impossible for Jada to stay in contact with

you. The last time she tried was about ten years ago. She didn't tell me at the time, but a few years later. There had been a news story about you and she saw a picture and recognised you.'

'Ugh, that creep who jumped out at me when I was... well, there was a time when I didn't look after myself very well. They did a story about the tragic girl, how sad her poor mother would be to see how low she'd sunk. I moved soon after, deliberately lost touch with people.'

'Jada found that story a month or so after it came out, then couldn't find you. It was hard. I wanted so much to reach out to you, but after that I just kind of accepted that we couldn't. They came down hard on all protesters, especially Claimants. There were more attacks, some deaths that they said were caused by the Claimants and though they always denied it, the damage was done. They made up a whole lot of stuff about them. People suddenly hated the Claimants as much as the others.'

'Do they threaten you now because of the link?'

'There isn't one really. And there's no point. They drone us, keep an eye. They'd know if anyone headed to town. They don't care I don't think. We have no way to prove anything. Jada was only a problem when she was looking for you. I think they are too arrogant to see us as a threat. But they've got a point. We don't threaten them because, well it would be hopeless. And we want to keep what we have here.'

Esther sits in quiet for a moment then speaks again, with restrained intent.

'Isolde, I don't want you to think we gave up on you, to keep life easy. I suppose that even when I hoped, I might've accepted that you were gone somehow. But we talked of you all the time. I think... thought, about you all the time.'

Isolde feels overwhelmed. How ruthlessly she had been co-opted into a role that, even as she had resented it, she had played to the best of her ability. The little lost victim with the difficult childhood, the robbed, inadequate prospects.

She feels a sweep of shame at her harsh words to Jesse, anguish as she remembers the relentless hatred spat in the urgent, quiet voice of the man in the pale mac. She wonders at what they all have lost.

'Let's go and see Jada.'

They cross the garden to two brick cottages on the far side of the yard. Esther knocks on the front door then opens it and calls out to Jada. They go upstairs, toward the light from a bedroom. Esther speaks as they enter the room.

'Jada, here we are; here is Isolde.'

The room is small, overrun with fabrics, drapes and scarves, small jars and vases with flowers in all stages of vivid life and dry decay. Disappearing under the folds of bed clothes, Jada lies propped up on pillows in an old metal-framed bed. She looks the same as Isolde remembers her, as she did in the photos. Finer, paler, her hair greyed, her brown skin a little ashen. Her face has deep lines on each side of her mouth, the memory of a frown on an otherwise smooth forehead. But she looks the same. She smiles at Isolde but says nothing. A tear falls. Isolde feels shy, confused, but is overtaken; she reaches forward to hug Jada.

When she does finally speak, Jada's voice is steady, quiet. 'I see you, Little Iso; I'd know you anywhere.'

Isolde sits back on the edge of the bed. Jada turns to Esther in the doorway saying, 'Your sister, Little Esi, she's here!' Esther's expression of stricken joy means she can only nod rapidly in response.

'I thought I'd lost you for good. It broke my heart, Iso, and now, here you are! A chance for me to put it right. I thought you were living with a family, moved away, and Esther tells me you were there all the time.'

'You have nothing to put right. We just landed up here, didn't we?'

Esther moves to the other side of the bed and perches on the edge, the two sisters sit like guardians, gate posts either side of the older woman so small under the covers. They talk in strange patterns, finding a gentle way through all that needs to be said. Isolde tells them about the walk. They answer questions about the farm, she about London, and then why Isolde has finally come. She struggles, both with the heartache that drove her to this unlikely journey and a sudden awareness of its ordinariness – the end of love. She holds back when she comes to the part about the child. The sense of failure feels like a private burden, a weight, where none is, in her belly.

She tells them about visiting the prison, the man she now knows as Jesse. Jada reaches for her, clutches her hand when she first speaks of him.

'Did you know him?' Isolde asked.

'Yes. Yes, I knew him.'

'I feel so bad that I blamed him.'

'How could you know? I missed him for so long, and so much. And I know that they put him there because it suited their story. But I blame myself because I took him too close.'

They talk on of lives that have passed in unknown arcs. They make new understanding, add to old. Isolde notices Jada closing her eyes. The sister's voices lower and talk slows down, and soon Esther says, 'We should leave her now.'

Esther explains that Jada has a rare and stubborn cancer. Treatment has been difficult, though she had moved back to the city when it first appeared ten years ago, managing to reactivate her official citizen status for long months of what had seemed a cure. It was during those months that she had tried once again to find Isolde. Now, she no longer wants to leave the farm. They are able to get painkillers, other treatments that

make living bearable, but the treatments won't make it enduring. She has accepted the coming of death.

'We all try to accept it too, as she wants us to, but she is better at it than I am,' says Esther, sadly.

Chorus

why is it so hard for you?
we take it through, one to the other
share the burden
we all carry what must be carried
until it belongs to all

if only you could learn our ways

Throughout an evening that stretches long into the darkness,
Isolde meets other members of her sudden family – the children
Bert and Amber. Their father, Esther's partner Clifford, and
his brother Pete. There are more people – people she barely
registers. People who live in other buildings, with other children, coming by to say hello, to share the meal cooked by Pete,
to bring or borrow something. The children, allowed to stay
up for the momentous occasion, gaze shyly at Isolde and flock
joyously to Lee who whoops and plays and chases them into
happy night-time weariness. The children are eventually taken
up to bed. The kitchen quiets to the chatter of adults, happy to
be together in curious wonderment and new kinship.

25

Isolde wakes early the next morning, before everyone else. She goes downstairs, into the garden. The sky is grey, pushing pink. Birds sing, a million tiny facets shaping the air. Her sleep-warm feet feel a shock of cold from the dew on the grass. She notices a cherry tree in the garden, plump fruits, gold and red, hang in clusters. The ground is littered, she can feel pips under her bare feet. She tries to place herself here with her mother. It seems possible. She reaches for some cherries, bites into the sweet sourness. Yes, it does seem possible.

A flash of white passes her, an owl flying by, at head-height, into the woods over the lane. The feathers glow with pearly vividness in the low light. Being out of the city isn't new, but it is exotic. The trips she has made were rare and left her with memories that she cherished. She wonders if the people living here would feel the same in the city. In what would they find wonder? Perhaps in the hum of the trains, the boundless energy harvested in the milky glass of the suntiles, the crowds that shift and bloom unknowingly with the grace and flock harmony of starlings as they negotiate the city streets. The colossal endeavour it takes to build somewhere so huge. Or would they just find anxiety, claustrophobia, noise?

She wonders what she will do now. Now she has a family. What it will mean for her. Obligations? Foundations? Could she stay here? Or will she repack her bag, tuck her new story into a pocket, then walk back to London? That seems plausible, until she thinks of her flat and its drab echoes. She feels that she would be happy never to go there again.

Her feet in the dewy grass are tingling, the cold radiates a little shock up her calves that enlivens her body, takes her away from fretful thoughts. She walks to the back of the house, toward the yard, treading carefully over cement that is scattered with small stones. There is the barn, converted into a series of living spaces. How many people live here? She can't remember. She had met maybe ten the evening before. Further on, the paired cottages, where Jada will be asleep in her old-fashioned, high bed.

She comes to a field, grazed to ankle height. The sun is beginning to appear above distant trees. Outcrops of thistles stand sculptural and bold. The downy seed heads catch a halo of early sunlight. Behind her, she hears the noises of someone starting work in one of the sheds. A life hooked onto the cycles of dark and light. No interruptions from city lights and home screens. People in the cities live on any number of shift patterns. Life never stops. Days don't revolve though light and dark, they spin through a restless, pixilated grey of blended night and day.

Chorus

we wake from herd dreams, the kinship of sleep

we wake in the luxury of our own time
it rolls as gently as the hills

stay here, girl, learn the luxury of time

Isolde lies down. The grass is long enough to tickle her ear and cheek, to bend into the nape of her neck when she pushes her hair out from under her head. She spreads her arms, ruffles fingers through the dewy grass. She rolls her ankles so that the blades meet the sensitive skin of her feet. She feels the space around her, stretches into it. She feels pressed, thin as a membrane between earth and sky, between liquid and light. She feels the warming of the sun as it rises higher into the sky.

Bumps of earth press indents into the skin of her back. One stone meets a vertebra. Another under the plate of her skull. She shifts her neck a little, the grass whispers against her skin. The sun rises higher, the leaves spreading themselves wide and green and greedy for the light. The wood pigeon breaks briefly then resumes its soft phrase in the shade of the branches.

The light comes up, slides into his eyes, burns up his dreams in a cold electric glare. He stretches on the narrow bunk.

His hands rest palm down. He scrunches a fist, traces the movement up his arm; fibre and muscles that pull from the elbow. He feels the tension in tendons strung along the twin bones, the slight twist and pull, a judder as the machinery of his hand is pulled into action.

The bones are old and dry like hollowed trunks. The tendons, too, have lost their suppleness. He feels brittle, decayed.

Later, Esther shows Lee and Isolde around the farm. Reintroductions are made and new faces named. After breakfast, Isolde goes with Lee and three of the children, Misha, Bert and another girl, Cara, for a walk to see the stream. The children have been making a miniature homestead for fairies on the bank. An area of mud is cleared, within a boundary of stones. The children have built the fairy houses with sticks poked into the ground, cross beams laid into the forks of twigs. In the time since the children have last tended the miniature township, the leaf roofs have blown away, woodland debris has blown in. The children begin the repairs.

Isolde sits at the foot of a tree a few feet from the stream bank, the bumps of bark a pleasant scratch at her back. She strips a slender twig, finds leaves that are still flexible enough to pierce, threads them onto the stick, in then out, making a roof cover weighted by the central twig. Not heavy enough to defy all weather but good enough to beat today's flippant breeze. The children are delighted. Misha, with natural authority, designates Lee, Bert and Cara as component gatherers, to supply herself and Isolde with what they need for the important job of making the roofs. Misha sits next to Isolde, leaning back against the same trunk. Their shoulders touching. In the angle between their legs, Misha places the gathered twigs and leaves. The two of them build fairy roofs while Bert, Cara and Lee, their duties done, scramble splashily in the stream.

When they return to the house, Esther is working in the vegetable garden with Cara's mother Leanne, laying compost between rows of vegetables. Isolde sits on her haunches, taking in the wonderful variety of plants, all of them to eat. With a small thrill, she spots pak choi, seen in the market, carrots that she had learned to identify just a few days before, where they grew wild in a garden back down the road. Misha appears with a glass of water and sits next to her, shoulder to shoulder once again. Isolde asks her about the plants growing up poles. Misha is delighted to show off her knowledge, gives names, when to plant, when to harvest. Some of them she knows how to cook too. Isolde, hand shading her eyes from the sun, smiles, her admiration, desired and easily earned. Her connection with Misha is already a joy – pure, unselfconscious, new, not impeded by the tight burr of ancient knots.

Later in the day, Misha helps Isolde wash her few items of clothing. She borrows a sarong from Esther and puts everything into solar heated stream water with a scoop of commercial powder from a box on the sill above the sink. Misha tells her that when the pedlars come, sometimes they pay for boxes of multi-purpose soap, sometimes they make their own, depending on whether they have money or items to trade. Isolde rinses her clothes and Misha helps her ring them out for the line, a knotted stretch of rope and twine scraps pulled across the garden.

The day is clear and hot. Her clothes dry quickly in the sunshine, there are bumps where the wet fabric has dried over a knot in the line. She sees Lee sitting under an apple tree, leaning back on his arms, shoulders bunched up at his ears. A stalk of grass hangs from his mouth. She sits next to him as she folds her clothes.

'It's interesting. Nice here, isn't it?'

'Yeah, it is.'

'I'm thinking I might stay a bit longer. There's more than I expected, what with the surprise sister. And I don't want to head back to London tomorrow. The food isn't going to run out now, so there's no rush. What do you think?'

Lee squints in thought. 'I guess it's a good idea to stick with you.' He looks at her quickly, anxious that his slip into vulnerability not be unwelcome. 'I mean, if that's OK with you? I don't want to get in the way of all this new family stuff.'

'That's fine with me, Lee.' She smiles at him. 'I just was worried that you'd be disappointed about not getting to London.'

'I think, after a while, they'll all go home, stop looking for me. And London will still be there. It's nice here. Everyone is nice. And there's no oath swearing!' He makes a comical, exaggerated face to show his relief.

'Hey, that can be arranged if you miss it!' jokes Isolde.

'An oath to the fairy people.'

'An oath to not sleeping on the ground!'

'An oath to no uniforms!'

'An oath to unexpected sisters.'

'An oath to not getting whipped in the town square!'

Chorus

be wary boy
their anger echoes across the land

26

A small table, leaves of paper and an oblong of paints. Paper is safe even for terrorists. Paper doesn't sneak through the ether on invisible waves. A tray of children's paints in ten round blocks of colour. The red plastic brush looks awkwardly small in his hand. He dips the splayed bristles in a bottle cap of water and wipes it on his dark green t-shirt. He dabs blue onto the brush.

The etched, dark outline printed on the page describes mandalas. Fig 95. – Varieties of White Blood corpuscles; a, Eosinophils; b, (neutrophils); c, hyaline cell or monocyte; d, lymphocytes (large and small). He thins the blue with water, fills the bubble of the first cell, laboriously working with a tool that is both clumsy and fiddly. Each of the eight uneven spheres are filled with painted blue. Blue behind the red of his own blood. He hears the hum of it in his ears, a waterfall cascading past the bony outcrop of his skull.

Blood-red, then blue. He puts down the red brush and turns over his hand, flexes it backward to expose the pale beds of his wrist where the blue veins flow delta slow. To his hand or to his heart? He can't remember. He pictures blood oozing around the rocks of his hand, the complex bones washed in an uncontained river flow. Blue then red.

He pictures cells moving, the steady flow of his own blood. He wraps his thumb and fore-finger round his left wrist, squeezing hard. The veins fatten in his hand, above the thrum of his grip. A small, sweet relief in feeling, a physical sensation of even this meagre measure.

There was a dam he had built, with the other children. He yearns for the cold of the stream, the damp of a soaked coat cuff zinging against the bone-cold of wrists that have spent too long in winter water. They had always hoped for the miracle of perfect containment, a discovery of woodland engineering, of moss or mulch that would defeat the pull of gravity on the rushing stream water. One time they had gathered stones, thinking that choice of material would give their engineering the advantage. There had been many pools, but none efficient enough that the flow of water spilled over the top of their wall rather than through it. There were always gaps. The water was slowed, not halted. He remembers with longing the joy of friendship, of shared adventure.

He lets go of his now painful wrist, imagines the blue rush home to the heart. As though on the bank of a river he watches the flow. He walks the bank in his mind. The stream running smoothly now, one either side of him. He sits, eyes almost closed, still softly holding his wrist for company, waiting for a jay to fly from the woods he conjures.

Chorus

come to sleep
sweet dreams of sugar stems

we move in fields where boundaries once pinched, stung

held us, like you are held

those boundaries are gone, and we belong to sunny glades
that keep us because we choose them

come to sleep and join us here

Lee and Isolde go with others to pull wild oats growing among
the wheat in the field. The sun is burning. Isolde's hands soon
ache from pulling the stems from the ground. She is hot under
the cloth and hat that keeps the sun from her shoulders. Her
eyes ping with the effort of distinguishing the dots of one plant
next to the dashes of another.

Later in the day, the rain comes. Soon, thunder and light-
ning catch up with the herald rain. The workers retreat into a
barn. Lee goes straight off to find more work, well adjusted to
the efforts that such a life requires. Isolde rests a while, content
to take the privileges of a city guest. One of the men is working at a bench that runs along an end of the shed. His work
surface is littered with an array of technologies from different
eras. Wooden handles for iron tools lie next to data boards and
the skinny colourful wires of solar electrics. Isolde is drawn by
the potent chaos of the mix.

His name is Ben. He is in his late thirties. He has been at the
farm for fifteen years. His childhood had been unhappy. Hating
the city and the jangle of constant crisis, he had simply walked
out one day, looking for a different way to live. He brought
with him skills in electronics learnt in college as a young man.
These skills made him welcome most places, but he didn't settle
until he crossed the country and found the farm.

'And here I am,' he concludes cheerfully. She asks what he is
working on.

'I'm mending a part of a tractor. It's a bit of a beast and we can't really cope with it misbehaving. Not winning at the moment, but I will,' he says, waving a circuit board around. 'Do you know anything about—' he pauses, looking over the array on the table, including it all with a gesture— 'anything?'

'I'm afraid not. But I'm willing to learn.'

'Oh. OK.' Ben looks crestfallen at the thought of another inadequate student. 'Well, perhaps you can help me on something simpler than the tractor innards for starters.'

Esther and Isolde sit together in the garden under the cherry tree, their faces catching the low flare of the setting sun. In these neutral moments, Isolde finds small, tiptoe steps toward her sister, toward the love she knows is waiting but has never had the chance to inhabit, to dream of, or to miss.

But for all the wonder, the unexpected bounty of such a discovery, she struggles with an underlying anger; the difficulty of accepting that such harsh choices had been made about her life. Who had been present at the conversation? Which state employees had decided she was more of an asset in the children's home? Or was it simply carelessly administrative, the inability to recognise a family that existed off the records in their systems?

And lying another layer below, what calculations had been made about the reach of a bomb, the careless creation of dead bodies to serve as winning points in a propaganda war? She has been given a beautiful, unexpected gift but in receiving it, the world has been revealed as a darker place.

But what is she to do about it? What are any of them to do? To set oneself to fight is impossible, she can't climb such a sheer wall. The higher you climb, the more densely burnished the surface.

Lee walks past without a comet tail of children, for once.

Esther calls him over. He sits down with them. Isolde switches back to the present moment, puts her anger aside once again.

'Am I right in thinking you come from a White Town?'

Lee looks defensive. 'Yes. But I left it.'

'I understand, it's no problem. You are welcome here and I can see that you don't share White Town views from the way you are with everyone here. I was just curious, so that I could, I don't know, be more welcoming I suppose, by knowing your story.'

'I had to leave. I hated it. And I...' He breaks off, the conditioning of shame he has grown up with catching his words on the way. 'I'm gay. I'm a taint, as they say at home.'

'You know we don't say that here, don't you?' Esther put a hand gently on Lee's arm.

'Yeah, I know. It's just, I dunno, stuck in me.'

'Which town was it? Where you're from?'

'Drake's Drum. It's a long way. I got way off course by taking a couple of rides with pedlars. I think one of them must have passed it back, because the ones looking for me would never have come this far east by chance.'

'Pedlars trade in any grade.' Esther trots out a saying familiar to those living Out. 'Is Drake's Drum what it was always called? It's a strange name.'

'The first people came from Leicester, between the pandemics. I don't know what the place was called before we recolonised it. It was named by my grandparents, and others. The drum was on our shield and flag. And here.' He slides down the ribbon at his neck, showing the tattoo. Isolde understands now the meaning of the black square with zig zag marks across it. The cords that held the skin of a drum in place.

'What is the drum?'

Lee adopts a bored recitative voice. 'When Drake's drum is beat, then Drake, Old England's hero, will return to strike our enemies down. We are the drum. We are Drake's soldiers. We are the heroes of England.' He looks at them both. 'No, never made much sense to me either. But they were all pretty emotional about it, working themselves up to a fist-clenching shout at the end.'

'So, was there a plan? Was there an idea that one day you would, I don't know, take back England?'

'I think that was the plan. Kind of. But there was more effort put into keeping our stock pure, our whiteness. It was like most people knew, secretly, we were never going to be a big enough group. I think most people knew we were freaks, really, though they never admitted it. But everyone liked to get excited about joining up with the brothers in other towns and they'd talk about taking back the land. Or about the whites in the cities coming to join the cause. Round the fire after some ceremony or other. Then they'd wake up with a headache and go back to worrying about how to keep a few dozen people in and a few million out.'

'So they don't like it when people leave?'

'No. They try very hard to make an example of them. It was a risk getting a ride with a pedlar, but he seemed uninterested. I thought he thought I was just visiting. I guess he knew the score, and seeing my neck, took the initiative. If he'd seen the tattoo he would know which town I was from.'

'Do you think they will look for you here?'

'I don't want to cause any trouble.'

'Lee, you're welcome here and we'll be glad for you to stay as long as you like. I only ask because we should know what to expect.'

'They'll probably come if they know I'm here. But they don't know where I am, yet. I guess the sooner I can get rid of the tattoo the better, too.'

'I know a few places in London where it's easy, and not too

expensive. But would there be anyone in Cambridge, Esther? Or somewhere near?'

'Maybe. Cambridge is a bit of a limbo town. The University still functions but it's a retreat, an add-on. There are permanent residents but they live more or less as we do – small holdings, but in city plots. We can ask though. I can get Pete to ask about removing one of his self-made disasters so no one asks about us harbouring a White Towner, just in case people talk at some gathering.'

'Thanks. If you can find out, it'd be great. I can't wait to get rid of it.'

Chorus

they hear the word, the buzz, the telltale
they will return

their thirst –
there is nothing that will slake it, no pull,
no sweet clear water
that will dampen such a rage

to gore and draw hot blood
even that is not enough

27

Isolde creeps up the wooden stairs of the cottage. The light is on and the door open. She peers through, to see Jada sitting up against a stack of pillows, sewing.

'Iso, Iso, come in.' She pulls the fabric onto her lap, making room on the edge of the bed.

'What are you doing?'

'Embroidery. It soothes me, gives me just enough to do. Though if I last much longer I will need stronger glasses.' She smiles over the top of the glasses perched on her nose. Esther says that Jada isn't afraid of death, but Isolde hopes she will need new glasses.

On the bed are pieces of white fabric. Sections of old bed-sheets, Isolde guesses. She lifts a corner, looks over the designs stitched into them. Some delicately detailed, some crude shapes in simple outline stitched in dashes. There is a strange variety.

'You will have to add something, Iso. I ask all my visitors who will spare the time to add something to my collection.'

'I've never done embroidery, I'll make a mess of it.'

'No, you won't. Look at this one.' She holds out a piece, a simply stitched face, a wonky oval, a big smile. Round black eyes with eyelashes standing like quills. The word Mummy rendered in awkward straight lines. 'Bert made this, with a little help from me. If Bert can, you can!' She smiles at Isolde.

'OK, what do you want me to do?'

'Whatever you like. There are no rules. Something that makes sense to you.'

Isolde thinks about what caused her to come, about the man she now knows as Jesse, and the woman lying in the bed before her, people tied by new-drawn paths and ancient threads.

'Does it have to be something beautiful?'

'No darling, the doing, the action is the beauty.'

'OK then, I think I know.' Isolde reaches into her pocket for the map drawn by Jesse.

Isolde and Lee settle into the routine of working for the harvest. Isolde starts to feel a pleasure in the strength in her limbs, muscles responding, her body enjoying the satisfaction of physical work. In the early evenings she visits Jada, slowly stitching her embroidery. The map is taking shape. Jada is really pleased that something from Jesse will be included in the collection. Isolde finds that she improves, can more subtly sew the designs. She has a piece of material, an oblong narrowed at one end. Along one of the edges, Petra, a woman who has been at the farm since the early days, has embroidered a strip of grass. Long, open stitches in the front getting smaller and denser behind. Hovering above the grass are the simplified forms of pink blossoms and bees in black and yellow. They stop half way across the strip of grass. Jada asks Isolde to remind Petra that she is due a visit to finish it.

'She doesn't really have the patience for it, but she's done a lovely job, and we had the chance to talk about the old days, about all the things we used to talk about in the young days. I would like to continue that talk.' Jada puts down her work and looks over her glasses at Isolde.

'It was your mum who brought us here Iso. I wouldn't have been brave enough to leave the city, I don't think. But with you in her belly she became fierce about finding a different, better life. She didn't believe the consensus, that life was impossible Out, that life had gone back to the middle ages in the countryside.' She laughs. 'Though of course in some ways it has. Ben mends as many scythes and hoes as he does solar panels.'

'And you did go back to the city when you were first ill, Esther told me.' Not wanting to be intrusive, she speaks carefully. 'Did – would you have been cured if you had stayed in the city?'

'I don't know. Really, I don't know.' Jada smiles. 'I love it here. I have lost my sense of city life. I never liked it that much anyway. Kept trying to build the countryside in the city, when all I had to do was walk out into all of this beautiful empty space.' She smiles again, taking up Isolde's hand. 'Three metres of poor cloth can be traded for one metre of quality without anyone feeling hard done by.'

Jada asks Isolde to pass her a box from the chest of drawers. Slim fingers sort through trinkets, parting scraps of silver and gold, fishing out a small silver anchor with a loop for hanging on a chain. She closes the box, gestures for Isolde to replace it. She gives the anchor to Isolde.

'This was your mum's. She wore it on a chain that broke. She thought it was lost, but I found it after she died. Esther has other things of hers, but I think you should take this.'

Isolde looks, a barbed smile, a spar, a symbol of safety and wandering. She wraps her fingers around it, feels a point catch onto the inside fold of her closed hand.

Isolde finishes the line she's stitching as Jada has shown her, with a few small over-stitches, then snips the leftover thread at the back. For a moment she studies the reverse side of the piece, a rough mirror of the front. She runs the pads of her fingers over the knotty chunks of stitching, the in-between space of the design. Her map, crude as it is the right way, is cruder in its mirror, here where it is all held together.

She turns it back over. She has copied the pencil lines drawn by Jesse, a curve of coast, the straight line of the road, an inlet, where she and Lee had crossed on the pontoon of storm-wrecked boats. The lane that leads to the farm.

Just above the star that marks where she met Lee would be the empty brick sprawl of the town. She begins to stitch in criss-crossing lines, as small as she can manage, intersecting and overlapping. An irregular grid made with dark red thread. Jada lies back, her hands, still holding the needle she works with, resting on the bed covers. She has fallen asleep. Isolde carefully removes the needle, tucking it into a fold of the fabric, then folding it into the bag. She picks a grey woollen thread, coarser than the red, and makes an overlaying design of the same crossing stitches. The empty town of Chelmsford blooms around the stem of the road, a disappointing brick and cement flower.

Chorus

there is a place in this land where we belong
and it is here
always here
where we are – we map it by existing

you map it with earth drawings on cave walls, you map with stitches and with paints
you mark it with your hands

with patterns that you make, on our emptied hides, on pots
of clay twirled like galaxies,
    you mark it with beads cut from shell, this shell, this beach
    thus, you map where you belong
    you map it with the branding on your skin
    with the braiding of your hair
    in the colours of your painted faces
    in words
    in names

    we map it by being here

28

Jesse is grateful for the books he's allowed, has made an art of escaping into them. He looks at the diagram on the page in front of him. So many things, rivers from streams, from runnels of rain down leaf and rock. Tree trunks branching, and again, spindling out to twigs that waver upwards, lifting leaves up so they might breathe the sky. These twin shapes describe what's inside his own body, that puzzle of wet, rounded lozenges, each primed with different pumps and suctions and chemical prompts. This drawing, the black webs caught in mirror pools show the path that air takes, sucked in and down and in until it becomes an entity small enough and divided enough that it is able to slip below the surface and into the wetlands of his body.

He remembers someone describing trees as the lungs of the earth. He lets the patterns form on his softly closed eyelids, lets the damp bumps of grass and stone be found at his back. He feels the blanket. No, it's not the blanket. He feels the nap, guiding his hand, the smooth brindle pelt of Mister. He plays his fingers across the splay of ribs under the skin. Wolf lungs, caged, buried somewhere deep in time beneath. He looks upwards, above them, to a dark tracery of twigs against a feather sky. His lungs fill and empty as his own breath billows through his body.

Everyone works, harvesting the field crops and preparing bucket-loads of vegetable for preservation. Leanne frets over apportioning ingredients between her trade pickles and relishes, and what is for winter use on the farm. The children are roped in, after their hours of lessons in the morning, to ferry food to workers, to clean jars for Leanne, to write labels and chop herbs. Pete stops working earlier than the others and, with some helpers, prepares an evening meal, large enough to be breakfast the next morning, eaten with slabs of Petra's bread. She is baker and miller. The mill has been in use for fifteen years but Ben has recently harnessed solar power to augment the sails rigged on the roof of the building where the stones are housed.

Petra is small, quiet and intense. She has long, grey hair that, when it is not tied back into two plaits curls around a delicately lined and angular face. She wears black trousers over work boots and, in spite of the heat, a black, holed jersey. There are floury finger marks on the black. When Isolde comes to find her, she is hefting a bag to the door. Isolde offers to help, picks up a second. It is heavy, tests the grip of her hands. She lifts and shunts with a knee. They move more sacks then Petra offers her coffee. They sit in two mismatched chairs either side of a small, overflowing table.

'I'm going to have to learn to make this stuff soon,' says Petra, leafing through scrap sheets of paper. Isolde looks around, at the wooden cogs, the burlap, the ropes.

'Would you have time?'

'Ha! No, I wouldn't. Perhaps that's for someone else. We can probably find more notebooks in one of the towns, anyway.'

'How do you know how to do this?' Isolde looks at the wooden gears, the chutes and levers. Shelves on the walls with tools, a jar marked beeswax. Such transformations, such a machine.

'I didn't have a clue when I started. I trained as a midwife, lived in a small town further west. But I ended up here, and one thing I have learnt, if you can find something useful to do, it makes a life run smoothly. There's refuge in it, do you know what I mean?' Isolde doesn't. But she's pulled in, curious.

'How did you learn it all?'

'Trial and error, and error and error!' She laughs. 'But when I could easily grind my flour, then make my bread, it was worth it.'

Petra tells the story of her mill. She keeps her grindstones like hearth gods – she worked hard to get them, long trade walks, travelling across the land to find them. The mechanism was fitted together from salvage and addition in a series of errors and gradual improvements. They have been turned by different powers over the years – pushed by hand, pulled for a while by a stubborn donkey who didn't long for fresh bread as much as Petra did and soon became a grouchy, elderly farm pet. They eventually built mill sails to use wind. The canvas sails scoop through the sky, scraping out energy like spatulas. Petra has decked the inside walls of the mill with corn dollies, experimentally woven as she watches over her machine.

The steady flow of work is the reason she gives for not visiting Jada. Wheat cut a few weeks before is dried and threshed, ready to mill. Setting up a new solar-power drive with Ben has been absorbing all her attention.

Isolde offers to oversee the mill so Petra can be with Jada. Petra insists Isolde first needs some lessons, to hear the sounds of the machine, to know the responses, learn the touch of the flour. Read the wind through the medium of grain. Over a day and a half of emergency apprenticeship, Petra confides that part of the avoidance is because her love for Jada has made her afraid of the loss to come. She prefers busyness to keep feelings at bay. But once her stern instruction seems to be fully taken on by Isolde, love takes her back to the side of her friend.

29

A traveller comes to the farm. Francis, an intense, young, white man in his early twenties with a downcast gaze and dark copper hair, is searching for a place, finding it currently on the road. He asks if he can swap his labour for a bed for a week or so. He hardly talks, focusing his curiosity like a thirst on the innovations and techniques developed by the problem-solvers of the group. He spends three days in the mill with Petra, watching after her with something like adoration. He drives Ben mad with relentless, barely audible questions. But Ben is won over by the intelligence of the queries and soon provides commentary while he works, their two heads together over machine guts and wiring scattered across his table.

Isolde is finishing up some tidying in the rows of fruit canes. She's struggling to untie old knots so she can reuse the string, picking in frustration at the dense, weathered burrs. She wonders what the next pedlar to call might take in exchange for a new supply. Francis passes by and, always demonstrably overpaying the debt of his bed and board, offers to help.

'We can make some twine,' he offers.

'OK, how?'

He beckons her to follow, walks to the lane. He pulls work

gloves from a pocket, reaches into the verge, gathers some nettles, stripping the leaves with a downward pull.

'Let me see what you're doing.'

'You have to be a bit careful, but it's quite easy to make them
non-stinging.' He speaks as though it's a private, neutral commentary of his own actions. Though he clearly dislikes attention he sets to the task earnestly, making sure that Isolde can see
what he is doing. Soon the leaves are rubbed from the stems.

'Now crush the stems and split off the long fibres from the
outside,' Francis continues, speaking as though to his hands,
but he stands so that Isolde can see. He crouches to the ground
and, finding two stones, drags the reddish stems between, flattening them. Then he splits them open lengthways. He bends
them and pushes a finger along between the divide, separating
inner from outer fibres, end to end.

'You might want to come a bit closer.' He still doesn't look
at Isolde. She's drawn into the process, curious to see how it
works. Francis plays the green outer fibres across his thigh, and
with a combination of rolling and pinching, a length of twine
is twisted into being. Isolde is beguiled. One kind of order,
with a specific usefulness transformed into another, with new
utility. For the first time he looks up, holding and pulling the
short length of twine before him, demonstrating its strength
before handing it over for her to examine.

'You can wait for it to dry first, and that will make it more
slender.'

'That's great! Can I have a go?'

As Francis pulls some more fibres, Ben comes over.

'What are you two up to?'

'We're making string!' says Isolde, as though announcing a
long-awaited celebration ball.

Isolde bends to watch the movement Francis makes with the
fibres, the direction of the twists, the order of the turns. Her

first piece is short and bumpy, but she picks more nettles and soon has enough to tie the raspberry canes.

Later, she finds Ben and Francis in the workshop. She brings a home brew for each of them. They talk about rope-making. Francis shares his limited knowledge, and tells them of a homestead that makes hemp rope, uses it as a trade good with other farmers. They speculate with fresh interest on the importance of rope, a material none of them had ever really considered before. They examine the idea of a world without it – what of trade if there were no cords to tie down goods borne to markets, no sails held tight to the winds?

Chorus

> you used our hides since you first stuck a spear in our ribs
> since you painted us on your cave walls
> – yes, we remember our wild selves

> we remember a time, when we were there,
> and you were not
> we remember when you first built walls around us

> we remember our kind who feed you now
> never in the sun
> farrowed and crated

> you who can make ropes to sail the seas
> you who capture sun in plates, like leaves

> your feet that cannot walk without our hide
> your hands that cannot carry all that you need

your hairless skins that do not keep you warm enough
tss

Isolde gathers a fistful of nettle stems. She feels in her pocket for the silver anchor. Under the work light, she threads nettle fibres through the top loop, rolling and twisting, adding in lengths to make a foot of twine that twists in a natural curve, smelling of growth, green and dense. *An anchor, untethered, on its own, does nothing,* she thinks. The silver isn't weighty enough to stretch out the natural spring of the cord. She twirls it from the top. The metal skitters shiny in the light.

One morning, Petra asks Isolde to keep an eye on the mill. Isolde sits on the platform above the stones, preparing a bowl of vegetables for Leanne. She eyes the fetish-like figures tacked to the timber structure, the corn dollies, essential human forms twisted from straw stalks.

She peels and chops the carrot and beetroot into the bowl, her fingers stained an unsettling deep red. She keeps an eye on the steady grind of the stones, listens to the pitch of wood and stone as Petra had taught her.

By the door is a bundle of straw. She sets the bowl down once the preparation is complete, takes a few stalks, rolls and twists them. They are too brittle for a slender cord but with practice she finds the touch and pull, bunching the right number of stems to make rope. It is uneven, ungainly, but it feels strong. The smell is earthy, the warmth of summer turning to autumn. The sweetness of grass preserved in the drying of the sun. Soon her hands ache from imprisoning the twists that will give the rope its strength.

She ties the ends with string scraps, knots it around her waist.

Later she hangs the rope, curved like a blonde bow, on a board hung on the wall of the barn. It is the thickest and longest piece yet. She writes with a stub of pencil, makes notes about the workability, where she made it, that it smells nice. She has become absorbed by these experiments. It is a pleasure that is new to her, interacting with materials, noticing details inherent to each – when a leaf or piece of bark splits, how long the strands, how pliable a fibre will become with handling. She is finding a new language that is spoken by touch.

Through the summer months, the flow of new experience and new closeness carries Isolde. She loves the work and the time out of doors. She loves learning about nature and food. There are moments when she feels out of step with the close-knit group but she enjoys the days. Sometimes she longs for solitude again, and is glad that the many group discussions, so laboriously played out, so politely and politically teased through the collective don't need to include her. How they have the patience for such compromise is beyond her. She stifles sometimes a rising criticism of the group's earnest carefulness that can shade into a kind of righteous piety. But she is happy in the company of all as individuals.

They have a carefully orchestrated plan for Jada's care and with this, she gladly cooperates. Their aim is to entice her to eat without being seen to do so and without overwhelming, so they take ordered turns bringing her varied treats and favourites.

Isolde takes Jada some mint tea and a plate of freshly picked peas, hot and buttered. Though her appetite is patchy she welcomes the visit. She picks up one pea at a time. 'It's like bursting a bubble of sweetness,' she says. She holds the plate out to Isolde who takes one as though selecting from an offering of after-dinner Turkish delights. And though it is delicious, her enthusiasm is in the service of encouraging Jada to eat more. She eats enough to keep their enjoyment going, not enough to diminish the quantity available for Jada. 'Look, Iso, that green, it's extraordinary!' They share out the peas; this most basic of food is experienced as miraculous. But Jada tires, lies back, sighing contentedly, as though she has shovelled trenchers of pie and potato, not young peas picked one at a time from a dark blue plate.

Crossing the yard back to the farmhouse kitchen, Isolde sees Ben, crossing the back field on the solar quad bike, behind him a silhouette cockerel tail bouncing as he crosses the field. She stops, holding the tray, unable to respond to the high wave he gives her. He pulls up, beaming, nods backwards over his shoulder. 'Flax!' he says. Isolde puts the tray down on the rabbit hutch at the edge of the yard and goes to inspect. Tied onto the back of the bike are three plant sections, clumped earth and roots bound in old fabric and tattered blue tarpaulin. Isolde is excited. On an earlier trip, Ben had brought back a clip on his device, showing a traditional Maori way of making flax twine strong enough to catch fish with bone hooks, and beautiful enough to hang heirloom amulets around the necks of royalty. Next to the plants is a bundle of cut leaves. Ben hands them over to her. 'In case you want to start right away,' he says. 'I found a bunch of them outside an old hall, Bingo or something, and I thought it would be worth transplanting some for a regular supply. We should get them into the ground.'

They choose a spot behind the cottages, open and unused. A space they can grow into, grow big enough to be cropped for fibres.

Later that evening Misha feeds her rabbit, Ty, the leftover peas left on top of the hutch. She strokes his back, feels the soft pelt run below her palm. 'Goodnight Ty,' she says, then takes the tray and the plate back to the kitchen.

30

Esther comes in to the workshop, joins Isolde who is looking at her board of twine samples and experiments, wondering how thick she could make the nettle cords.

'That's amazing, Iso!' She puts her arm around Isolde. 'It makes me sad that you weren't allowed to grow up here. But you're a natural!' Esther beams, rubs her sister's arm and leaves the workshop.

Isolde is irritated; she is reduced, thinned out by this praise. Not for the first time, Esther, in welcoming the addition to her own life, has left no room for Isolde's. As Misha said when she first arrived, it's as though she had been lost in London for thirty years. She understands that she is fitting into an existing set-up. But there is the irritating presumption of this being an upgrade, the correction of a fault.

The life she had lived before had not been a placeholder, it had been her life. London is her home. The farm isn't a perfect antidote to that imperfect place. She hadn't been waiting, deprived, to live the same life as her sister. Living in the children's home had been difficult but it had certainly been valid. Her wild youth, it had been risky, fractured, but it had been spectacular. She knows, somewhere that only good is meant, and doesn't fully understand the strength of her response so she pushes her irritation aside and goes to help Leanne with the vegetables again.

A pedlar comes to the yard, greeting all in turn. Leanne hollers for him to come into the barn kitchen where preserves are made, shows him all the jars and recipes she is working on. She pulls out a little jar from the year before, handing it over to him.

'For you, Jost, your fave garlic and tomato from last year – to remind you to keep putting in a word up and down the line about what I've got!'

'Leanne, your pickles sell themselves, my darling, but I will gladly take it.' He blows her a kiss and stashes the jar in the bag over his shoulder in a continuous performative sweep.

'But a warning.' He lowers his voice. 'Those whiteys are hopping. They are looking for a boy; Lee, is it? They may come here, after hearing whispers from one of my road brothers. Take care, they're dangerous.'

Leanne shakes her head wearily. 'Thanks for the warning, Jost. I'll let the others know.'

A few days later, Isolde comes into the kitchen. She hears the last of what Clifford says, before he's hushed by Esther when Isolde appears. Isolde feels sure that they are talking about the news from the pedlar, about the risk to Lee, and, by extension, to all of them.

'Look, maybe it's time Lee and I went to London, I'd hate for us to cause you any harm.'

'No! No, don't go. You belong here,' says Esther.

'Esi's right. I am worried about it, but we've had trouble with others before and I don't want to give in to those bastards. Just want to be ready for any trouble that might come along. I'd be glad of a chance to have a go,' says Clifford.

'But it's not fair on you all.'

'It's not fair that you would have to go back to London. Iso, it's not fair that you would have to leave here because of them. I don't want you to go back to that place.'

'Well, OK, but you know, it's not so bad.'

'Yes, but you don't have to live there now – you can stay here.'

Isolde bristles, again, against Esther's easy winnowing; the role of sister kept; the rest, all she has been, is chaff, left to the breeze.

'I know you don't like the cities, but part of me misses it. I had a whole life there. Those years aren't wasted because I wasn't growing up here, in someone else's perfect place.'

Esther is hurt by the implied criticism. As so often, when people are hurt, she pushes her argument further.

'Are you seriously saying you'd rather have grown up in the kid's home you're so dismissive about? That you wouldn't rather have been here, with us, with Mum alive, as she had planned?'

Isolde is further provoked by what seems deliberate misunderstanding.

'I wish I didn't have to defend my inferior childhood all the time! Actually some of it was pretty blinding and an awful lot more fun than making bloody corn dollies.'

Esther's face sinks in hurt, but the same quick anger rises in her.

'I'm sorry we have so little to offer you.'

'Oh, for god's sake, Esther, just try to understand that not all of my life was a complete failure, will you?'

Clifford cuts in.

'Wait, Iso, you don't have to be so damn prickly. All she's

done is offer you love and a place to live. What's wrong with that?'

'I'm not "prickly", as you put it. I'm just sick of how sanctimonious you can all be.'

Esther, more distressed by observing disagreement between the two, tries to sooth the flare up. She reaches a hand for Isolde, but Isolde is angry and speaks harshly.

'Listen. I may have been pretty low when I arrived, and I may have been overjoyed to find you all, but I didn't bloody need you OK? Or this place. I came here for some answers, so I could sort myself out, like I always have done, and now, I can leave again.'

She turns abruptly, walking out of the farm toward the beach.

The edge of the land is a raw cut of earth. None of the boundaries of long-settled coastal areas, the promenades, the decks and quaysides of towns, exist here. The sea comes in, negotiates with the land on its own terms. The land, tired of resistance, concedes chunk by chunk; dark soil washes down with a sigh into rattling amber shingle.

Why had she been so harsh? She admonishes herself for the outburst. But irritation trumps regret. She walks across a field toward the beach. Right here, a field where peas had grown last, before the sea came. The tender curl of leaves had sneaked prettily from the ground, like a crop of embellishments. A storm flood washed in to drown them first, with salt. The wash had left the soil flat, curiously primed and smoothed for a new medium. No longer a fit surface for the green curls of pea plants. A crescent at the western edge of the field remained undamaged. But not enough of a crop to live by. The farmer, Mary, sold and exchanged the peas in small lots with local families. A kind of coin, a barter. The money she didn't make from selling to the supermarkets didn't mend her roof and didn't repair the boiler. She grew colder, angrier, sullen with silent rage over a harsh winter. The second time the field flooded, dressed in three jumpers that restrained as much as they warmed, she had walked into the sea and never came out.

The farmhouse still stands, approximately; it sags, at least, in a nest of brambles. A rabbit hops through the doorless gloom of the entrance, pausing at the foot of the stairs, just at the spot where Mary used to hold the bannister, the wood worn dark from the contact, while she kicked off her heavy work boots and put on a pair of slippers for the end of a hard-working day. The bannister dangles now, fallen from softened plaster, crumbling brick. The rabbit smells the air, hops carelessly through into the living room. A mouse skitters along the top edge of the blank, black television screen.

Isolde looks up from the beach, up the step of raw earth marking the sea's most recent reach. In the flattening mist the house and clamber of brambles look dense, like an outcrop of rock. She turns slowly, the world arranging itself in two semi-circles, loosely joined by a vertical strip of mud; in some places recently enough fallen that pale roots, tender from growth encased in soft ground, protrude to waver over the beach, feeble-looking, unready for a life exposed to the battering of the weather and the inconsistencies of the physical world.

The bank that edges the beach comes up to her hips. She imagines the step of land folding around her, burying her to the waist in earth. She is slowed to dragging by some subtle geography that seems to be taking shape from within and around her. Something more than her frustrations with Esther's certainty, something more than the hurt, masked by irritation, caused by their argument.

Something nags, an undertow pulls at her ankles, imperceptibly makes balance more difficult as she walks this new landscape. Something laps at the edges. She sits on a dip in the step between shore and field. A flat silver disc of sun, robbed of heat by the sea fret damping the air, is held above, a halo for an invisible deity.

Her fingers rest on the edge of the drop. She pulls a shoot, mindlessly. The earth gives it up with such ease. She realises that it is almost exactly a year since she lost her child, its arrival unnoticed, buried in the loss of her lover. The thing she had hoped for most was gone. Had it stayed, she would have been in London, brimming with love and joy for this new life, part of both of them. Esther's easy dismissal, as though the past were an aberration left no room for this loss, this secret pain. She would choose the life in London, with her child, over being here without. It's not something even a sister has the right to dismiss.

She turns the grass between her fingers, the stem and little fronds of roots. Above and below life. Air and water, dark and light.

31

It's dark by the time she heads back to the farm. She walks up the lane, noticing that ahead, in the yard, an arc of light swings through the blackness. She can hear voices, a clamour, something urgent. She hurries to find out what is happening.

Pete, Clifford and Leanne stand near the entrance to the yard, the backs of three men between her and them. She stops before she is seen. She waits quietly, listening to the conversation.

'I've told you, there is no one here by that name.'

'Yes, and we're saying that's not enough to satisfy our curiosity. I ask you again, is there anyone here with a tattoo?' Isolde sees the silhouette raise an arm and point to his neck, to a place where Lee wears a ribbon.

'There is no one here who you need concern yourselves with in any way. Now fuck off.' Clifford takes a step forward as he speaks, squared and tense, imposing.

'There's no need for that my friend.'

'We are not friends. You people will never be friends to me or anyone here, do you understand? Now leave.'

Behind them, others from the farm come to stand. Leanne steps forward, and speaks with a steady voice.

'Do not come here again. You have no rights over anyone here, or anywhere. Stay away from us. Don't mistake us for passive people just because we don't parade around with weapons and rules and uniforms.' She gestures with contempt at the three men. 'We'll protect our own, you can be sure – however long they've been here. We're not here to be pushed around by little thugs who are too afraid of the world to live in it.'

'Big words. I can see why you wouldn't see eye to eye with us. But we will be looking for him. You can pass that on.' The three men turn abruptly and walk out of the yard onto the lane, heading for the main road. One of them looks hard at Isolde as they pass, tilts his head and gestures with a flat hand in a slicing motion at the side of his neck. He hisses the words, 'If he doesn't want our fellowship, tell him we will remove the tattoo from him.'

She joins the others in the yard, their defiant line become a circle. Others come out of the stable. Esther from the kitchen door, with Misha behind her, calls across to ask if they are gone. Ben comes out from the stable and joins the group. Leanne is furious.

'I've told Lee to stay indoors in case they keep an eye on the place. He's pretty shaken up.' Isolde crosses to the barn and goes to Lee's room. He is sitting on the bed, head in his hands, fingers pushing up tufts of short hair. The end of a kingfisher blue silk tie loops over his shoulder, hangs down the back of his orange t shirt. She sits on the bed next to him, putting an arm around him. She leans her head on his shoulder, needing comfort from him as much as offering it. They sit in the darkness until Ben comes with two cups of honey-sweetened tea. He sits down on the bed next to Isolde. Ben reaches his arm behind Isolde and pats Lee's back.

'You're going to be alright, Lee. You're safe here, and we'll help you be safe wherever else you want to be.'

Chorus

we lie together on the grass, birds chitter their boundaries,
in the hedges and the trees
we hear the fear whispering through you

we hear the anger

we keep an eye
for each other
as should you

your kind are dangerous

The next morning, people talk about the visit of the White Towners the evening before. Isolde doesn't have a chance to put right yesterday's row. Esther is anxious and fretful about the children, about the rest of the group, about Lee and Isolde. She wants them to stay on the farm, in the house ideally. Isolde feels stifled by the attention and guilty that their arrival has caused these difficulties. She longs for time on her own.

She walks through the yard to the cottages and up the stairs to the calm of Jada's room. Jada is sleeping. Isolde picks up the cotton bag that holds the pieces of embroidered cloth, sits in the small armchair in the corner of the room. Her hands rest on the worn nap of the arms, faded coral velvet, buttoned and creased over the horsehair stuffing of the chair. Her fingers fold over the edge and find the brass studs that pin the fabric in place. For some minutes, she sits, with the bag on her lap, fingers playing out a silent tune on the metal studs. She sighs impatiently, fishes around in the bag for her piece of embroidery, unhooks the threaded needle from a fold and continues a line of stitches.

Later in the day, after working in the vegetable garden and helping Ben in the repair workshop, she goes to check on Lee. He hasn't worked as he usually does in the fields but has spent the day in one of the barns with Leanne as she cooked trays of tomatoes down into a peppery pickle. He is distant and quiet. They walk out to the garden together, but Isolde can see he is nervous.

'Lets go into the woods, keep out of sight that way,' suggests Isolde.

They slink through the yard and across the lane into the woodland. It is foggy, colours desaturated by the weather and the time of year. Leaves are turning and falling, brambles ragged, sprayed with the weak acid of autumn. The remaining berries, dense and dark, shrink into potent bitterness.

'What do you want to do Lee? Do you think it is safe to stay here?'

'I don't know. I can't tell if they know I am here or if they are just trying to find out.'

'What about London? Is that still your plan?'

'I guess. It seems hard though, to think about going there on my own when there are so many nice people here. But I would like to know what it's like. I don't know.' Lee kicks at some bracken in frustration.

'They won't keep after you for ever and no one here is going to let them get you. Or take you back. Just sit tight for now, don't go off the farm on your own.'

'I hate them. Those bastards. I saw them out of the top window in the barn. Two of them weren't even from home.'

He looks forlorn. Young. Isolde hopes she can protect him,

let him find the way to be himself, safely. Not compromised by fear. The White Towns are a danger, a pathogen, stored in pockets of the land like a contagious rash.

Two days later, the quiet of the morning is interrupted by screams. Isolde runs down the stairs and into a scene of hysteria. Bert is sobbing into Esther's shoulder as she crouches, folding herself around him. She is speaking to Misha, a hand out behind her, telling her not to come through from the kitchen, to go out of the kitchen and get Clifford now. Esther stands, picking up Bert and gestures to the door, telling Isolde to shut it.

Isolde leaves the house, a wide step over the threshold, closing the door behind her. On the doorstep is Misha's pet rabbit, Ty, lying on its side in a pool of blood. Around its neck, soaking up the blood spilled from its throat, is a strip of orange fabric tied in a bow. She picks the rabbit up, feeling the lean muscular body under the soft fur. Feeling how the clotting blood has matted the underside, making her fingers sticky. She strokes her thumb across the cheek of the dead animal.

A moment later, Clifford joins her, coming round the side of the house from the kitchen.

'Fucking bastards. Those fucking bastards. Where's Lee?'

Isolde feels panic, doesn't know what to do with the body of the animal. She lays it on the grass next to the doorstep and races to check on him.

As she runs into the yard, she can see Lee, among several others, alerted by the children's screams from the house. Relief is brief, followed by horrible compassion for the boy, knowing he will have to be told what has happened.

Chorus

blood runs like poison
the spill is what they crave
watch out, watch out – that thirst will never die

32

Everyone on the farm is nervous and watchful. Five days pass, people go about their work, in pairs or groups. Ben and Clifford set up hoses, in case the White Towners use fire, as they heard they have done in the past. Lee stays in the workshop most of the time, working with Ben. As though in defiance, he adds an extra flourish to the ties at his neck, combining silk scarves and neck ties or ribbons in bold, harmonious hues. But his heart is cheerless.

Ben calls around to some of the neighbouring settlements and they agree to lend people to the farm, promising a return of labour at a later date. Five men and women bunk down in the barn, swelling the numbers. No one knows if such measures are necessary, but not many believe they have heard the last from the White Towners and the scattered farmsteads have much to gain by helping to protect each other.

At dusk on the sixth day, they return. Seventeen men and boys come toward the farm across the field. Some hold torches, flames burning above their heads. When they get near enough, the people of the farm see that they wear as close to a uniform as their resources allow. The six men from Drake's Drum wear an armband over dark grey shirts, with the design of a zig-zagged square that matches the tattoo on Lee's neck. Six men who should be putting their shoulders into farm work. Almost three days' walk from the fields that sustain them. Their numbers have been boosted by eleven men from the nearest White Town to the farm, several hours' walk to the north. Eleven men, more easily spared because their absence will be shorter, from a village renamed Churchill Cross. On their chests, bizarrely buttoned on at each corner using hand-stitched holes for what they named Donning the Flag, an oblong of white with a red cross emblazoned across it, the spars extended along the edges to make a variant of the swastika. So much meaning put into that securement, that act of attaching fabric to a shirt carefully primed with buttons scavenged from a department store in Norwich fourteen years before. So much invented value had been put into that absurd moment; boys getting their buttons when they got their tattoos. Grown men and women crying when their sons attached the flag for the first time; some men experience a tightening of the throat each time they put the flag onto their chests. A ritual come to such power in only fourteen years. A ritual that gained its form because a bag of buttons from a haberdashery department in an abandoned store in Norwich had been taken on a whim, in case by sheer volume, they should turn out to be useful. No matter that to others it looks foolish, like a nursery bib. The ritual is made.

Anger glitters in the hearts and throats of these men, learnt as boys at their father's sides. The anger of betrayal, that fatally false reading of the world, has led them into all their acts of misery. It has caged them in with their fears.

Hopeless creatures – our search for meaning takes us down such dark roads.

Armed with some foreknowledge of how the farm is run, they head past the house to the yard, making for the barn.

Isolde, in the house with Esther and the children hears clamour, shouts, the urgent prelude to violence. Esther pulls the children with her upstairs to the bedroom, screaming for Amber and Cara to come from another room.

Isolde, her heart pounding, thinks first of Lee, then of Jada. She runs from the house into the yard. Through the door of the workshop she sees Ben holding on to Lee, struggling to keep him inside. She runs in, begs him to stay quietly there with Ben, that it will be safest for him and for the rest of the people. Isolde then rushes over to find Petra in the doorway of Jada's house. She shows Isolde the long knife in her hand, tells her that she will go in, bolt the door behind her and stay there with Jada.

The numbers of the farm people in the yard are growing. The six children, hurried into the house are upstairs with Esther. Ben joins the others in the yard, once he has persuaded Lee to stay hidden in the workshop.

Violence erupts from the wary circling and shouting. People start fighting, shouting, pulling each other to help and hinder. Two of the White Towners brandish knives. Clifford, grabbing a large piece of wood goes after one of them. There are more of the people from the farm. The women are fighting alongside the men. Clifford disarms the man with the knife, knocking him to the ground. As he scrabbles to get up, Pete and Ben drag him, twisting and bucking, into a small outhouse and lock him in. Pete picks up the knife he dropped.

Leanne and two others skirmish with more of the marauders. Somewhere in the mayhem, Isolde looks over and sees two of the younger men trying to burn the barn. One screams through a window, smashing it with his torch, trying to light the curtain.

'Come out you fucker, you dirty taint!'

Isolde tries to dodge through the chaos to get to the barn. It is built of stone, but the roof and lining could catch. She is calling out, trying to reason with the two, who can't be more than twenty. The one shouting turns his insults on her. The other, caught in a moment, looks confused, fleetingly ashamed.

'No! Stop it! There might be people in there!' she shouts, running the last bit of yard to try to pull out the curtain that the torches have lit. She hears a roar behind her as Leanne charges across the yard at full speed and punches the one who is shouting square on the temple. He drops, out cold, to the ground. The other, in fright, runs away back across the field.

Isolde goes into the barn with a woman from the nearby homestead, between them they pull down and douse the flaming curtain, using a dustbin lid and the hose that is coiled and connected by the barn door, before it catches further. There is another fire, a timber stack in the yard, flames spit and crackle hot glee among the confusion of voices.

Clifford and Ben throw another of the men into the outhouse. Two are out, on the ground. There are five of their men still standing and a number who have scuttled off back into the woods, or retreated to the field to nurse an arm or head, their bravado and their torches guttering on the hardstand.

A storm. Called up by the mayhem, black smoke met by black cloud, and merciful rain. The flames dance, they roar. But the rain comes and the burning timber is kicked over the ground to fizzle out. The five men try to keep the fight going. But they are outnumbered. There is a stand-off. A bitter smell of douse and burn. Ash. Wet faces glower at each other. The rain takes up all the sound. In that moment of stillness Lee comes out from the workshop, walks toward the men.

'Dad,' he says, looking at one of the men.

Gesturing at his comrades, the older man says, 'Some of them may wish you harm, but I won't let them. You don't just leave your folk. Come back with us, we'll speak of it no more.'

'But you're not my folk, Dad. You don't want me as I am, so how can I be your folk?'

'You are my son. You should be with your people. Not these – these traitors. You'll be lost.'

Lee looks at him, incredulously. He laughs. 'Lost? Here? You're the one who is lost. You make no sense. You are pathetic. All of you. I will never, ever see you again.'

'Lee, I can't guarantee that they won't come for you.' Once again, Leanne strides across the hardstand, coming to a stop inches from Lee's father. She looks into his face. She speaks without anger, but with such a brute edge of force that all are swept before her words. She becomes taller, louder in the measured quiet of her words.

'You don't need to guarantee his safety, because I will guarantee it. I guarantee this boy,' she turns, pointing at Lee— 'that you will do him no harm. I guarantee that for all here. I guarantee that if you come here again, I will kill you. Do you understand me? I told your friends once before that you are not welcome here. This time you must understand my words.'

They see the man trying not to flinch, trying not to back down.

'Dad, I don't want any part of it – what you are, what you believe. You are all so wrong. I hope you leave and cause no more harm. But I will fight you, with Leanne, with everyone here, if you come back again.'

The older man struggles with a mess of emotion and belief, trying to maintain a strong exterior. It seems, for a second, in his beseeching look at his son that love is part of the mess. But love is not ascendent.

'We are done then. I am sorry. You're my only child. Yet, you turn from me with such hate.'

The people of the farm shake their heads, gasp at such a telling. But belief can make anything true.

Clifford speaks next. 'I have your two comrades; we will keep them until you are gone. They won't be harmed. But understand this, you best keep yourselves away.'

He turns to another of the men, the red and white flag on his chest hanging down at one corner, blood from a cut on his head darkening his shirt collar.

'You are from a way north of here, aren't you?' The man nods. His face a resentful blank. Clifford continues. 'You don't want trouble with your neighbours.'

One of the men from the nearby homestead speaks too. 'We're three miles from this place, there are more of us than you can trouble. Cliff is right, if you can't learn to button your hate'— he gestures dismissively at the man's chest— 'then stay behind your fucking walls. Keep your poison for yourselves.'

'Now you should go,' says Leanne. The men turn. Two of them drag the boy who set the fire to his feet, one nudges another groaning knife-wielder until he too stands, staggering, for the long walk home. One of the men looks around at the ground, comically pats himself as if he might have absentmindedly left something, then turns to leave with the others.

There is a moment's silence. Lee suddenly breaks, shame and bitterness pours from him. He turns to Leanne, Clifford, looks at all of them.

'I'm so sorry. I'm so sorry. I didn't mean to make such trouble for you; I'm so sorry.' Tears stream down his face. Leanne puts a hand on each of his shoulders. She speaks without emotion, in focused, weary calm.

'Lee, look at me. This isn't just about you, this is everyone's fight. It's mine... This has been my fight since I was seven when the Sons of Boudicca killed and burnt the body of my aunt, since I was fourteen when I was chased and beaten by some other gang that looked just like those men. This fight is bigger and longer than what happened just now, and you are a

part of it, a good part of it. But you being here is not the cause.'
Then she turns and leaves for the farm house to check on Cara
and the other children.

33

There are two days of reordering. People are edgy and upset, a fearful heightening that leads also to the carnival shimmer of a strange joy and the extra energy means that repairs are easily completed. There are several injuries – cuts and bruises and a couple of burns. Isolde discovers a tender bump on the back of her head but can't remember how it got there. Pete's arm is in a sling for a few days.

Jada frets, from her bed, about the safety of all, but the tales are retold at her bedside, comedy added to the exploits of the intruders, heroism dusting the actions of the defenders. After two days, the men trapped in the outhouse are let out and told to leave. They walk across the field, two dark shadows, unlit by the certainty of their rage.

A few days later, Isolde finds Lee and Ben in the workshop. Ben is putting together a piece of machinery. Lee sits on a crate shaving a haft of timber to set inside a pickaxe head that lies on the floor next to him. Ben looks over at him now and then.

'Remember to check it, Lee; don't make it too small to hold the head.'

Lee picks up the metal axe, measuring it against the wood he is shaping. He doesn't speak. Isolde goes to a pile of brambles in a corner. She pulls on work gloves and begins squashing the stems to lift the fibres, glad for something to occupy her. The three of them work in solemn silence.

'I'm thinking, why don't I take you to London, Lee, and we can get the tattoo removed? We could all go, Iso, you could get your stuff so that you can move here properly – I don't know, if that's your plan? We could be there and back in a few days.'

'But would it be safe on the road?'

Lee puts the pretend work to the ground and sits, elbows on knees, listening to Ben and Isolde.

'There are so many roads. We don't even have to touch the main one.'

'We could just go ourselves, Ben. I do need to sort out stuff, make a decision about what I'm doing. I'm not sure I'll stay here.' Isolde is wary of obligation, longing, in part, for the quiet haven of independence. The kindness of people at the farm, given freely, sits like a burden she is not ready to carry. And in a secret she keeps from herself, the presence of people she cares for is a risk that life has taught her to dampen.

'I know you would be OK Iso, but I don't like to think of you being alone when those bastards might still be about. If you don't want the company, that's fine, but I have a couple of contacts in London I need to see any way, so it wouldn't be a wasted trip for me.'

'That would be good. I'd like to go.' Lee speaks quietly. Ben comes out from behind his bench and walks over to give Lee's shoulder a squeeze.

'We'll do it then.'

There is some relief in the certainty of a plan. She will go back to London, to end the trouble, to help Lee, to escape doubts about what she wants in favour of what she knows. It is a disappointing solution but it has been decided. She'd only meant to be gone for a week, after all, and months have passed. Going back to London is the logical thing to do. She bends over her work, twisting fibres into twine. Her heart sinks a little but she will make changes, she will get used to it.

Jesse

34

Jesse wonders whether he should be leaving Marshal alone in an empty house. But he is always so distantly busy that he can't see it will make a difference. The two have, in grief, lost the knack of reading each other. And Jesse longs to get out of the city. Marshal has given him the keys to the old house and that seems blessing enough.

Jesse and Mister take a train then wait some hours for a slower train. They call the community taxi at the station. A woman arrives twenty minutes later, driving an electric car with a Community Vehicle licence propped on the dash and a child's car seat, a few bits of clothing and litter in the back. She takes them to the village, giving Jesse an overview of the changes in the area. Few have held out but there are handfuls of people living in the town and the villages round and about. They have meetings once a month, with a representative from each community, trying to work out how to sustain the life they have.

The road to the village is worse than when they left, the scatter of green islands along the centre is now a causeway. She drives the robust vehicle with familiar confidence. All the roads out of the town are pitted and overgrown. He sees no one as they arrive in the village. He checks he has a signal before she leaves. There are enough bars to call up a return journey; he won't be stuck.

It is darkening when they arrive. The timber shuttering looks worn but the structure is intact. Jesse feels a fluttering of anxiety. Perhaps someone has moved in through a back window, perhaps they will come back when he is sleeping. Perhaps the inside is rotten and darkly ruined. Memories contaminated with slime and stink or the grubby overprint of other bodies. He unlocks the heavy padlock over the door, slides the board out of its metal housing, pulling at a shroud of cobwebs behind. Mister pokes around in the thick growth of the front garden as Jesse struggles in the cold with the stiff lock of the front door.

As he goes into the house, he is suddenly reminded of entering the cool, deserted emptiness of Mr Arnott's house, a chill feeling he associates with death. A flash, a twang of pain as he thinks of Lena joining Mr Arnott in death, that strange, incomprehensibly distant place. He remembers the revulsion he felt at Mr Arnott's empty coats, feels a strange tug imagining having the same reaction to anything of Lena's. But in moments, the memories of life reassert, flood his senses as they take in and log the familiar sights. *Yes, this. And this, oh yes, I remember this.* The sound of his feet on the hall floor. The worn paint in the centre of each stair tread. He puts his hand on the post at the bottom of the bannister, where coats would be hung until one of Lena's occasional frenzies for order would stir and she'd insist that all coats be put away. Jesse was always perplexed by this, thinking that the bannister post was already put away.

In the living room, he sits on the sofa, the corner where Lena sat. He pulls the yellow cushion onto his lap, and escaping the perplexing twists of the present he leans back into the embrace of the past.

Mister circles, twice, then sits on the floor at Jesse's feet. Their breath dents the chill of the stagnant air.

Jesse wakes early in his old bed. He takes in the surroundings, stretches out the sleep from his limbs. The day before had been long. He had been, he now sees, tense. He hadn't known what to expect. He had felt scared of how he would feel, whether he would be overwhelmed by loss. There is so much, of course, to remember – new things that he hasn't practised the bearing of, newly woken memories. Lena is vividly here. But he feels peace; he feels he can manage whatever comes. This is the place to come to terms with it all. To work things out. He is at home.

He stretches, gets out of bed, pulls on jeans, wraps himself in the bed cover for extra warmth. Downstairs, Mister sleeps in the corner he always slept in. Jesse smiles, wondering about Mister's memories. He rummages in his bag, pulls out food for both of them. Mister yawns and stretches, beats his tail on the ground in greeting as he looks over his shoulder at Jesse. Jesse nearly calls Jada but puts it off. He sends Marshal a message: *All good, hope you are too.*

They set out, walking down the lane opposite the house, past the empty farm and the overgrown fields. Part of the barn roof has fallen in. Some of the farmhouse windows are broken. The yard is becoming overgrown, young saplings poke up through cracks in the hardstand. The lane too is choked with growth; Jesse picks up a stick to beat his way through.

They pass the field where the cows had been, the gate he had swung from now hanging at the bottom hinge, slantways on the ground, buried in brambles and grass. They pass the stone barn, the clearing where they first met and into the second field, now elbow high with thistle, grasses, yarrow. They walk across, down the slight incline. What had been a dark and clearly drawn line of woods now smudges into the field as layers of smaller growth, a peppering of young trees and shrubs spreads into the open space, blurring the edges. On one side of the field, he sees a bump, a glint of colour: Marshal's car. Three cows watch him, then amble into the tree line, the white patches of their hides moving through wooded darkness.

Chorus

welcome, boy

the weary mother hordes
who, patient,
heartsore
waited lifelong in this field

now are joined
by sons and daughters, children
yes, and fathers too

in groups that grow, or shrink on nature's watch
– a chosen family

not always easy, these new old ways – you find it too?
we get it wrong sometimes
but we learn

we learn again
what we once knew

The car is surrounded, roof-high, by plants. The handle is cold; it sticks, but the secure, reassuringly mechanical click of the handle releases with a tug and the door swings open. Inside there is a scatter of dead, black insects on the dashboard. Otherwise the interior is intact. No fox hole, no mouse corpses, no decay. Only the insects. It is musty, but almost perfectly clean. So sweetly made that death and decay have been defied, even when abandoned in the wild. Jesse slides into the driving seat, Mister his companion passenger. He shuts the doors. Grasses, dulled for winter brush wavering on the tempered glass. The glittered trails of slugs and snails snake over the dashboard. Snail shells stuck, overwintering, on the inside of the door as if the sleek leather had sprouted moles – the only sign of age. The low-slung vehicle hunkers down into the greenery, gloriously engineered speed dawdling in a field of dreams.

Later, they walk into the village. He finds Mikel, Giana, Chetna, a couple of other residents still hanging on to their homes. They greet him with such joy, and he reciprocates, though his heart drags with the telling of Lena's death. There are the customary curt and solemn exchanges – my brother, Mrs Pym, the family from Waverly lost three. And they tell him that the families with children have all moved away. Chetna invites him for a meal later that day. He visits the churchyard, makes a tally of those he can remember, Sep and Euan, other less clearly defined people from the village past. He wishes Lena could have a stone here. They aren't a religious family, but he thinks she would like that.

Isolde

35

There is quiet at last, everyone is settled for the night. Only Isolde and Esther sit at the kitchen table. Isolde pours wine, emptying the bottle into their glasses. She picks at the edge of the handwritten label. The fire of anger is long gone, but they wait to find the words that will clear the smoke between them. Esther speaks first.

'I've been thinking about how selfish I've been, acting like everything is solved for you now, just because you've done what I've always longed for. I know you've had so much happen and have so many memories, and I haven't really been interested in the real you, just the sister I always longed to find again.'

'Oh, Esther, please don't say that. I've been prickly and doing my usual repel all boarders thing, and I'm sorry, I just got overwhelmed.'

'Of course you were; how could you not be? I know you don't necessarily want to stay here. I know it's been hard for you to cope with everything, when you're still trying to sort stuff out. I can see you haven't really found a home here, and I don't want you to think I expect you to stay.'

Isolde feels flat and heavy with failure. Even the discovery of this marvellous bounty, this kind and loving woman, trying to make amends, trying to give her all she can, it isn't enough for her to build a happy life; she perceives it with regret at her own inadequacy. And she feels the weight of disappointing Esther. But these last few months have been Esther's idea of a happy ending. Isolde hasn't had the chance to make that dream and doesn't have the right edges to fit into it. Her edges, she sees now, are formed for solitude. It feels a sad inevitability.

'It's not exactly, or only, that I want to leave, but also that I have to. I can't let Lee go on his own. And I need to sort myself out. It's not just about getting depressed after the break-up, needing somewhere to start again. Not anymore. I've as many questions as when I came, no sense of what to do, where I should be. But I do have to help Lee, at least to make some connections.'

'Yes, I can see that. He'll be better off if you go with him. It's too big a change to manage on his own.'

'I have so much to be thankful for, all that I've found here. I wish I could just stay. And maybe I'll come back for visits. I've got a sister now, and I will never let that go. You and the kids, and everyone here.' She feels emotion clamour at her throat.

'If you need that to be a distant connection Iso, that's OK. We can send messages. Henk, the pedlar takes messages. He travels up and down to London every week at least. And if Ben's latest project takes off, we may have a net connection. Though we probably haven't stopped arguing about whether that is a good thing or not since it first dropped out years ago. Now I think I'd definitely like it back.'

She smiles a little at Isolde who reaches a hand over to rest on her sister's knee.

'I'll come back soon, I promise. But it will be better for you too – those thugs will leave you all alone.'

'Hey, we have no problem with you being here on that

score. No problem. There's only about half of us who are white enough for them so they're already enemies.'

'I know. But with the kids. It feels like such a horrible risk, and I know Lee feels guilty too.'

'They'll be OK soon enough. This world isn't always able to provide the prefect childhood, and we do OK, don't we?' Esther smiled sadly at her sister.

Isolde spends her last evening with Jada, finishing her section of embroidery. She knows that Jada doesn't want her to leave and feels guilty that this isn't enough to keep her. Jada is quiet, she doesn't work on the embroidery. She lies on her side, curled round to see Isolde sitting in the armchair. Isolde senses she is trying to give her the freedom to leave, but she is withdrawn, melancholy. Soon she drifts into sleep.

Her embroidered copy of the full page that Jesse sent is almost complete. She had finished the lines of the map and then just carried on. The diagram of the eye, printed more than a century before on the page of the book has become a vivid abstract pattern, a wild planet, stitched in bright colours, not the careful black of the illustration. Isolde begins to stitch the message, written in Jesse's strange script: I'm sorry. She thinks that though Jesse had nothing to be sorry for, she in leaving owes Jada those words.

She stays long after Jada has fallen asleep. A senseless, necessary logic compels her to finish the whole page before she leaves, an unreadable gesture of atonement to the man, confused about his own innocence, and to the women she is leaving behind.

She makes the final stitch, pushes the needle through to the back and ties off the thread on the last letter, the Y of sorry. Jada has been sleeping for many hours. She folds the piece of cloth, tucking it into the bag with the others beside the bed. She leans over the sleeping woman, kisses her on her hair and leaves the silent room, one light by the bed still glowing, as Jada likes it.

The yard is lit by a high moon; uncertain shapes at the edges, waiting to be useful or to be repaired, are silver gilded. Against the wall of the barn, the empty rabbit hutch, its door still open, has a fresh bunch of wildflowers on the top, still clumped at the stem, from the hot and earnest little hands of the children in their solemn ritual. Isolde walks through the vegetable garden, says goodbye to it all; she hopes it will make the morning's parting easier.

36

The next day, after an early start and sunrise breakfast, Lee, Isolde and Ben set off for London. Goodbyes are muted, a sense of anxiety, failure, dragging further the sadness of parting. They say goodbye quietly, with love and promises. Perhaps, tucked under layers of pragmatic veiling, there is also hope. But they will be two days walk apart, trusting messages to pedlars who might be self-serving or forgetful, blown off course by any number of unexpected opportunities glimmering from a turning off the road.

They walk the compass route, the crow road. Lee is quiet, trailing behind the other two as they walk through woods and fields. Isolde and Ben talk, letting loose connections lead them into new conversations. The plants they pass – their uses. Isolde looks over the patches of nettles with a quick, greedy assessment, so that Ben begins to tease her about it. He tells her about memories of a bakery in Liverpool, how he would look through the window with the same kind of longing; dreaming of buns, seduced by the sheen of icing dotted with sugared gems, the cream and jam that oozed from layers of yellow sponge or sheets of light pastry. She promises to buy him pastries when they reach London.

Conversation between them is easy. They make each other laugh, and they share many enthusiasms. Isolde's interest in making twine and rope has opened in her a new curiosity for materials, for their useful or problem-solving capacities. They talk about the way wood reacts in different circumstances, about the age of beams still holding up the mediaeval churches they pass, churches that survived years, plagues, wars, declines in faith, and, finally, abandonment. Isolde tells Ben about camp-making with the children – tentative, playful structures made from twine and hazel, experiments with binding stems of wood together with cord she had made from brambles. Ben tells her about the requirements for fixings when using oak, its durability and power to decay steel.

Lee hangs back, still quiet. Because of his silence she forgets for a moment why she is leaving. She sees her experiments have given her a sense of purpose and the first intimations of pride in her work, something that she has not experienced before. But she slows, turns back to wait for Lee. It feels suddenly like an indulgence, a dream, in such a misaligned world. Better return to the imperfect reality of the city.

Chorus

wake up girl!
all reality is imperfect

just what is it you seek?

Time for Jesse passes like a dull ache. But the boredom of years in prison sometimes flares into an intolerable itch. The light irritates him. The walls, those flat receptors bore him. His eyes, what he can see, bore him. Bore into him. He presses the pads of his fingers into his eyes, pushing the heel of his hand up under his jaw. Teeth clamped. An ache beginning in his eyeballs. He pushes into the soft and springy resistance of his eyes until it feels dangerous. Waves and fans of interior light dance in the shuttered black. He eases the pressure, lets the pain become an ache, watches the fireworks his fingers have pressed into his eyes.

When he stops, his eyes groggy, flashing still; when he blinks, the same dull and tepid light still floods the space. Sitting on the floor, the trunks of his legs splay before him, he reaches behind, catches a corner of the blanket and pulls it onto his lap. He wraps his head, pulls darkness around himself. Leaning back, cushioned by the turban wrap of the blanket, he lies in the darkness, the edge of the bed pushing into his upper back.

Eyes are so greedy for light. They find it in any corner. Through any imperfect barrier. Though wrapped in layers of fabric, the darkness is still made more complete when he presses his hands over the wad of blanket swaddling his head.

He wonders if blindness would save him from the boredom of the light.

There are paths through the woodland. Enough used to keep the way clear. Some are even cut, the effort of labour speaking of regular usage. Ben tells Isolde that more people are coming to the area. In the last year two smallholdings have sprung up, each claiming a patch of land a couple of miles from the farm.

'Soon you won't be able to call it "the farm", when it is surrounded by others.'

'There was an old sign on a gate that fell apart. But the sign is still kicking around the workshop somewhere: Cherry Tree

Farm. We could always go back to that. We'll definitely need a name now more people are returning to the countryside.'

Isolde can't help a dose of cynicism at the idea of returning to the land. Like there really is a way out from under the restrictive dominion of the city. And now, she sees the land as contaminated by the bleak hearts of the White Towners. She sees belief in the possibility as naivety, a false cheer won by a refusal to look at the darkness. Her weary pessimism leaves her sad.

Where they walk now, through dogwood, hazel and birch, their breath visible on the cold air, there had in the past been a succession of farms; back into time and perhaps now forward again, into the future. The first smallholding to work the land was set close among trees. The first farmer a woman. She walked her plot, crossing their path. One of the palings had fallen. She went to her home to get twine, to re-secure the fencing to keep the cattle in while they churned and cleared the ground. She stepped over her children, the youngest caught hold of her skirt as it swept like sudden night over his head. They were playing, making a pattern with leaves and stones on the flagstone placed in a doorway, centuries under the feet of Lee who pauses for a rest.

She only needed to fix the paling for a while. Half the plot would be planted soon with flax seed. Flax that made the linen of her skirts. The fencing would move, to a different plot, for different containment. Her breath rose on the cold air as she bound the cross piece of hazel into place.

On the kitchen shelf of the newest farm, a quarter of a mile west, flax seeds, a trade swap from one of the gatherings, wait in an old mayonnaise jar for next season's planting.

They walk for two days. Approaching the city with no distant view, it creeps toward them in the trees. Empty houses defy the forest with decayed determination. They stop in an outpost. A little nest of streets so completely paved that the green invasion creeps over, patchily, across the surfaces, in alpine nooks. Front gardens cemented for cars, back gardens covered with terra-cotta concrete slabs, wooden decking. Thus, the reclamation of the forest was slowed.

The wide canopy of a petrol station replaces the shade of the trees. They sit on the ground. A zigzag of greenery shoots through, hardy meadow weeds growing in the shallow soil of a split in the cement. The rusted case of a car waits at the pumps as though a skeletal driver might still, one day, return from the empty shop, clutching a doughnut seeping with sugar, and coffee in a throw-away cup that will last forever. A bird has built a nest on the dash board, the neat structure pushed against the windscreen as though sliced in cross-section.

Lee has become more animated, asking questions about London, about Isolde's apartment, the location, the amenities. He is excited. It is easy to see, in the wide clarity of his eyes and the flurry of questions, that he is nervous too.

Chorus

edgelands, the tailing off of all your work
– time and weather wearing, the never-ending work of roots
that press into tiny gaps, ferocious for a place

water that seeps from sea and sky

the land creeps in on slow and shallow waves
we follow, a flotilla,
once the land has pulled the towns under

Jesse

37

After the ravages of the October Night Flu, there is a blurry hiatus. Individual miseries remain tattooed on the hearts of those left behind, but society is fed up with dread and worry. The state discovers a useful libertarian strand and the populace take as though born to the ways of the libertine. Why think about the declining birth rates? The deaths we still all feel? The tightening of control? The snip-snip-snipping away of freedom? Let's cavort, cabaret, and let's toast the us that remain. The state, a wily schemer, learns quickly that certain freedoms can stand in for others. Sure, party, take drugs, get high; who are we to stop you? The concessions are offered with insincere, man-of-the-world smiles: we share your appetites; who are we to judge? But slowly, quietly, stealthily, control is exerted. The internet is pruned. Soon it takes an espalier shape, dropping tight little fruits of uniform size and shape. The voices of those who notice, who rail, who warn, soon are only heard on street corners. The rest come to in the months and years after the second pandemic with a hangover, to find everything, once more has changed.

Food importation is almost total. Alternative options wither and as soon as this profound dependence has been created, the provision changes. Vegetables can be reheated; they don't need to be cooked in the same place as the plate on which they are served! It doesn't need to be fresh! Just heat it up. Food comes only in boxes: easier to stack and import. No one buys ingredients, they buy servings. Soon enough, ingredients are referenced in blurb but no longer required to be listed accountably on the boxes.

Lives readjust, new ways emerge and, soon enough, become the default. Not all of it is for the better, certainly not, but people move on, life takes turns, patterns shift and become familiar again. People find ways to manage the shock. When all suffer, the pain is not lessened, but the extraordinary isolation of grief is at least tempered.

Jesse returns to London, fits himself back into this strange world, a little less sure of himself, a little less certain about what it is he wants. He thinks about moving out of the city but secretly can't bear the idea of separation from Jada, so continues his work with the gardeners, which at least gives him purpose. In time, he meets Brita, a new volunteer. She is tall, with pale skin and sharp features, freckles across her nose. She plants marigolds among the carrots to keep away the eelworms. Jesse smiles at this new, or resurgent folk language of growing and planting. He jokes that eelworms sound grim but if they can be defeated by marigolds they can't be all that. Brita laughs, a surprisingly rough and raucous sound. They get to know each other, fall into regular companionship. They quickly discover that both, after childhoods in small villages, hanker for a return to the countryside. Over the next few weeks they become a couple.

Jesse is happy with Brita – she makes him feel good. They talk about how things could be, how they could return to the countryside. They map out the possibilities and share hope for life outside of the city. Brita gives him the sense that after the emptiness and loss of the last few years there is still the possibility of a happy future. There is suddenly intimacy and love in his life, and someone close to him who doesn't confuse him.

Chorus

yes, we all need kin
the bodies at our side, the breathing souls that flank us

not always this one, boy

but good,
you're practising the way of it

38

The gardeners agree to work with a community group founded and run by women, mostly single mothers. A garden is planned for the concreted outside area of an empty, unfunded nursery they have taken over. Jada was first to connect with them, through her oldest and best friend, Stella. Stella is white, small and skinny, with brown hair complicated with braids and tangles. She is fierce, disorganised and passionate. She cares with emotional abandon about unfairness. She lets her life slide into serial chaos on whims of concocted love that end in despair and tumult. She lives on the estate where she was born, and where the women have set up their group.

Jada's dreams are fine, gold threads, coiled, ready to string across a sturdy frame that she is carefully constructing. She finds the optimism and mistakes of her friend's choices spend-thrift, foolish, but she has always been protective of Stella. She has stood by her, pulled her out of pell-mell chaos, held her hand, her hair back from her face, her heart when it broke again. In return, Stella has watered and nurtured Jada's dreams least she abandon them in the search for their safekeeping. Stella's relentless love has made Jada value herself.

Jada is drawn to working with the group of women not just

because of this friendship but for their determination for the future of their kids, their ferocious dignity, the simple articulacy in their message: poverty is a function of the system, not a failing of those living within that system. The women refuse to take the slap-down that society confers on them as a caste birthright.

Chorus

mothers –
you can't decide whether
you adore or despise them, can you?

like one of your machines or one of your sins

in our unnatural herds, a thousand mothers
not revered
but valued

you flatten dangers, keep the wolves at bay
take the babies and their food for yourselves
our mothers mother you

your own mothers too
– elevate them, beat them down –

giving birth, they write the biggest story of the world
and still, reshaped by others greedy for their power,
that story even,
is not their own

The group take the name, the Claimants, a designator that has long been a pejorative, an expression of spite for those forced to get financial support in a system that offers them no other options. All societal harms and insults are snuck in behind that word; laziness, selfishness, unfitness for decent family life. And so, the women feel it.

Until one day, Dyan speaks. A dual-heritage woman dressed in shielding layers, a silent and meek presence, motherly and bovine, they had thought. Until she stands tall and wide at the back of a meeting and lets forth a tirade. 'Curse them,' she says. 'Damn right, I am a claimant – I claim for my kids what they have for theirs. I claim my dignity. And I claim the right to feed where they gorge. Curse them all. Damn right, I'm a claimant.' Dyan suddenly quietens, looks about her in confusion. There is stunned silence for the briefest moment, then the other women begin clapping. They cheer, 'Claimant! Claimant! Claimant!'

A few weeks later, a small hand-painted and hand-stitched banner is hung outside the nursery. It says:

We are the Claimants

We claim our right, our place

The letters have been stitched by many hands. Not too big, hand-crafted and beautiful. It speaks of intention, labour, dedication to improving their choices, rather than raising a dangerous flag of rebellion. And the name sticks. The women work collectively under that banner, under that name. They proceed carefully within the law, as a support group. Dyan grows from her moment of inspiration into the role of one of the leaders and then mentor for other groups. Though they feel enough anger for all forms of opposition, they know the state will tolerate little in the way of it. They have families and children to care for. They ask only to be listened to. But with energy and creative force, they ask in a manner that ensures many hear.

Over a year, the group strengthens. They become advocates

and advisers for those so often and so easily left behind by societal changes that protect and place benefits elsewhere. Stella is often the battery charge, her idealism and Dyan's implacable belief in what they can do keeps their carefully negotiated place thriving. Jada creates the garden, eventually taking Stella's share of the work as she rests in the later stages of a pregnancy that is the blessing left over from another disastrous affair.

The women of the group meet each day, share responsibility for each other's children, take turns working in the garden, teaching the children how to grow the vegetables and herbs. They work out steps they can safely, effectively take in their careful dance – wanting to be heard, wanting the injustices they encounter to be recognised, wanting to fight for the dignity so carelessly wiped out by the complacent, raucous, goose-fat voices honking for the state.

News outlets, they are still called. The women scoff, knowing full well the inadequacy of such a title. What about the news that they are forced to live in damp and deterioration, that their children are post-coded out of decent jobs, that their health, their life expectancy and that of their children is declining at an increasingly fast rate, decade on decade? That they die of breast cancer, ovarian cancer, lung cancer, heart disease; they die of poverty. They die of complications, they die of illnesses that in a different part of town, pass merely as a stretched-out inconvenience. What about the news that, yes, a beautiful new hospital has been built, just streets away from where they live? What about it? Somehow, though they could walk three short streets to arrive at the glass cliff face, the modern, clean eternity of care, a different kind of map is at work for these women. The streets it would take them less than ten minutes to walk are blocked. They don't find their way to the consultants and nurses, the scans and therapies and drug treatments. Not until it is too late. What about that news?

Here is the late news. Mirelle died of treatable cancer today. She was admitted to hospital just in time for some painkillers and the regret of medical staff that it was too late to save her. Mirelle, of Groundsel Way, leaves three children.

A day dawns that should have been a celebration, a naming day for Stella's daughter. A brand-new baby girl. Jada, godmother to the girl and as present as any parent, has grown flowers for the ceremony. But they gather now also to say a last goodbye to Mirelle. The women weep as they hold the baby, kiss her forehead, dampen her straight, black shock of hair with the brush of a teary cheek.

The women hold and console Mirelle's children, Kaia, Kye and Akaan, they name one of the new beds in the garden for Mirelle and the children solemnly plant a morello cherry tree in honour of their mother.

Jesse is there, with some of the other gardeners. To cheer up the confused gaggle of children, they plan another bed, asking them to choose what they would plant. 'Dragon seeds,' says Noor, thinking of her latest adventure book.

'Monkey puzzle trees.'

'Eurgh, not cabbages! Cabbages are stinky!'

'But you like coleslaw?'

'Yes, let's grow some coleslaw plants! And some big, big, great big sunflowers.'

39

There is plenty to keep them busy in London, but Jesse and Brita long to leave. They decide they will move back to the village, if Marshal will agree. They know a lot about growing vegetables now. They know something about preserving them for later use. There is still a serviceable solar connection and enough people to avoid isolation. In the happy flush of a young relationship they plan an idyllic life, the two of them and Mister. Regular trips back to London while they find their feet. Brita is on a temporary teaching contract that will end in a few months; she signs up for a distance learning agency. Jesse saves what he can from work and learns all he can about plumbing, solar, building, eco-heating, renewable small scale energy, water harvesting. It is this, in the end – the planning, the conversations he has with Marshal, the questioning, the seeking out of old books on food foraging – this earnest dedication that finally brings Marshal around. He knows that they will leave, whether he allows them to use the house or not, so he gives them a grudging blessing.

Jesse and Brita know it will take time to grow all the food they need. They plan a phased retreat, coming back to London to work in one of the gardens for a share of the crops, and to stock up on other foods. There are several forums where information about the process of going self-sufficient is updated and, just as quickly, taken down. The state is ambivalent. There is a don't-ask-don't-tell approach to the hardy, the stubborn, the romantics who head back out to the fields. Official policy is discouragement – there are dangers in being in isolated communities, there are no funds to invest in small and distant settlements. There are even rumours of wolves. And it turns out, most people are not willing to risk their connection to the safety and advantages of city life. As traffic and combustion engines decline, there are countryside parks growing up around the city, chalets to hire, long and safely wild walks. There's no need to actually go and live there, out in the wilds. But people still own houses; they still have rights. Nothing is technically out of bounds.

After several months of planning, they are ready to leave. Marshal pays for a van to take them and their belongings. He comes with them, helps unpack, then drifts into silent corners of the house, remembering his wife. He brisks himself out of his sorrow with a tool in hand, checking taps, connections, searching for the fixable to mark his love. Early next morning, he heads back to London waving from the van window. Jesse has a lump in his throat.

The first weeks are blissful. A sense of freedom and achievement garnishes every action of the couple. Jesse gets extra solar power working on the third day, enough with the new battery to heat some water. They clear and make a start on the old vegetable patch. Brita has brought carefully packed boxes of plants. Only a few, but enough to make the veg patch look like it is underway. They clear a sunny windowsill upstairs and add two shelves within the frame. Boxes of seeds fill up the space.

Jesse and Mister walk the familiar walks, fitting back into the landscape on a deep breath. The loops of their walks are shorter now that Mister is so old. They don't spend all day in the woods, but they rediscover familiar patterns – stop, sit on logs, lie down on dry leaves, look up through bare branches at the careless sky.

He takes Mister to visit Chetna and the shop, which is less like a shop now, more like Giana and Mikel's home with an open front door. Chetna always tries to give Jesse something, early cabbage, seedlings, last year's jam, bags of flour she earned helping a cooperative a few miles away. He doesn't want to take her supplies but she is so glad to see the numbers rise in the village that she insists.

Brita works in the evenings. There is still a connection that allows her to collect essays and upload critiques and personal learning plans. Jesse gets the details of the cooperative to find out if they might be able to work together. As they settle in, they feel a deep sense of satisfaction, a thrill of the adventure. But both feel unspoken anxiety about what they have taken on, and they secretly worry about the test of being so much in each other's lives, so little in other people's.

They settle into a necessary pattern. Most of Jesse's time is spent working on the vegetable garden. Mister lies on the grass next to him. Jesse looks over every now and then. 'How you doing, Micksmaliks?' His greying snout stays on his greying paws, his sad, wise eyebrows flick up to Jesse, and Jesse hears, 'Yeah, I'm doing OK, Jess.'

Brita is growing wheat in the neighbouring plot, in the once-perfect lawn where Paul and Arty would have a summer evening drink sitting on their smart garden chairs, occasionally popping their heads over the fence for a cheery chat like characters from a children's tv show. Jesse and Brita have pulled a section of the fence away. It's possible that a long lost relative will turn up and claim the house, but why would they bother? It has no value.

They both work hard, putting in many hours of physical labour and evening planning time, trying to see troubles before they arise, anticipating lean days and gluts. They create a plot that will soon feed them and have enough to swap and share with the handful of neighbours. They do a day's work at the cooperative, earning extra food. They begin to need trips to London less often. By the time the restrictions of winter have settled, both secretly miss those trips, the freedom of absence, but there is always work that needs to be done in the village.

They neglect to plan for the heart. During darker evenings and colder, shorter days, life becomes routine, and then stale. The first awareness of a growing distance is pushed away, by both of them. It's because we're busy. We'll have more time for each other when this and that and this are done. I can't be bothered today. The work, the tightness of their shared company starts to wear them down. They fall into tiredness and a torpor with each other. Which should come first? Love uplifts and gives energy, the joy of company too. But tiredness can rob us of the desire to bother. Either way, the chord that links them lengthens as each day passes. They don't fight; they are too tied down for fights. But after months, though they don't make each other miserable, each finds little joy in the other.

Those months keep rolling by. Jesse and Brita work through another day, remind each other that this is bliss, isn't it? Yes, this is bliss. And yet, their anxiety when they started out, for once, was foresight. Brita can't tell if it is Jesse or where they are living. Jesse, trying not to think about Jada, can't understand why Brita is not enough. Perhaps the concentrated circle of their life together turbocharges what would have been the natural demise of their bond. Perhaps it's the hard work. Perhaps the boredom. Brita's raucous laugh is no longer heard, but they tell each other, this is bliss, long after they have stopped bothering to delight each other.

They work, as though by consent, with the aim of politely avoiding the rupture of a break-up, rather than with any desire to properly resolve their difficulties. Jesse's walks become longer. Brita feels abandoned by his unreachable self-sufficiency. He avoids her because he feels bad; he feels that he is letting her down.

They lie each night in bed, allowing the pretence of exhaustion to keep their bodies apart. But they are so damn polite, so frustratingly careful with each other that neither can decide what to do. They both drown quietly in the frustration of it.

One day, desperate to break through the impasse, Brita goes to London on the pretext of swapping seeds to enrich the next sowing. She visits the old crew, the city garden builders and gets blind drunk on the latest batch of their almost-drinkable blackberry wine. At the end of the night she goes to bed with Halm, chosen perhaps because, of all the men in the group, he is the one that Jesse doesn't like. Nor does she, particularly. He is arrogant, annoying, a bit of a prick, or so she'd decided, before they'd left for the village. That's what made him perfect. She fucked him and let it be discoverable. In fact, she calls Jesse the next morning and tells him herself. She doesn't like Halm enough to have to carefully extricate herself from the connection. They had each used the other. And she had found it fun. And it did the trick. The stale pretence of her relationship with Jesse is over.

She goes back to the village to finish up. They argue for a few bitter weeks, just to be sure, just to pay out the dues owed to their time together. Then Brita packs a bag and leaves. Jesse understands Brita, her need to force a change. He doesn't feel angry, or not with her, but he is wounded and feels that he has failed; the price of failure is being alone.

Over the following months, Brita and Jesse started to write messages, neutral descriptions of what they are doing, what is before them, a description of a crop, a few lines about some gathering or other – little missives that demanded only the recognition that they had cared for each other, and still do. They send these notes every few weeks, until sometime later, Jesse stops replying, and Brita, forever after, wonders what became of him.

Chorus

life can be so simple, boy
but be aware
it's not enough
to roam and eat

Isolde

40

Isolde closes the door behind Ben and Lee. For all that she is ambivalent about her return she is longing for some time alone and glad to have the apartment to herself. They will be gone for a while, chasing up a contact of Ben's and looking for information on papers for Lee. Though the White Towns have no legal jurisdiction, they want to be sure that as a paperless arrival, he won't be escorted back. The problem with his tattoo is it acts as a mark of provenance. As soon as they arrived, the evening before, Lee used Isolde's device to track down tattoo removals. He has made an appointment for later that day and will be back in time for Isolde to take him there.

Her bed is rumpled. Faisal, the temporary tenant has left, for now, alerted by her message on the road. She hadn't wanted to make him homeless on such short notice, but he had offered to be out of the way. He has gone to his girlfriend's, leaving a smear of his presence over the bathroom, without putting away his clothes, without changing the bed. The two rooms would have to accommodate her, Lee, and if not Faisal, the litter of his belongings that overlie her own. She pulls off all the bedding, bunching it irritably on top of the mound of Faisal's clothes on the chair in the corner. She checks and damps her criticism;

Faisal is the one paying the rent, had carried on doing so when she decided to stay at the farm. He has left without fuss to give them space. He has the right to act as if he is at home.

Lying on fresh sheets, she tries to feel that coming back is the right choice. The city, the world, reality, it can't be escaped. There is an ugliness that surely can't be coyly covered with hand-made stitches or flavoured with herbs grown all year round in pretty pots tucked in all the corners of a garden. There is hatred and loss and danger. At least here in the city, there is no pretence. *We are all in the same dream*, she thinks, *here in this island of cement. We know our limits, our boundaries. We know our imperfect options, the shape we are supposed to fill.* What would be the point of hoping for any more than that?

The sound of the door and Lee and Ben talking in the living room wakes her a few hours later. She sighs, longing for enough time to slip into the restful peace of boredom. Not to account for the collective. Not to have to listen to the needs and wishes of other people. It is a feeling she carried from the children's home and had experienced again on the farm. A box, a caravan, a cupboard, an empty park; her frustration elevated any solitude so that it seemed it would be a paradise. On the farm they had embraced thinking and acting collectively. She had run away from it.

And yet, she loved the complex patterns, the connections, the fitted-together lights of each person, like all are part of a stained glass window in one of the empty churches. The fragments of voices, ideas, roles shared between people made a thing of beauty. She currently longs for the clarity of the big, plain sheet of glass that squares off a distant view of the city, its step up and down horizon. But she brought with her from the farm a sense of the beauty of the mosaic – cooperation that the babble of the children's home had never come close to.

Later, she and Lee go to the parlour for his tattoo reversal.

They ride three stops on the citytrain. Lee sits with his shoulders hunched up, his eyes flick around the carriage self-consciously. He keeps fingering the ends of the ribbon covering the black words beneath. What does it mean, to mark people in such a way? Why do they do it? A brand for breeding. A stamp of some impractical, esoteric authenticity. A method of claiming ownership of that strange irrelevance they define as a commodity – their whiteness. The boundary of skin, a barrier that is fragile, utilitarian, indifferent to anything other than the biological performance that is its destiny, policed as though to make it strong enough to hide the fear within. What an absurdity.

At the parlour, Lee is shy. He is ashamed, she can see, of the task he is asking the dark-skinned woman who runs the parlour to perform. She smiles at him, often, trying to convey her reassurance; he won't be judged for what was done by others. He sits in the chair, pulling the bow out of the ribbon, sliding it away from his neck reluctantly. He hands it to Isolde who winds it into a loop and puts it in her pocket. Her fingers find there the twine she had made with nettle. Two strings, olive-green and orange, rough and silken, two loops of colour nesting in the dark.

'Oh, I haven't seen one of these before. But you're not the first. I've done about three of these removals. I had a woman about a month ago, in her late fifties, had the inner arm tattoo removed. Said, what was it... can't remember, but there was a cross with rays behind it.'

'Fire of St George. They come from further up country than us. There's a lot of them.'

'She said. She was an angry woman, cursed a lot of people, then cried and hugged me when it was gone. She didn't have enough money, so I said no worries, but she came back the next day, tried to give me a gold necklace to pay. Cried and hugged me again when she left that time too!'

'I can definitely pay.' Lee starts scrabbling in his pocket. 'I've got—'

'Hey, no worries! I believe you! Now relax, this will sting a bit.'

41

Ben reluctantly concludes his business, in the form of a large hessian bag of solar tile fascias, digital components and a couple of antennae that protrudes from each side of the bag like horns. Two buckles suggesting eyes make the assemblage look like a hastily assembled representation of a gormless god. The contents of the bag, their potential for connection to the sky, their bringing of power and words have more in common with the gods than just its eerie anthropomorphic form. Ben explains how he hopes to use the antennae to make a connection to the grid so that messages and conversations can be exchanged. Perhaps, he hopes tentatively, they will be able to speak, now and then.

Isolde takes the citytrain to the edge of London to see Ben off on his return walk. She finds herself walking with him for the first part of the journey. She goes far as the garden where she first rested a few months before. Now it is colder. Distant trees look drawn onto the sky with a pen dipped in thin ink. The colours of late autumn, growth died back and muted, are perhaps more abundant in decay than in the green of summer, but except for splashy dots of red and yellow, or the dark swipe of a stem, they come from a subtle range. Intimate colours that require close attention to be noticed, tones shifting in tiny fragments.

Back in her apartment, she twirls a leaf, picked up as they walked. There is a tracery of holes on one side of the central stem. On the other, only the fragile veins remained. A marker perhaps of how much has passed, since the summer only a little more than half a year before when she had first walked that way. She felt sad saying goodbye to Ben. He is steady and kind, unobtrusively giving his friendship with love and care. She doesn't want to lose that, she had realised quite suddenly as they stood awkwardly at the side of the old A12. In the end they hugged, for longer than expected. She watched him leave, the face of the gormless god lolling on his back, waiting to be charged up with mighty power, with sacred usefulness. For what is a god, if he or she is not useful?

Lee to begin with is morose, afraid he will never find a way that will shield him from the past and take him into a new future. But soon, like so many other seventeen-year-old he has met people, is at loose in the city, skidding from friend to friend. He has quite a bit of money after all: stolen, he confides, from the village on the night he left. But it isn't going to last long and Isolde is anxious about him in a number of ways. She worries that he will fall into trouble, or meet an unscrupulous man keen to exploit a naive newcomer. She worries that he will get stopped, deported, imprisoned even. She feels responsible for him, happy when things go well, glad to be able to help him when she can, anxious when she can't. She begins to feel something like a parent.

But she has her own knots to untangle. The ease with which she returns to normal, back where she has started, leaves her with a heavy heart. She signs up for three weeks' worth of employment that thankfully she can complete from home. Dull days in the apartment while Lee skips excitedly around his new playground with reckless abandon is not what she wants, but she wants even less to be among a new crowd of co-workers, either getting through the weeks in the temp space with their heads down, or trying to bond with the others working on small pieces of a puzzle they'll never see complete.

She opens a screen, logs in. A message arrives – her opportunity to take up her rights under the Restoration of Justice Act, should she wish to do so, is available to her the following day.

The door opens and Faisal calls out a greeting. She comes out of the bedroom. They hug, awkward in a new closeness that comes from sharing a home.

'Hey Fais, how are you doing? Good to see you. We should probably talk about the apartment.'

'To be honest, it's no problem at the moment. It's working out quite well staying with Becca.' He smiles happily, checking through shopping he puts on the table. 'I thought, if you don't mind, I'd just leave a bit of my stuff here, come back now and then when I need it and, you never know, maybe move in with Becca full-time soon.'

'That's no problem, yeah, great.'

Faisal makes them both a coffee then tidies and gathers his belongings into two large bags. Isolde sits, twiddling a teaspoon, doing nothing. Soon Faisal is done – two bags: one for the cupboard, one to take with him.

'I'll let you know if I'm going to be back, and stay in touch, won't you?'

'Of course. Good luck at Becca's; hope it works out.'

'So, are you back for good? I thought you were going to stay Out.'

'I don't know, Fais. Nothing seems to be the logical answer at the moment.'

'Well, you've had a bit of a hard time, from what I can gather, so, take it easy on your bones.'

Isolde feels an unexpected drop, a pulse in her throat. Faisal and she have not known each other well enough to become close friends, but something about the sincerity and kindness of a happy man connects her weary words to the deeper part of her soul. She holds herself in check until it passes.

'I'm getting there. And yeah, I'll try.' She smiles back at him then, after a brief hug, goes to the bathroom to wash her face. He picks up his bag and leaves for his optimistic new home.

She pushes her hair back, grown well past her eyebrows since her last fringe crop, the rest is past her shoulders. She smooths the black hair flat against her head. The clippers are in a cupboard under the sink. She reaches for them, starts to run the cold buzz across her temple, the slightly sickening vibrations humming against her skull as the hair drops onto the counter and the floor. She shears her head methodically, staring at herself in the glass. When the hair is gone there is a strange combination of paleness and dark shadow across her scalp. Vulnerable, newly exposed skin speckled with black.

She collects up the hair, lays it on the table. It isn't quite long enough to twist easily, it requires a tight grip that soon makes her fingers ache. But with care, she twists it into twine, adding length as she goes. She binds the ends with a needle and thread. She marvels at the strength of the slender cord, its animal roughness as she pulls it across the bridge of her nose, feeling the prickle of single hairs that protrude like bristles, losing their softness. She goes to the pocket of her jacket, pulls out the nettle twine with the anchor and Lee's orange ribbon. She finds a plain cotton bag, part of a gift set of beauty products that she had thrown away after three years of standing untouched on the bathroom counter. She coils the different fibres and places them in the bag, folding over the top. She wonders how the flax is growing, whether Ben is keeping an eye on it.

Jesse

42

Mister's head hangs forward, a low incline along his spine, across the planes of his skull. His eyes have lost interest in the sights and movements and chase-ables around him. His nose follows only that which is directly ahead, ignoring the temptations, the scents and stories that line the path. He remembers them. *That smell, yes I have known that one. That is new, or perhaps not. Who can tell?* He walks, steadily, in Jesse's wake.

Chorus

patient old friend
you will be missed

another chance to learn
that love
weaves across what first seems unbridgeable divides
and binds all living things

They walk at an amble down the lane, past the cows' field. Jesse is thinking back over the last months, trying to learn the lessons, to find something that will reduce the score of failure. The ease of their parting is a relief. But that ease, it echoes too, like a warning. How natural it seems for him to be alone. How likely it seems that he will stay that way. He looks at his old friend, his companion. He fears their parting most of all, knowing it can't be far off.

After a few days he calls Jada. They take to having long conversations where not much is said. Jada works between the raised beds; he catches glimpses of her passing across the screen, a blur of leaves as she picks up the phone and moves to a different part of the garden. They pass intermittent comments across the waves. Sometimes she shows Jesse something, a bone she has dug up or a curled leaf sheltering the dense white gauze of a web, the startling colour shots of acid that burn in a fallen leaf. Her gloved fingers fumble close to the screen to show these little treasures. Jesse sits in the gloomy house, on the floor next to Mister's bed, his back against the wall. The contact with Jada soothes him. He misses her with a longing that takes him by surprise. He imagines her, next to him, one of his hands resting as it now is on Mister, the other holding one of the miraculous, strong hands inside the too-big work gloves. It makes him feel a strange kind of guilt, and it makes him sadder. But he acknowledges properly for the first time that he carries Jada in a pocket of longing sewn into his heart. He sees that he always has. He pushes such hopeless thoughts aside, in shock at the revelation, in disgust at his betrayal of their friendship.

Chorus

yes
love for us is safe, a simple thread
that binds the world

for you, it twists, contains so many strands
love for you is a complex, plaited cord

a tangle
a fetter
a lifeline

As they are about to hang up, she asks if he is OK. His reassurances don't convince her, because she asks again.

'I'm OK, Jay, I'm just a bit... well, just deciding what to do.' He longs to ask her to come. He longs to go to see her but dreads it. She would be horrified.

He and Mister go for a walk. He sits in Marshal's car until he can see stars in a thin strip of sky above the tree line, below the low-slung roof line. Mister snores gently, curled up on the passenger seat. Snails crawl out from the dark caves of the wheel arches, trail silky ways across the windscreen.

He wonders in unsettling snatches what it will mean to be himself without Mister, but he swerves from the thought, the savage intrusion. Depression sinks into him. He is weighed down by a sense of failure. He becomes essential in a joyless, passive manner, reduced to the most basic needs of living. There is work, there is food to be eaten, there is work. The worst thing would be going back to the city, sitting across a gulf from Marshal, unable to sustain any connections, hampered by the terrible desire to blow up his friendship with Jada, wrecking even that bond. He will just stay. There is work; there is food to be grown and eaten – at least therein lies an achievement.

43

In the reclaimed pre-school, the women have created a vibrant community. They grow enough food to make a fresh daily meal for themselves and for the elderly residents of the estate. There is a Saturday lunch for all who want to attend. A buzz gathers around them – a sense of hope. And hope is precious. Hope can be so easily swept aside by reality. Jada feels energised by the women, the Claimants. They are proud of what they have achieved and the standing it has given them among their community, and as the word spreads, further afield. They look outward, increase the ambition of their plans.

But she always feels the tug of caution, held close to her chest as though it is a betrayal. She has spent time around other political groups, enough to know that the state can be a spiteful enemy. It adds the scratch of fear for friends like Stella who stray into talk of rebellion, change, protest. *Small victories are safest*, she thinks, *small hopes that sneak under reality's radar*. Reality is the power of the state, and it is defended, passively, by a wide, sludgy moat of acceptance.

Jada sits on her bench, or the edge of a bed, she thinks hard, fingers fidgeting, strategies rearranging and bumping. She would love to be free, working in her own garden, unfettered by the dreary caution of city life. She works out where she is, what can be done, what next. She examines pitfalls and carefully polishes her hopes. And then she stops, drifts for benediction into no thought, lets it all curl away to be lost in the sky, like the smoke, catching light, shaping shadows.

And thus, she is primed, when Stella, her idealism turning away from the wrongs of society and toward the future of her daughter, introduces her to a group who have moved out to an abandoned farm to live self-sufficiently. They are part of a small and scattered movement, the New Agrarians. They draw a parallel with the Claimants, saying they are Reclaimants. They reclaim the land and the right to farm it.

Stella, a firestarter by nature, is full of enthusiasm for the possibility of a fresh start, a new beginning. Jada, though used to tempering her friend's wild enthusiasms, starts to feel it too. And both women are drawn to this vision of a place for a girl to grow up.

The women under their Claimants banner have taken over the work in the garden, they know all they need to know to keep it going without her. She has the choice to start anew in another unpromising corner of the city, or as she sees it clearly, suddenly, to start her own life. The two friends, with growing excitement, plan a visit to the farm.

Isolde

44

Jada had made Isolde promise that she will visit Jesse, that she will pass on a message. Isolde had tried to wriggle out from this horribly intimate chore. But Jada had become fierce. Manipulative even. She had talked of the nearness of her death, of her need for Isolde to help her, that she is the only one who can, it is a great wrong that has been done, is she really unwilling to put this small, tiny piece of it right? Hiding her crossness, Isolde had promised.

So tomorrow Isolde will go to the prison. But it troubles her, what she will say, how she can in any way make amends. Unable to sleep, she walks, out into the lulling business of the night. The city grits and rolls, like shingle. A clatter, constant enough to soothe – with a certain caution, as the waves can knock a person over, the multitude of stones can singly bruise. Not all the edges get taken off.

The city hums. A miracle of collaboration. She sits on a bench in the park. Her shadow cast by the moon is kept company by two more, from dim sensor lights lining the path.

No one made the moon, no hand, not a god or devil or angel put the moon together. The lights, everything about them other than that which names them – they are touched by so many hands. Metal dug and cast and recast and reclaimed and binned and sorted and finally cast one more time. So many men and women have made that story. The last time, coming to the current form, the hands were few, didn't touch the metal that made the shade and the pole so often. It had slid on conveyer belts, through presses that spat the correct forms into existence. One hand of a man who oversaw the transport had rested on the pyramid of lamp posts belted to a pallet. Another had leaned on the cylinder that became the light behind her, eight years ago in a depot, as he checked the screen, the destination mapped in codes and instructions read without his interpretation. Another two had guided with the barest touch as it was placed into the hole next to the cement path. Boys on blades had stopped to watch, a woman jogged, took a path across the grass around the workers, noticed the light the next day when she jogged past again. Now other joggers sometimes stop to hold it as they stretched their legs in balletic poses, children grab and swing in games of chase. Sometimes a furtive hand will stick to it a protest, a call to arms, too small and too quickly removed to ferment a revolution.

Electronic battery circuits inside, stripped from a mirror-form Babel tower that spiralled down into the ancient earth of Australia. Not touched but accounted for, passed along, by many eyes and fingers that swiped screens to send them on. Plastic cooked up from oils watched over by eyes half-shut and gritty in desert sun. Eyes that watched meters, checked calculations, overlooked reports of financiers and markets analysts. Oil driven in one, two, three lorries, made by countless other machine-operating men and women who walked on feet cased in boots made by other men and women, who ate bread baked by other men and women.

The light will fade, if she sits still enough, or walks away from the bench, made from old bottles and wrappers, stripped, blasted and bonded into a semi-useful material in a factory in the Ukraine where, now, one woman sits in a small control room, drinking coffee-flavoured hot drink, reading a letter from an old friend, losing herself in dreams of their young days as she babysits the machines.

The infernal connections. No one could make a city deliberately.

Isolde doesn't stay in the park for long. It's cold and damp. Tomorrow she will walk south again. Through the city toward Purley Maximum Security Prison. Tomorrow, she will go and meet the man who did not kill her mother.

Chorus

a complex pattern and a simple sight
night sky and stars
or the patterns of roots under sweet meadow herbs

you can't expect to grasp it all
– just find your patch in the sun, under the stars, and
be glad of it

45

The bag Isolde took on her travels is still propped by the front door – a sop to uncertainty. Perhaps a reminder that she could pick it up to leave again. She pulls out packets of dried food that she hadn't eaten, the cloth she had used for summer bedding. Twigs still snag, prickles of dry leaf fall to the floor. Clothes she wore last to work on the farm. She pulls everything out and puts it to wash. Tucked in an inside pocket she finds what she is searching for. Isolde had told Jada she wouldn't be able to give anything to Jesse, but Jada had insisted, saying that she would do this thing for him even so.

Isolde pulls out the square of hemmed cloth that Jada had embroidered with two initials, two letter Js. They are boldly stitched with curlicues that reach out to the raw edges of the white square of fabric then trail off as loose thread, as though to exist beyond their confines. The letters are delicately and richly embroidered, magnificent. Each is like an initial from a medi-aeval manuscript, telling of two mysterious lives. She smooths the cloth, presses out the creases across her thigh. She folds it carefully and tucks it into the fabric bag with the anchor on its loop of twine, the ribbon and the rough tail of twisted black hair. Talismans – though she shies away from the thought, feeling foolish.

The streets gleam. Low winter sun skids in under a cover of dark clouds, the remnants of a downpour in the early hours, soaking Isolde as she walks back from the park. The light is silver; railings pour like mercury, the streets clad with a steel sheen. Faces are bright, as though cheerful, with the cold.

She doesn't know how to talk to Jesse, now that she no longer holds him responsible for killing her mother. She doesn't know how to talk to someone wronged so badly, when she has no resources, nor the power of will for the fight to put it right. She feels ashamed that she can't even start such a fight. She feels ashamed of the years he has spent, of her unknowing collusion in the injustice. She feels shame and sadness for the hate she has directed at him. What a thing it is, to be so malleable in the face of a persuasive story.

Lights blink to guide her through to the corridor. She walks toward the cell. She's as nervous as she had been on the other visits, but her anxiety this time is cooked from a different recipe. However uncomfortable the situation had been, she felt she knew her place, her status within it. Now she has lost that certainty, the horrible clarity of righteousness.

She sits carefully, in the middle of the bench, facing the cell. Jesse is bent over the small table. He doesn't notice her arrival, though he must have seen the shutters rising a few feet in front of him. She sits quietly, waiting for him to become aware of her. Voices clatter from the other end of the corridor; she looks up to see a man jabbing his forefinger toward the mesh. His voice cries loud, joined by a cautionary beeping when he gets too close. When she turns back, Jesse is looking at her, paintbrush poised above the page.

'Hello, it's… I'm Isolde.'

He looks at her. 'I know that.'

'Sorry, it's just you said you sometimes forget, and you looked a bit unsure.'

'Yes, well, I am that too.'

'Is it often noisy, like that?' She gestures with a dip of her head along the corridor.

'Sometimes.' He turns back to his painting.

'Jesse, I…' She tails off, uncertain about what she can say. He doesn't seem to hear. She wonders if he is ever called by his name. All the letters she has been sent refer to him as Prisoner D191-H14.

'I've been to see Jada.' He looks up at this. 'She asked me to give you a message.' She holds her fingers together in her lap, a clinched home for awkward anxiety. She feels exposed, her shaved head suddenly vulnerable and raw.

'Jada, how… where is she? She's OK?'

'Yes, though she is very ill. But she is alive and she is happy, I think. She wanted me to show you something that she made for you.' She pushes a hand into her pocket, unfolds the fabric.

'I'll bring it up so that you can see.' Isolde walks toward the mesh, keeping careful distance, holding the square of fabric at the two top corners. She turns it around to check it is the right way up. Jesse peers, leans over the corner of the table.

'I can't come too close, it will buzz me,' he says. She holds it up higher, so that he isn't stooping, holds it up to his eye level, above her own. The handkerchief-sized square obscures her view of his face. She doesn't know if he is still gazing at the design, but he doesn't move. She peers round and sees his face, rough skin, battered with emotion. His eyes deep with tears.

'I wish I could give it to you. She asked me to tell you that she has never loved anyone as much as she loved you.'

'We… when Mister died. She came. We went to the seawall, we ran. She said she loved me then, too. She—'

Jesse crumples. He steadies himself from a fall by reaching for the upright of the bunk bed, resisting gravity's temporary assault. The effort holds him still, then he speaks again.

'I think of that day. Impossible to be happier. Everything was beautiful on that white wall, walking over the sea. Our shadows on the waves.'

'I don't know what to do with this. I just wish I could give it to you, but I've checked and they won't let me.'

Jesse stands, clutching the bed-frame.

'I wish there was something I could do.'

He remains silent, his hand gripping firmly, his eyes reaching somewhere distant in time and space over Isolde's shoulder. Then the door at the end of the corridor opens, the man in the pale mac heads toward them. Isolde feels a horrible panic rising. She turns toward him, tries to explain the mistaken nature of his blame. But the man just nods toward her, unhearing, as though to a colleague seen daily, a person sharing the same routine chores, a collaborator in the same dull grind. He ignores Isolde's words, sits on the bench and begins to spit his hatred.

She watches with a new horror. Over the hissing torrent of the words, she hears Jesse speaking.

'He lost his wife, Barbara. It's almost as if I've come to know her over all these years.'

Jesse looks up at Isolde as she tries to protest the unfairness.

'He may as well blame me,' he says, with no bitterness. 'It makes no difference.'

Isolde feels her tough resolve, the shield so tightly held for so many years, slip. She feels the hideous injustice in the real and the mistaken pain of the two men before her. She retreats into the dark end of the corridor, lays her palms over her eyes. As she gathers herself, the visitor stands to leave. She is torn between staying to talk to Jesse, and following him, to try and engineer a way to reshape his understanding. Jesse is painting again, his head bent over the table. He shows no signs of waiting for her to return, so she walks along to the exit, behind the old man.

He walks painfully slowly, drifting slightly, listing, to the left. She follows him onto a train, then to a residential block of quiet streets. He lives on the ground floor in a grid block of narrow, single-occupancy apartments. She watches him from across the street as he checks a bird feeder hanging on a pole in the tiny strip of front garden then opens the door and disappears inside.

She marks the address. But for what? How to tell a man who hasn't forgiven, hasn't moved on, hasn't learned to let go, that all of his hatred is wasted?

She sits on the low wall of a garden opposite. She sinks her hands into her pockets, finding the cloth Jada has made. Her eyes roam over the detail of the stitches, the array of choices made in response to previous choices or in pursuit of new. The threads make numerous, beguiling patterns. Stitches splay out in a spray at the ends of the letters, reach the edge of the cloth and trail off over the edge. She smooths and carefully folds it back into the cotton bag.

The cold creeps inside her clothing. Her mind races. *Ring the door bell, explain his mistake. Write a letter. Bring Arthur with his research to explain; watch the man crumble with shame as he realises he has been unfair to an innocent man. Persuade him to stop going to the prison without explaining why. Talk to him. Heal him. Make him better.*

What difference would it make? Someone has left a bomb because the death of someone, of that man's wife, it turns out, suited their purposes. How could that ever be made better? She shivers, wrapping herself smaller, pressing her body against itself to squeeze out the cold. But the cold is too much. She stands, looks around to get her bearings and heads for the walk home.

46

Isolde tries to distract herself with work. Lee comes and goes, sleeps when he is in the apartment, is evasive about his time, his progress with getting papers but is not around enough for Isolde to be able to help him make any headway. She hides her annoyance with him, knows really she is just finding a target for her own dissatisfactions.

The mark on Lee's neck fades – the tattoo is gone. There is a patch of skin that is paler, an outline that could represent a natural, uneven distribution of skin tone. He still wears scarves and ties, is still self-conscious, as though his history can be read in that small island of light skin. But he is happy, and he is having fun. Isolde wants to scold him into getting his papers, wants to voice her own frustration that he is still precariously balanced. But she doesn't know how; she can't quite grasp her own position – she has no rights to make demands.

The torpor that had sent her to the prison all those months before, that has been shaken out. But it hasn't gone. It has taken a different form. What she has learned, the options it has put before her, the facts that have been changed – it's a new kind of problem. So she distracts herself with work, putting in long and determined hours. It is a suitable strategy, for a number of days. But the intensity of her effort means that she finishes the project early, has a week paid at the end of the contract with nothing to do.

Chorus

come out
come back out to the fields and grasses
come out to where there is space for hearts to open

In the prison, when there are no people in the corridor and the grille is down, there's a blank wall before the little table. He stares into the off-white paint, then looks down at the imperfectly torn-out pages on the table. A diagram shows a river flow around the body. Where is there room for it all? Miles of tubes, gallons of liquid, strata of fat and muscle and bone. Ropes and pulleys, hinges, sieves, sensors and builders. Trails of liquid that start from the meat, from fat organs, reach out, as though to beyond, so small do they become. So infinite.

He stands, facing the blank wall where, on other days, people look at him, speak with him or at him through a fine mesh grille. He stands, pulls into his mind the image of the hemmed white cloth with the two letters. J, for Jada, for Jesse. He stands, tall, stretches his arms up, like the trailing curling threads that spill out of the letter, reach the edge. Splays his fingers, reaching to overspill the space that contains him.

Jesse

47

As the days shorten, Mister stops going outside. He doesn't want to walk. In the deep of winter, a few days before Christmas, Mister stops eating. Jesse stays by Mister's side. He pulls the blankets from his bed onto the floor, next to the sofa, nests Mister into them, so that Jesse can get close, sleep curled protectively around him. Jesse uses a spoon to try and get Mister to take some water. Mister doesn't lift his head, and doesn't swallow. Little scoops of water dampen the blanket under his chin.

Mister's light fades; he dies, he runs into the woods, he swerves through long grass, chasing the pounding feet of a small boy. A breath rumbles from him one final time. Jesse curls like a teardrop around the body of his dearest companion and friend, so still, so different, so familiar.

Weak sun eases through curtains. It is Christmas Eve. Jesse calls Marshal. He tells him haltingly, that Mister has died. He tells him that he wishes he were there. Marshal wishes he were too. There is little to say. After some moments of awkward silence, Marshal makes to leave, even on Christmas Eve, reaching for his coat to go to work.

'Dad, please don't go, not yet,' Jesse asks. Marshal nods,

smiles a watery smile at his son. He sits on the arm of a chair. Jesse props the screen and moves restlessly around the living room. Marshal is moved by the scene, the sight of his son in the house where he had been a child. He marvels at the man his son has become. His memory floods with all the ages of boyhood, the lifts and hugs and carries, the easy way they embraced each other. Playing and chasing, talking about rivers, a seagull, why the house was safe from floods. He longs to remove the burden of sadness from Jesse, but knows, perhaps for the first time, that he can't. And with that understanding comes relief. At last, he feels no guilt. He can't protect his son from the pain of loss. All he can do is love him. A burden lifts from Marshal; he struggles to hold back tears that, though formed in sorrow, are a kind of gratitude and a kind of breathtaking relief. He simply has to love Jesse, and that he can do.

Jesse buries Mister in the clearing at the back of the old stone barn. He picks flints out of the grass, makes a small cairn. He walks through the woods, along the stream. He tries to lose himself, but an awkwardness of body won't let him slip into the being of the world. He is clunky, mortal; he is alone.

48

Not so far away, Jada and Stella begin a new and hopeful year on the farm. They maintain the safety net of a city connection, and at the end of January, Stella goes back to London for a few weeks until the birth of her second daughter.

So much is happening on the farm, and Jada is thrilled by the possibilities. Possibilities are where all Jada's notions of happiness rest. Hope not undone by reality, that is what she asks for. And that is what she has.

The barn becomes a living space, with a new raised floor, a lining of timber and a patchwork of reclaimed plasterboard and plywood. As it gets colder, they scavenge and add curtains, like tapestries in an ancient castle. The walls are too thin to defeat the chill, so they build indoor tents for themselves, reducing the spaces until their own breath and bodies become the engine of warmth.

Jada becomes central to life at the farm. She brings knowledge and an evident passion to the work that leads others to defer to her. Stella brings a fierce ideology and different skills, having studied preserving, making jams and pickles, ways to store excess for future use or barter. They designate an outhouse as a storage and preparation room for the preserving of fruit and veg – the empty shelves a promissory note to success. The daughter of a group founder, a serious child of twelve named Leanne becomes Stella's apprentice in the pickle room as they make a start on a batch of cabbages. The first hurdle is storage vessels as most equivalent food coming on the freights is brought in compostable and non-reusable packs. When people make speculative gathering trips to nearby empty villages or the deserted parts of towns, Stella always puts in a request for glass jars with lids, full or empty. Sometimes people have a shelf of them, tucked away in a shed, or the back of a garage. People who once made jam, or who thought they might one day. As she gathers her supply, she guards them with jealous care.

Jada calls Jesse often. And often he doesn't reply. She worries about him. She wonders if she can persuade him to switch his strange and lonely existence for life with them at the farm. After weeks of distance and infrequent, listless conversations, she tells him that she will visit. Two weeks later, she sets off.

It is thirty-two miles. The train takes out twenty-five and Jada walks the rest. She is shocked when Jesse answers the door. The beard and old clothing are standard; for those living Out – distance from mirrors, shops, razors, washing machines leads to a natural run down of the finer points of fashion and style. But Jesse looks so changed her heart sinks. Thin, unkept in a way that worries her. He looks hollow, like a winter stalk. They hug. She wants to protectively cup the shoulder blade that sticks out under the thin shirt and worn old jumper, the wafer skin. She is glad she didn't leave her visit any longer.

And indeed, her presence is a cure. They spend two days, walking, talking over shared memories, filling the gaps since Jesse had first left. Before long, though still thin, still scruffy, Jesse loses the lifeless pallor. Their days together feed the spark that Jada's presence has reignited.

Jesse shows Jada the clearing, now closing into woodland, where he found Mister, and the cairn where the dog is buried.

They smoke a joint, some home-grown that Jada brought with her, sitting in Marshal's car. The tall shadows of meadow weeds waver in the late winter sun, muting the outside world. The joint makes Jesse feel sick. And then it makes him feel sad. And then, sitting side by side in the front seats of the car, it makes him rashly confessional.

'Jada, you know, I think I am in love with you. I think, I think I always was.' He freezes, in dread at what may come.

She is shocked, so used has she become to an insulating padding, a cautionary layer between them. But in that instant, she recognises that caution has been a cover for deeper, more frightening feelings. Depths glimpsed in a dark crystal emerge, become light. She is moved by the look of misery on his face and sees instantaneously the possibility of love. Her face is open, astonished. Jesse looks at her quickly, registers only her surprise and looks away, afraid he has done injury to the connection he prizes above all others. But this moment, it spirals right into her heart. She lifts a hand uncertainly, places it against the hollow of Jesse's cheek. She passes her hand slowly through the tangle of his hair, the under-cliff of his skull. She pulls him toward her. They embrace in the most awkward way, over the gearstick and the handbrake. Jesse is stuck, side-on. He reaches his arm across himself, rests it on Jada's upper arm. For the longest, saddest time, he thinks he is being consoled. Until Jada says, 'I love you too,' and twists him to face her, and kisses him.

That night is the sweetest, the hungriest of Jesse's life. They don't sleep until early morning, but when Jada wakes, mid-morning, she can hear the sound of Jesse already working outside, the cut and ring of a spade digging earth, turning clods and shaking out by hand the spent roots of brassicas.

She watches him, the bend of his back. His light brown hair falls down in lank strands as he bends over the spade. He is so familiar to her, and now she sees, more precious than she had thought possible.

She goes back to bed, to puzzle, to wonder at the turn of events. The beautiful surprise of it, the suspicion that, had she listened better, she mayn't have been so surprised. She thinks about hope becoming a present state. About hope becoming reality. She thinks she might feel scared, if she didn't feel so excessively happy.

Jesse has never been happier. He slides back into himself, a grown expression of the boy slinking through the woodlands and fields. He observes the beauty of the world with no words or thoughts to mark the observation. He feels again, that he is this world. He is the woods and the creatures of the woods. When in London, he is the people walking the pavements; he is the hope and love and dreams. He is the trees and fields. He is the bite of cold in the air and the rising warmth. He is the sudden sting of February's freezing hail, the whip of slender twigs in the unruly March breeze. He is the soft rain of April, the happy group of friends he watches running for shelter. He is the glorious opening of May, the ripe revealing, the luscious invitation, the plea to renewal that all flowers make.

Jada, for once, feels herself carried effortlessly by a fair wind and a friendly current. She finds that she loves Jesse in return, more than she ever expected. Because she trusts him, love offers her refuge she never allowed herself with previous, carefully chosen, lovers. They were, she sees now, chosen for her ability to leave them. Their unsuitability, their obvious flaws were what made them viable. With Jesse, she too finds herself whole. Her anxiety about the state of the world is cushioned by her contentment in her own world. For the first time, she allows herself to welcome happiness, not defer it. She puts it on at last, like a garment made for her by midnight tailors and wish weavers. She grows into herself, accruing strands of being that make her more.

They talk about what they should do. Jesse is reluctant to move to the farm. He doesn't want to leave the work he has done, and the new memories he has made. He is still raw about the death of Mister and that keeps him tied for a little while. They split their time. Days and weeks between their countryside homes, visits to London. Marshal is always glad to see them. He and Jada become close.

But Jada is restless with life in the village. She needs action, a plan, a project to build. She is so excited by all the possibilities of a collaborative, collective life, and so persuasive, that he promises he will give it a try. Finally, after a few nights in the upstairs bedroom of a little cottage, still cluttered with the furniture and possessions of a long-gone former tenant, the farm takes hold of Jesse.

He is fascinated as the talk turns to all that they don't know. The weather inconveniences a city gardener, a smallholding grower, but it is ally or foe to a farmer. Clay, silt, loam, incline, drainage – these are new frontiers. They do understand their own limitations and in their planning, try in earnest to gather as much as they can to mitigate for their lack, and it is this that hooks him.

After days sitting in on group meetings, where a big vegetable garden is planned, watching with pride as Jada explains the potential for larger crops, he falls into it. Jesse and Jada walk the lanes and field edges and he knows that he has found the place he wants to make a home. He can shrug out of his solitude, if he wants to. He understands at last that it is a choice.

The group is keen to have him, and his knowledge. They are offered the room for good. Jesse shutters up the house in the village once again. He promises Chetna and Mikel that he will be back. He sits by Mister's burial place. He visits the graveyard and says goodbye again.

Jada moves her stuff from the shared accommodation in the barn up into the cottage. She takes a top drawer of the dresser and arranges her saved and salvaged seeds in it. She puts a jar of wildflowers on the window sill. Jesse lies on the bed, arms stretched behind his head, watches her make a home in the room.

They walk on the beach, swim in the gritty bite of brown sea, take tide treasure back to the windowsill. They go on trips, to a cooperative up country where they trade honey so Jada can learn about keeping bees. They go for long coastal walks back to the village where Jesse's old house can be seen poking from the water, down past new marshes, through the swirling of sea birds, rolling and sheering through the hefty grey squalls of sky. They walk for half a day to the new seawall. They buy fish from a man at one end, char cook it on an open fire, eat it in grubby fingers as they walk, then toss the bones to the waves and run to the middle of the long causeway. Their faces are bright with pure happiness. The sea birds extend their reach, express their wild, twinned joy up to the heavens and all the way to the never near horizon.

Work and life at the farm blend harmoniously for Jesse and Jada. Jada grows food, Jesse refines systems to help grow food, and with all members of the group working together, they make exciting progress. In the evenings, the group share a meal, sometimes spinning out the time afterward as a group. Jesse and Jada like to be alone sometimes, going for a walk on the beach. Or they lie in the old, metal-framed bed with its high, striped mattress base. Jada goes to sleep while Jesse reads into the night. In the morning, she gets up first, often before the dawn. She uses the quiet time in the kitchen to plan her crops, her seed swaps, her rotations. Jesse joins her, leans over her shoulder for a hug, slowly waking into a day that Jada already has in her grasp.

One morning, Jesse comes into the kitchen to find Jada talking via screen to Stella, who is in London with her two daughters. She wants to bring them back to the safety of the farm, but things are frantic and worrying for the women of the collective, and they are coming under great pressure. Stella tells Jada about a raid on two of the women's homes. Nothing was found, but the change in tone is ominous. In equal proportion to the growth of their good reputation among the disenfranchised, they are smeared by ludicrous and harmful press stories and harassed by the police.

Stella is staying with Milos, who works with the Claimants and is part of another more overtly political group. Jesse likes Milos, they get on well, but he is intense and too certain, too assertive. But so, most of the time, is Stella. Jesse has seen Milos in meetings. He is persuasive, charismatic, a good speaker. People look up to him. And Jesse has always suspected it is this, as much as justice, that Milos craves.

Jada is fretful. Her oldest friend, too often close to the edges of calamity, is in a vulnerable position, unwilling to leave equally vulnerable people in the lurch. She looks wrung out with misery, her face thinned and reddened by the exhaustion of a new baby and an anxious situation. The cry of her youngest causes her to end the call. Jada knows the patterns that may follow, has stood by her friend as, through younger years, she used drugs and damnation to counter the weight of growing up the child of an addicted mother and callous father. Jada secretly fears the lurking danger, not only of the state, to the two young girls she loves with the same ferocity she loves their mother. She tells Jesse that she has to go to London to bring Stella and the girls back to the farm. Jesse, in his turn, caring for Jada, decides to go too.

They arrive in London the next day. Outside the station, they hug before going their separate ways. Jada will go to Stella, Jesse is heading back to stay with Marshal. They will meet in a few days to return to the farm, Jada hopes with Stella and the girls. Jesse has often noticed how alive Jada is when she interacts with them. He thinks, suddenly, standing on the station forecourt with his arms around her shoulders, about them having their own child, one day, maybe soon. He tries not to smile for his own happiness when they are here for the unhappiness of her friend, but she catches it, and smiles herself.

'What?'

'Nothing Jay, you just look lovely.'

She beams at him. She looks around as though sniffing the air, listening.

'You know, it just doesn't feel right here anymore.'

'No, it doesn't. But we'll be back at the farm soon. We can build that seedbed by the end of the week, and then I'll make a start on a playhouse for the kids.'

They part ways, promising to speak later. Jesse walks the few miles to the apartment. Marshal has been waiting for him, and they embrace warmly. Jesse notices little signs of age, a slight tilt in the frame and hollowing of cheek, thinner hair perhaps. But he also looks fitter in some way, tanned and healthy. Jesse is amazed to learn that Marshal has taken the afternoon off work to spend time with him.

They sit in the living room, and Jesse tells Marshal what is happening at the farm, all the exciting possibilities that lie ahead. He gropes for a way to express the importance of it all, to make Marshal see what it all means and why it matters. He talks about the food they grow, how many people they can support. He talks in technical terms to convey a heartfelt message. He talks a language he thinks Marshal will understand, demonstrates that he has done the rational thinking, checked the numbers. He tells him that a doctor might be joining them soon. Jesse doesn't mention that the doctor refers to himself as a healer. He was a surgeon before he discovered a more spiritual aspect to his medical practice, and that is enough.

Marshal is delighted to see his son in such content and animated form. Jesse is gratified by Marshal's interest in his new life. He asks searching questions along familiar lines, which seem to be answered to his satisfaction. 'No, no one claims the stipend.' 'No, they don't pay taxes, but they do pay the first tier of health cover, and that is the only thing they get from the state.' 'No, it's not strictly legal, but the government has stated that no evictions will take place unless a specific claim from a previous landowner comes to court.'

They move on to talk about Jesse's current project. He has laid pipes and a pump to take water from a nearby stream to augment the rain harvest. The conversation stops being an interview, becomes the even-handed back and forth of enthusiasts talking over a shared passion. They go on to discuss the merits of various DIY water-heating systems. Marshal becomes almost as enthusiastic as Jesse is himself about the projects and the possibilities that lie ahead.

Jesse goes to the kitchen to get them both another beer. As is his habit, Marshal turns on a news channel. There is the usual fare – specialists in outrage pushing a hyped version of the party line. Jesse lets it go, for once allowing Marshal the age-old explanation that: yes, he knows it's suspect, manipulative, downright dishonest, but he still wants to know what is going on.

Jesse calls Jada every night before going to sleep. Stella is calm, a relieved Jada tells him, foregrounding her role as mother over the clamour of a new crisis. On the fourth day, Jada tells him they are ready to leave. The Claimants have quieted their collective gatherings, will wait for clearer waters. They can all go back to the farm the next day.

Isolde

50

Isolde leaves the apartment early on a cold morning and walks to the market, sits at one of the tables overlooking the stalls, orders a coffee and croissant. The stall holders are still setting up. The sky is only just beginning to lighten. Big lights in the roof warm the space but the wind reaches in from the open ends, pulls the warmth to swirl and dissipate on still empty streets.

The woman from the spice stall fills her bowls with domes of bright yellow, burning red, pale brown; powders and seeds are scooped into a precise cupola by her practised hand. The woman is tall, slim and dark. Her black hair, shot with grey at the temple, is cut square at her jaw and shaped by a loose curl. She chats with the man next to her as she works, easy conversation and laughter passing between them. He is older, ruddy complexioned, his thin, white hair scraped back with some kind of grease or dressing. He holds an enormous mug in one hand and gestures with the other as they chat.

Isolde watches them, their ordinary, daily connection. Such a simple thing. Not even the grand drama of love. Just the friendship of co-workers. But connection is everything. It is everything that Jesse has lost. Just in that light blessing of unimportant friendships, he has lost so much. A friendly arm across the shoulders, someone to talk to. And as for those grander dreams; a life with Jada, perhaps with children, grandchildren of their own. Such small changes and he might be with her now, fetching soothing tea, stopping by to help Ben plan a rebuild of the solar power, stashing little jars of Leanne's pickles to save for later in the year. Perhaps she would more jealously guard her time if Jesse were with her now. Such small changes and it would all be so different.

Jesse lies the whole day on the bunk, overwhelmed by a strange exhaustion. A dread pain, a heaviness, in his heart. It's been so long; he is so tired. He longs for escape. He turns inward, the only place he has to go. He blurs his mind, slides into nothing. He longs for it to be over.

He finds the shore. He waits, not wanting to hurry it for fear that he will lose what is coming.

He lies still, swaddled in what darkness the blanket can offer. He turns to the wall: away from here. As much away from here as he can be.

He watches a sea fret rise; it gathers softly, the sound of small waves blending with the blood in his ears. The imperfect darkness is overlaid with the brown of the North Sea and the beach that looks like builders' sand. The thin black of his imperfect darkness is a unifying filter. The thin white of the sea fret blends outwards to the dark, holds him, a membrane between two possible worlds.

He waits. Soon he feels his bare feet in the sand. Damp and grainy cold on his skin. He wonders where he has left his slippers. He leans down, bending his knees, with a suppleness that has been gone for years. Crouching on his heels he puts his hands into the sand, rubs damp grains between his fingers.

He picks up a piece of wood, a stick worn smooth and evenly brown by the water. It has one black line that circles a small knot in the wood. Each time he turns it, the pattern, so simple, shifts a little. The line dances ahead of his eyes, showing all the paths through the fibres of the wood. He puts it in his pocket. He catches site of Mister now and then, just ahead of him.

Further along the tidemark, a shell, soft pink inside a bone, and a razor-blade sharp edge, it is more of a shell, more bone, more pink, more razor. He knows it somehow, and marvels. He puts it in his pocket. A feather, bold as a sword, sticks from a knot of seaweed. He pulls it up. It twirls the flight lines of the sea birds, shimmering wakes revealing how those masters slice the air. The same slice cleaves his chest, as devastatingly light as an airborne wing. He puts the feather in his pocket.

A little further, a cloth, dampened and creased. He picks it up, smoothing it out to flatness, letting the fog soothe the creases away. Two letters, stitched in memory of love, in honour of not being forgotten. The stitches flicker with the joy he could have known and it fills him up. He puts it under his shirt, the damp cools his skin.

Mister waits, just ahead. Standing up tall, Jesse takes a deep breath, pulling the cold air, the fog, the droplets of sea and salt and youth and love into lungs that expand to take in more than he could possibly need in one last breath.

The sea filters into him; waterways, the reverse pattern of a river flowing into the ocean. The sea flows into him, branching first in the trachea, dividing, dividing again, flowing into all the spaces of his body in smaller and smaller channels. It takes him in, to blessed darkness.

51

An alert pings on Isolde's device. A reminder from the Justice Department. She opens it to check the time she can visit Jesse. But the letter is different, the shapes of the text unfamiliar. Her rights under the Restoration of Justice Act are void, Prisoner D191-H14 is now categorised deceased. This ends all rights granted under the Restoration of Justice Act. Rights of access to Purley Maximum Security Prison Facility are rescinded. Any attempts to gain access to the facility will now constitute a breach of law and may be punishable by fine or imprisonment.

Her hand freezes mid-air, holding the coffee. It takes two reads to grasp the meaning of the letter. Jesse is dead. There is nothing she can do for him; even if she had been able to formulate a way to help it is too late. He had lived for almost thirty years as an exhibit in a staged drama. Wheeled out in his cage to take part in the carney show. The state, that most unscrupulous of impresarios, had required his services. For what? Revenge, authority, power, safety. Roll up, roll up. A horrible side show to the official circus.

Isolde feels hollow. A bell with no clapper. A shape of nothing, empty and bottomless. She will have to tell Jada. The emptiness sways, like sickness, inside. She looks across the market. The woman from the spice stall is now talking to a customer, smiling as she points to one of the bowls, her fingers making a gesture of smallness – a pinch of this, a dab of extra taste. The man next to her holds his mug against his chest, other hand in his pocket. He gazes up into the rafters. She has a sudden urge to go over, to make a connection, to tell him about this new unfairness, about the man who died alone, slowly executed for a crime that he hadn't committed. She has the urge to tell him that she is implicated, stained by an unwitting collusion, that she doesn't know how to make amends.

She leaves the market. She feels a sadness, a loss that makes no sense to her. She has only seen Jesse three times. Spoken of him perhaps a handful more. But since she arrived at the farm and heard her past retold in a different voice, she has thought of him. Thoughts that intruded like a scratch on reading glasses, a small stone in a shoe. He had been wronged and she was somehow implicated in that wrong. And what was she to do about that? If there is an answer, it is too late.

She had heard him say that the man in the pale mac might as well blame him, Jesse. What had he meant? There was at least acceptance in that sentiment, but of what? Perhaps Jesse had felt himself guilty by association even in the clearer days when his muddled memory didn't tell him he was guilty. Perhaps his soul had accepted his fate. Perhaps he understood the anger of the other man, his need to pay out in his words, to hurt what had hurt him. Perhaps he felt in his reduced ability to connect with others, he was able to do this one thing for another human being.

Would that man be glad that Jesse is dead? So implacable, intractable is his performance of what once must have torn him apart, that she can't imagine him being able to let go. He must need the act of rage as much as he needs the idea of revenge.

Without a specific intention, she walks in the direction of his apartment.

Soon she is outside the door. She knocks. There is a quiet shuffle before it is opened.

'Did you hear? He's dead.'

'Yes, I… how are you here?'

'I followed you. I wanted to tell you something.'

'Well, this is strange. This is very strange.' He looks at Isolde, a knotted hand gripping the door as he leans toward her. She fishes in her pocket, pulling out the cotton bag, and the embroidered square.

'You see this? I don't want to cause trouble, or upset you, or anything really. But that man, the one who died in prison, he didn't plant the bomb. But I know that might be too much to go into now, to ask you to believe. But I just thought I'd show you this, and say that his name is Jesse, J for Jesse, you see?' She holds up the embroidery. 'This was made by Jada, who is probably going to die soon too. And she never got to visit Jesse. And it wasn't his fault. Your wife dying and my mum. All that. And I guess you don't want to hear it, so I won't go on about it, but he didn't do it. And it sounds stupid but I was worried about you. Because what are you going to do now?'

He stands still, a look of gentle concern on his face. The anger she feared stirring is nowhere. Isolde continues, spilling jumbled thoughts.

'He said to me that you and he had grown old together. And so I thought it might be a shock. And also, I hoped that one day you might understand that I'm not blaming you for being angry with him. It's just that he didn't do it. They did.'

The man reaches out a hand to slow her, to hush her torrent of words.

'I think it would be a good idea if you stopped, maybe went home to bed?'

Her words have been spent in force because she had antic-ipated an equal or greater force of resistance from him. His ferocity in the prison had seemed so implacable. She under-stands the absurdity of the moment, her incoherent babble, the peculiar connection between them.

'You're probably right.' She dithers, unwilling to leave. He tips his head to the side, watches her curiously as she stares along the street.

'I'm Isolde, my mother died in the bomb.'

'I'm Ray. My wife Barb died too.'

They share a look, kinship recognised in an expression that strangely approaches a smile. They stand together on the doorstep, unwilling to break the hold of this peculiar, newly realised bond.

Chorus

flank to flank, we wait out winter days
turns are made – choices, you would call them
one follows another, all are connected

on a whim, a new path is made
on the switch of a gait in one
read by all as a readiness to cross this field or stick to this edge

let the path find itself, beneath your feet

52

After the lights come up and the still form of Jesse Summers, Prisoner D191-H14, is noticed by the operator in the corridor control room and, on checking monitoring signals, is understood to be the body of a deceased prisoner, two orderlies are called in to take him away.

The door opens at the other end of the cell from the sliding shutter to let the workers wheel in the trolly for moving the body. A confirmation scan is made, into a hand-held monitor that logs the death up the line. The trolly is jacked to bed-height and the two white-clad, masked workers slide him onto the smooth, plastic surface. The bottle-green sweatshirt is ruched up in the move, revealing a pale, mottled side. One of the workers pulls the top down, gently, laying a hand briefly, in tenderness, on the now covered body. The state in all its cruelty is made of people capable of love and tenderness. That is what makes it so adaptable, so frightening. These are not automata, robots, dystopian drones. These are people who say, 'Yeah, I know, but what can you do?'

Jesse Summers's body is taken to the mortuary. Treatment is efficient, cursory. Two cleaners come into the cell. The pages from books are stacked, placed on top of the pile that is pulled out from underneath the table and left in the middle of the floor to be placed in an incinerator sack. Before bagging them, the cleaner looks at the top page, a diagram that could be the designs on tableware, but is labelled as the stages of cell division. She wonders, as she always does, about the lives of the men and women she cleans after. Why this page? What was he seeing? But she has a life outside these walls and corridors and her curiosity is passing. She thinks about her children, the oldest boy who won't work at school, the youngest, a girl, cast down by feuds within her friendship group. She thinks about the stories she listens to, the worlds that take her away from the drab ordinariness of her working life and dull marriage. She thinks of the man in this cell inventing worlds from the page of a mouldy old book. These solitary children, living like infants – like a cash crop. Fattened for the grave.

She bags the books, the last tray of food and beaker of weak tea. She bags the bottle of water. She bags the flannel, the worn toothbrush. The blanket and the mattress cover are stripped and bagged separately, with the prison-issue clothing, for chemical boiling. The mattress will be sprayed too. It retains, for now, the shape of Jesse Summers.

They empty and spray down the plastic walls, little chemical dots of cleaner settle on the flat plastic, like sea spray flicked onto the beach as a wave tumbles over before an offshore wind.

Jesse

53

It is time to go back to the farm and Jesse repacks his small bag before going to meet the others for the return trip. Jesse and Marshal have sketched out a plan for Marshal to visit the farm soon. Jesse is delighted by this turn, though privately, he half-fears his father getting too involved, taking over the water project. He smiles to himself, dismissing the anxiety, looks forward to showing him the workings of the farm; the burgeoning patterns for preparation, preservation and storage of food, the wind turbine, Jada's growing tunnels. Their goodbye is full of warmth, both have been buoyed by the visit. Jesse sets off to meet Jada, looking ahead to the happy prospect of pride, anticipating that Marshal will be impressed.

Chorus

take care, boy
stay behind
tend your father
let the heat
rise up and away, let the day die while you stay safe inside

He crosses London to meet up for a trip to a water park, a treat for Stella's oldest child, Isolde, before they head back to the farm. It is a beautiful day, hot but not punishingly so, the summer wind softly waltzes on street corners, rolls curtains in open windows and ruffles dress hems. Jesse feels buoyant.

But when he arrives, Milos's shared house is in turmoil. Dyan, founder of the Claimants, and several others, have been arrested. Perplexingly, the arrests have been linked by the news anchor to two bombs going off in city crowds that morning. They are confused. No one has ever got close to talking about bombs, but three people linked to Milos's group, the London Socialist Union, are among those arrested. Jada is hurriedly packing their things, trying to hasten their departure to the train station, but Stella begs them to stop on the way, so she can warn Milos at work. The stop is en-route to the station, she just wants to give him the chance to lie low, or maybe even come with them.

Grudgingly, Jada and Jesse agree. Jada offers to carry the baby, slings the papoose carrier onto her front, and Jesse picks up her bag.

They all feel tense. Of course, it could be nothing. A misunderstanding even. But Jada longs to be out of the city and heading back to the farm. Picking up on her mood, Jesse feels the same.

Milos works in a big outdoor and sports shop selling specialist clothing for climbing fake rock walls and running on the spot. Sportswear, energy bars and nutrition drinks. They get to the pedestrianised plaza where the huge store sits alongside other huge stores. Stella is trying to deal with a grumpy Isolde who has picked up on the anxiety of the adults. She clings determinedly to her mother's hand; she stamps and digs in her heels. Stella cajoles, and seeing a cheerful cart just down the pavement, falls back on the age-old bribe of ice cream.

Jada, still itching to leave, says she and Jesse will go in to warn Milos, meet Stella outside in five minutes and continue to the station. Stella, already being dragged to the ice-cream cart yells back at them over her shoulder.

'Tell him to be careful. Sensible. Tell him to lie low, or come with us!' Jada waves behind her as they head through the wide-open doors.

The store is crowded. The first shop assistant they ask doesn't know which floor Milos is on, the second thinks he's on three. They head up the escalator and, taking a side each, start to look, scanning the crowd for the blue baseball caps of workers. Jesse sees Milos, he turns to Jada, waves and points and makes his way over.

There is a bang. A loud bang. Downstairs? Outside? There is chaos, people move and surge in different directions. Jada panics in the unruly crowd, her responsibility for baby Esther and her ferocious wish to find Jesse crash and compete. She can't make sense of her own instructions. Everyone is scared. *We're all scared, I'm scared. Where's Jesse? Are those people terrorists or police? A second device? Stampede. How do I keep us safe in this mess? These people? I should go outside, we can't go that way, they're sending us down the back stairs. Where am I? Where is Jesse? Where is Stella? Where's Jesse?*

Inside the store people push and surge, the cruel whim of panic sending them first in one direction, then in another, following other bodies when the sense of what best to do is gone. Others fight their way on instinct, no longer acting with the courtesy of protection for those more frail. Slowly a consensus creates a rip tide to the back door, emptying them out onto an unfamiliar street, lined with returnable packaging and metal trolleys in front of grimy roller doors.

At the front of the building, it is more artful, more bloody.

The crowds have spread back to a wide perimeter drawn on the average tolerance of fear to curiosity. The wide apron-stage hosts a grisly scene. Glass is scattered like frost. A woman sits, her legs straight before her. She holds a hand to the side of her head then inspects the gore that covers her palm. A woman lies across the body of a child, her hair spilled across the pavement is sticky with blood. A man crouches over the prone body of a woman, he holds her shoulders, strokes her cheek.

'Barb, Barbara, my darling. Wake up.'

He intones his shocked and pointless hope for what seems an eternity.

When the bomb went off, Jesse and Milos had been standing at the corner of a display stanchion, talking over the morning's news. Within seconds of the chaos erupting, security police emerged from the manager's office, dragging Milos to the ground and then out to a vehicle. Jesse was taken too. When it was discovered he could be linked, however tentatively, to the Claimants, he became a bonus for the justice system. Their trials took place behind closed doors over a single afternoon. They were taken to separate prisons before either had a chance to really work out what was happening. Milos died in prison two days later, and Jesse began the slow catch-up of his own execution.

Isolde

54

The death of Jesse hits Isolde with a peculiar sadness. She shared a strange intimacy with this complete stranger, a man she had seen at first as the cause of her greatest harm. Someone she had come to know as a man patterned by all the beautiful complexities of any life. But someone whose luck or fate or destiny had turned on him. Someone who had been grievously wronged.

She obsesses over all the ways that Jesse might have sidestepped his fate. She had done the same as a teenager, mapping over and over all the imaginary paths that Stella had taken to her own end, all the turnings that might have saved her. She knows such tunnels end in darkness. But for a few days she can't help herself.

Isolde knows she must tell Jada that Jesse has died. It is a horrible chore, an obligation that sits heavily on her shoulders, robbing her of agency; the obligations of love once more snag, knot together as one peril. The lightest tied threads and the most stifling of bonds – all can be cut away in an instant when death slices the knot. The child in her belly, so young, so new. Catching light, a crystal pendant hanging in a ballroom, twirling in empty space on the end of a silken thread. If only she had caught the glitter of that light, she could have used all her love to swaddle the child, not wrung them both out with fatal misery.

She understands her dread finally, her fear, that she could have saved the baby from her grief.

Chorus

> we could tell you things
> you don't want to know
> about agency
> about emptiness
> about lost children

She is clear that at least she must tell Jada. She cuts a square out of the remaining sheet of paper and, uncertain about the words to use, writes an awkward message. She includes a promissory note on the out-facing side for Henk the pedlar, to aid the chances of delivery. Isolde feels guilty that she is sending the news in such an uncertain manner.

Lee, unusually, has offered to come with her to the market. They find Henk, pay him for taking the message, which he puts inside a leather bag slung over one shoulder, tucked against his side.

Chorus

> you are not so lost as you think, girl
> listen
> you have a voice
> listen inside, the hum of it, in your bones
> – you will find your way

They walk incuriously past tables and blankets. Carved lamp-stands, silver boxes, painted vases. Children's shoes, tools, bedding and clothing, small items of furniture, cutlery – all are abundantly available. A man is selling jacked VR chips that can be tried in a small booth made of bamboo and tarpaulins. They walk listlessly past the wares. Lee chatters, trying to overcome Isolde's morose mood; he speculates about the age of buildings, the history of an old pub, the name of a street. Isolde answers his questions when she can but is glad when he stops talking. They walk on. She pulls a scarf up around her ears and pulls down the hat that covers her cropped scalp. A few flakes of snow fall.

Lee, grown bored of Isolde's unresponsiveness, lapses into silence. He blows onto his hands and shoves them deep into his pockets. The snow falls feebly. They walk.

55

Isolde completes a small section of work returned for a few cor-rections. She gazes out of the window at city and sky, stares until lost focus creates a bleed between the two.

A message comes through from Henk. He has a reply for her and wants to claim the second part of his payment. She will find him at the market in the morning, for the next three days before he heads out again. The snow has been cleared but few people are out. The street market is quieter, thinner – fewer stalls, fewer customers. People dressed in their storm suits look uniform, simplified. Except for Henk, who Isolde sees a few stalls down. He wears an old coat with a blanket wrapped shawl-wise around his shoulders. He has the common pedlars' taste for eccentricity and showmanship. He is talking with a trader, negotiating over the price of some tubes of fast-lock glue. In one hand, he has a package of something – contraband tobacco perhaps, or weed. The trade is friendly enough. Isolde wonders how they could weigh the use value of glue against the worth of a plant-based high. They eventually make a swap without credits changing hands. Isolde reintroduces herself to Henk, as he flicks through his memory to place her.

'Ah yes! Wait, a sec.' He re-hoists his backpack and turns to the leather bag at his side.

'You owe me three credits for the completion of delivery and another five for the reply.' Isolde keys in the information and bites back a complaint about the price. Henk hands over a small package, thick paper covered in writing, folded into quarters and tied with a string of coral embroidery thread.

It is the same piece she had sent, now crowded with other handwriting. It starts on the blank side and continues running in a different direction around the message that Isolde had first given to Henk to deliver.

I am writing this on behalf of Jada

Petra

Little Iso, thank you for telling me the terribly sad news about Jesse. I know I couldn't have seen him, or helped him, or hoped for anything really, but I did so wish to have the chance to share something with him. I'm grateful that you went to him for me, that a little of that love was handed over, so thank you. I am getting to the end, Iso. Not sad. But near the end. I want to see you, girl. I want you to come back, please. I know you may not want to be here, but we miss you so, your sister misses you. I know we may not be able to keep you, but please come back one more time so I can say goodbye. Come back and try again. This is meant to be your home too. With love always,

Jada

Isolde, I think it would really be good for Jada if you came. She talks of you often. She has become weaker this last week – come soon if you are going to. P xx

Her home. Life would be so different now, if she had grown up at the farm. She would know all the same plants as Misha, would know some of the secrets of Leanne's preserving. She would know how much flour Petra used to make her bread, might know how much of a field went into a loaf. She might be able to make enough rope to bind a pontoon. She would know her sister Esther, would have had time to argue with her, dislike her sometimes. Take her for granted and know how to forgive it being done. She would know how to relate to her without a feeling of being crowded, of being under pressure. She would have known all that Jada could have told her about her mother. Isolde, who could remember the touch, the smell, the caress of her mother, knows less about her in some ways than Esther, who has grown up with stories from when they were little, from before they were born.

And she thinks of all that she wouldn't have known. Those moments of wild adventure, the sensational joy of not caring. The fear of realising she did care. She wouldn't have known the sublime happiness of those months and years of love, the hope that seemed a refuge; she wouldn't have watched it end. Perhaps she would've had a child with another man.

She knows as soon as she reads the letter that she will go back. There's no other choice. Not one that she can bring herself to make. It's too cold to walk all of the way. An ice storm on the road could be fatal unless she invests in better and bulkier equipment. Even without storms the hours of ordinary darkness are too long to sit out in a bivouac tent, the walking day too short. She walks back to the market, looking out for the dark felt hat of Henk among the snug hoods. She finds him further along the 25, seated at a little table outside a stall, checking messages on a device.

'Hi, do you fix transport?'

'I fix whatever people want to get fixed, my love.'

'For a fee?'

'For a fee. But for what you might also call a fair price.'

'I want to go back to the farm, where you picked up the message, in a few days or so.'

'The way it works is this. You pay me, and I connect you to what is available. I don't guarantee luxury travel or convenient schedules, but I do know where to ask, so your credits will be well spent. If you pay me now, another five credits, by the end of tomorrow I will tell you what is available and what price you will have to pay. The rest is up to you.'

Soon, as promised, Henk contacts her with a handful of options. The weather is set to get warmer over the coming days so she picks the earliest ride that takes her far enough and early enough that she can walk the rest in daylight. She feels anxious about Jada, angry with herself. She wishes she had left the minute the letter arrived. Or that she had never come back to London.

Lee comes back later in the evening. She asks if he wants to come with her. His money is on the point of running out, and they haven't found an affordable way to conjure papers. Lee doesn't want to go. She is worried about leaving him, but he says he will take care. She has to be satisfied with that. She isn't his mother. She turns on a distracting story and lies in her bed, staring at the lights of the city as they fade into the stars.

56

Chorus

find your way back by the stars
retrace the steps you made,
knowing now what you didn't then
find your way back

Cloud covers the sky, the light of day rises slow, diffuse. The world is grey, coolly neutral and the bitter cold has receded. Her ride had instructed her to be at the cafe of a heliport near Camden. The connector on her device leads her to a black woman in her forties. She wears a belted, blue work-overall and dark blue, leather gloves. She downs what is in her cup and stands up from the cafe table, gesturing Isolde to walk with her. She speaks in single words as Isolde transfers the necessary credits, except to say, 'I don't talk when I'm flying, you understand?' Isolde is glad for the lack of obligation. They exit the building to an open space the size of a football field, a transit hub for van drones. The ground is cement, criss-crossed with overlapping patterns, lines delineating landing areas and walkways.

They walk along a yellow cross-hatched path until they come to a transit in one of the painted bays. The woman opens a door and points to the second seat in the small cab. Isolde gets in and buckles up. Behind her, boxes and sections of obscure equipment, gleaming with the manufacturer's untouched paint work, take up the storage space.

True to her word, the woman doesn't speak for the forty-minute journey. Isolde leans into the corner of the seat, peers through the window. The light of the veiled sun still low on the eastern horizon seems to come closer as they lift off the ground. Her thoughts wander the sky, and the city below as it slides from underneath them. She traces a diagram, the path that brought her here, to this cab, flying at tower-height above London. She thinks about Jada and Stella – two young women, deciding to move to a roadless, school-less, hospital-less waste-land. Feral farmland that is a place of hope, to give her and her, as yet unborn, sister a better life, free from the grip of a politics that saps, taps the will from citizens. A little spile of fear knocked into them all, draining the syrup. She thinks about Jesse, curious and idealistic, a young man, a prisoner. She thinks of the map that Jesse had drawn, overlays it with where they are now headed. The destination isn't far from the seawall. She remembers his rambling words about it, its importance to him. What had he told her? How they had gone to the middle, like walking over the sea.

The end point of this leg of the journey is a resort built on what had, for a time, been a national nature reserve. As they descend, Isolde looks curiously over the organised neatness of the leisure park. The ground is tidy, shaped with defined boundaries drawn in the vector curves of a computer pen. Gardens and golf courses are linked by neat roads to the chalets, the bar and restaurants. On this ground, the shapes are smooth in comparison to the land that surrounds it. The countryside blends without definition, between states. The city is made of such complexity that the reasoning cannot always be mapped. Here, it is laid out, a series of boundried simplifications.

The land had been eaten into by some metres where the sea-level rise has broadened the river estuary on the southern edge. Two of the golf holes have been remodelled, and a stretch of cement banking has been built to prevent further erosion. Cement in a curve, poured and packed onto the land. So many ways to isolate people from harm. If there is a will. If there is a budget. If they are the right people.

A light flashes on the ground at the northern edge. They descend, landing with a small bump.

'You're here.'

'Oh, do you mind if I…' She needs a minute, pulling out her device and trying to get a bearing on her location using the drone's connection. The woman sighs, stares ahead, hands still on the infinity-figure wheel, the blue leather stretched taught over her knuckles. Isolde finds her place, checks her pocket for the compass and another hand-drawn map. She pulls her bag off the seat and they both climb out of the cab.

A man waves to them. He is next to a quad bike with the flashing light mounted on the trailer at the back.

'Hi, name's Jim. Henk says you might want to organise a ride onward?'

Isolde hesitates, not certain enough of the terrain to know what kind of lift will be useful. She pictures the map, the overlay of Jesse's map. It is still early. She has enough time to get to the farm before daylight ends.

'The power station sea wall, is it near?'

'Yep, 'bout fifteen minutes. I'll do it for two credits?'

'OK, good.'

'Well, wait over there for a bit, while I take this load, then I'll pick you up. Won't be long.' He points at an area a few yards down the metalled drive, a flat area of mown grass with a couple of picnic tables and a rubbish bin.

The pilot is standing, hands on hips, next to the open freight doors on the drone. Isolde picks up her bag and turns to her.

'Thanks, and bye.'

'Luck,' says the woman. She and Jim turn to the back door of the drone, taking out the packages and bits of machinery, loading them into the trailer hitched to the back of his quad bike. Jim drives off with a wave, and the pilot returns to the drone, lifts up and away back to London.

While she waits, Isolde checks her belongings. In her pocket, a couple of energy bars, a knife and lighter, the cotton bag of twines and the embroidery Jada made for Jesse. The compass weighs on the other side. Her pack is light, just a few changes of clothes. She doesn't need camping equipment or spare water; she doesn't need food. All that will be provided when she reaches the farm. She searches in her pack and finds the map that Jesse had made, putting that too in the small, cotton bag.

It seems fitting to go to the wall though she can't explain to herself why. She feels the accusation of empty gesture, even of impudence; the idea that her own actions might mean anything in the wrongness of Jesse's death. It's just that she needs to choose something, make a thing happen on account of him. A way to mark the passing of the chance to offer more. A way to say to herself I would have done more if I could.

The solar-battery quad bike appears silently behind her over a grassy hill; she is startled by Jim's voice calling a greeting.

'Hello! So, you want a ride to the wall?'

'Yes please.'

'Well, hop on. Stick your bag on the back there.'

As they bump along tracks across scrubland and through woods, Jim gives her a potted summary of the history of the controversial wall project. He enjoys his authoritative knowledge and after a morose and irritated five minutes, Isolde begins to listen and appreciate his explanations.

Despite contested scientific benefit, dwelt on in greater detail than Isolde finds necessary, building work had been completed, just, before the pandemics had rendered the protection of property unnecessary and done the work of protecting nature with a different strategy. Human kind, in its reduction, discovered that the best way to protect wildlife is to disappear a little.

But the wall still stands, failed and forlorn now, creating a brackish lagoon that covers the wetlands where birds have blown and cried. The birds, indifferent to human success or failure, have moved inland to the fields – new marshy areas, new spaces, new sea for them to glide over, dip and dive into, to float upon, neutral and serene.

The wall stretches four miles in a direct line toward her destination. She asks whether it will be possible to walk the full length, saving an inland detour. He tells her that there is a section that has deteriorated, about two thirds along, crumbled but it is still passable. With this reassurance she changes her route. It will save some time.

Jim stops at the top of steps that lead down into an area that had once been a car park. The wall runs straight to the north, a steady line of off-white cement, two metres wide, flaring out toward the base. At this end there is a scruffy beach on the seaward side and a jumble of foliage scrabbling at the leeward side, as though the barrier is protecting the sea against the invading hooks and curls of thirsty plants.

Jim takes his leave of Isolde, then unnecessarily points along the wall, demonstrating her direction of travel. She pays him and thanks him for the lift.

57

She adjusts a strap on her shoulder and heads north onto the causeway. Ahead of her the looming shape of a decommissioned, cement-cased nuclear power station, its eerie dome like a message on a scale she can't understand. As she gets closer, the vegetation on the landward side of the wall gives way to a promontory of cement ringed with high fences. The outside is blank, sealed off, unbreached by the fermenting dangers of the core. The gulls arc a lazy hurricane above the unnatural cliffs.

The landward side becomes marshy, then water, lapping lightly at the cement precipice. Once past the power station everything she can see is lower than the wall, as far as distant trees that smudge the horizon.

The two bodies of water, east and west, have different qualities, different textures. The sea, swelled from distant winds, beats against the wall in an endless surging metre. The landward side is smoother, flatter, with a ruckle on the surface flicked up by local wind. The cries of sea birds ring in the grey sky, a thrill in the air. Reaching out across a flat plane of land and sea it sounds like distance, like walking a gangplank.

She imagines Jesse as a young man, in love with Jada. She free of cancer and he not in peril. She pushes the thoughts of injustice aside and pictures them. Seeing Jada again had refreshed memories and brought new ones to the surface. Jada young, vivid, and laughing with Stella. She tries to remember Jesse; he must have been there. She must have him in her mind somewhere. It is hard to imagine what he had looked like. Hard to imagine Jada in love with the stolid, bulky, baffled man she had spoken to in the prison.

She comes to a widened section of the wall, a relief design of a compass pressed into the cement under her feet marks it as the halfway point. The pattern is partly obscured by stones and seaweed trash thrown up by storms. There is graffiti etched into the solid balustrade on both sides of the gangway. She stops, putting down her bag. Names and dates, some that woz 'ere, pairings with hearts, true lovers and the boastful proclamations of self-lovers – all had stopped long enough to gouge words into the pale structure. She digs in her bag for her pocketknife.

She takes the fabric bag, pulling out the embroidery Jada had made for Jesse. She studies the letters, then crouching down, she finds a gap and begins to gouge two Js into the parapet of the wall. It isn't hard to make an impression, but she sticks at it so as to make it enduring, visibly present. She adds the lines that reach out from the letters, little tendrils that snake into freedom.

She straightens up, lets the blood flow back to her legs, shakes them out. She takes an energy bar and a flask of coffee from her bag. Leaning her elbows on the parapet she looks down the slope of the wall, curved to absorb the beat of the waves. The sea rises and falls, an oscilloscope slide along the wall. No smacks or sprays of water but a steady, relentless heave. The high-tide line is marked with a thickening of green, the top line of a band of discolouration. Though even on the calmest days, the surface of the sea is never completely flat, the line is as true as the horizon before her.

She speaks to Jesse.

'I'm sorry you were treated so… that your life was so unfair. I'm sorry for my arrogance the first time I came to see you. I'm sorry that I didn't have time to bring you more of the world, to show that I cared about what happened. I'm sorry I didn't have the chance to care more for you.'

She pictures Jesse as a young man. He is running, the blood moves in smooth joy around his body, muscles working with pleasure and certainty. There is a world of hope before him.

She finishes the dregs of the coffee, folds the square of fabric and replaces it in the bag. There are around two miles left to walk along the wall. She wants to make it to the farm in daylight.

After a while, she notices an anomaly in the causeway, it is the breach in the wall. Her heart sinks, imagining walking back and round the long way. But as she gets closer, it's clear that the gap is not impassable. It doesn't reach deep into the water. A crumbled chunk is missing. At low tide, she guesses, it will be a matter of simply climbing down and across, then back up to the causeway which resumes a few metres away. Now there is perhaps half a metre depth of sea water to either wade through, or cross above on gangplanks laid over a breach that is less than three metres wide. A hand rope has been strung across and secured at waist-height. It is a careful walk of a few metres.

She is cautious, aware of the backpack, ready to counter the imbalance. There are uneven footholds down a few feet of crumbled wall onto to the planks, a little way above the water and just above the high-tide mark. She tests their steadiness with her foot, anxious not to dislodge anything.

She forces herself to imagine that the planks are lying on the ground. She could hop or skip along them, bag or not.

They might bounce, but they don't look like they will fall. The rope handrail will swing some; she schools herself in advance to anticipate the movement and not to put her weight into the holding of it. She steps out, looking ahead and down in turn, slides a hand, steps a foot, flicks a glance. But when nearly across, her foot slips, the wet wood offering no hold for the grip of her boots. She staggers, tips to her right, pushing the rope out away from her, plunges into the water. She goes down, under the water. Far further than she expected. The gloom of it, the paleness of the wall fading down into the depths.

Cold rushes into her hood, down her neck. The shock of cold and fear ring through her and drop her in the perfect dead-centre of a hurricane. It freezes her for a moment that measures not in seconds. A moment of profound time. A moment of reckoning. A moment of connection, the flash of joining contact, and recognition, back to the start of her real life, that ripping moment on a London street that she had survived but others had not.

It is like panic. Like balm. Like nothing.

A dim shriek from the corner of her soul tells her to push. Into the hurricane. She needs the storm of it, not the still, cold, roaring silence of the centre. Panic elevates her, her arms and legs grow a motion that takes her upward, bursting into the air.

She can't move freely in the suit, with the bag on her so she wriggles free, kicking desperately with her legs while her arms are untangling. Her feet feel stupid, ungainly in the boots. But she keeps her head above the surface. Free of the bag, she sees that she is only a little way from where she had fallen in. She marshals her heavy feet, and pushes forward until she holds a break in the cement. With a bit of manoeuvring she pulls herself up onto it, and then up onto the northern stretch of the wall.

She is dazed. But the spark of a memory in that awful emptiness, the cold retreat of shock has lit a fire. This time, she won't
be passive. She has to be warm. She has to try to get dry. That
means moving. She is frighteningly aware of her isolation out
here on the wall. But for certain, there will be buildings, maybe
even people at the far end. She has to get there as soon as possible.

She stops long enough to take off and drain her boots, to
wring out what she can from her suit. The inner layer is ther-
mal. If she can generate body heat it will perhaps keep her
warm enough. Rationally she counts all that is on her side. It
isn't a freezing day. She is perhaps only a mile from shelter.
There is no wind. She is strong and healthy. She reaches behind
her head, wrings out the water from the suit's hood, rubs her
hands over the short nap of hair, pulls up the hood and sets off
at a brisk pace.

A glow of heat begins in the small of her back. It travels outward, radiates through her just under the skin. She hopes it will
last until she becomes dry or finds shelter. The flesh of her face
feels raw but her body provides some warmth, caring for itself
as she focuses on reaching the end of the wall. She walks and
jogs, conserving energy but heeding time.

It takes quarter of an hour to reach the end of the wall. Her
teeth chatter. Cold extremities, not reached by the burning
core, are painfully numb. She sees a row of houses set back
from the shore but closer to the sea now than when they were
built. She's not sure if she wants to find them occupied or
empty. The windows are dark, some empty of glass. She pats
down her pockets, hoping she has adopted the safety-first policy of keeping basic items on her. The pockets of the storm suit
should be waterproof and she hopes that they will have stood
up to a submersion as she touches the reassuring outline of her
pocket knife and a lighter.

Calling out, she approaches the nearest house. No one responds. The interior is fusty, some plaster dust, the blackening of a fire that did not catch the whole building in a corner of the downstairs room. She is torn between staying and pushing on. Building a fire to dry out the inner layer of clothing is tempting but will push her arrival into darkness and perhaps greater cold. She begins a search of the house.

There are three bedrooms. Two still have beds in them. She is tempted to lie down and shiver herself back into animal warmth, but she can't afford to spend a night here. Most of the last occupant's possessions are gone. In the second bedroom, there is a chest at the end of a bare single bed. She steps over a storm of feathers, the corpse of a trapped wood pigeon. Inside the trunk is an assortment of bedding. Counterpanes and blankets. One of the blankets is cotton. She pulls it out, anxious not to find the further resting places of wildlife. It is corpse free, clean even. She shakes it out then pulls out a second woollen blanket.

Stripping off her clothes quickly she lays the still damp under-layers out on one end of the cotton blanket then dresses again in the storm suit, a fabric that doesn't retain moisture and provides more warmth than its light weight implies. She throws the woollen blanket across her shoulders then rolls up the cotton and damp clothes, stepping on the roll to squeeze out as much moisture as she can.

In the last room, there are some clothes among a small pile of belongings in a corner, for a child, perhaps twelve or thirteen. No socks, but she takes all the t-shirts and jumpers and a pair of long shorts. Her feet are freezing; she works on drying out the inside of her boots as much as possible. She cuts a t-shirt into two jagged strips of fabric with her penknife and wraps her feet as thoroughly as she can. Two sleeves of a sweatshirt are pulled over her feet and up her calves under the storm suit. Her damp clothes, though drier, have become chilled. She decides to improvise, cutting items and wrapping her body under the suit with a mixture of the clothes and strips of fabric from blankets and counterpanes. She makes strips from the stretch fabric of one of the t-shirts to use as belting and binding. Her body is wrapped as though in doll's clothes, made by an imaginative six-year-old child. She hopes that the suit will keep the improvised base layer in place.

Lastly she takes a strip of floral counterpane, wraps it around her head under the hood. The improvisations give her a strange awareness of her body; it feels peculiar, both naked and bound. She has a few hours walking in which to get used to it. All she has is the cotton bag, the little pocketknife and the compass. The thought of what she doesn't have makes her hungry.

Chorus

set a path, girl
if you want to find a way

we told you before
it's not your belly that needs feeding

An old road snakes subtly through the woods. As the cloud thins and the day gets brighter the bracken becomes saturated, foxy and red, birch bark gleams in pearly contrast. Soon the trees give way to open ground. She stops several times to resettle the fabric wrapping her feet, but it slips and ruches, wedges under her sole. Her knees and feet are cold. The sweatshirt sleeves don't stay up, and the shorts don't reach down. But otherwise, she is warm enough.

58

Finally she reaches the farm. Knocking on the door again, she feels an uplift, wondering who will answer. It's Misha who comes, Misha who, after a moment of shy assessment, throws herself into Isolde for a hug, then drags her into the kitchen, running to get Esther. Isolde unwinds the stiff floral scarf from her head and neck. She realises how much she is looking forward to seeing her sister. She turns, smiling as Esther and Misha comes toward her. She feels relief that almost makes her cry as the three of them embrace.

She tells them about her fall into the sea and, in the warm kitchen, takes off the outer layer, causing great hilarity for the children as she reveals her patched-together outfit. Bert is particularly delighted with the leg-sleeves and runs to get a jumper that he can wear as trousers, adding the floral strip wrapped around his head. Esther runs a bath, checks hot water, finds clean clothes and towels. She makes food, hot drinks, questions Isolde anxiously as though to make sure, in hindsight, that nothing more dangerous will rewrite this moment of reconnection.

Isolde lies in a hot bath. It is good to be back, among the sounds of people she cares for. It is good to hear the children talking and playing. By now they are all racing about and falling over in jumper-trousers. An air of excitement has swept in with her return. *What a blessing to be the cause of joy*, she thinks. The still, warm water embraces her. She goes back for an anxious moment to the swallowing of the sea. As though to remind herself, her neck stretches, her head moves, reminding her fears that she is in the water, not under it.

The clothes borrowed from Esther – soft, comfortable, forgiving shapes – feel good, return a sense of her body being whole. It is as though she had been wearing the stiff fabrications for days rather than hours.

She and Esther visit Jada. She seems smaller, quieter, her dark brown skin ashen. She smiles at the two women, who sit once again on each side of the bed. She takes a hand of each of them.

'Little Iso and Little Esi.' She smiles slowly.

Chorus

trust us – we see things simply and know what matters
– for us little changes

it was, is, always was always is so

we are tiny sparks
we join to make a dim and precious light through the black of unexistence

we don't have the words to tell you why it is this way,
we don't have the words to make you feel the safe light of existence, so bold in the darkness
but we know it

59

The next day Isolde sits with Jada through a quiet morning. The few words they speak spread out over gentle hours. Regrets and sadness drift through the window, the faint light of distant joys dust the sill. Jada sleeps between fragments of conversation. Isolde sits, patient, making amends for her absence.

In the middle of the day Petra comes. She smiles a greeting at Isolde, sits in the corner armchair.

'It's good that you've come back.'

'Yes, and thank you for telling me I should. You were right.'

'I know this place can be a bit full on, but Jada is so happy you are here.' Petra pauses, looks across the room past Isolde. 'I found it difficult myself when I first came here. Took me a while to get used to having so many people around. People weren't really my thing. But,'— she looks over at Jada in the bed— 'then you start to care anyway.'

Isolde asks around for Ben. She finds him crouched over a pump housing, next to the stream. He mutters a curse under his breath until the snap of twigs under Isolde's feet makes him look up. He leaps to his feet with a smile, giving Isolde a warm hug. She returns the warmth but portions it out, carefully, illustratively. Reading her, Ben caps his exuberance but keeps his smile.

'Pump's got clogged. Whoever built the system did a good job but it gets blocked with leaves or mud now and then.'

Isolde steps over and peers into the hole lined with board. An incongruous square hole in the roots and burrows of the woodland stream's bank. Ben carries on poking through one of the pipes with a length of cleaner fashioned from wire and plastic bristles cut from an old bottle.

'I did have a proper set of drain rods but lent them to a guy at the fair, he hasn't brought them back yet.'

'Will you be able to chase him up?'

'Maybe, if I can't bodge it. Listen, what are your plans? Are you free this afternoon?'

Isolde smiles, thinking of the work she has just signed off and left behind, trying to come up with anything, other than seeing Jada, that will feel like an obligation.

'Yes, I'm free this afternoon.'

'OK, I wanted to show you something. I'll be done here in a little while.'

They arrange to meet later at the workshop. Isolde leaves, walking up stream, further into the woods and around the top of the field back to the farm. Clifford and Esther are in the yard moving boxes between buildings. Isolde gives Clifford a hug, he tells her he is glad to see her back, asks after Lee. Bert comes hurtling around the corner, his little legs flying. Both arms trail out behind him. He throws a glance over his shoulder now and then to check that the speed of his run is making Isolde's improvised floral head wrap fly out behind him. It's too long and trails on the ground.

'Hey, Bert, shall we make it into a proper cloak?' she asks.

'Yes! A cloak!'

They go into the house to find scissors and sewing thread. She cuts the middle out of one end, turns the remainder over to make arm holes. The back of the neck is stitched with a pleat, then cut the bottom in a curve. Bert is delighted with his cloak. She helps him tie the off-cut around his head to make a matching hat. And he is gone, sturdy booted feet charging across the hardstand of the yard.

She wanders over to the workshop to wait for Ben. He comes back, muddy-kneed, rubbing red-cold hands pulled from wet work gloves.

'Hey, do you want to get washed up?'

'No, no, I'm fine. So, come with me.'

They walk the lane toward the sea. Taking a turn into the woods, after less than half a mile they soon find themselves in an open space before a small row of houses Isolde has not seen before, facing onto what had once been a wide-verged road. There is a partly ruined church in a spacious graveyard on the other side. There had been a hedge demarcating the church-yard but a wide section is missing and the spaces blend.

'I don't know how you feel about being really alone, but look, I thought that if you wanted to stay a bit longer, it would be easy to set one of these houses up for you. They are all sound, and I could easily get lights and water up. If you like?' He looks at her, cautious of over-stepping but wanting to give her something, something precious. Instinctively she rejects what he is offering, her impulse is to slam the door shut on his kindness, brush away the tender hook of obligation that it casts out toward her. But the houses, three of them, are so con-tained, so inviting. Three old, brick cottages with low win-dows and brick paths, opposite the ghostly, beautiful ruin of an old church.

'No one has lived here for years. Not in any of the houses. There's a couple of bigger ones.' He gestures further past the church. 'But they're not in such a good state. Some people stayed there for a while, two summers ago, they helped with the harvest. We thought they might stay, but they left. One of them nicked some of my tools too.' He shrugs – the unknowable risks of other people. And that is the sticking point for Isolde too. People have different ways of leaving you. But Ben, she realises, isn't going anywhere. The house isn't going anywhere.

He walks over to the middle of the three front doors, through an overgrown garden. There is a wall. Held open and buried deep in the brambles there is still a gate. The path to the door has been cleared. Inside is clean of cobwebs and plaster dust, no animals have left their homes or graves. It is clean, as though in mastery of its story. The past lives witnessed by this house are tidied away, in their proper place. There are three rooms, two at the front with a small hall between, one built on at the back, the former kitchen.

'There's no water at the moment, but it will be easy enough to set up.' Ben goes over and twists the old tap handle, inviting her to imagine it flowing, once he'd had the chance to work on the connection.

Through the back window is a tangle of shrubs, and, further, some fruit trees. Ben follows her gaze. 'Those are actually really good cider apples. A couple of times Pete has brewed a batch with them; it's pretty tasty actually.'

The orderly neutrality of the empty house is beguiling. It is old, faded, but not stained with the residue of a previous tenant. And it is too isolated to be grubbied with the leavings of temporary inhabitants taking time off the road.

'Come and look at the upstairs. There's a bit of a leak in the roof next door but it's all sound here.'

On the ground floor, the boards are stripped and had been varnished. The stairs, like the rest of the floors, are bare of carpets. The treads are painted at the edges; in the centre, where there used to be carpet, they are the soft grey-brown of old wood. Upstairs is the same orderly, faded cleanliness, bare boards on the floor and sound walls. There are two bedrooms with a bathroom over the kitchen.

'We'd have to build a loo out back and use a compost system, but you could build it into a lean-to or wall it in, like at the farm.'

Isolde is touched by Ben's gently proffered consideration. There is no denying the house would be a good place to live. Ideas stir, pictures of how it could be – a desk here, an armchair there. Peace and nearby company. She crosses to the window that looks over the front of the house. The church is mournful but beautiful. Trees behind it mark the boundary between land and sky. A small group of cattle have wandered in and are dragging patiently at the grass in the lea of the tumbled stone wall. She looks down on their backs, the broad flanks sweeping from the ridge of a spine. Necks moving as blunt teeth snag and pull, their breath warming the insects in the grass. Such a steady gait. They roll like fluid for all their heft, in slow harmony one with another.

She turns to Ben, smiling in thanks.

'It would be great Ben, thank you. If I stayed, I think it would be a great place to live. I will think about it.'

Ben smiles, a big smile, then turns away, feigning dissatisfied interest in the workings of a perfectly adequate window latch. They leave to go back to the farm. The cattle have moved on from the door into the graveyard of the church, a couple of them watch behind, dark eyes following the direction of the two humans.

'You know, in that stuff I found about rope-making, there was the plans for making a rope walk. If you're interested, we can set one up, grow the right crops, start making ropes of a decent length.' He stands before the three cottages, laying out with his hand an image of the rope walk running down the former road at the heart of the village. Isolde imagines working, maybe year-round, with a cover from the weather, with a second cottage open for storing and drying and sorting materials, a room filled with great coils of twisted rope, spun into being out here. She pictures threads, coming into their strength and purpose, growing from this little patch of land, down over the fields to the sea, reaching out to a sail of canvas, catching the wind, making a boat fly across the water.

Chorus

Some of it, girl, is courage

60

The arc tips as the earth moves around the sun. The north gets slowly warmer. The surface shifts by tiny degrees, in concert with the grand and slow movements of the solar system. The weather paints in washes and daubs; systems zing at the boundaries, or change one the other, blend to make a new tone.

Plants react to temperature and hours of light, signals pulse in the dense hub of a seed buried in the earth. A wakening begins, in grains lying among the winter mash on the ground. A dormant tree reads messages to itself, *hello hello*, checks its network. Not yet, but soon. Soon will be the time to break out, invade the horizon, to occupy the space where the sky touches. To reach for the sun and inhale the light.

On the farm, there is preparatory work for new planting, the next cycle of growing. The jobs of winter, work on buildings and maintenance, checking resources, are being hurried to a conclusion. It is still cold. Mornings are frosty, misty, cloudy. Days are grey. Jada sleeps. Drugs for pain, checked by Esther, by Petra, by Leanne, are in good enough supply to see her through to the end. There is sadness for all, plotting out remaining days in the small bottles on the top of the chest of drawers.

Short moments come and go, Jada talks with a visitor, or holds onto their hand as she sleeps. Isolde realises with a horrible wrench that she has not heard all that Jada could tell her, about Stella, about her childhood, about what is behind the blank that closes off her own memory, the white tent over a crime scene. The two sisters find consolation, sitting together in the evenings, sometimes with the others, once the house is quiet, talking about Jada and Stella.

Lying in bed before sleep, she sees that what she does now with Esther is like a knitting of yarn. They are twisting their love of Jada into something secure, durable, ensuring its continued existence. The memories become anchored to both, secured at different points, different people.

Her grieving for her child, for the end of her nearly family had been solitary. A crochet of fine thread that stretched only to measure the hollow space within her.

The next morning, she finds Esther, asking her to walk with her. As they cross the fields, walk along the stream, making a route with no logic but with steady, necessary movement, Isolde tells Esther about her childhood in the home. The fun and games of misadventure, the daring, the chutzpah, the tedium, the loneliness. She tells her about the glorious, reckless wildness of her early adult life.

They sit on a battered tree trunk, smoothed dark by the sea. Isolde tells Esther about her lover, the slow path to trust, their hopes for a child. And how their hope had become loveless determination. Finally she speaks of that loss. She tells her sister of her deep regret, of her sense of loss and shame that she had not been able to keep a hold of the child that glittered for a few weeks, unseen and, she is afraid, unprotected, as that love slid away.

Esther puts an arm around Isolde. Isolde turns her head into the warmth of her sister, clutching at the lapel of her jacket. She lets her sorrow go, lets it out to sea.

61

Ten days later, Jada dies. A lengthening of sleep that finally takes her away. On the last morning, all the people living at the farm come to pay their love and their respects. Some are unable to leave. The room is hushed, people making room for a new soul, their faces pinched with sadness. People try not to be selfish, to respect the needs of others. An elaborate, loving courtesy overtakes them all. Speaking in whispers, moving slowly, they try to make each other cups of tea, try to stand so another can sit. They hold on to the one who cries.

The children come and make earnest goodbyes, unable to keep to the whispered tone of the adults but full of solemn understanding. Misha sits on the floor at the foot of Jada's bed, tucked in as small as she can and won't leave. For some time, Bert sits on her lap, resting his head on his older sister's chest. He pulls her hair down, over his own face. Isolde remembers Stella.

Leanne, speaking still to Jada, marks the moment of her death.

'I'm just here, Jada; it's my hand you can feel at your neck. I just need to keep it here for a second. You are gone, aren't you, my dear friend. Thank you, Jada, for your wonderful life.' She places both hands gently on each side of Jada's face, then turns to the others, smiling and crying.

Misha's sobs fill the room. She jumps up and grabs her mother. Bert picks himself up, stands forlorn and serious at the foot of the bed until Esther reaches out an arm to him. He walks over slowly then launches himself into her embrace. Isolde sits on the sill of the window. There are seven people in the room. Clifford stands with a hand on Esther's back, looking down at Jada.

'I'll go and tell the others. Will you be OK?' He says to Esther. She nods, her face between the heads of the two children. Isolde goes to find Amber who hadn't wanted to come to Jada's room. She finds her in the kitchen, drawing on a strip of timber board.

'Jada has died hasn't she?' Amber says, hardly looking up as Isolde enters.

'Yes, darling.'

'I heard the others crying.'

'What are you doing?'

'I'm making a picture for Jada to take with her; it's all of us so she remembers that we love her.'

The day passes in strange fragmentation. The courtesy continues, people making room for each other, finding space for themselves. They observe, looking out for anyone who may need help, or love. Isolde fits herself into the group. Her own connection to Jada is spectacular, magical in some way, built as it is on the wonderful surprise of reconnection. But for the people at the farm, Jada was a part of every single day since they had been there. Her loss to them is fundamental.

Isolde goes out to be away from it all for a while. She walks down the lane to the hamlet, empty but for the crows and cows and the ghosts of a future, plans drawn in the air by Ben's hand. She is glad to see that the cattle haven't left. They are behind the church. She sits on the wall outside the house she has unconsciously begun to think of as hers.

She watches the cows. *Perhaps,* she thinks, *their simplicity, their trust in life as it is spread out before them, is after all the intelligent option.* She is tired of the solipsistic clanking of her thoughts, the testing and pulling apart of options, the examining of dissatisfactions. She wishes she could be more animal. She wishes she could roll through the landscape, caught in a series of moments. Free of an ancient grief that somehow pulls at the shape of a loss that happened just that morning, as if it would greedily reshape even that. She wishes she could just let herself get on with life, its sorrows and beauties. Get out of a head that has become tedious, self-absorbed, unrewarding.

She knows Esther is heart-stricken. All of them are. Leanne too has known Jada since childhood. For Esther, Jada has been what Stella could not. Isolde determines that, whatever she herself feels, whatever choices she will make, trying to help them, help her sister, will for now be at the forefront.

It is a relief to put the weight of herself down. To lower the magnifying glass that she has been holding over herself for so long. Here she is, nothing else can be changed. She is, in becoming finally bored of herself, suddenly thirsty for the people around her.

The people of the farm meet in the evening in the barn where there is a huge table, a kitchen with pans big enough to feed everyone. Isolde goes to help prepare a simple meal made by those whose sadness is best served by action. Esther sits, with the group but removed, her face a startled mask, red-eyed and lost. Petra comes and goes, silent, pale in her dark clothes. Pete makes food for everyone, pressing at his eyes with the back of his hand now and then. As the meal takes shape and nears readiness, Isolde goes to find Ben. She expects him to be in the workshop. He hadn't been with Jada when she died. Isolde had presumed him busy as always. She has a sudden anxiety that he won't know of her death. She searches the farm but can't find him. Eventually, she goes up to ask Leanne, who had been sitting with Jada. As she approaches, she hears a low voice. It is Ben, sitting on the bed, talking quietly to Jada, saying goodbye.

'She took me in when I was lost. Showed me how to be OK again.'

Isolde goes to comfort him, hugging him awkwardly as he sits on the bed. She realises that this too is a story she wants to hear. How a man who has shown her such kindness, whose kindness she has sometimes pushed away as an intrusion, had come to feel lost and how the dead woman, the dear friend of both, had helped him find what he needed.

She takes Ben's hand gently, leading him to the door.

'There's food for everyone, come and eat.'

The meal is unexpectedly joyous when it isn't desperate and silent. They open wine and cider, some made from the apples in what is becoming Isolde's garden. Petra stays with Jada; Leanne speaks to them all about tomorrow when they will bury her. Isolde learns that they have a kind of ritual. The handful of people who have died at the farm are buried at the field edges. Their resting place is marked with a plant, a flowering shrub or rose. Isolde had never noticed this, but now she can see the markers in her mind's eye, a row of plants edging the far end of the wheat field. Almost natural, but now she can understand the pattern of the markers. Leanne reminds them all of what will be done, to fulfil the practical and emotional needs of the day. To facilitate a transition from presence to absence. To bring a beloved body to its new realm.

The evening goes on, children fall asleep on the laps of adults and are carried to bed. Glasses are refilled with sharp cider and musky wine. Memories are retold by smiling faces with tearful eyes. The familiar stories spin up the chimney with the sparks from the fire to make patterns with the stars.

62

It has rained in the night. Wet grass sops trouser legs as they walk to the far end of the field. Before digging, people talk of the others buried at the field edge. There are enough hands to do the work, so Isolde returns to the kitchen, to find Esther, to help with the children. Misha is eating bread and jam with Clifford who tells Isolde that Esther is still upstairs. He gives her a mug of sweetened tea to take up. In their bedroom, Esther is lying in the bed, watching Amber finish her drawing, colouring each section with care. Esther's eyes and nose are red from crying, but she is calm, stroking the neat head of her middle child as she bends over her work.

Isolde sits on the bed with them for a while, then feeling the need to be useful, she kisses both of them on the cheek and goes out to the workshop. Ben is picking something apart. Cleaning it. He smiles a sad greeting to Isolde. She offers to make him tea, but he lifts a full mug. She sits on a battered chair in the corner, just waiting.

In the middle of the day, Petra comes to find Isolde and asks if she and Esther would like to help her prepare Jada for the field. Her heart thumps, in anticipation of her first close contact with a dead person, but she wants very much to have a role, to offer something. She finds Esther, still red-eyed, still tangle-haired, but up and helping Pete and Clifford prepare food in the kitchen. The two of them walk over to Jada's room.

Petra or Leanne has tidied the room, pulled the bed straight. Jada lies as she did the night before, with her mouth comfortably closed, her hands resting on her solar plexus. Esther lightly touches her cheek with her finger tips.

Isolde remembers the first time she had been in the room, the golden glow of full summer flooding it, catching light on the jars, the little vases. The jars are still there, a trail of ivy, a collection of dried meadow grasses, a stem of tough winter greenery. Petra follows them in to the room.

'I would like to wash her body, just with plain water, and brush her hair. She has a gown that she asked me to put on her. You'll find it in that drawer, Esther.'

Esther turns and opens the drawer, lifting out a folded white garment.

'Shake it out. It was what she made out of all the embroidery. All the pieces of fabric were cut right from the start, for the making of this gown. In the last weeks, around Christmas when she stopped wanting to work on it any more, she asked me to help her make it up into this. She called it her field robe.'

Esther shakes out the gown, holds it up at the shoulders. It is full-length, white, and loosely shaped. The sleeves are long and wide. At the back it overlaps, with ties of white ribbon at the neck and halfway down to secure it. The garment is patterned, all over, in connected uneven designs of embroidery that all the visitors and residents of the farm have contributed to over the previous year. Esther can't hold back tears. Isolde thinks she has never seen such a beautiful thing. She sees the part she worked on, the map copied from the drawing by Jesse, next to the stitched hem of the right sleeve. None of them were designed to fit together, but there is a harmony, a completion in the whole. The tenderness of clumsy attempts and equally of finely executed skills, the slippage from meanings to abstractions. From Bert's inch-long dashes and square-sided curves to the intricate workings of tiny stitches, blended colour added by Jada herself. Jada's intention had made it whole.

Petra pulls back the cover on the bed slowly, folding it at the foot of the bed. She weighs the gesture with deliberate consciousness.

'Isolde,' asks Petra, 'Can you fetch some water in a bowl? I know it's silly, but make it nice and warm. There is a wash bowl under the basin and cloths in that drawer.'

She takes clean flannels from the drawer. Under the basin in the small bathroom is an enamel bowl. She unfolds a flannel and wets it, waiting for the water to run warm. Carefully, she carries the bowl back to the bedroom with the cloth folded over the edge.

Jada lies on a single pillow, her dark grey-black cloud of hair, fans out like thunder anticipated, on the horizon. Her face is serene. Her eyebrows curve in lazy flight below her still-smooth forehead. Isolde holds the bowl while Petra washes her tenderly, removing the sheet only where she washes the body. Esther combs out her hair. Pulling the sheet down and lifting her arms, Petra asks the two sisters to help her dress Jada in the gown.

Lying on the bed, the white sheet behind her and the embroidered gown of white, Jada looks to be floating in a meadow of spells. She is held by the coloured threads, the network she had created. Each thread spins out of the room and to the hand of someone. Isolde remembers the time sitting on the bed, stitching the pattern, finding from the work of the others the way to make the design. She knows she will feel that thread, that connection, for all time.

Later, wrapped in a linen sheet, they carry her on a board to the edge of the field. All say goodbye once more. Items are passed down to lie next to Jada. The piece of wood with Amber's drawing. A corn wreath from Petra, the heads of seeds spinning out like sparks from a Catherine wheel. Ben passes over a square of paper from his precious scrap pile, folded to hide his words. Isolde takes out the cotton bag from her pocket. She smooths out the embroidery with two Js, uncoils the slender length of cord made from her own hair. She passes them both to Clifford to lay in the ground with Jada. She feels it is her role suddenly to bring Jesse to the place, to wish him here, to insist to the stars that he is. She thinks of his face staring into the past, into an impossible alternative, into the memories of his love. She weeps for them both.

Soon the grave is covered over. They stand next to the raw earth, some still tethered to the scene but drifting into their own thoughts, gazing into the distance. People cry or hug each other. Laughter bubbles, ordinary conversation too. Bert resumes his running, restores his child's excited chatter. In the kitchen, they open bottles and pass around glasses. There is music, a playlist made by Jada years before still stored on the system. There is the merriment that follows death. A particular, fragmented joy.

They open more bottles, build a fire in the barn fireplace and also outside at the field edge near the yard. Visitors arrive to pay their respects, bringing wine and food. Others come from the nearby settlements as the evening goes on. Isolde drinks; she tells Pete about Jesse. She drinks some more. They all do. Early in the evening she feels ill with it. She is sitting on the sofa in the barn next to Ben, when she begins to feel a little sick. He stands with her and walks her into the garden. It is a clear night, more than half a moon makes the world visible. It is still cold, the end of February. Ben goes inside to get a blanket that he wraps around Isolde. She leans against the post of the porch, her head hanging, letting the cold air on the back of her neck wake her.

She pulls the blanket, wraps it shawl-style around her shoulders, and says, 'Let's walk. I want to walk off the drink. Fresh air.'

They walk down the lane to the sea. The sound of the waves meets them in the darkness of the woods. The waves are edged with moonlight. Isolde breathes in the sea air. They stand together as the wind pulls in from the sea. From here to there the air moves, a shifting skin across the surface of the whole earth.

'Can we get to the house, to my house, from the beach?' she asks, once the wind has revived, once the sea has stilled the sickness in her belly.

'Yes, just along a bit and across.'

Isolde turns to the north and Ben falls in step beside her. It is peaceful in the hamlet. The church shaped roughly by the moonlight in front of the trees seems to hold the place steady. *This is a place for us*, it says in the silence. The house is dark. Ben finds a candle and lighter that he must have left there on a previous visit. The pale glow, warmer than the moonlight, makes a vessel of the empty room. Isolde walks through the ground floor of the house. It feels like hers. She comes back to where Ben stands, leans into him. The knot of the blanket keeps between them like a buoy on a boat. She pulls it off her shoulders, sinks down to the floor and pulls the edges out, squares it over the boards. Ben, his hand in hers, lowers down to floor level. They lie on the blanket, facing each other. Ben's face is in shadow, his curly hair silhouetted against the candlelight. It feels reckless, necessary, and hopeful, pulling Ben to her. Their hands reach under layers of jumpers to caress each other's skin. The emotions of the day, the alcohol, make her greedy; they rush toward each other, making love with bulky winter clothing only partly removed. Isolde gets her head stuck in a jumper. They laugh, they reach hungrily for each other, race toward the conclusion of a tension that has been between them since the summer, hiding respectfully behind her caution.

It feels so good to be unguarded, to let something happen without fear of the consequences. It feels good to be held and touched, to be loved. It feels good to enjoy sex, drunkenly, freely. It feels so good not to manage their connection but just to enjoy it, to enjoy him. She lies on her back, cold where her skin meets the air, covered in part by discarded clothes. Ben rolls off the blanket and covers her with the edge of it. She pushes it back, fits herself to him for warmth. But they don't stay long. The floor is cold. The air is cold. The excitement that has kept them warm becomes a glow that cheers hearts but leaves feet to freeze. They walk back to the house, both wrapped in the blanket, as far as it will reach across two sets of shoulders. As they get near, Ben stops, pulls it from them and wraps it around Isolde, guessing discretion will, as usual, be her chosen mode.

Chorus

we see you, girl
from our leeward sleep
we see you in your dreams
and in our own
let us share this stretch of land
and make it home

She smiles at him, grateful for the space and time he allows. They walk back into the farm to rejoin the others, rejoin fires that warm and lights that glow, keeping them all together in the dark of the night.

63

February ends with three days of storm. Isolde has made no plans to leave after the burial and the bad weather makes it impossible. She thinks more and more about staying, but can't come to a decision. Outside, the weather rages but the people of the farm are steady and quiet, as though waiting, simply, for an easier time. It is both content and melancholy; they move around quietly, checking in with each other, spending time alone and together. Everyone finds chores to get on with. *Keeping their hands busy*, Isolde thinks.

She has managed to talk to Lee; he isn't making much progress. She is worried about him. No one can reassure them about whether papers will be available or not. He may have been reported officially missing, and could be sent back. It pulls at her, this anxiety. It gets in the way of fully making a decision to stay.

The quiet days when they are all held in check by the storm give her time to get to know Ben better. She knows now that whatever happens between them they will be able to work it out. Being uncertain about what lies ahead, she schools herself out of thoughts that drift to imagining them together, sometimes stops herself from wandering over to the workshop. But her thoughts and her feet defy her often, taking her toward him anyway. She trusts him; they will be able to find a way to each other, and she trusts they will manage it safely if they do not. She hopes in serene moments that perhaps their story isn't over yet.

March arrives with a break in the weather. The storm abates in the night, and spring is suddenly beckoning. The sun warms but is held in check by thin mist, a veil of silver voile draped across the fields. Later in the day, Henk comes into the yard and is met by all who expect something from him, and some who are just curious for news. He delivers books to Leanne and Misha, razors to Clifford, news of other homesteads to all. He has a verbal message from Lee:

'He wants to know, would you be happy to have him back?'

'Yes!' says Isolde, then glances around at the others. More practised cooperative decision-makers, they look at each other, giving small nods of agreement before Leanne speaks for them, telling Henk that yes, they would be happy for him to come back anytime. Isolde is delighted. She walks over to the workshop and, sitting on the battered chair, gives Ben a summary of Henk's news.

'Hey, that's great about Lee,' says Ben.

'Yes.' She smiles. 'I'd love it if he did come, I feel like it's more his home. And I could stop worrying.'

'And maybe I'll get my most promising apprentice back,' says Ben.

'So how easy will it be to set up lights and water at my... at the house?'

'It will take me about four or five days, if I work in the afternoons and with you helping. Maybe more, if I need more pipe than I have, but that will only add another day or two.'

'OK, and when would you be free to start that?'

He smiles. 'How about this afternoon?'

'OK. Good. And in return, you can tell me what to do to help you with what you are working on in the mornings, and I'll try to be your second best apprentice.'

Later, she wanders down to her house. The cows are down the lane. She greets them silently as she steps over pipes that will be installed for water. Inside, the armchair from Jada's room is in front of the fire place. She sits, taking in the room. She pulls the cotton bag from her pocket. The map is creased, corners buckled, but she smooths it carefully and places it on the mantlepiece behind a candle. Later, she'll look in one of the other houses for a frame.

She walks back, past the farmhouse and along the field edge. Birds sing, criss-crossing the air with silver threads. Pale grasses held over from the last season are shot through with new bright green. Soon, the way to the bottom of the field will need to be cleared to be passable. She goes to where Jada is.

Threads will unwind, unstitch, the new yarns of plants and the paths of insects will work their way, take her into the ground. Tender roots, pale and persistent, will reach through, welcome her back. Stitch her into the meadow, make her forever part of the world.

The cells inside Isolde have uncurled too. They stir, making the first connections, the expressions of a wish to exist. A new human life reaching out to become.

And so, new growth unfurls in both the living and the dead.

Acknowledgements

Thank you to all of you who pledged to support the publication of *Salt Lick*, either from faith in the project or kindness. I am so grateful for your part in making it happen, and I hope you will find something to like in a book that is partly yours.

Thank you to early readers for your time and insights. Mary Monro, who put me straight on farming matters and helped me learn about the loveliness of cows. Virginia Moffat, whose encouragement and observations helped me shape the book in its early form. Rónán Hession and Heidi James, thank you for taking time to read *Salt Lick* and sharing your thoughts – I'm honoured.

Jane and Mike (aka Giana and Mikel), thank you once again for your wonderful support and generosity. It is so very appreciated. I hope you will like your namesakes, keeping the village going with wine, wood and a plan. I can't thank you enough for your kindness.

All my family. You are all wonderful, and your support and love means everything and comes in so many precious forms. Joe, thank you for your generosity – it means so much.

Pierre, you keep me safe, sane and happy.

One of the starting points for this book was a song by the *Handsome Family* called 'Peace in the Valley Once Again'. Though not used, I would like to thank Rennie Sparks for responding so generously to my request to quote the lyrics and also for having written one of my favourite songs.

To my editor Emma Howard, your insights and guidance have been invaluable – thank you. You made *Salt Lick* a better book.

The Unbound Authors Social Club – diamonds and champions one and all.

Everyone at Unbound, John, Anna, Caitlin, Julia, and many others, it has doubtless been a time of anxiety and frantic plate spinning – and you have kept us all up in the air. I hope you know that your work on our behalf is so appreciated in what must be hugely difficult times. And I hope your marvellous dedication to books and authors is as rewarding for you as it is for so many of us.

It has been a strange and for many people devastatingly difficult couple of years. The two pandemics in *Salt Lick* were already written before the real-life version came along. I learned about more than how a pandemic works in real life. Perhaps we all learned something of how resilient, how brave, how fragile, how blessed and how perilous our lives can be. We are all more or less always just muddling along, with a measure of wonder and a dash of disaster, in a stumble or a glide – here's to us.

Unbound Supporters

Unbound is the world's first crowdfunding publisher, established in 2011.

We believe that wonderful things can happen when you clear a path for people who share a passion. That's why we've built a platform that brings together readers and authors to crowdfund books they believe in – and give fresh ideas that don't fit the traditional mould the chance they deserve.

This book is in your hands because readers made it possible. Everyone who pledged their support is listed at the front of the book and below. Join them by visiting unbound.com and supporting a book today.

Lucy Cage
Matthew Carter
Jamie Chipperfield
Laura Clark
Mathew Clayton
Jason Cobley
Tamsen Courtenay
The Crafty Hen
Jessica Crowley
Gill Cummings
Suzanne Day
Lilian Deans Allison
Phoebe Deans Allison
Sarah Dibb-Fuller
Angela Dickson
Samantha Drouin-Aspden
Natalie Fergie
Emma Grae
Thomas Graml
Eamonn Griffin
Suzanne Harrington
Maximilian Hawker
Kate Henriques
E O Higgins
Paul Holbrook
Sara Jaffer
Dan Kieran

Helene Kreysa
Pippa Lewis
Buster Maroney
Katie Mather
Liza McCarron
Julie Meredith
Max Michaelides
Mary Monro
Carlo Navato
Ivy Ngeow
Kate Orson
Justin Pollard
Frances Ratcliffe
Antonia Redding
M.E. Rolle
Anne K. Scott
Nicole Snepp
Christine Sylla
Emma Taylor
Eve Taylor
That I Love
Valerie Wallis
Julie Warren
Wendy Whidden
Terry Wilson
Joshua Winning